Jiana stopped
Radience. The s
the eye, lips pre
arm was tucked inside her tunic again.

"What do you want?" demanded Jiana.

"Nothing, Most High."

"What do you *want?*"

This time, Radience lowered her eyes and contemplated the ground before her feet. But Jiana could see that this was not a sign of humbleness; she was thinking.

She looked. Her face was bloody and beginning to swell, and she could barely talk. But she was not cowed.

"My freedom," she said, "Most High."

"But what do you want *from me?*"

Radience looked past Jiana, through the camp, over the bridge, and into Bay Bay, south past the floating city to the ocean, across the waves to the other side of the bay, and even farther south to the hot, still desert of Tool, the Five Sands, the tiny town of Jabal Saq, just two weeks east of Deh Bid.

Her face was an enigma, but without even thinking about it, her left arm pulled out in full view.

She spoke again, almost whispering through swollen lips.

"From you, Most High, I wish . . ." She closed her eyes, seeking the right word; she knew the wrong word would finish her chances.

Jiana took a moment to visually examine the girl's face. Make-up would not cover the bruises; questions would surely be asked.

"Alliance," the girl concluded.

WARRIORWARDS

Dafydd ab Hugh

WARRIORWARDS

Copyright © 1990 by Dafydd ab Hugh

A Baen Books Original

Baen Publishing Enterprises
P.O. 1403
Riverdale, N.Y. 10471

ISBN: 0-671-72019-8

Cover art by Larry Elmore

First printing, October 1990

Mr. ab Hugh is not available for personal correspondence,
but letters of comment may be sent to
4216 Beverly Blvd. #177, Los Angeles, CA 90004

Distributed by
SIMON & SCHUSTER
1230 Avenue of the Americas
New York, N.Y. 10020

Printed in the United States of America

the mind builds a maze
and the body runs through it
                            like a rat

every night in our dreams
we escape the maze
                        like a dream of birds

There is no maze.
We are free
                even from dreams of freedom

Vani Bustamante
December 23, 1989

"Before the Beginning"

Toq grinned, barely able to contain himself. The order surrounded him, waiting for him to speak.

"Sleeping Tifniz . . ." Toq giggled, then continued, "Sleeps. And sleeps!! He wakes not. I am the only and the one. It's mine! You can't have it."

The others said nothing, kept their heads bowed as Toq continued. Pieces of the boy-god spilled onto the ground. "Some of you opposed my succession. I forgive you all, though regretably I must destroy the lot of you."

He gestured sadly, every inch the regal, all-forgiving godking. Five minor deities flickered and tore apart as the abyss entered their souls.

Some who remained blubbered in fear, prostrating themselves before Toq. Two held their subservient posture in proud silence, twitched nervously and strained. Only Magadauthan Full-of-Oceans seemed at ease.

Magadauthan knelt serene, unmoved by Toq's rhetoric or authority. The albino boy-god chewed his lip, unable to think of anything diabolical enough to temper Magadauthan's arrogance.

"The rest of you motley pile of dung—you too, Waterbelly—shall be given much time to regret your inability to recognize my claims earlier, when that soon-to-be-damned Snoring Tifniz pretended to this seat." He turned his eyes in disgust, waved his hand and the order departed swiftly, all but one.

"Have you chosen to stay and apologize, Magadauthan?" asked Toq without looking up.

"Oceans are deep," rumbled a voice like crashing waves.

Toq raised his head and glared furiously. "What is *that* supposed to mean?" Bubbles formed on the boy-god's alabaster skin, blisters of hatred that burst, spewed venom across the floor to etch channels in the marble.

"I know what you intend," said Magadauthan. "I know her that tears your pride."

No need to specify the woman in question. Toq puffed up like a furious air bladder. "Then you also know what that thing did to me!"

"You did yourself, new boy."

Toq raised a fist, but checked his first, violent reaction. Magadauthan was crafty. Tides would freeze before the Goddess of Oceans tempted destiny without a backup plan. "This is a challenge," Toq marveled. "You challenge me!"

"Piece to piece."

"Spawn to spawn. Winner break all."

She looked up, eyes black as the vasty deep. Magadauthan's face was unreadable, even by Toq the boy-god. Toq grinned nastily, spoke quickly before She could. "I'll not make the same mistake, you wet slut. This time, *I'll* take Jiana Analena herself, against herself. Her own nature will destroy her! A test she'll fail!"

After a pause, Magadauthan Full-of-Oceans smiled. "You have spoken . . . lord." She swirled her blue-grey cloak and flowed from the meetroom.

Toq stared after her departing form. A nasty suspicion bubbled in Toq's stomach that he had been taken. . . .

Chapter I:

Prophet and Lass, a balance in the sheeting

A long, mournful cry settled across the tent-khayma; the wind, crying for the dead past: toooooo looooong, whoooo? bego-o-ne. The sound smothered the slave girl, wrapping around her mouth like a shroud, catching at her breath like a black silk veil.

Did he hear? Will he wake?

Radience crept silently with utmost humility, as she had been taught, into the tent, the khayma of the Caliph of Dokamaj Tool. The walls of the khayma puffed slowly in and out, and creatures too tiny to see clearly scurried at the edges of her vision.

Radience held the weighty bowl of candied mushrooms close to her left side, so her left arm would be able to help, too. The bowl was one of the lead pieces, ugly and heavy. Most of the girls could not carry it. Not even with two good arms.

Pressed against her side as it was, the bowl also offered excellent cover for the long dagger, sharp as a needle, as the sins of Arhatman.

Bodies pressed against the khayma walls, scratching with their claws, weeping to be let in. It was their breath that puffed the canvas, their pushing that billowed the tentwalk to a moist crawl.

I won't be humiliated anymore. I won't!

But there she was, at the door to the Caliph's bedchamber. How had she come so far, without passing the intervening distance?

3

Radience pushed through the beaded metal curtain; a lifetime of skulking to avoid the Overman allowed her to pass through with not a clink, not a single, silver tone. Behind her, the furry things she could never see chittered and nipped at her heels.

The Caliph was asleep, laid upon his furs. His arms were folded as if in death, his head tipped against the luminous, alabaster resting block. Some said the glyphs on the side of the block were the Caliph's eyes, when his eyes were shut.

Ripples rolled across the alabaster, radiating out from the Caliph's sleepy head. The block ticked with each ripple, like the mandibles of a stingtail clicking together.

The slave girl stepped closer, her teeth chattering until she gritted them. She rolled the weight from back foot to front foot, for she *had* been taught. Holding her breath to not flutter his eyelids, she leaned over and studied the face of the man she would kill.

The Caliph's eyes were wide open. Radience waited in silence; he often slept this way. She allowed one hundred heartbeats to pass before she dared breathe. *But if his eyes never shut,* she wondered, *when do the glyphs watch me?*

She put her good, right arm under the grey bowl and used her left to steady and guide. She lowered the candies to the chess table beside her master, so carefully and slowly that a watcher would have wondered if she were merely one more statue the Caliph had collected.

"Is she another stone Rakdare, carrying the waters of life to the Underdwell, to buy her dead brother's soul back?" *Who spoke?* demanded Radience. Silence was her only answer.

A lifelike Tooquo san Toq, masterpiece of the divine Tokogare, glared at Radience across the dozing body of the man who owned both statue and slave. The statue's eyes were alive, cold and watchful. She shuddered and looked away, almost catching the brittle flicker, the *bricker* of a tiny creature.

Stone statues in a traveling khayma! The man was a beast, but the Caliph's word was the roar of the wind and

the bite of the sand. The male slaves broke their backs
lugging the thing along the caravan route. But Radience
had enough worries, plotting to kill her master.

"She's plotting to kill her master!" screamed the non-
voice that Radience could not quite hear. Radience slapped
the side of her shaved head, knocking the voice loose to
fall upon the ground and shrivel. She put the bowl down
to free her arm, then slid the heavy, businesslike dagger
out of her robe.

*Moons gone by, an old foot-soldier of the Elect had
idled in the kitchen. A fat, randy kitchen maid caught his
flirting fancy, and he tried his luck.*

*But a schemer with hollow cheeks, greased hair, and a
withered arm whispered sins and wickedness in the old
maid's ear, lies about her fancied soldier. She knew her
pans and pork, this kitchen maid, but her wit was not
known to dim the moons with its light. She believed every
word and spurned the bold rogue.*

*The soldier was a philosopher. "If it is not one maid,
then it is the other," he mused. But he meant the daughter
of the vine, and he swilled down three bottles, tumbled in
a stupor.*

When he woke, thought Radience, *he found the long,
hard dagger missing from between his legs.*

She held it in her hand now—in the whole, right hand—a
dagger towards the heart of Hal'Addad, Caliph of Dokamaj
Tool. She fought the shakes out of her arm, doubts and
worries sent by Arhatman to tear at her decisiveness.

Tiny snakes like long, black hairs fell from her body and
slithered across the floor. *Snakes or shakes?* she thought,
then pushed the question deep into the lair of her stomach.

Radience heard a footscrape across the room, and the
Caliph's eyelids fluttered. *Will he wake from the sheer
savagery of my thoughts?* It was only the wind, the bodies, fluffing the walls of the khayma.

The Caliph was *Lord of the Wind*. He was Hal'Addad
bin Kerat bin El al'Sophiate, Lord of the Wind and the

Five Sands, Prince of the Waters, Caliph of the Elect from Qomsheh to Yazd to the oasis of Deh Bid, Master of Arts and Letters, and Caliph of the Elect of Dokamaj Tool.

"Snakes!" shouted the voice. "Snakes and quakes and rakes!" Radience gritted her teeth, thinking *I will not surrender to terror, agony, and despair this time, and to hell with the Overman!*

She lowered the tip of the flat, steel blade until it kissed the Caliph's saffron robe, just left of his sternum. Then she suddenly remembered she was looking *down* upon him and moved the point to the other side, where his heart actually lay.

She inhaled deeply, sucking the iron of the blade up into her own heart, but her muscles turned limp, and her bowels contracted. An invisible thing sank its needle teeth into her ankle.

Her heart beat like Horsemen at a fast trot, with an extra thump as one of the brutes stumbled.

The step scraped again, heavily. She looked up.

The black eyes of the stone Tokogare glared at her, his hand outstretched as if to stay her arm. *Was he bent like that just a moment ago?* she marveled. It did not seem possible. He looked different.

She looked down at the Caliph, symbol of her enslavement, and even brought her tiny, left arm up to help hold the wooden hilt, hoping the sight of the limb would give her courage to thrust. But a loud, grinding scrape drove her eyes back to Tooquo san Toq, warrior king of the First Men, ten thousand turns dead.

The statue *did* move. It moved again as she watched it. It clutched at her, seized a sleeve!

Radience backed away, losing her balance in astonishment. The juggernaut lurched forward, still clutching her sleeve. It tottered off the pedestal, gnashing stone teeth like an avalanche. As Tooquo's foot impacted the canvas floor of the khayma, the world shook and boomed hollowly.

Radience stared full at the stone face and saw the malevolent glitter of the dusty, carven eyes. The crowds whooped and laughed around her, laughing at the cripple, laughing at the poor little girl not even fully one of the Elect. Never do it, never make it, never 'mount to nothing—

"*Damn* you!" she cried, more fury than fear. She flipped the dagger and thrust it at the statue's chest. Her hands numbed as she struck a stone wall. She dropped the knife; it shattered like a glass goblet full of thick red wine.

She remembered—*why doesn't he wake up? why don't I wake up?*—but no, she remembered nothing. Sleep, black sleep, gripped her stomach and even the brickers were dark.

Radience woke from nothingness to find . . .
Did I dream it all?

She lay on her own mat, in her own khayma. She pulled at her dress; it was dry, and her feet were clean of mud. The night smelled old, waiting for the dawn.

Late, she thought. *Too late to still be abed!* The Overman would draw stripes on her hide. *Still alive . . . the bastard's still alive. I failed, even in the dreamworld!*

She leaned over, hyperventilating, and felt her throat constrict. A moment later, she lost what little she had eaten for supper. Then she wiped the bile from her mouth and shuffled away, through the flap and into the paling night, toward the kitchen khayma a dozen strides away.

She felt the pallor in her cheeks replaced by a warm flush of shame and humiliation. *I am a slave*, she thought,*0 and a slave I am. I will murder the bastard*, she promised. *Perhaps tomorrow.*

She clenched her teeth so hard that she locked her jaw, and could not open her mouth for an hour.

2

Jiana stood still, listening for the swordsman. He was as silent as a horse on cobblestones.

The man was heavy, his breath labored. He shambled back and forth on the wooden floor, which creaked and complained beneath his metal-shod feet.

He slid closer in a lunge. Jiana parried easily, even blind, and flicked her own blade toward his face.

Tugga grunted and lost his balance, stumbling back another two steps. Jiana pressed, anticipating his every twist. Blindly, she nicked him again and again as the crowd pressed closer.

She smelled their sweat, the stench of their hot breath. They hungered for a good cut. So many, so many were the crowd that the floor shifted and rolled on its pontoons.

Tugga sucked in a gasping breath, and Jiana *felt* rather than heard the slice. She took one giant-step forward, letting her weight roll with the waves, carrying her own Wave.

She felt the ineffectual slap of the top third of Tugga's sword against her upper thigh. But her own Wave bowed like a palace arch as she reached over his arm, pressed the tip against his chest, and thrust.

Had Wave been bare, Tugga's blood would have slaked its thirst. Even with the point guard, he whooped with pain as the hard blow struck his sternum. He called blood and urine upon Jiana and her ancestors.

Jiana slowly ran her finger under her blindfold, removing it with an elegant, studied motion that the audience loved. They began to chant: HU-hu-hu-hu HU-hu-hu-hu. . . . Her stomach tightened, and she swallowed bile.

"Champeen takes it in two," said Maqtan. "Lay them out, boys, big ends first."

"Hi, hi!" cried one fat woman, as she gathered her winnings from the teakeep of the Squatting Dog. "She's invulceable, that's what she is I says."

Maq said nothing, but toted the ledgers. He smiled, and Jiana thought he must have covered the house edge.

Silently, he handed Jiana her fourth-share. It was a bit more than the price of a Bay Bay dueling permit, an errand she dared not neglect. Two miserable days spent white-washing public buildings was enough. Dueling with an expired license was a serious offense, and had not Judge "Tan Tan" Dutillai as much as told her she would sure be jugged next time?

"Good call, that blindfold," said Maq, admiring his cut.

"What next, do I have to tie my hands and hold a bucket of horsefeed between my teeth?"

"It'd bring in the chums."

"Face it, Maq. No one wants to duel me anymore. Soon they won't duel at all but just surround me and wait for me to walk across the waves."

Then the ghouls, the watchers, the lurkers would not come, and Maq would let her go as cheerfully as he had booked her, two moons back.

Then what? Who hires a hero?

Jiana held the long, clay pipe steadily, keeping the tremor out of her hands, breathing deep. She held the glowing taper to the bowl, drawing long—long and hard though it bit at her throat like sand in a whirlwind. Violence crackled through her body, turning eyes to fire and toes to ice, black hair to grey embers and bold blood to cold ocean.

Peering through the smoke and the buzzbees (were they there? sure, were they there?) He looked at her taut face, His black eyes peeking through a placid smile, waiting for the tindersmoke to ignite her stomach. He: Tong Aouyong, the Tunk, supreme high something-or-other muckety-muck of one of the thousands of TRUE successors of the Old Ways, the First Men, the Ti-Ji Tul. He says.

At least he baths and doesn't drool, she thought. At least the son of a bachelor actually seems to know more than I and packs a mean pipe, but—

The world became a bend, Focus Number One at the Tunk (for precision, at his smile), Focus Number Two at Jiana, She Herself. She leaned a gentle back, leaning back, taking the tip of the clay in her mouth once again, drawing deep of the thousand thousand thousand thousand magic sandsmoke.

The shapes in the roof-thatching stepped off, came alive, came off and into the air: dancing triangles, squares interloving a circle, spinning a child's hoop, banking and rounding, so round, so bridge. The shapes (their hooves crashing, flashing sparks against the wooden planks of the Floating City) stepped off, turned to longs and shorts as she drew again on the long, white clay pipe, turned to faces jeering, laughing—

*   *   *

—Caterwauling, "hey, girlie," growled Maq from behind the bar, "wanna drink?"

Jiana ignored the patronizing term. Maq was what he was.

"If I start drinking, I'll wind up walking another day on these blood-slippery pontoons without a stamp on my permit."

"You gotta do that every moon?"

"Yeah, it's a twenty-eight day curse." She smiled at Maq's puzzled frown as he looked up, feeling it sail over his head.

"You going out?" he asked. "You better shave."

Jiana blinked, and a fat troll sat across from her in the smokey hut, smoking, puffing on a great clay pipe, intelligent eyes like bright buttons watching, looking through the windows of her soul—but another blink and it was gone—she was with Maq in the Squatting Dog.

Jiana gingerly pulled her right boot on, trying not to rub the tender scab below the knee. It had taken a long time to heal this far.

"Maybe I'll just grow it all back."

"Fuck no! It's distinctual. Want me to shave it?"

She smiled, wincing as she put weight back on the leg. She looked dubiously at her cloak, still soaked from the pitcher of ale, cheaper than strongtea.

"Give me your coat. It stinks outside."

"There's been some waves, and you got that bum knee."

"If I can walk home after a dozen of your Baby Boilers, I bet I can get to the Bureau of Duels and Marriages. Anyway, even after the stamp I have a copper claw for the ferry."

"Well, at least let me shave your head."

Jiana closed her eyes and slowly ran her fingers along her scalp, feeling the rough stubble that surrounded the long, black strip of hair in the middle.

"I like doing it myself," she whispered towards the ceiling. Maq would understand. She never let him shave her. His hands shook (and he was who he was).

Jiana cupped her hands over her face, and tilted her head back. She reveled in the bubble of privacy formed by her tented fingers, warmed by her boozy breath. Then the conversational jumble pierced the peace like a bagpipe joining a quiet flute.

I am a billboard, she thought, cold denunciation razoring through contentment. *I'm a sword-whore. I have a headache.*

I see horses, cheered, a thousand thousand . . . Too many thousands, she feared. *No more thousands.* Jiana inhaled deeply from the water pipe, holding the smoke in her lungs as long as she could.

"Do you see souls? or horses?" Sure and it must have been the Tunk who spoke, but the voice was lost from whence it came, coming from now here and again there, and mostly from Jiana's own stomach.

"Well—honest, no, they just look like horses. Should I be seeing snakes?" Jiana started to inhale again, changed her thoughts and put the stem down; she had already flown too far and worried about finding her way back.

"Snakes?"

"I mean souls. Why did I say snakes? I drove them out. I drove Tooqa the Nameless Serpentine out of the water and out of this sphere. Where is It now? With Toq in his wretched ivory city? Is my God hissing with Sleeping Tifniz?"

"You're babbling. Let the talker go. Give your stomach over to the listener for a while."

"What should I listen to?"

She wished her eyes worked. She wished she could see the Tunk, for she thought he might have shrugged.

"What should you not listen to? The buzzbees, the water waves lap lapping against the planks, the creaking of the timbers. Your heart beating. Your stomach thinking. That voice inside of you—what is its name?"

"Jianabel. Haven't heard her much lately. Haven't heard her at all for nearly a full turn."

"But who is the One who makes the grass green?"

"*Perhaps she needs listening to.*"

"*You're a sword-whore, not a billboard!*" A familiar familiar would have laughed.

"*O Jianabel, you have such a gentle and understanding view.*" The Voice was silent, but Jiana heard her own thoughts, filling in for that separate part of her. "*I call the coin the way it falls,*" Jianabel would have rejoined. As it was, she did not need to; Jiana answered from her own Wolf Self.

"*What do you see? Now?*" asked the Tunk. He asked in Jiana's dreamtime as she drifted armless and legless in the timeless.

Saw herself step to the window in answer; saw herself naked, fling wide the shutters. Saw the pane, frozen sugar as if spun by a candy spider. Pushed she did and out it popped, to fall to the cobblestones and brittle into a thousand thousand thousand thousand pieces.

"*Bricker it is,*" she snarled, thinking of her coiling god the Nameless Serpentine. "*My (Tunk), my teacher, what is this crumbly bricker I've been smoking?*"

But already through the window, already leaning way, way out the empty, looking down, down, down the distance. Sill presses against her stomach, gouged by the latch, splinter in her wrist. Slowly stretching until fingers grip sill, sharps of pain through the knuckles, feeling center now panting over three and twenty man-stands, three and twenty times, say, six feet equaling well more than one hundred twenty to fall. Strains, pulls back at last, too late; overbalanced; falls. . . .

Slowly do the fingers give.

Strange, She thinks, how not to be afraid; strange to look Old Death the Barber in the eyes, if eyes is the word. Old Him that I shit on so many times and laughed at, and not to feel fear. What's on the other side? I don't care. I just don't care care.

Slips. Fingers slip.

Sees cobblestones. Harder than a prince's heart, she thinks. The fingers slip.

Falls—a long moment heart in mouth, light as a feather, gossamer ladder. Ground rushes up. Hands outstretched, *reaction, bypassing even the stomach and a scream rips out of her face like skin torn from the skull.*

March march marches time to the beat of a snail drum. First the hand strikes, savage wrench up the arm culminates in a horror of pain at the elbow tells her all she needs to know that her arm has shattered.

But still her body pushes down, feeling as if it is pushing up 'gainst a cobblestone ceiling. Now the arm folds under her and the horror rushes up to her shoulder.

Face strikes, the moment slows yet further. First the left then the right, feels the front teeth smashed, snapped clean out of jaw. Jaw, faceplate of skull collapse inward.

The body has its own agenda, momentum pushing back and over, folding body in half to snap neck like a poorly-made sword with too much carbon. Ribs snap one by one by one, though that surely is the least of hers.

Thighs counter-rotate to grind kneecaps into powder.

(BUT—she reached around and bit his neck, not quite hard enough to break the skin. She ran her tongue lightly across the fold of flesh stretched tight by her teeth.

Dilai took hold of her buttocks, sinking his fingers inside, touching the tiny, black hairs. Almost despite his intentions, he grew excited, and rubbed himself against her thigh.

She spat out the powder and kissed him again. He responded, and their tongues entwined. At the edges of her hearing the trumpets sounded, still too faint, but louder than before. Closer, the circus turned back. A memory? Of the future?)

Coughs, spits, drags again on the pipe, looking again at tent walls and a figure in the smoke.

"What do you see? Now?" he asks again—or is it the first time still?

"One future, from many; not mine I think. Another's, or another's present. What do you see?"

(BUT SHE SEES—She was inside of him, even as he was inside of her. The future memory continued. She looked out through Dilai's eyes, heard with his ears the warpipes that called him up, called him out.

He rises. Rises up out of his body. Rises up, the him-ness of it; looks down—*Jiana my love, farewell—my time—learned what it is to have, learned what it is to lose.*

Rising, rising above her (me) and what was once mine. Rising, and across the room, they stretch out their hands to me. Pipes, I hear you! I hear them!

In the end, in the last days. In the truth. Rising, and I walk across the room, drifting in smoke, drop in the ocean. She is behind me; Dilai is behind me.

The door opens, and I pass through.)

"I see certain," says the Tunk, "war woman on road to Ruoy Oudin, meeting the eyes of slave girl."

"What slave girl? What are you talking about?"

"Not know, but you will, when meet her. She very important. Your next step."

"There are no slaves in Bay Bay."

"Slaves everywhere. Get goose out of bottle. She your next mountain."

"There are no mountains in Bay Bay."

"Mountains everywhere," corrected the Tunk.

A cold drizzle fluttered from the sky, iron sky, as Jiana pushed through the real, wooden door onto the sidewalk. Despite the rain, the ocean was calm. She felt no need to hold the rope rail, even after the tea and ale she had slugged.

Dilai. Dilai, silky hair spun black like a spiderweb of a glistening coal gossamer.

Dilai, get out of my stomach. I didn't want this. . . . I only wanted you. I only wanted to taste your lips, your spit, your cock, all of you. Drink you in. Breathe your air, laugh at your foolish japes and read wretched poetry at you.

I didn't want love, you fucking bastard serpent.

She walked the plank, headed for one of the public walks.

"Thirty-two turns old today," she said, "and a shit day it is, too. Thirty-two is twice sixteen. Do I remember when I was sixteen? I stabbed a sergeant. And four times eight, but that was in the wolf time, lost now. Thirty-two, happy birthday to me."

There was no answering, hectoring voice. Jianabel was conquered. The entity that once infested her stomach, living with her like two snakes coiled, was gone. Or, as fat Toldo would say, the schism in her personality was healed. Either way, it made for a lonely monologue.

"Thirty-two, and today." She stretched, rubbing the hurt from her still-healing leg, and stared at the water.

Black, silky hair looked back, though the ocean was far too dark to reflect. It was Dilai . . . or was it the mouse, Dida? So easy to confuse the two: Dilai, the aristocratic, polished decadence of Bay Bay's third oldest family; and Dida, rough, home-woven, innocent naif, an over-excited puppy.

Jiana wrapped her arms around her stomach, trying to hold the images inside.

"Bastards," she prayed.

3

"Fuck the license," Jiana snarled.

The sun sank into the waves, and she abruptly decided to leave Bay Bay, City of the Floating Dead. Her future was as grey and formless as the iron sky. She stopped in the busy thoroughfare and leaned against the railing, causing the walkway to tilt alarmingly on its pontoons. A fat merchant took a stumblestep and swore.

"Hup!" cried the man, "You move or whut?"

"Sorry. I was just thinking . . ."

"Nah, nah, you no think. You soldier-boy, girlie! You police! You a footgrab, you whiteface marine!"

"Look, I said I was sorry. I want to go back that way. Get out of my way, will you?"

"No, you from get outa *my* way! You go that way, go to end! Go!"

He stepped forward and butted her with his potato-sack belly. Jiana reached for Wave, but caught herself. Her permit did not allow duels with unarmed louts.

"That was a gimmie, you spherical thug. Now get out of my way and out of my life."

"You from get out, get out that way, or whut? Or whut, *hunh?*"

Grinning like a demented leper, the man eagerly thrust himself at her again, trying to butt her another blow. Jiana stepped nimbly aside, and the man sprawled against the rail. She put her foot against his tailbone, and gently pushed.

The rail was old and sea-worn; it splintered easily, and the man tumbled into the sea. Jiana stalked away, not even checking to see if he could swim.

"What," she answered decisively.

She side-hopped to another floating walk, and followed it to the courtyard of a hostelery. Jiana slowed her pace and trotted south towards the Eagle Causeway that led to the Prince's Drillgrounds, across the bay on dry land.

The city reeled and staggered in the swells from an offshore squall. The buildings swayed like drunken sailors, and the walks twisted and slid treacherously. Jiana shuffled like a pro; she had lived in the Floating City nearly eight turns, hating every hour, every moment.

Some buildings were bright with color, splashed with paint and dye from a hundred faraway lands, purchased from the ships that prowled the harbor by the sun and the moons. Most buildings were grey and scored, stripped by the raging winds and salt spray, torn asunder by centuries of neglect. Derelects and drunkards made homes in the worst of them, seizing their tiny islands from the armies of the apathetic.

Jiana scarcely glanced at the murals and paintings, works of art, obscenities scrawled in haste and despair; she had seen them all before. She trotted, eyes half shut, and soon found herself across the Prince's Causeway, on the upper-class landfill island between the mainland and the Maze.

There were a dozen stables there; she could buy a horse. Or she could change her mind and buy the bloody license, as she had every moon for four turns. *Yeah. That was my World's Dream. Yeah, fuck Dilai. Fuck Dida.*

Fuck Toldo and Prince Alanai. Traded blood for shit. Now who hires a hero?

For a year following her remarkable adventure for the World's Dream, she lived like a princess. But then Alanai grew silent and depressed, and withdrew into his palace. His band of heroes drifted apart, and Jiana discovered that being a hero had a downside.

What could she do? Certainly not the army; they would treat her either with awe or with sadistic abuse, and she would surely feed some colonel a yard of his own steel within a moon.

Jiana freelanced for a while, drifting from job to job; but she was expensive, and how often did a spice merchant need a true hero to guard his warehouse?

Broke and proud, she found Maqtan. Her name was enough to drag in the bored and sated, a few of them at least. For some moons, the Squatting Dog was *the* tea-room to frequent.

Dilai found her again. They took up where they had left off, but she was restless. She did not want his money, and he wanted for nothing. Soon she was back at the Squatting Dog, but the crowds were not. Maq kept her on to diminish his lifedebt, and she began dueling clods and foreigners for action on the side.

Jiana slogged through the mud of the landfill, her eyes fixed on the stables, far in the distance. She might reach them by the time darkness was complete, if she made no stops along the way.

"Slave girls on the road to Bay Din. . . ." But what did he mean? Two weeks had passed since that smokey night in the Tunk's house, and the Bay Din road was full of mud and pilgrims, as usual. She saw the first stars, and began to hurry.

As Jiana ran, she put a hand on Wave; it was securely wrapped around her waist, looking more like a belt than the twisting, razor-sharp sword that it was.

As she touched the sword, a spark of memory contracted her fingers. The taste and pain of every kill she had ever taken flashed in her stomach. She saw them hovering in the air around her, their eyes watched mournfully from sunken sockets in bare, bleached skulls. They worked their broken jaws as if trying to speak; but no sounds came forth. Jiana ignored their pleas.

She saw an inn across the street, the Jackanape. It was unfamiliar, but she began to thirst.

"I ought to stop in for a moment, just to ask around about slave girls in Bay Din. A drop. Maybe just one drop. . . ." She trotted on by, licking her lips. The stables did not look noticibly closer.

(But *what* was the dream? She had dreamed it last night. It was a horrid dream, and He, Toq, the blooded boy-god, was in it.

(So what had he said? What about casting his shade three times? Three times, thrice before—before—no, it was gone.)

Jiana passed under the Great Arch of Lilies, black stone frosted with the white flowers. The arch carried the Ruoy Mava Cemetery across the five great thoroughfares of Bay Bay. Jiana slowed to a cautious walk, for the Cenotaph was dark and evil, filled with footgrabs with queer ideas.

She passed the Hung Stallion Tavern and then Knicker Pickers, low dives both, and resolved to stop at the next teahouse for a tightener.

A deep, still eddy from the canal passed around three sides of the Pregnant Bull. Jiana paused on the walkway, and stared down into the blackness, drawn by an irresistable curiosity. Something was *down there;* she knew it.

Slowly, like an old wound pulling open again, she began to realize why the building and the pool looked familiar: it was where an old lover of hers, Tawn, had sunk to his death, clutching to his breast the stolen chest of gold he would not loose.

She stared at the rippling, oily water,. and an icy chill crawled along her spine. Something *was* under the water, and it was rising.

Tawn? Come back to accuse with silent eyes and pointing finger?

Tiny, white things broke the surface; they rose higher,

and Jiana gasped as she realized they were bloated, water-bleached hands.

"No!" she said through clenched teeth, anger overwhelming fear. She clutched her sword hilt and thumbed aside the catchlock. "You are dead, bucko, and that is how you are going to stay!"

The hands rose higher, and they were not the hands of Tawn after all. Instead, they were the hands, then the arms of a little girl.

She rose slowly from the waves, her long, black hair dripping down her face and back.

Jiana bit her lip, and dropped her hand nervelessly to her side. She tried to speak, but the words caught in her throat.

The little girl smiled, and her teeth were all filed to points. The Wolf Hour struck.

"I'll *never* be very far," laughed Jianabel, spitting out water. "And you'll always be mine!"

"Where the hell have you been?"

"Yes, my dearest sister; hell, indeed."

"Like it? You're going to stay there."

"It's tolerable," said Jianabel, stifling a yawn, "but I'll be ever so glad when you join me here. We belong together, you and I! Kiss kiss!" She blew two kisses at Jiana; they smelled like the gas from a bloated, watery corpse washed upon a beach.

Jiana looked at the girl; she felt none of the old helplessness, still in control.

"I slew you, once. I'm not ready to deal with you again, so piss off."

"I *was* you, once," whispered the hideous little girl. "You were me. I am the wolf within you still." Her eyes rolled up, and her tongue lolled out of her mouth. It was thick and black, as if she had been poisoned. She sank slowly into the oily water.

". . . never too far . . ." she promised, ". . . and you'll always be *mine.*" The final word was lost in the gurgle of the water.

Jiana stared at the water; there was no trace now of the

apparition. The shakes she had suppressed during the encounter returned with a vengeance.

(It was crawling. Something was crawling. Something was *crawling down her throat*. . . .

(It was a sort of a rhyme she dreamed—Toq dancing and singing a song of triumph. He would cast his shade three times over her life, before . . . before something, whackity-whackity, thirty-third.)

Taking a deep breath, Jiana moved quickly towards the teahouse, cursing at the top of her voice the son of a bachelor who had nailed the walkway boards.

4

The strongtea was hot, but not cheap. The Pregnant Bull, unlike its predecessor, was one of the more expensive establishments in the Maze, frequented by the sorts of successful thieves, traitors, and highwaymen who were given nick-names by the constables: Black Mask, Gentleman Jarak, Mistress Catch-It.

But another batch haunted such tearooms and hid in the shadows. They were Briars, once rulers of the land, now ploughers in other people's gardens. They hid and they plotted, and plotted and planned. The Eagle dynasty followed their progress with amused contempt, for once in a few moons a Briar would kill an officer or a tax collector. Then slumming became hell, for the Eagles would beat the bushes for any Briars they could find, tearing apart tearooms and private houses with an energetic fervor.

Jiana spotted them at once in the Pregnant Bull; they sat in the open, listening to a small, dark singer. Jiana waited for her eyes to adjust to the light; then she sat at the bar and ordered a pot of tea all for herself.

A gentle man was passin' by,
He asked for a drink as he got dry at the well below the valley-o,
Green grows the lilly-o,
Right among the bushes-o . . .

"Can you spare a moment, master?"

The Briar was old and a bit deaf; at least he did not respond or turn to her.

"Old man," said Jiana, touching his hand. He turned, and blinked at her a few times. He was past his cups and into his pitchers, Jiana saw.

"Arah? I didna catch it, mistress."

"What do you know about slaves, somewhere around Bay Bay? I keep hearing about. . . ."

They chatted, Jiana pressing him for information in the guise of teatalk. She drank as she talked, *the better to loosen my tongue and lubricate my ears,* she told herself.

> *I say tae you maid, yer swarin' wrong,*
> *For six fine children ha' ye brung at the well below the*
> *   valley-o,*
> *Green grows the lilly-o,*
> *Right among the bushes-o. . . .*

Soon the room began to darken, though the paper lanterns burned as bright as ever. She lost interest in the conversation, which led her to no one and nothing, and she slid back on her stool.

She sipped another cup of tea, and sang a quiet spell into her cup:

> *Ricki-ticki pay-the-bill,*
> *Here I sit invisible,*
> *Hiding in my hidden hill*
> *Fast!*

The singer responded, his own eyes shut as he lost himself near the well below the valley-o.

> *If you be a man of noble fame,*
> *You'll tell to me the fayther of them at the well below the*
> *   valley-o,*
> *Green grows the lilly-o,*
> *Right among the bushes, oh.*

The magic was deceptively simple, and thus good practice. Three things had to balance: the song (that served to *focus* the mind), the mental image she held of herself shrinking smaller and smaller, disappearing finally into the twinkle of an extinguished candleflame (that served to *direct* the magical energy), and finally, the power itself, that had to be drawn from the reservoir up and down her spine like water from a desert well: carefully, lovingly, without spilling so much as a drop.

There's two of them by yer uncle Dan at the well below
     the valley-o,
Green grows the lilly-o,
Right among the bushes, oh.

It worked so long as Jiana banished her fears that it would not. All eyes slid past her, as if she truly had become invisible. She was glad now that she had ordered an entire pot, for the teakeep no longer remembered her or asked to refill her cup.

I bloom and know myself, I bloom and lose myself, she thought. *Why do these songs have such an effect on me? Why do they creep about inside my guts like spiders in an old house, maggots in rotten meat?*

She pulled deeper within herself, chilling at the words as they razored through her.

If you be a man of noble steam,
You'll tell tae me what did happen to them at the well
     below the valley-o,
Green grows the lilly-o,
Right among the bushes, oh.

She turned around at the bar (. . . *sit invisible, hiding in my hidden hill* . . .) and leaned back against it.

Her Briar friend was named Padrag, and he was involved in an animated conversation with another of his countrymen. They spoke in *Curyc*, dead tongue of the

Dead, learned language of the Briars (their native tongue, though none spoke it as a native).

"Aye, Toolians; from the deserts, my friend, far south." Padrag, coughed, and swallowed the rest of his ale.

"Tents, they live in. Tents, Padrag—think upon it! Carry them all upon huge, hideous beasties, what they call *jamals*. Horses with humps and evil lips."

"Sure and you're telling a story, lad."

"May the Lord strike off my testicles if it is not true."

Toolians, thought Jiana in disgust; she had spent a long, hot summer in Tool, fighting the wily tribesmen. They were brutal but intelligent, and never knew when to die gracefully. *And they keep slaves . . .*

There's two buried 'neath the stable door at the well below
    the valley-o,
Green grows the lilly-o,
Right among the bushes, oh.

"It's caused the butchers a terrible embarrassment," said Padrag's friend with a laugh. "They fear if a slave should escape—should they return the slave and save a valuable ally, or keep their own law and declare him free?"

Jiana smiled. The *old* (pre-World's Dream) Prince Alanai would never even have tolerated Toolians in the Water Kingdom, let alone allow them to bring their slaves.

Jiana frowned, remembering Tool—ugly, brutal Tool, Dung of the Desert. She had raided across the sandy border from Door, in a small troop of horsemen led by Warkai the Witty, who naturally led them into a trap (his men called him Warkai the Witless).

Sliced and bleeding, Jiana had lain with the dead for a day and a night, out-waiting the Toolian scavangers. When they fled, she rose shakily and stumbled across the sands, a split wine-skin over her head to shade her from the sun.

Foul memories, she thought. *I wonder if they've civilized any over the seasons?*

Oh snakes, she wished, feeling them crawling down her

throat and writhing in her stomach. *Oh loves, I wish I could remember that horrible, horrible dream this morning. I think there might have been something in there for me. Something awful. Something I need to know.*

> *Another two 'neath the kitchen door at the well below the valley-o,*
> *Green grows the lilly-o,*
> *Right among the bushes, oh.*

She tilted her head back until her neck bones cracked. Against the dirty, soot-stained ceiling of the Pregnant Bull she saw a shape—black on black. It was a spider, the size of her spread-fingered hand.

Behind Jiana, the Briars whispered. Their conspiratorial tone attracted her attention at once.

"Sure and they must know they can't."

"They're not cowards, the lot."

"Arrah."

"To the children."

"End to the Troubles."

> *Another two 'neath the well itsel', at the well below the valley-o,*
> *Green grows the lilly-o,*
> *Right among the bushes, oh.*

A pair of glasses clinked together, cracking Jiana's ears.

Jiana eyed the newcomer. Padrag had completely forgotten her, for he did not know that Jiana spoke *Curyc*.

The monk spider, she thought, looking again at the ceiling. *Terrifying of mien, nothing to back it up. You're well-named, you hideous bugger. I wonder what Toldo Mondo is doing these days?* She shivered with a premonition as she thought of her friend, apostate of the "True Church."

> *If you be a man of noble fame,*
> *You'll tell tae me what will happen mesel' at the well below the valley-o,*

Green grows the lilly-o,
Right among the bushes-o.

You'll be seven years a-ringin' the bell at the well below
the valley-o,
Green grows the lilly-o,
Right among the bushes-o.

You'll be seven more a-portin' in hell at the well below
the valley-o,
Green grows the lilly-o,
Right among the bushes-o.

As if in response to Jiana's arachnid musings, the canvas door of the Pregnant Bull burst open. A strange and wonderful little man entered. Tied around his waist was a rope, stretched tight as a gossamer strand behind him. Light streamed through the doorway around him, making web patterns on the wooden floor.

The man was short and stumpy, and marched like a soldier towards the bar, trailing his strand of rope. He wore neither armor nor weapons, but a rough homespun tunic and cracked, leather breeks. His boots were wooden strips, bound by cloth and stitching.

I'll be seven years a-ringin' the bell,
But the Lord above may save my soul,
From portin' in hell at the well below the valley-o,
Green grows the lilly-o,
Right among the bushes-o!

The rope stopped him just a stride from the counter.

"How many in your troop?" demanded the tea-master in a haughty voice. Only then did Jiana notice the brand on the spider-man's forehead; he was a Prisoner of the Guard.

"Who's the jack?" asked the older *Curyc* voice.

"My people are with them, even cousin Niam who

hasn't been the same since the last uprising," continued Padrag, unhearing.

"Who's the jack, the bastard on the rope?"

"Arrah, he's on a rope," said Padrag, blinking and squinting his eyes.

Jiana frowned. *I've been too quick to say the Eagle bastards have outlawed slavery. I forgot about these ones.*

"Prisoner of the Guard," said Padrag's friend. "Taken during a holy crusade, sure, for the Eagles call them all heretics and unbelievers."

They were held as POGs, and suffered a dubious status as neither citizens nor criminals.

"Sox mens in platoon," answered the spider-Pog with a distinct accent of Tooltak, the language of Tool.

Jiana jumped as something scuttered across her foot. She looked down; it was a tiny, white mouse. It sat on its haunches and looked back at her, twitching its vibrissae.

"But children, sure," continued Padrag, who had forgotten about the Pog. The dead past called. "What good can children, and sure an even score of them, prevail against the red and blacks in their fortress of stone, heart-hard? Even *lads*. Lads, but not a one among them more than thirteen turns old, Calem."

Calem laid his face in his hands, and his voice shook. But something in his mien aroused Jiana's suspicions. *He bears watching, this one,* she thought.

"They'll be butchered, Padrag. They'll be butchered for sure, b' Gad, for sure and sure."

"The Newlies did it before. Thirty turns back it was, before your beard even. Children again, another crusade of lads. They stood against the Eagles, and may the Lord strike me where I sit if my own son was not a-one with them."

"They died?"

"To the last, true to the last. They held a bridge for half a day, and I still never cross without wiping a tear and taking a drop in loving memory for my lad. Sure and may God strike the spit from my tongue if they were not among them, my people were."

Jiana rolled her head to the side, watching the tea-master.

He began to set out the six teapots that the Pog requested. The rope went slack as the grinning master sergeant and his five men passed under the still-open canvas flap. They wore the red shirts of the Waterfall spearsmen, and the red and black badges of Colonel Cosuss, brother-in-law of Prince Alanai, who still sat on the throne of Bay Bay, in a legal sense.

Too many voices, now that the singer had quit. He glared at the spearsmen as they entered, a venomous look shielded only by the darkness of the Pregnant Bull.

Jiana too studied each face as it passed through the light from the doorway. She was curious whether she knew any of them from her own days in the army, though she had been a horseman and never fought under Cosuss.

"Craven bastards and bloody butchers, they are," pronounced the younger, Calem. He raised his voice a bit, not to be seen a coward in the presence of the Newlies with their hated red and black uniforms.

Padrag spoke quietly, not to draw down the familiar wrath.

"Cut down the children, they would. Cut the shoots, wither the briar patch. Bastards. Butchers and bastards, and heathens sure."

When the sixth and last soldier finally stepped in the light, Jiana gagged on the lees of the tea she had just drained, spraying the liquid across the candle-dipper who sat next to her at the bar. He turned around angrily, and seemed to see her for the first time; but she was too busy choking in amazement to worry about having lost the "Rikki Tikki" invisibility spell.

The sixth soldier was taller than she remembered, and he had the beginnings of a scraggily beard. But it was undeniably Dida.

"Oh lord," she moaned aloud, "it's come to *this*? A stick-flinger for Colonel Cosuss?"

She watched Dida cross the room, feeling no compulsion to call out to her former student. She shrank into the shadows, but could not muster the calmness to sing the spell again.

Dida! How long ago had he danced around her, slaying pretend-enemies with his longknife? Now he swaggered and brayed with the rest of the bully-boys. Four turns ago, he blushed when Jiana dropped her clothes. Now he pushed a grimy hand down the bodice of a young girl, as she sat at a table with her boyfriend.

The boyfriend half stood, moving his hand uncertainly towards the knife at his belt; but Dida laughed, a short, ugly sound, and grabbed his own crotch in response.

The kid looked at the six soldiers, and at his terrified date, who cringed from Dida while staring fixedly into her glass. Then he sat down, glaring at Dida in impotent rage. Dida bulled his way to the bar, still braying. The master sergeant followed, gathering the rope as he walked.

Jiana watched Dida swill two cups of tea in rapid succession. She kept her seat and her silence, trusting to his unobservant nature.

This is my punishment for setting him on this path in the first place, watching the little shit act-up. Four turns back, Jiana had plucked him from a farm south of the city. She was twenty-eight then, and Dida was fourteen.

Too young, too ignorant, no blame, says the Tunk, snakeshit . . . I am to blame.

Dida had left her. Kidnapped at first, but in only two weeks he fully joined his captors, Prince Alanai and his men. They raided the City of Sickness, and Dida took soldier's spoils on a young girl there.

Jiana shut her eyes, hoping to block out the inexorable vision, the sight that her eyes would not let her forget, no matter how her stomach pleaded. Unconsciously, she balled her fist and drew her knuckles savagely along the rough, wooden bar, tearing off the skin and leaving a long, bloody streak.

She did not want to see Dida, Dida bloody, Dida with the knife in his belly and his guts trailing behind him like the rope trailed behind the Pog. Dida the suicide.

Shutting her eyes was no help; without the sight of the

teahouse, they had free reign to show her the blood again and again, like a conjurer endlessly stuck on the single trick of the Cut and Restored Chicken. She opened her eyes again, watching Dida drink himself as sick as any other soldier.

You were better than this, you bastard. You owed me more than this, you ingrate serpent!

But she could not shake the feeling that she was to blame. After all, she had undertaken his "illumination" voluntarily . . . no one forced her; no one asked her.

I botched you. Go away, please lord by the Nameless Serpentine, don't let him stay here to remind me of my failure!

She felt a tear roll down her cheek. She had not wept in four turns. She had not seen Dida in that time, either.

Jiana pressed her lips tight together, trying to hold back the rising lump in her throat. It was a battle lost. She kept the tears quiet. She wanted neither company nor sympathy.

She need not have worried, not in Bay Bay.

How many people get the chances you got? she demanded, not aloud. *You got a chance to expiate your crime. You got to kill yourself and start over, you piece of shit! I have to live with my mistakes. So why did you throw away your "heart an unbound page" and become a hard-ass soldier-boy like me? Snakes. I'm drunk. This tea is deadly. Eat turd and kill yourself, Dida, but do it somewhere where I can't see you.*

She kept her face buried in her arms for a long time, noticing how the teahouse was rocking more than usual in the waves. It spun in the current, around and around, and she wondered whether it had come loose from its moorings.

Meadows of green lie stained with blood,
Farmhouses burned and razed;
The howl of the hunt and green of the hood,
Ashes and snow where the farrow once stood,
And the babe-queen stands amazed . . .

He was at it again, the Briar singer. Jiana looked up, but
Dida was still with the boys, and Padrag and Calem sat
silent, heads bowed to hide murder in their eyes, hands
fondling ale mugs that ought to have been daggers. She
looked around the room; a score of young men and not a
few women sat in identical postures, looking any direction
but at the Eagles.

Jiana swallowed another cupful of tea, and the Squatting
Dog fell into thick darkness. For a moment, she felt the
rough wood of the table, pressing against her cheek.

At last she woke, her tears dry. The tea was cold anyway, and the room seemed chillier than it should with so
many lamps and bodies.

She stole a glance at the bar; Dida and the Eagles were
gone, and conversations had resumed around her.

"Good Lord, Calem," whispered Padrag, "they'll all be
dead, b'Gad. Dead by sunup."

There was a long, silent pause in the Pregnant Bull.

"Dead," agreed Calem, a quaver in his voice, "and my
own son among them."

"Your lad stands with them?"

"He stands. He is a Briar, God rest his soul."

"Killed by those heartless bastards, may they rot in
the lowest hell, and they not even knowing the light of
God."

"Still," mused Calem, but fell silent again.

"Another drop?"

"Pour away. Still, they'll make a bonny batch of martyrs. To the Cause, you know."

"To the Cause."

"End to the Troubles!"

The glasses clinked. Jiana felt a tightness in her stomach, and her throat closed. Martyrs. The Cause.

She stood quickly and ghosted out of the teahouse.
*Tooqa, name of the Nameless Serpentine. How many of us
aren't slaves anymore?*

"I ought to get the dueling license," she said, shivering
on the walkway in the chilly night breeze. She enunciated
carefully, "They close at midnight."

She pulled her coins from her pouch and fingered them in the waning sunlight, chewing on her lip drunkenly.

She looked across the water, watching the cracked and bloated sun fall into the ocean, quenching its fires again for the night.

"No, I'm a warrior, and I need a horse, not a fucking piece of paper. License! A horse, just a horse, b'Gad. Maybe I *am* a Briar, in the center of my breath. My dead past is no worse than this living hell." She spat on the sidewalk and staggered towards the Causeway. She crossed the Prince's Causeway on willpower alone.

She saw the world through a tunnel, as though she wore horse blinders. She swum through the air, hands out to steady herself, calculating each step. *No sir, no sir, no one is going to know that I have had a drop or two. We heroes, we heroes must set an* example.

She staggered along the gravel-built Causeway and eventually, after an indeterminate time, she left the wetlands behind her. The buildings were all of white stone, with not a splash, not a scribble, not a chip to mar their surface. This was the Prince's quarter.

When she set her foot on truly dry land again, it was the first time in six moons. She stooped, scooped up some sand, and swallowed a mouthful. Sobered a bit, she began walking towards the ranches while there was still sufficient twilight to pick her way.

She followed her nose to the nearest stable and refused to think about a little bird she had held in her hand and thrown in the air, but never quite taught how to fly.

The brisk walk to the stable did not sober Jiana, but it woke her up a bit. She walked up then down the row of stalls. Jiana did not know what she sought, but she did not find it.

"Don't you have—have any other horses?" she asked, a hiccough spoiling the illusion of sobriety.

The stableboy peeked at her cleavage and mumbled, "No, ma'am, all we have is yan stable-stalls in." A Souther, by his voice. He pushed past her, squeezed close though he had plenty of room. He showed her a horse she had passed.

"This one is fine, fine! See not his silvery coat, cockleburrs all combed out? See his sharp and shiny hooves?"

"I'm not buying a sword, kid. Show me a horse with muscle and bree—brains, that is." She took the beast by his bridle and looked him in the eye. He lowered his gaze and tried to pull from her grasp, shivered in submissive fear. "No, he won't do at all. Damn your wandering eyes, find me something for a warrior queen!"

A sudden scream from the back of the stable caught her attention. A horse cried again in terror and agony, then fell heavily to the ground. A brute stallion, black and red as firey coals, burst open the gate to his stall and charged into the walkway. Left behind was a maimed and bloody gelding that kicked and crawled feebly.

"God's cock!" the stable boy cried and ran to Jiana. He threw his arms around her, terrified.

She put him behind her protectively and faced the snarling brute. They closed, he unblinking and she unyielding, and stood nose to nose. The horse bared its teeth.

Stone sober, Jiana swung her fist too fast for the eye to follow. She connected with a right cross, and the horse staggered from the unexpected blow. It shook its head, then reared.

Jiana charged the rampant beast. She threw a shield-press without the shield, and the horse fell to the ground.

It rose, regal and calm as the Nameless Serpentine rising before the Hero-Queen of Scale Mountains. The beast approached gently. It rested its nose on Jiana's shoulder and nickered. She seized its bridle, holding the great head steady.

"You're a horse among horses," she whispered. "Why didn't I see you before? I'd have noticed a double-stalled pair, I'm sure."

The boy still cowered behind her, pressed close, but through fear, not desire. "Ma'am . . . is that n-not the horse for you? D'you want to take him the stables from?"

"How much?" she asked without turning.

Some trace of manliness returned to the boy. His heart beat less rapidly against her back, and she felt the beginning of a lump in his crotch. "Ah, such a horse, it's only twelve you for—I mean ten Eagles!"

"How much?" she repeated, menace creeping into her voice.

"Nine serpents. Eight! He is yours eight Eagles for. Or Serpents! Eight Serpents."

"This beast just killed that gelding," she pointed out. "Your price is high. Perhaps I'll simply let him go, and *you* can put him back in his stall."

The horse jerked against her hand and laid his ears back, whinnying savagely. The boy staggered back away from Jiana and fell to his buttocks on the floor.

"Take him!" he cried. "Take him away the stables from! He is yours, sure, and never to see him again herein!"

She turned and looked at the Souther. He was young, as innocent as anybody could be in the wickedest city afloat. She led the horse away, but as she passed the poor boy, she pried a silver stud from her gambeson and threw it to him. It was worth at least five claws in the Maze, more than the value of the slain gelding.

"I'd have given two," she explained, "if you had had the simple courage to look this gift in the mouth. Good life, kid."

She grabbed up a servicable saddle with her free hand and left without a glance behind. She followed the road to Bay Din, towards the Toolian camp.

5

How long Radience sat, she did not know. But all at once she leaped up in shock, seeing the growing darkness. *The lights! The lamps! The fire in the kitchen!*

She darted from the slave khayma to the great khayma, her heart squeezing down to her stomach. As she ran, she tucked her left arm inside her shirt.

She sped through the tent flap, rounded the turn and

realized, a fraction of a heartbeat too late, that she was going to collide with Lord Giathudin, Overman of Slaves.

Giathudin had once been a soldier, until he had grown old, fat, and lazy. But, apparently, he had never lost the reflexes taught by a lifetime of striking from horseback.

As Radience darted through the flap, the Overman turned and straight-armed her. The back of her head had already slammed into the canvas before her feet realized they no longer touched the ground.

Giathudin eyed her narrowly for a moment; then he returned to his discussion with Ruhol the eunuch.

Radience tried to sit up, but her body would not work. Her legs seemed severed from her body—or at least, they would not obey her dazed commands. Her head throbbed, as if a blacksmith were beating it into shape with his hammer.

Finally, Giathudin finished issuing his instructions and dismissed Ruhol. He turned his full attention to Radience again.

The Overman reached down and seized her shirt, yanking her roughly to her feet. He held her while she wobbled and tried to stand. His eyes were the color of coals, with streaks of fire burning through the whites.

"Where is the sun?" he asked, in a cold, quiet voice. He raised his single, thick eyebrow that crossed his entire forehead.

Radience was still stunned into silence, and could not answer. She felt his icy fingers gripping her throat, right through her shirt.

"I see stars," said the Overman, his face flushing. "The West is a red glow! Why do we all stumble about in the dark still?"

"I—because—I—was just . . ."

"Just do it any old way—that your motto now?"

The girl said nothing, sensing that any words now would only compound the crime. She knew what to expect. She had lived through it many times, as had they all (except Teenja, who had *not* lived through it. Radience cringed as her dead lover's face floated momentarily over the Overman's shoulder, hurt and accusing). Her heart pounded. *Please,* she begged of the Sand Lords; *let there be someone— anyone! Let us not be alone.*

But they remained aloof, as was their habit. Radience heard no welcoming voice, no sandal scuffing on the canvas floor. Giathudin dragged her inside the eunuch's chamber, his hand still gripping her shirt, trapping her tiny left arm under a fist the size of a *jamal's* heart.

Ruhol looked up as they entered, his slack face betraying nothing. He had seen many secrets, and every one remained hidden in the folds of his pendulous stomach. The Overman had nothing to fear from the eunuch, as all three of them knew.

"Bring me the whip of retraining," he ordered, and Ruhol waddled across the canvass to the horse chest. He selected carefully—the single-strand crop—and Radience felt a faint relief. He could have brought the flaying stick.

Giathudin accepted the whip without complaint, which either meant he was not particularly angry or too angry to think straight. *Probably the first,* she thought. Forgetting to light the lamps was not a great crime.

The Overman released her, and she stood silent, her head bowed. She made no outward signs of resistance. *Only makes it worse,* whispered the spectral voice of Mother Lhana from beneath the burial sand. (But in dream-thoughts buried deep inside her stomach, Radience "retrained" the Overman, again and again, starting at the toes and moving methodically to the crown of his head, which received a tent-stake.)

"Prepare," ordered the Overman. Moving carefully to avoid waking herself from the dream-thoughts, Radience untied her belt and pulled her longshirt over her head. She stepped out of her sandals and stood naked with her back to her tormentor.

"Twice seven," he declared, and Radience braced for twenty-one stripes. He coiled the whip, swung it twice to gain the rhythm, and began the retraining.

The first seven blows were savagely hard, and Radience held her breath and her cries, hoping the Overman would

continue in that fashion. She timed the whip's swing, and
fell beneath each beat, stealing much of the force. Each
such blow bruised and dazed her; but she knew the inju-
ries would heal quicker than the careful, slicing stripes
that a dispassionate man might deliver.

Giathudin *was* angry—a broken tryst with a Horseman's
favorite wife?

Ruhol counted the blows, his nasal "one your terror,
two your terror" warning Radience a heartbeat before the
whip landed.

After counting the first seven, the eunuch paused for
the customary rest. Radience sobbed a bit, in spite of her
resolve. She pushed up to her knees, and rose shakily. By
the time she turned to thank Giathudin, she had swallowed her tears and crushed them in her stomach.

"I thank the Overman for this correction," she whispered, envisioning a screw drilled slowly through his face.
Then she turned and breathed deeply, willing her heart to
slow and her back to relax in preparation for the next set of
blows.

As expected, when Ruhol began to count "one Your
Anguish," Giathudin interrupted him in fury, saying, "you
are mistaken in your count, eunuch! We are still at terror,
not anguish."

The next blow was counted as "two your terror," and
the count proceeded.

After the second blow of the second whipping, the
Overman paused. Radience could hear him panting, even
over her own choked sobs. She found the strength to
struggle up again and waited, eyes tightly shut against the
light, which had become bright as the sun at midday.

After a pause, she heard the whip turning in the air
again, and when Ruhol counted three, a line of coldness
passed across her back, barely moving her at all.

An instant later, the ice turned to fire, and Radience
gasped aloud at the sudden agony. The Overman's resolve
had hardened; his blows were no longer as savage as a
sandstorm, but as subtle and deadly as the shaker-snake.

The next four slices were anguish indeed. Radience

began to whimper and cry aloud by the sixth terror. As many times as she had stood for three, she never could get used to the agony of cold-striping.

The third anguish, which should have been the third despair, cut from her withered shoulder all the way across to her right buttocks, and the whip and the khayma and the eunuch and even the Overman himself vanished into blackness.

Radience awoke sputtering, choking on the salted water. She barely had time to realize that Ruhol had doused her before the pain hit. She felt like a single, twisted, burning ember as the salt-agony wrapped around her body from legs to neck.

She wrapped her good arm across her breasts, cradling the left against her stomach. She had gotten to her knees somehow; she did not remember. At last, the white heat receded, like the sand uncovering the dead, and she rose aimlessly to her feet. She stared vacantly at a wall of yellow, a rough texture, which slowly became the canvas floor of the khayma.

Something took her hand; she only noticed after several moments. Something—someone, Ruhol, the eunuch. "Go," he prodded in his emotionless, nasal voice; "the salt burns but heals. Go to the kitchen with the other women. He won't go there while the coffee flows." Radience understood what Ruhol meant by "coffee."

He tucked her shirt under her arm, her good arm, and gave her a not-so-gentle push. She continued walking in the direction he chose, towards the tent flap and outside.

She found herself again, standing outside in the night. The sun had fully set, though the western sky and the salt sea both still glowed a dull red. She felt the bite of the wind off the water, the smell of brine, so different from the alkalai stench of the sand-zephyr.

It was dark where she stood. No moon exposed her, and no torches revealed her.

Radience looked west, across the ocean towards the blood-red light for which she had been named, then she

looked north to the white Icenpeaks, south to the floating
city of Bay Bay, and east, to the ends of the earth.

The wind blew again across her naked body, cooling and
soothing her wounds. They still ached, but her stomach
ached more as she thought of the world and freedom.

Far to the south was home, the hell of Tool. But east
were the grasslands, north was the snow, and west was the
sea, the ships, and the mythical Flower Empire, which
probably was nothing but a story to sing the children
asleep.

So easy, she thought, *so quick, so easy.* Just a step—
another—across the gravel road, then lose herself in the
twisty streets. *They wouldn't catch me; they couldn't. . . .*
They don't even keep slaves there!

She felt eyes. Turning, she saw the glow of the Empire
khayma, heard the harsh whine of the Tooltak tongue as
the horsemen bellowed for *kaf* coffee and challenged each
other to wrestling matches.

Feeling suddenly ashamed at her ugly, bare body, she
pulled the shirt over her head and tied the belt, her hands
shaking so violently that she almost could not pull it tight.
Her face felt flushed, and she almost fell from the dizziness that had crept upon her unnoticed.

The Khayma watched her with a thousand eyes and held
her tight with a thousand arms. *Nine hundred and ninety-
nine arms,* she thought bitterly, burying her withered left
arm beneath her shirt.

She turned in despair towards the kitchen, and caught
sight of a horseman.

He was a stranger; his face and head were covered by a
wound cloth, as if he feared a sandstorm. . . . But there
was no sand in Bay Bay.

He watched her for a few moments, and she grew
ashamed. He was not of the Khayma. Had he seen her
naked? She dropped her eyes out of politeness; but when
she sneaked a peak, he was still watching her. Did he not
even know enough to ignore a slave?

She felt a strange tremble in her stomach then, as if the
wind had blown grave-sand across her face. There was a

peculiar sense of connectedness between Radience and this mysterious horseman. Was he going to buy her?

He looked foreign, dressed like a citizen of Bay Bay. With a shock, she realized that he must be thinking the same of her, since she too had been born in this city.

Radience looked up, throwing all civilized behavior to the sand-zephyr, and stared him full in the eyes. *Let him look*, she thought triumphantly. *Let him see me! He's no better than I am, the bastard.*

Then she walked pridefully towards the kitchen, dismissing him from her life.

Chapter II:

The radience of silverblades,
destiny through the door

1

Jiana sat unmoving atop her horse, watching the young boy with the withered arm walk back into the tent—*the khayma,* she corrected herself. *A "tent" is a pup-tent for solitary journeys.*

Dressed as he was, he was probably a slave. Only two years before, Jiana would have burned with the ambition to liberate him. But today, she only watched, wondering if he would ever liberate himself.

Pretty likely, the way he looked at me. He knows anger and resolve. He's been hurt.

She shook her head, clearing her mind of ephemera. Was this what the Tunk meant? *There are no other slaves within a hundred leagues,* she thought.

Jiana paused for a long moment, watching the rhythm of the camp. There were two or three hundred men, women, and children strolling about the grounds on errands. The women generally carried pots and goatskin sacks, the men more often than not wheeled barrows full of flour, buckets of milk, skins, or truck.

Jiana could tell the slaves, because they all wore identifying collars—*like horses,* she thought angrily. But aside from the markers, they seemed no worse off than the rest of the Toolians.

One class rose above the rest, literally, since they spent most of their time atop horses. They were the Horsemen, Jiana remembered. Unlike the rest of the Toolians, the aristocratic Horsemen grew immense beards and braided them into complicated patterns that signified their ancient houses and arcane patrimony.

Jiana made sure her cloth was tight around her face, concealing her features (and her gender) completely. Then she clucked to the magical horse who had chosen her. He walked forward implacably, directly towards a group of five Horsemen.

Two of them turned to face her. The others deliberately kept their backs turned, pointedly ignoring Jiana. Her own horse did not stop, and he laid back his ears and refused to turn aside when she tugged on the reins.

He ploughed into the batch of Horsemen, pushing through them as easily as if they were the wickets and he was the ball.

"Watch yourself, whiteface bastard!" yelled one of the Toolians. The rest swore liberally in Tooltak, and the biggest one reached out and seized Jiana's bridle.

Jiana sat quietly atop her own horse, a hand and a half above the largest Toolian beast.

"Here for the physical?" asked a young man with barely a beard to braid.

"Physical?" asked Jiana, pitching her voice low and hoarse.

The Toolian pointed at a sign, so tiny it was invisible until a stride or two away. It was written in Tooltak, and in a broken version of the Tongue of Eagles:

TEST OF PHYSICAL PROWESS
COME ENTER AND TEST YOUR SKILLS AGAINST
OTHER WARRIORS
WINNING WARRIOR JOINS ELECT AS BROTHER
TRAVELING WITH THE CALIPH OF THE ELECT
OF DOKOMAJ TOOL

(CONFER WITH LISTMASTER WITHIN) VISIT
EXOTIC DESERT

This last was a subtle insult. In Tool, a tribeless Horseman could join a "nation" by proving his valor in a physical.
With his dry, ascerbic wit, the Caliph suggested that
citizens of the Water Kingdom were by nature *tribeless*.

No doubt the Prince and his viziers basked in the trib-
ute to Bay Bay bravery.

Jiana absently massaged her elbow, which ached whenever the Fool Caller caught her ear. *Join the caravan . . .
why not? Even the reptilian cooking of Tool is preferable
to watercress and shoretonies*, she reasoned.

As she thought of cooking, she shuddered and stiffened.
She remembered that she dreamed the same, horrible
dream again last night that she had the night before. But
this time, she remembered a bit of it. She remembered
pushing something live and squirming into her mouth and
choking it down, bits and pieces wriggling and writhing as
they slid reluctantly down her throat.

The horse turned its head enough to watch Jiana, his
gaze intelligent, but cold as Toq's heart. Jiana gazed back
at the strange beast.

She reached up and once again felt at the cloth binding
her head and face, as much for the tactile comfort of
feeling something as to check the integrity of her guise.

It was tight. With her loose clothing, it was unlikely
anyone would realize her gender. She was challenge enough,
a stranger in the camp.

"Well?" demanded the great Toolian, suspiciously, "are
you here to join in the physical?"

Jiana ignored him and clucked for the horse to continue.
The animal responded instantly, ripping the bridle out of
the man's grasp so swiftly that the Toolian staggered in his
saddle and nearly fell to the ground. By the time he regained his balance, Jiana and her horse were long past them.

"Cute," she said, softly. "I suppose this means I'll have
to name you."

Away! Jiana ordered, fanning the air with her free hand.

Idle thoughts kept invading her mind, speculations which interfered with her concentration.

If my stomach needs a thought to stew upon, let it be one from the Tunk: "we must go out of our minds to come to our senses." It was that remark that induced her to share a pipe and an evening with the laughing master.

What else did he say? A sacred space . . . he suggested creating a safe haven in her mind, a place she could go when she needed peace to concentrate. *Well too late now; file it for tomorrow.* The khayma loomed.

It was actually a series of five tents, with the great khayma at the center. Jiana watched for a few moments, identifying the cooking khayma, the horsemen's khayma, and one that seemed to be for women of all types, slave and free. The green silks and scarves that hung from the guy lines barely flickered in the sullen air; once in a while, a modest breath from the sea would puff them out like sails, then let them deflate and droop.

She started to flick the reins, but before she could, the horse walked forward, his ears rotated back flat. She felt his powerful muscles between her legs, and shivered.

A stream of horsemen galloped around the cluster of khaymas. There were at least fifty of them, and they quickly encircled her. The large Toolian from her previous encounter led the group.

"Halt!" he commanded in Tooltak. Jiana halted and sat impassively.

"You must either respond to my question this time, or we shall declare you an enemy. *Are you here for the physical, or not?*" He sounded genuinely furious.

He wore a cream-colored robe, as did the rest. But a well-worn tulwar dangled from his sash, sheathed in silver-banded leather. His beard was tied into three braids which looped and joined at about his sternum. He wore no head covering, which was unusual, and he had shaved all the hair from his head. Still, it was grown back enough that Jiana could see he had lost all but a small fringe, young though he was.

"Are you the Listmaster?" she responded.

"I am the Overman of the Eastern Star Hundred. If you would sign up, *that* is the *khayma* you seek." He pointed at the largest khayma. "My men and I shall lead you there, sir."

"I believe I can find my way now, sir," Jiana said.

"Allow us to lead you," said the Overman, his voice as full of menace as he could make it.

Jiana smiled, but before she could move, her horse charged the mob. He rose into the air and fell upon the animals, cascading over the line of Horsemen like a waterfall splashing over a shoal of buried rocks.

The men grabbed at her, and several were unhorsed. One man barely managed to leap clear as his mount was knocked to the ground. In a moment, she was through, and her horse slowed to an unconcerned trot, as if he had merely picked his way through some bushes.

Jiana turned in the saddle and looked back in amazement. She caught the eyes of a few of Hal'Addad's Horsemen, who were looking back, just as surprised.

She turned back, grinning beneath her cloth mask.

"Cascade," she declared, "you've found your own name, horse!" She touched her sword, still wrapped around her waist. "Wave and Cascade, I like the motif."

Cascade did not answer. Jiana allowed him to lead her to the great khayma, where she dismounted and found the list.

As she expected, fifty or more men were ahead of her. Jiana paused for a moment, inventing a suitable name— "Jiana" was too well-known in Bay Bay. She decided upon "Kidi Tondenar," and signed in Tooltak, which impressed the Listmaster. She thought of poor Kidi, dripping his life's blood away in the Ghoul's Pass, and wished she had been able to think of another name instead.

Jiana decided to circumnavigate the camp before entering into the revelry. Taking Cascade by his reins, she strolled around the khayma towards the rest of the encampment.

There were fifteen large khaymas, and innumerable smaller tents. Besides the great khayma, which served as the feast hall, there was an Empire or household khayma, which housed the Caliph himself and his retinue, the Horsemen's khayma, the slaves' khayma, a stables-tent, and ten others which Jiana did not recognize. They were laid out in a star pattern with the Empire and great khaymas at the center.

The grounds were full of suspicious Toolians, narrowly watching an unruly mob of drunken, frightened, bragging, mugging contestants there for the physical.

The contestants naturally split into five groups. First, there were the Teenage Terrors, anxious to fight, to win gold and renown, but above all else to get the hell out of Bay Bay. Most were Dida's age or a bit younger, sixteen to nineteen. A few looked as young as fourteen.

One of these was a girl, and Jiana smiled wistfully beneath her facecloth, remembering her own first "physical."
Good luck, kid, she thought. *Hope yours goes better than mine did.*

Jiana remained on foot, leading Cascade. The khaymas were painted with strange, spiral motifs, skillfully interwoven with scenes from the works of the Prophet of Astatul. She reached out and ran her fingers lightly over the figures; the paint was rough and thick. It would surely suffer from the sandstorms in the Toolian desert. *Wonder if the slaves repaint it?* she thought. *Maybe not, maybe that's a religious duty of the tent's owner.*

The "kids" were easy to identify. They all sat or stood in groups, nervously drinking hard tea and ale until they were near to passing out. There were more of them than any other group, as many as the rest of the groups combined.

The second class of entrant Jiana spotted was made up of embittered, battle-hardened Bay Bay Vets. They sat together, and were easy to identify, for she knew most of them by name.

Jiana stepped over a taut rope, and gently plucked it. It barely moved, so tightly was it strung. She was thankful for her facecloth, for it blocked out the dust kicked up by Cascade's hooves in the dry parade field.

The third group consisted of the Unknown Quantities:

obviously soldiers, but from "somewhere else." This was the most dangerous group to fight. Sometimes they did not understand the list etiquette, and would actually treat the game as a serious battle.

Fourth were the Desperados. All were old; some were old in seasons. Once she would have put herself in that category: desperate, frightened, dead inside. They were merely "good" in a contest, such as the physical, but horrific in a real scrap. No feelings—fear, pity, battle-rage. They would slit a throat or watch a buddy bleed to death, all without changing expression.

Once, Jiana would have classified herself in that group, but on this day, she fit into the last category, the Watchers. The Watchers sat; they drank; they watched, and spoke not.

Jiana completed her circuit of the camp, and found herself back at the great khayma. The smell of exotic food began to intoxicate her: pungent spices she had never tasted, peppers and curries . . . mutton and goatsmeat, speared and dipped in a sweet, tangy sauce, then burned quickly in a very hot oven . . . pastries and sweetmeats, some as light and airy as a cloud, others as thick and earthy as a warm hearth in midwinter. *Kaf* coffee, laced with a particularly strong liqueur made from fermented goat's milk (though nobody was supposed to know that, since alcohol was forbidden under strict interpretation of the words of the Seer).

She entered the khayma, and after a long moment of indecision, drew a goblet of blueberry juice. She briefly considered a potato, but prudence won over gluttony, and she just pulled the skin off and ate that. The rest of her meal consisted of a small piece of bread, to absorb the acid in her stomach that might block her thoughts from roaming freely.

There were four other representatives of the Watchers, besides Jiana herself. The Watchers sat in corners, spoke to no one, and watched everyone. She caught each of their eyes in turn and smiled in recognition. To each she tipped her goblet fractionally in silent salute. It was a strange camaraderie. She had seen none of them before, but knew them all, knew what they drank, better than she knew most of her erstwhile soldier buddies.

What did the Watchers watch? *The lives of others guys flowing by, fear like waves rolling across this bloody khayma, who's hot, and who spills the butter, who eats with his left hand, who's careless with his weapons, who's a brute, who could not bear to kill a stray dog, who might be good in the bedroll after the fight, who might pick a purse, whose purse dangles unnoticed and tempting, the other four groups, the other Watchers, the exits, and where the canvas could be cut if a torch fell in the oil, people they knew, people they wish they didn't know, but never themselves, Great Snake—never me, nor me!*

The Listmaster paraded into the khayma and called the first round. Jiana was to fight third, paired against a Teenage Terror. This was normal; the Listmaster wanted to eliminate as many of the kids in the first round as possible.

Jiana moved outside before the crowd, for a good vantage point (to Watch). The sun was just beginning to get uncomfortably hot, especially under Jiana's thick, black clothing. She pulled the headcloth lower over her eyes to shade them from the brutal sun.

The first rounds were to be fought two at a time to speed things up. One of the first four fighters was Dorj, who used to run with Tawn back before Jiana knew gods could be killed.

She checked the list and spotted her own man, watching the setup. He was very tall, overweight, and wore a thick, leather butcher's apron—possibly as a passing nod towards the concept of armor. His face was scarred with pimples and the remains of the pox.

Under his leather apron, he shook with fear. Since Jiana could not pronounce his name, she decided to call him "Butcher Boy."

Silly to let a golden opportunity like this go to waste, she thought, as he nervously paced and wrung his hands in an agony of uncertainty.

She stood behind him and began raising the cold reservoir of magical power up her spine to her eyes.

Cheater, whispered a voice in her stomach. Startled, she almost let the power fall. The voice sounded so *much* like—but Jianabel was dead. She never even lived. It was a memory, or some undigested food on the rocky shoals of her intestinal tract.

Cheat? I outgrew "fair play" before I ever left White Falls, so don't even try.

Dorj tipped his head to watch his opponent, a powerful, stocky kid, through the slits in his helm. The kid stepped into the diamond with a sword in each hand, and he was big enough to heft them both equally. "Two Swords," Jiana dubbed him.

In the other contest, a fat spearsman faced a skinny fisherman's boy who had a fishing net fitted with fish-hooks; he seemed to think they would have some effect on an armored man.

Two Swords whirled his blades in a complicated pattern. Dorj tracked him for a moment, then charged straight into the kid, shield first. Two Swords flew to the ground, his blades whirling into the crowd amid general laughter. He tried to stand, but his legs were suddenly made of noodles. The Listmaster called Dorj the winner.

During the fight, Jiana's own opponent watched intently. *Probably knows the kid*, she thought.

She let her eyes unfocus, and found the Oversphere, a plain slightly above what Toldo Mondo called "Reality Prime." From the frozen reserve running along her spine, she drew out a long ice-needle of fear. She visioned it turning in the air, pricking the nape of the butcher's neck, and sliding downward, slowly, towards his stomach.

Worry, worry,
Hurry, hurry,
Prickle tickle, needle stickle;
Hear me, hear me,
Fear me, fear me,
Needle wide—run and hide!

His trembling became more severe, nearly a palsy. He

pulled and clutched at his pantaloons, and rocked from one foot to the other.

On the field, the fisherman's son cast his net, and the spearsman caught it and ripped it in half. Finding himself unarmed, the kid came to his senses and conceded.

Jiana noticed a rope-end draped across a stump. It was looped, and the single end was heavily laquered. Acting on an unconscious inspiration, she picked it up.

Not Wave . . . don't draw her out just yet.

Jiana took the field, intensifying the needles into frigid, iron daggers. *Hear me! hear me! Fear me! fear me!* she thought. Butcher Boy's sword wavered like a ribbon in the Prince's wind.

Only after she actually stood in the center of the battle-square did she realize why she had taken the rope end. Wave had become so well-known of late that the moment she drew her, everyone would know who Jiana was. She was not yet ready to reveal herself.

Butcher Boy struck first, a heavy, clumsy blow aimed at Jiana's shoulder. She stepped slightly off-line, and the blow whistled harmlessly past her.

He followed with a thrust, and a complicated and obviously memorized pattern of blows, none of which landed. The apron slowed him and made every motion a grand gesture. Jiana had plenty of time to side-step.

After his third attempt, Jiana had seen enough of his style to end the match quickly. On his next overhead strike, she stepped in past his tip, slid her hand up the outside of his dull blade, and seized his sword-hand. She pulled her rope end in short and beat him back and forth across his face.

At that same instant, she thrust forward viciously with the magic, envisioning a barbed and frozen icicle piercing him from front to back.

He cried out in a terror that approached ecstasy, turned, and forced his way back through the lists. He tripped over a guy rope, and for a moment Jiana wondered if he would actually pull it down. But the rope was as taut as the one Jiana had plucked earlier, and it only twanged musically.

Butcher Boy crawled a few feet, then jumped to his feet
and continued to run back across the Drilling Bridge,
crying.

The Listmaster watched him for a moment, then shrugged
and advanced Jiana ("Kidi") to the second round, to be
posted later. As she left the field, she was given a yellow
ribbon which would re-admit her to the main khayma,
from which she heard Toolian belly-dance music.

She visited Cascade and held her hand along his face.

"Told you I'd get the bugger," she said. She pulled from
her pouch a sugar-candy from the great khayma. He seemed
to find it an acceptable offering, and nickered.

The trick will not work twice, she imagined he said. It
was such a realistic visioning that she laughed. Then she
tightened her facecloth, followed the weird, wailing music
back to the khayma, and pushed through the tent flap.

2

As soon as she entered, she slid along the canvas wall
into a dark recess, to Watch. The hookah smoke was so thick,
the noise so cacophonous, that she began to see utility
in the Toolian custom of wrapping the face and head with
a cloth. It saved her sanity while she adjusted to the chaos.

The thick walls blocked out most of the light, but the
mass of human bodies raised the temperature far above
that outside. Jiana felt trickles of sweat roll down her neck,
where the cloth did not touch. She sucked a bite of the
facecloth into her mouth, wet it with saliva, and breathed
through it; it screened the smoke.

She peered through the haze, blinking her stinging
eyes. In the center of the khayma were eight female
belly-dancers. Two were passable, one was positively stun-
ning. They danced in various states of undress and
intoxication.

Jiana smiled. Something in the way the beautiful dancer
looked at the slavering men told Jiana that they would
none of them find luck that night; not unless they brought
along a girlfriend.

Hypocrites, she thought, smiling beneath her facecloth. She began to edge towards the slave boys with their trays of sweetmeats, gluttony winning after all.

Surrounding the dancers were about forty men, mostly Toolian, but a dozen from the lists as well. As the physical continued, the khayma would actually begin to fill. All were talking, yelling at peak volume to be heard over the *tual-guth* flute players, the singers, the spirit-drum beaters, and the other conversers.

Jiana heard Tooltak mostly, but she detected smatterings of the Tongue of Eagles from the Water Kingdom, Tzu from the Flower Empire, Flaet and Trade-talk from over the mountains to the East, Duj of the steamy, southern jungles, and even Tuk Atuktu, the allegedly dead language of the Ti Ji Tul, the "First People." She knew only a few words of the latter two.

The conversations were cryptic, but predictable: "Lost it in the sand; the tip broke . . . tastes like bad fish . . . *u-urtan'g (!kg)uuth* [bury them] . . . turned and ran, the little shit . . . twenty-three copper Rizulis . . . peed his pants and ran off . . . wanted to stop and look but we were moving on . . . twenty-eight Rizulis . . . ran away, didn't even look back . . . back in the sand . . . always wants it . . . no matter how many snakes are on them . . . *to-opu taku* [I am/I was] *t'ai* [death-cold] *chikiki* . . . thirty-two Rizulis . . . had it made special in al'Jemhaen, the fatherless bastards,"

Jiana felt woozy from the hallucinogenic smoke and oppressive heat. She gripped the front of her shirt and fanned it rapidly against her chest; the sweat drenched her.

As she approached the hors d'ouevres, the slave with the shriveled arm threaded his way up to her with a tray full of suspicious looking lumps with grey butter on them. As he pulled up in front of Jiana, she discovered the slave was a girl, not a boy.

"Ah," stalled Jiana, looking over the proffered sweetmeats warily, "what are they?" she asked in Tooltak. She studied the slave girl's face. It seemed very pale for a desert Toolian.

The slave's eyes widened when she heard Jiana's voice and realized that the warrior was a woman. But the girl maintained her professional demeanor.

"Each is a different bread made with dates and other fruits," she answered. Jiana hesitated, then took the darkest one and stepped back so the slave could squeeze past. Jiana watched curiously as she balanced the tray on her one good arm, using the other only to steady the tray when she was jostled.

Something looked funny. Though the conversation was entirely in Tooltak, the girl's hair was definitely blond, albeit dirty. Her skin was very light, too, though both flesh and hair were liberally smeared with dark grease.

She was such a striking contrast to the other slaves, with her withered arm and her northern ancestry, that Jiana found her eyes seeking the girl out again and again, watching with consuming interest as she performed her duties around the khayma.

The bread was spongy, and Jiana managed to drop it down the pantaloons of a fat, bearded swordsman who squatted near a hookah, his backside bare from the tailbone to halfway down. He was so busy begging for a puff that he never noticed the nutritional addition to his ensemble.

The Listmaster entered the khayma, tucking a folded ribbon of vellum inside his robe. Jiana moved quickly, weaving around the cross-legged warriors and horsemen. They were transfixed as the beautiful dancer removed the last of her costume, and danced naked in the lanterns. Jiana saw a dozen purses cut at that moment.

The warrior hopped lightly over a sprawling boy who was paired against one of his peers, and had advanced to the second round—the only youngster to do so. She caught the Listmaster just before he could escape again, wineskin in hand.

She grabbed at his arm, and though he looked chubby (*rolly-polly*, was the phrase that sprang into her mind), his muscles were as hard as tortoise shell. He turned, not angered by the touch; Toolians were very tactile.

He waited silently for her to speak first, since she had initiated contact.

She whispered, as if she had a throat-devil, to disguise her sex.

"Who be next me for?" She feigned a Souther accent, wondering if it was even necessary.

He smiled slightly, and slid slowly away from her grasp. She was unfazed. Of course it was illegal for him to reveal such information to one participant ahead of the others.

She held up a silver serpent, half of her change from buying Cascade with what should have been permit money. The Listmaster squinted at the coin, pursing his lips, then he held out his hand. She held her hand over his, but did not drop the coin.

After a beat, he understood and slid the vellum list from his robe and extended it to her.

She scanned the tree quickly and found her assumed name. Her opponent, Nilrinai the Loose, was unfamiliar to her.

"Who is?" she whispered. The Listmaster shrugged, and she believed his ignorance. She returned his list and dropped the snake in his palm, and they parted even.

Back in the khayma, the crowd had nearly doubled. The final two first-round bouts had ended.

She began to circulate, asking after Nilrinai. She drew a blank until she gave his full name; then the old man she asked curled his lip and pointed her towards "the *Louse*." She sidled up to him.

He was a brash, young soldier, ten years her junior but clearly experienced: he had beaten an old sergeant in the first round.

Nilrinai the Loose had a thin, cruel mustache and running sores on his face. She began to wonder whether the Doorian pox was a requirement to enter the physical.

He was sharing a hookah with an ugly horseman and chatting in Tooltak, so he was probably a campaigner.

"No, the sands of the Water Kingdom are totally different from Qomsheh," he insisted, correctly. "You would starve if you waited for *far gul*. Now their tortoises, however—"

Jiana looked at their water pipe. Something stirred in the back of her stomach, something worthy of the devious, priestly scheming of her old friend Toldo (*what's become of that fat apostate?*). A "rube's trick," he would call it.

Nilrinai and his friend sucked ascetically at straight tobacco. *An Eagle, through and through,* she thought. What was that scheme that flickered through her belly? Something to do with a trunk.

"Try another?" queried a voice nearly in Jiana's ear. She turned too quickly, upset the tray and spilled the bread. It was the crippled girl.

The girl's face flushed and she dropped to her knees, frantically scooping the hors d'ouevres onto the silver tray, along with handfuls of sand. She seemed terrified.

As she leaned over, Jiana saw an ugly welt sticking up her neck from under her robe. She had been whipped, recently and brutally. An image thrust violently from the girl's stomach, hitting Jiana like a physical blow. The warrior saw the girl hovering over an old man who lay dead on a concrete slab. She was about to thrust a dagger into the corpse.

Jiana jumped at the vision, and felt an instant empathy for the frightened slave, but she made no move to help the girl. It was the slave's place to pick up, not the guest's.

The warrior crouched down beside the slave and spoke quietly, for her ears alone.

"Did you try to kill your master?" The words were a blind stab in the night; there was a buried streak of rebellion as sharp as her scars. It lay behind the image Jiana caught.

The slave froze and stared up at her. Behind the fear was wondering admiration.

"My name is Jiana."

The girl hesitated, weighing her need to talk against the memory of the beating.

"I am Radience," she answered—in the Tongue of Eagles.

Trunk. Trunk? *Tunk* . . .

Jiana gently plucked a piece of bread from the tray and

popped it in her mouth, sand and all. She chewed slowly, and was rewarded with a grateful smile.

Then she was gone, Radience the Rebellious. Jiana turned back to continue eavesdropping, and the scheme bloomed like a flower.

She reached into her belt pouch and rummaged around for the packet of leaves that she and the Tunk had shared, days ago. For a moment, she could find everything but the Heui Dan-Dan tobacco. But at last, she found the velvet-wrapped package and extracted a pinch.

Jiana trapped the pinch between the index and second fingers of her right hand. Then she picked up a glass goblet and hurled it to the ground behind Nilrinai.

He turned at the sudden sound, and while his attention was diverted, Jiana casually reached out and "moved" the hookah slightly, taking the opportunity to wedge the Heui Dan-Dan into the bowl.

After a moment, he turned back and tried to inhale, and swore gently about the fire going out.

She held her breath as he relighted it. The newly added tobacco was reddish in color, totally unlike the old, which was black. But she counted on the dim light, and on Nilrinai not paying much attention.

He took a deep drag, and frowned at the taste.

Like burning tar, Jiana remembered. She watched to see how he would react to the flavor.

He grimaced as the aftertaste flooded his mouth, but he evidently thought it was the pipe, for he politely took another drag and said nothing about the wretched taste.

It gets easier after the second puff, Louse, she encouraged. *Taste doesn't matter much then. Breathe deep, Pretty Boy.*

After a reflective moment, the young, aristocrat Nilrinai inquired of his companion, "Say—do you think that the tea merchants might be in league with the fishmongers? Just imagine how cold it would be if they were scaling the fish before boiling them in strongtea."

At first the Toolian looked puzzled, but then he too smoked another lungfull, and the point carried.

Jiana smiled. She drifted away, content to let the snake

slither its own path. With the second round taken care of, she decided to seek out Radience and draw her out a bit about her bruises.

3

The fight with Nilrinai was short and peculiar. After watching him wander aimlessly around the khayma, Jiana decided to see how far she could get with no weapon at all.

Under ideal circumstances, Nilrinai the Loose would hardly have been a challenge. With his drug-induced infirmary, the fight was comical.

The Louse took the field wiping sweat from his brow and snapping his head left and right to locate imaginary tormentors. The Tunk's tobacco accentuated the natural fear and trepidation any fighter feels before a match against an unknown opponent.

Nilrinai charged at Jiana, but he forgot to draw his sword. Instead, he tried to gut her with an invisible blade. Jiana walked slowly around him in a circle while he cut, thrust, and parried. When the crowd began booing and whistling, the young aristocrat seemed to come to his senses.

He drew his sword, but became fascinated by it. He stood still, examining the blade until Jiana rapped it sharply with the heel of her hand, knocking it to the ground.

When Nilrinai bent to pick it up, she threw her arms out, raised up on her toes, and roared. She accompanied this startling behavior with a powerful projection of a charging *elphas,* bearing down upon the young man.

Nilrinai screamed and crawled backward half the length of the battle square. Then he stood up, looking dazed and confused. He turned and wandered into the crowd, as if he had forgotten where he was, and why. The disgusted crowd angrily debated whether to dunk the Louse into a horsetrough, but no one could find him, so they let the subject drop. The Listmaster declared Jiana the winner by confusion.

For her third bout, Jiana "borrowed" a fencing blade from a stuporous loser in the previous round. The sword was nicely balanced, a tool for finesse, not brute strength. It suited her better than a broadsword, though not nearly as well as Wave would have.

It was so hot that the khaymas shimmered when she looked at them, as if they were under water. Her clothes were cotton and loose, yet she was drenched with sweat.

She stood steady in the battle square, blade out in the standard Third Position. She awaited Tourdi's attack. In the third round, she had finally drawn an acquaintance as opponent.

Tourdi was a good, smart fighter. She had not spoken to him for several turns, not since they campaigned together before her great quest for the World's Dream.

He feinted, and Jiana countered sufficiently to guard the false attack, then anticipated Tourdi and side-stepped to meet the real threat.

Tourdi crossed her, rebounding his feint, cutting an arc to the other side, and then pulling the blow up over her head to curl around from her left again.

She leaped backward, off balance, and his sword point still contacted her salted leather vambrace. It was a skillful blow. Tourdi opted for weight over edge, so her left forearm was numbed, not severed.

Jiana backed away, swearing softly, staying on the periphery of the battle circle. She put her useless arm behind her, and managed to get it tucked into her belt after a few tries. She could feel nothing below the shoulder.

Damn your scales, don't let it be broken, she prayed. She deliberately winced, though she felt nothing yet, and pretended to stagger and almost drop her sword.

Tourdi stepped in for the kill; *always a buggerer,* she thought, nearly aloud. She thrust her sword inside his guard, aiming carefully. The blade sliced through buckles and gambeson and left his brigantine hanging open at the chest, tangling his sword arm.

She backpedaled, nimbly this time, and thrust, rolling

her wrist to arc the blade in a gentle curve that ended at his bare chest, the same blow she had used in the Squatting Dog.

Tourdi fell backward heavily, clutching his minor but very painful wound. Jiana began to follow to press her advantage, but at the first step she suddenly collapsed to one knee in exhaustion. The heat did not help. The fight had been brutal, lasting five full bells.

The marshall stepped in to examine Tourdi. Jiana leaned on the ground, panting heavily.

Tourdi staggered to his feet, his face white. He seemed unsteady. The marshall held out his sword arm, and looked into his eyes.

"You alright?" he asked, in Tooltak. Tourdi looked at him uncomprehendingly, blinking slowly.

"Hey, you alright, Water man?"

"Hunh?" asked Tourdi, his eyes drifting.

Ridiculous armor, Jiana thought. *I would've warned you not to wear it, if you'd asked. Not in this heat!*

The marshall shook his head and made a chopping sign with his hands. The Listmaster nodded, pointed at Jiana, and said, "Final round, by torchlight."

She had made it.

The other semi-final was to be fought in a while, after the participants and the Horsemen had a chance to make book and place their wagers. They still did not realize that she was a woman, so the odds were running well in her favor.

Jiana walked away slowly, massaging feeling back into her left arm. It did not feel broken, and she could make a weak fist.

This time, Radience carried a bucket of orange juice through the khayma, serving the Elect and those foreigners who did not drink ale or strongtea. Jiana intercepted her when she headed towards the kitchen with the empty bucket.

"Why do you stay?" the warrior asked.

Radience stared, her mouth an unvoiced "oh."

"Stay," repeated Jiana, "here. Here, in the khayma. Why do you stay?"

Jiana realized that she was enjoying the girl's turmoil, and she listened expectantly for Jianabel's accusatory gloat. But the wolf-side was silent.

"I—I must," stammered Radience, "My master—"

"Who made him your master?"

Radience grew angry at the question.

"No one, most honored. It has always been!"

"Somebody must have made him master."

"The Wind. He is Lord of the Winds. Why are you asking such things? It is forbidden to question—"

"Who forbade it?"

With a half-strangled cry of exasperation, Radience turned and ran past Jiana towards the kitchen-khayma.

Halfway between the two tents, the girl slowed to a stop, her right arm cradling her left. She looked south, towards Bay Bay, then reluctantly, she resumed her path with leaden steps.

Brave Jiana! Frightening children, doping opponents, and now bickering with a slave! Whatever shall be next— wrestling the cripple?

"At this point, we're about even," Jiana retorted, weakly curling her mug with her left arm. It still hurt, and still shook; but the tingles told her it would be alright by her fourth round. The lists were posted for the finals.

Jiana's opponent had an unpronounceable, Doorish name. She knew who he was.

He had once arrested her for vagrancy and drunkenness, before she attained her hero-hood. He took a detour on the way to the jail and tried to rape her.

Her left arm began to ache. It would not fully open, even before today's blow. The Doorian she would shortly face had shattered her elbow two turns ago.

But she did not begrudge him the injury; he was amply provoked. At least he would never reproduce.

He was both huge and agile. It would be a brutal fight, despite the "no maiming" rule. He was probably broke, and wanted to get back down to Door, only a week south of the caravan's destination, the Deh Bid oasis.

If Tool is hell, Door is the Void. Why would anyone want to go there?

A thought gnawed at her, drifting upward and prickling her scalp. Something that just happened.

Memory surged: "Brave Jiana . . . !"

Jianabel had spoken to her. Aloud. Again.

"Nameless bastard Tooqa," she whispered, *the bitch is supposed to be dead!*

The hookah smoke was thick, and it began to seem like the coils of a *(thousand thousand)* dozen snakes, rolling and squeezing all courage from her heart and all thought from her stomach.

You're dead. I murdered you.

Jianabel . . .

No, just the shit-tobacco they're smoking. No, it is *she!*

Jiana jumped up and shoved her way through the mob surrounding the notice board. But as she gained the open air, she realized that she was not frightened anymore.

She felt as if a lost friend was back.

Jianabel! You're alive.

Of course, silly! spoke the familiar voice in Jiana's stomach.

Jiana paced in the hot, white sand, willing the churning thoughts to settle.

"It was inevitable," she said, speaking aloud to herself and her other. "How could I kill you? You *are* me. You're parts of me, at least. Toldo's right. Damn."

She worked her fingers inside her headdress and rubbed the bare scalp on either side of her crest.

You'll never be rid of me, and I shall haunt you forever, o sister mine.

Jiana searched her stomach. She sought for the fear, the sick paralysis that always accompanied the child from the Wolf Time.

She found nothing.

"I can live with it."

There was a long silence from within.

You're not warring? Not fighting me?

"Nope."

That's not playing fair!

"Sorry."

And will you stop apologizing? Must I do everything?

Jiana laughed.

"It was wrong to think you dead, and I apologize for that. Why fight? Let's work together. We're sisters under the skin. That's a good one, ain't it? Under the skin."

Silence again. The inquisitor ignored the outburst of charity.

"I accept myself, Jianabel. I really love myself, and that means I must love you, too."

Jiana felt a sharp, stabbing pain in her belly, as if she had eaten too much *tanszanones* and curry. It only lasted a moment.

"Can we work as one?"

No one ever did before.

"No one's ever loved you? Perhaps they did, and you didn't see."

No one ever has before.

"Mom did. She tried. Stupidly, but then she was a pretty stupid woman. Jianabel? Did you drift away, like Nilrinai?"

The presence was gone. In a dim corner of her own stomach, Jiana could feel a monumental sulk.

Jianabel was alive, and Jianabel was *Jiana!* It never sank in when it was just the fat priest prattling. Calm descended upon her. A torn piece of herself was healing.

As the worry and the fear loosed their hold, she felt a coolness blow through her body. She was clear, like glass. She was light, she was fire. She was the wind through the heather.

I do love you, you little pig, she thought. *Come back when you can. Come together with me, grow. Snakeshit, don't stay out in the snow. I'm open—come in.*

4

Jiana stood, arms wrapped around her even in the heat, for her heart was full. In the long of the afternoon, the air was stifling. At least the dust had died down. She sniffed, but could smell only spices and horses, nothing green or growing on the Prince's parade ground.

A sound disturbed her silence. She looked toward the kitchen khayma. Did a sound come? The cries of a woman?

Then her ears deciphered them. A slave was being beaten, the slave master screaming incoherently. She heard the phrase "prideful cripple," and nothing else intelligible.

"Radience," Jiana said, her voice grim. She ran to the tent flap, and saw the girl crouching on the ground, her clothing torn from her. She was sobbing, but otherwise not saying anything. A paunchy ex-warrior stood over her like an angry child over a cowering puppy.

"What does your blood-time have to do with anything?" demanded her tormentor. "You're no household slave! You've no rank—why do you make trouble? Bitch!" He kicked her in the ribs with the heel of his boots, and Jiana's eyes widened in astonishment.

Does the Caliph know how you're treating his property, you hairy ape? Maybe someone should tell him. . . .

Then she put her hand on Wave, and began to make more direct, immediate plans.

But she drew the sword no more than a hand's width from her belt sheathe before a new thought crossed her stomach. Who appointed Jiana savior of the world?

The Horseman bent down and slapped at the girl's face, and Jiana could see that he was awkward, slow compared to herself. She could sever his neck before he even raised his tulwar to block.

But what if Radience did not *deserve* to be rescued?

Dida. He had depended upon her, and one day she was not there for him. Just one day.

She pushed the blade back into the sheathe. It slid reluctantly, as if it smelled blood and wanted to drink.

The master kicked at Radience again, and this time he caught her in her face. She would have a beauty of a bruise in a few hours.

The same thought obviously crossed the stomach of the slave master, for he stopped and stepped back, looking rather worried. He bent over to hiss in her ear.

"Listen, you little pig," he said, "when next I offer you to an important client, you better bare your arse, or you'll bare your bones to the kites and the kuzakim. Go find a nurse and get something on that cheek. Tell her you fell." He grinned coldly and added, in a nasty tone of voice, "Surely you do not want to mar your wonderful beauty . . ."

Then he laughed, braying like a donkey, and turned to leave.

He caught sight of Jiana and froze. He parted his lips as if to speak, and his cheeks paled. Then he regained his composure and pushed past her, out of the khayma and into the waning sun.

Jiana's eyes bored like ice-daggers into his face the whole way. Even through her face wrapping, he must have known that she saw everything.

Radience saw her, too, and her sobs became more piteous. She held her good arm out to the warrior, begging help in standing.

"You've got legs," Jiana said. "Don't play your slave-games with me."

Radience stopped sobbing in puzzlement, then she stood up, annoyed.

"My games are forever games," Jiana said. "I'll see you in your dreams."

She turned and walked away. A flower of thought sprouted in her stomach. Jiana strode towards the proving grounds and heard the girl's timid footsteps behind her.

She stopped abruptly and turned to face Radience. The slave girl looked her back in the eye, lips pressed tight. Her left arm was tucked inside her tunic again.

"What do you want?" demanded Jiana.

"Nothing, Most High."

"What do you *want?*"

This time, Radience lowered her eyes and contemplated the ground before her feet. But Jiana could see that this was not a sign of humbleness; she was thinking.

She looked. Her face was bloody and beginning to swell, and she could barely talk. But she was not cowed.

"My freedom," she said, "Most High."

"But what do you want *from me?*"

Radience looked past Jiana, through the camp, over the bridge and into Bay Bay, south past the floating city to the ocean, across the waves to the other side of the bay, and even farther south to the hot, still desert of Tool, the Five Sands, the tiny town of Jabal Saq, just two weeks east of Deh Bid.

Her face was an enigma, but without even thinking about it, her left arm pulled out in full view.

She spoke again, almost whispering through swollen lips.

"From you, Most High, I wish . . ." She closed her eyes, seeking the right word; she knew the wrong word would finish her chances.

Jiana took a moment to visually examine the girl's face. Make-up would not cover the bruises; questions would surely be asked.

"Alliance," the girl concluded. Unlike the rest of her answer, the word was spoken with finality.

Jiana smiled beneath her veil. *Watch me,* she told Jianabel. *This time I'll do it proper. This time, no Didas.* The beast was silent, brooding and biding.

"My road is broken," said Jiana, "and my shit stinks. But I *do* have a path."

"What is your path, Most High?"

Jiana reached up and pulled the cloth from her face and head, letting her Warrior's Crest cascade along one side of her face, the side with the scar.

"My way is the way of the edge," she said. "I am blood. I'm death on a black horse. I'm the midnight sky above a freezing desert."

Then she laughed, mocking her own awe-full-ness.

"Wait 'til tomorrow's morrow; you'll know me, though the others won't. Anyway, my *real* name is Jiana. But don't tell anyone."

She turned and walked away, covering her face and hair again.

5

Radience watched the woman depart, staring at the long, ink-black crest that grew from the center strip of the woman's head.

She had heard of the Flower Empire, and the horrible rituals and initiations that gave a few the right to shave a crest like that. Could this Jiana truly be one of them? It was an exciting thought, and Radience felt a chill.

She walked at a respectful distance, following Jiana to the finals, but she found herself visioning the warrior's back bare and white, her legs short and muscular, but lithe nonetheless.

Her arm felt cold, and she tucked it back inside of her *kaf*, frightened by her own thoughts.

For the finals, the woman had drawn a gigantic Doorian with a head like a pumpkin. He stared curiously at the woman as she stepped into the diamond, as did the rest of the crowd. They hushed.

Radience's heart began to race, and she felt a sick fear that she had never felt before, not even when the Overman "prepared" her for a client. Rather than a sword, or spear, or other decent weapon, the woman chose a short, light herding stick. The Doorian would have a huge weapon advantage. He could slay her.

You can't! Not now! Not when she's my hope, the one that finally came!

The first blow was struck, before the Listmaster even opened the match. The Doorian whirled his unguarded blade in a short arc, designed to cut Jiana in two and never mind the no-maiming rule.

But he cut through nought but the wind, for she stepped aside as casually as if allowing a drunk to stumble past.

He swung and she ducked, and ducked, and ducked. *Why doesn't she fight?* Radience wondered, her throat constricting with fear.

The beautiful warrior seemed determined not to strike a blow. But neither did she intend for one to land. She wove a complicated pattern, a dance whose steps repeated endlessly, yet never allowed the Doorian to predict where they would fall next.

After four complete circuits of the battle square, he panted like a winded horse, and Radience began to believe that perhaps Jiana knew what she was doing.

The crowd was cheering lustily. Most favored the Doorian, but a very vocal faction began chanting "Kidi! Kidi!" as soon as she stepped onto the field. Radience felt a strange annoyance at them. What right had *they* to cheer? They did not even know her true name!

She almost spoke out. She almost shouted at them to go away, to stop being such hypocrites.

But then Radience turned her eyes towards the Empire khayma, towards the black, impenetrable doorflap. She saw him there, the Overman. She saw him looming, angrily watching her, barely able to contain himself or wait for an opportune moment to finish the job he began earlier.

She saw him with her stomach, not with her eyes, for in truth the doorflap was empty. But he was so easy to envision that she shuddered nonetheless.

She turned bitterly back to the fight. *What's it matter? Tomorrow you'll be down there and I'll be up here, and then I'll have an "accident." Or maybe the morrow's morrow.*

Radience watched Jiana, and felt cold resentment fill her thoughts.

And why did you come to torment me with what can't be?

Anything *can be*, whispered a *daeva* in her stomach, using Jiana's voice. *Just play the forever game with me. . . .*

Radience gasped and grabbed her abdomen, forgetting for a moment to breathe.

She looked at Jiana, and the warrior turned to look at her. They locked eyes for an instant.

In that moment, half a heartbeat, Radience saw worlds enclosing worlds, space within space. She saw the dim, shadowy figures of the gods, their dancing fingers dangling strings to their human puppets below, and above these, even longer strings, even more clever hands, far away and above.

And then? What above them?

It's no good, said the *daeva* within (and now she was certain it was Jiana). *It's turtles turtles turtles, all the way up.*

The girl wrapped her arms around her stomach and backed away from the warrior, frightened. Turtles? What did she mean turtles?

Jiana still watched her fixedly, when she should have been watching her opponent. But the Doorian seemed strangely frozen, as if something held him back and kept him from the winning blow.

The crowd had grown silent, puzzled and bewildered. Most still stared at the statue-like combatants, but a few, following Jiana's gaze, now looked at Radience.

Then slowly Jiana let her herding stick droop, a ghostly half-smile on her lips. In a moment, its tip touched the dirt.

At once, the Doorian shook his head and sputtered, as if he had been dunked in a well.

With a grunt of effort, he raised his huge tulwar to his right shoulder and swung the sword like an axe.

Jiana reacted easily; she had clearly anticipated the blow. She raised her stick . . . but the parry did not carry far enough!

Though the bulk of the swing was checked, the sheer weight still pushed through her defenses and battered her arm—the same one that had been wounded in the last fight, Radience remembered.

Jiana dropped to one knee, cradling her useless, shattered arm.

The savage Doorian took a step forward and raised his sword for the killing blow. But before the devil could smite her, the Listmaster charged across the field and tackled him. Four Horsemen piled on, virtually crushing the brute.

Somehow, injured though she obviously was, Jiana rolled out of the path of the crashing bodies, which would probably have squashed her like a horse atop a careless child.

"The physical is finished!" yelled the Listmaster, angrily. The Doorian looked confused until the Listmaster said something in Doorish, then announced the man the winner.

Speaking again in human speech, the Listmaster recited the names of the opponents of the huge oaf, whose own name was apparently Faisal al'Tuq Barouk. Both he and Jiana, who seemed astonishingly recovered, were surrounded by the mob and inaccessible.

Radience blinked back tears. Clearly, Jiana was the better, yet the merest mischance had cost her the fight and nearly her life.

And is this how I want to live my life?

The slave girl turned her back on the woman and the crowd of gloaters and well-wishers, and walked slowly back towards the kitchen khayma, which seemed to have receded from her by the width of the Great Sands.

Would you rather live your days dodging the Overman?

Damn al'Tuq Barouk! she thought. *Why couldn't he have missed, just that single blow? Why didn't she block it? What's the matter with her?*

"Nothing," said a voice at her back. "I am much recovered."

Radience turned to stare.

"But thank you for your concern," Jiana added politely.

"I—I didn't say any—any—" She realized she was babbling, and closed her mouth quickly.

"Your questions were clear enough. I played my move in the game."

"What game?" Radience demanded. "Do you listen to my stomach? You're a *daeva!*"

"Just a survivor. I mean the Great Game, the forever game, all this." She gestured vaguely at the khaymas. "I suddenly realized what the Tunk meant when he talked about meeting my destiny on the road to Tool."

"What trunk?"

"How can I expect you to join me until I join you?"

"I don't understand you. Were you wounded?"

Jiana smiled, and scratched her crest of hair, using her injured arm. It seemed to work fine.

"You'll understand day after tomorrow. Soon enough. Meantime, keep your left up."

Jiana struck a quick blow at Radience's left cheek. The girl raised her hand to block, but Jiana pulled the blow at the last moment. Then the pale-skinned, black-crested warrior turned and walked away, as serene as any Horsemaster on a cloudy day.

For a long time Radience watched as the woman walked through the camp, retrieved her horse, and rode back over the bridge. No one else paid her any attention; they were too busy pouring goat's milk on Barouk's head and slapping him on his back.

The gargantuan warrior was formally inducted into the Caliph's Body of the Elect and al'Sophiate's Horsemen, and they gave him a silver bridle. He was invited to ride with the people.

Radience felt a hot glare on her back. It was the Overman, and this time he stood at the flap for real. Without looking back, she ran back towards the kitchen, tucking her bad arm inside her shirt again.

She said I'd understand tomorrow's morrow, she thought; and clutching that promise to her stomach like a newborn pup, she pushed through a day's work in half the time.

6

Damn, Jiana thought as she walked, pretending to be her old master in the Flower Empire. *Why'd I make that snakeshit comment about keeping her left up, probably thinks I was making fun, don't know how to handle these fucking cripples. No, she's not crippled. Probably still hurt by it. Shit, I've seen a thousand worse off guys from the wars. Why did I say it?*

She kept her face impassive and her thoughts to herself, weaving her way through the throngs (*not cheering me today, cheering that pumpkinhead bastard, thinks he won, the slug*) towards the stables, towards Cascade.

Nameless Serp, what am I going to do with Cascade? Jiana stopped at the flap to the stable khayma, pondering.

What was she going to do with her horse?

The plan had sprung full-grown from her stomach, as Tooqa the Nameless Serpentine had sprung, full sized and eggless, from the belly of its father.

How free a slave? Only the slave can free herself, so Jiana must become a slave to free the slave.

It made so much more sense in the battle square!

You can STEAL a slave, she had thought, her feet slipping on the bloody hard-dirt. *You can kill a slave, beat a slave, sell a slave, and loose a slave. But to FREE a slave . . .*

She had stepped around the creeping Doorian, letting her hands and feet do the fighting while her stomach mulled more important thoughts.

Freedom, she thought. *Free the slave. Free the soul and the belly will follow, he told me. Free state. Overlord. Kill your own gods—who can kill the other gal's gods?*

And then the thought had pushed through her stomach like a beer-belch: only Radience can free Radience.

Followed in an instant by the sister-thought: *the warrior trains the warrior. The baker teaches the baker. Who teaches the slave?*

Jiana pushed through the flap. Slaves fanned the air inside, keeping the horses cool and comfortable.

Cascade looked up when she entered and nickered. He watched her cross the canvas floor, seeming oddly sentient.

She tugged at the knot; it was reassuringly tight. She gripped his bridle, gently but firmly, and whispered to his eyes: you're mine—I'm yours—you're mine.

Glancing into the stall, Jiana saw that the water was criminally low, and there was no trace of any oats.

She turned to berate the stablehand, but he was breathlessly pulling a horse away from its new found mortal enemy in the next stall.

Hell with it, she thought. *Another time.* She turned back to Cascade.

Somehow, he was untied, the reins tossed lightly back over his neck.

He looked at her, expressionless, something deeper than a horse in his eyes.

"Come on," Jiana said, but she realized as soon as she heard her own voice that it was a suggestion, not an order.

She unhooked the rope gate, and Cascade stepped out of his stall. She reached for his bridle, but then dropped her hand to her side and strolled out of the khayma. Cascade followed, his hooves making a harsh, grinding noise against the sand and canvas floor.

Outside he stopped, and turned his left side towards her. She stepped into the stirrup and mounted cavalry-style, with a forward kick.

Cascade walked towards the bridge until Jiana said, "Bay Bay," then he began to canter.

Over the bridge the town began, south of the Prince's drill-grounds where al'Sophiate camped. Here the houses were massive, built of slave-hauled stone back in the days (it was said) of the Ti Ji Tul, the First People of the world.

Here was Old Bay Bay, solid-ground Bay Bay. If she were to journey to the Market Maze, she would pass through the financial district, over two bridges or a pay-the-troll causeway, and then pass through the gate onto the floats and streets that spread across the bay, the "Maze."

The Maze was home. She had not been born there, but reborn surely, and twice-eight turns she had called it more or less "Prime Base." Even the biannual mass suicide of shoretonies in Bay Bay harbor no longer made her want to tear her nose from her face; she simply buried it in a snoot of strongtea, like everyone else, until the smell dissipated.

But she did not turn Cascade towards the bridges, or even along the echoing flagstones of the financial district, deserted at such an hour.

Instead, she hooked west along the Street of Dreams, negotiated the perennial vending carts along Apple Pack Road, and galloped through Tanny's Garden of Romance before the jacks could seize her and make her pay "admission."

She tried to rein Cascade in before the far wall of

Tanny's; but he laid back his ears, picked up his hooves, and cleared it by a hand's breadth with a wicked leap.

When Jiana had swallowed her heart back down her throat, she nudged him and he turned into Tsil Jan Lane, where he walked under the shades and oaks and across a carpet of browning, rustling leaves. Once every ten steps, the less moon could be seen glimmering through the tree top canopy.

Dilai lived along the lane (Lord Dilai now) if he had not yet left for Door. *Why is the bastard going to Door?*

His house was in an uproar. Lanterns and torches ringed it 'round. The neighbors out on the Lane in the sleeping caps, glowering and polishing their eyelenses.

Carts everywhere; two dozen servants heaping the household goods into some semblance of traveling order. Orders were barked, oaths and denunciations of slackery, but all in a whisper, which gave the scene the ominous undertones of an ambush or a sickroom. It simply was not *done* to raise a ruckus along the Tsil Jan!

Jiana dismounted and approached the door. A servant took Cascade's bridle. After a moment of suspicion, the horse allowed himself to be led away to the stables. Jiana had the most disconcerting thought that he had expected to be put up in the big house.

At the door, she paused. The butler and Dilai's valet were engaged in a spirited yet dignified discussion of who had been at fault in the recent collision between a parlor maid and the cook.

Jiana cleared her throat, and the argument broke off as if the litigants had suddenly been strangled.

"May I help you?" inquired the butler.

"Dilai," she said, tugging off her gloves.

"Lord Dilai is indisposed at present," said the valet.

"Well dispose of him," she suggested, "and get his lazy butt out here to talk to his favorite bitch."

The valet stiffened, and turned away, muttering "very good, madam" almost too softly to be heard. The butler maintained a post in the doorway, eyeing her unpleasantly.

"Moving out?" Jiana inquired, trying to pass the time politely.

"It would appear so, madam," grumped the butler. He did not sound pleased, though his stone-face would have won many a hand of cards.

"Going to Door?"

"The master has not taken me into his confidence, madam," the butler lied, unaware that Dilai had been telling everyone from the Maze, to the docks, to the floats, to the royal castle.

"Leaving in the morning?" It looked doubtful, unless they planned to work the night through.

"That is our earnest intention, madam."

After a long, uncomfortable silence, the gentleman's gentleman reappeared with an obviously hungover Dilai.

"God," he whined, "what do *you* want this early in the bloody morning?"

Jiana looked in puzzlement at the blackness around her and the moons in the sky. She let the remark pass; his eyes were tightly shut, anyway.

"Do me a favor," she begged.

"Anything, if I don't have to wake up."

"Can we make up long enough for you to sell my sweet, young arse to the Toolians as a slave?"

One of Dilai's eyelids popped open. Slowly the other pulled, as if stuck together, then opened, too. After a few beats, each eye separately found Jiana and focused.

"Sell? You? Slave?"

"I'll have to shave my crest. Shit. Slaves shave their heads, though—not so far apart, slave and warrior, what? Just a crest of hair down the middle. Snakes. Sorry to spring this on you, but you're credible—rich, you know, and bugging out anyway, to Door. He'll believe it, coming from you. Am I babbling? I sound like I'm babbling. Look, Dilai, I'm not used to asking favors . . . know what I mean?"

Jiana realized she was tugging at her pantaloons, so she squeezed her hand into a fist and pressed it against her thigh.

*This is lame. This is really fucking lame. Where's that
fat bastard priest, now that I need his tongue?*

Jiana watched the light begin to dawn across Marblehead.

"You want me to sell you to the Satrap as a slave,
what?"

"You got it."

"Why? That is, if it's any of my business, seeing as
you're involving me."

"Ask me in and I'll talk."

Dilai seemed to shrink a few inches in height as he
cringed at the thought of the ordeal.

"As you in? Now?"

"Now. I don't plan to spend the night in the stables."

He scowled, rubbing the stubble on his chin.

"Night? In the stables?"

"I really wish you wouldn't repeat everything I say. It's
disconcerting."

"Well—you know there are no rooms, Jinny."

She smiled; he rarely called her that anymore.

"Sure, sleep on the floor. Better than a cell or a bar-
racks, anyway. In the morning we can breakfast, and . . .
plan things."

He nodded, and stepped aside. Jiana entered, and settled by the unlit fireplace. She leaned back against her
saddlesack and composed herself for sleep.

Plan things, she thought, or was it the voice of her other
self, timidly creeping from her hiding den?

Plan things: like, what to do with Cascade?

And oh snakes, what about my sword? What of Wave?

Jiana had a sinking feeling that slaves were not generally
allowed to carry swords.

The floor proved uncomfortable, and after watching the
less moon creep to the top of the sky, Jiana arose, crossed
the room, and sat heavily on Dilai's knees.

He was awake already, watching her. She looked at him
and inclined her head slightly. Dilai pulled back the covers, and she climbed inside.

She kissed his forehead first, her lips dry. Then she
worked her way down his face, his lips, his throat. She

gently licked his chest, and she felt him grow hard beneath her pelvis.

But there was no fire.

They made elegant love, and were both quite considerate of each other's feelings. Jiana felt a great surge of politeness, and she would have tipped her hat, had she worn one to bed.

When it was over, she knew it was over.

Cascade paced nervously in the barn. He had been summoned, why? Who was this human, the master human? What horrible place would give him only dried vegetable matter to eat?

He decided to stay quiet; an unknown sphere afforded unpredictable dangers.

A tiny, four-legged furry creature scampered across his stall. Quick as sin, Cascade leaned down and caught the rat in teeth of iron. He rolled it around his tongue for a while, sucking the last drop of juice from its body and chewing the bones carefully, to avoid a splinter.

Chapter III:

Slaving over the bonding,
She bites the hand what frees

Jiana walked briskly alongside Cascade. Dilai walked, too, on the other side of the horse.

Cascade would not allow Dilai to mount, and Dilai would not walk when a soldier rode.

"So *both* our feet are sore," Jiana muttered. If he heard, he did not react.

She listened to Cascade's hooves on the gravel for a time. Then she broke the verbal silence.

"Why Door? It's such a hellish, damn place. Hot and sandy. Snakes, too."

"Sorry? I thought you *liked* snakes."

"I . . . well, I *used to* worship them as children of the Nameless Serpentine. But I slew him four years ago, so now I have no religion. Anyway, I always hated the slithering, slimy bastards. Gave me strange thoughts."

"I think I know what kind of thoughts you mean, and I thought you had those all day long, with or without reptiles. And anyway, snakes are not slimy. You're thinking of worms."

"Worms, then. Snakes. What's the difference? You didn't answer about why you're going to fucking Door."

Dilai did not answer for a number of steps. When Jiana

76

peered over the horse at him, he was smiling, his eyes fixed on the middle distance.

"I say, it gets me away from the Court. Away from the Hollow Prince."

"That what they're calling him now?"

"Oh, this and that. Here and there. We began dubbing him nicknames directly he came back from that quest you officiated."

"I was just a player, like all the others. Like the Prince, what's his name, Alanai."

"Odd you should forget."

"Why? I haven't seen him for four years."

"No one has, not outside the Court. I say odd, because I forgot his name only last week, when he offered me the ambassadorship of Door."

"Hah! So you *do* have a reason."

"Ruddy yes, it gets me out of the Court!"

"What are your qualifications for ambassador?"

Dilai stopped and looked at her quizzically.

"Qualifications? It's an ambassadorship, not a smithy job. One doesn't need qualifications, save a clever choice of parentage."

Jiana rested her arms against Cascade's back, and nestled her chin on her wrists. She looked through Lord Dilai towards the Drilling Bridge. Once over the bridge, she would be a slave.

"I guess it's time," she sighed.

She rummaged in her saddlesack until she found her razor. It was still quite sharp, but soon it would be as dull as the Prince.

She ran her fingers through the long, lush crest that ran down the middle of her scalp, feeling the tugging at the roots and the wind on the bare sides of her head.

"Nameless Serp, this is going to feel weird. I've never just shaved it all off before. Not the hair on my head, I mean."

"I shan't even ask. Er, it occurs to me that you had better cut the lion's share off with a knife before you tackle it with the razor. You'll dull it too soon, otherwise."

"I know. I've shaved the sides, remember?" *Good-bye,* she thought, as she pulled the hair tight and began to slice through it with her skinning knife.

Dilai watched her every cut, entranced and vaguely disturbed. Jiana did not mind as much as she had feared she would.

I've a good face for it, she thought, *rounded and symmetrical. Eyes planted in the center, not high or low. Nose okay, cheeks pale. Why worry? It all grows back. . . .*

When she had sliced the hair down to a finger joint in length, she poured water into a basin and wet her head, soaped it, then began the job.

The razor scraped across her scalp, making noises like a polishing stone on wooden furniture. As she shaved, she ran her hands over her head, feeling for the long, stray wisps that would give her away. Neither she nor Dilai had thought to bring a mirror.

"Cast his shadow three times across my life," she mumbled. She could not for her life remember where she had heard the phrase; but she knew it was something dreadfully important, something she *should* remember.

She surveyed the damage done to her reflection in the water basin.

"Can't say I find it attractive," she said.

"That isn't its purpose," Dilai said with a smile.

"Hm." Jiana removed her pantaloons, carefully folded them, and put them in her saddle sack. Then she removed her tunic and shirt, and stood naked and bald as the day she was born. *Except Momma always told me I was born with blonde hair, so I guess I'm balder than the day I was born.*

"Now what?" Both she and Dilai asked the question at the same time.

"Now for the hard part," Jiana answered, "you have to ride Cascade."

"And you have to dress and walk behind. Trot behind."

And what of Wave? The problem had been worrying her since the previous night.

"What about my sword?" she asked.

"Ah, what's the problem? Can't be that expensive. I'll get you another one later, if you're hard up."

Jiana smiled. Dilai was Dilai.

"It doesn't work that way, L.D. I've used and suffused this sword with—" She stopped, remembering the cold force coursing through her womb, flowing up through stomach and heart and down her sword arm, spilling out of Wave as blood spurts from a heart wound.

She closed her eyes, but the connection remained between her and the blade. It was a sword the storysingers call "twice-forged," once by fire and again by blood. It was an arm, a hand. Jiana did not wield it; she allied it.

"No. Even to free that dumb cripple I won't ditch Wave. She stays—as what?"

"Can you disguise it?"

A thought began to prick at her stomach, a rose with a persistent thorn that jabbed at a piece of forgotten arcana. A lark. A laugh from the Flower Empire days.

What had Tsu Hsi done?

A rush of remembrance. Jiana's training partner from the Pit. The girl had once "hidden" her brother's sword, a fine Crescent Moon blade, by shrouding it in a simple illusion of ivory. Xiau Tsu had searched the room for hours, raging and threatening, and never once picked up the intricately-carved elephant tusk that to Jiana and Tsu Hsi still looked like nothing more than a blue-glowing crescent sword.

"Let me talk to Cascade," Jiana requested. Dilai withdrew two steps, respectfully.

She took the horse by his bridle and held his head steady. She pressed her cheek against his, and imagined that he could hear and understand: *It will be a day or so. I cannot let anyone know about me. Please remember, and please watch over Wave as if she were yours . . .*

Don't be stupid, she imagined him responding. *I know what you're up to. Sneak me a treat, let me know you still remember, too.*

Jiana picked up Wave and held the sword aloft, gently rippling it in the still air. She closed her eyes and began to prepare the spell.

A touch, a whisper of leather, a taste of wooden buckle. She envisioned a Toolian horse collar, worn and oiled, but still serviceable. The collars identified the owners, and were not removed. Slaves, too, wore collars, for the same reason.

Jiana wasted no time trying to remember the specifics of Tsu Hsi's incantation; it was irrelevant anyway.

The essence of magic was purity of will. The mantras and mudras were nothing more than tricks to calm the body and *focus the will*.

Jiana reached deep within herself, into the Wolf Time itself—into the Jianabel Night of her spirit—and plucked therefrom a tendril of power.

She spun the strand, spun it into a confectioner's spiral, then looped it into a twisting, coiling snake.

She opened her eyes cautiously, left then right, and found herself peering into the Overrealm that sat atop Reality Prime.

The strand-snake spun before her, eerily glowing with the blue radiance cast by magical power. It hovered in the air directly below Wave.

Jiana lowered the sheathed sword into the center of the prismatic spiral, holding the sharper, harder image of the horse collar firmly in her mind. When the sword was completely covered, she began to contract the spirals.

The strand-snake spun faster and faster as it contacted the metal. Soon it vanished into a thin thread that spun its way into the center of the blade. Jiana began to tremble with the strain of the Overrealm; it had been many turns since she had breathed such power.

Soon, even the thin thread above the sword was merged. All that remained when Jiana looked at Wave was a sparkle so faint that she only saw it when looking elsewhere. The sparkle, and of course the blue glow that now hugged the contours of her sheathed blade.

Jiana cautiously pulled back her consciousness from the now-disguised sword, afraid of perturbing the delicate balance of forces she had set around it.

"Well?" she asked, looking at Dilai.

He was staring curiously at her and at Wave.

"Well what?"

"What's it look like?"

Dilai studied the blade for a few beats.

"Well, it looks like a sheathed sword."

She eyed him reproachfully.

"Wait," he added, "it's sort of rippling in the breeze. Is it supposed to ripple? Is that a kind of disguise?"

She continued to scowl at him.

"Magic doesn't affect you, does it?"

Dilai tugged at his lip.

"Not really," he said, trying to be polite (*last night, last night,* she thought. *What's happened to us?*). "I mean, I say, it hasn't ever. I don't even really believe in it. Actually."

She turned back to the sword. It still glowed strongly, despite the vote of no confidence from her aristocratic companion.

"You're not representative, Dilai. Those nomads are all *terrified* of magic; think it's a sure sign of a pact with Arhatman, like burying corpses." She smiled, as much to convince herself as Dilai. "They'll buy into it. Yes, they will."

She buckled Wave around Cascade's neck. Dilai watched dubiously.

"If you say so. What's it supposed to look like?"

"Horse collar. You ready?"

He took a deep breath, looking even less certain about his personal future.

"You sure I have to ride that beast? Look at the size of it!"

"No way around it, Lord D., old chum. I think I can keep him calm."

"Think?"

"He seems to listen to me."

"*Seems?*" Dilai's voice was sharp-edged, and his face the merest shade paler than her own.

"Get on."

She cupped Cascade's nose in her hands, and looked into his eyes. She was still seeing the Overrealm, and the horse's eyes brimmed with intelligence and knowingness.

For me, she asked.

"*For you*."

She started; had he spoken aloud? But no, Dilai had not heard anything.

Horses speaking aloud? Oh Jiana, you are a pip!

You've finished your sulk? Glad to hear you again. I really mean that, kid.

You invaded my realm, Jiana-dearest. Mine! *You had no right!*

I am you, remember? Your very words, Wolf Girl.

There was a long, silent pause in Jiana's stomach. She grinned. For once, Jianabel had nothing to answer.

Jiana felt a tingling in her hands. She glanced down at them, and saw them both trembling uncontrollably.

Time to come down from the clouds, she thought. Her physical body ached with the strain. Over the turns, she had learned to heed such warnings, rather than brutally repressing her fears and feelings. Harmony still eluded her, but at least her spirit and flesh no longer fought an active war.

She relaxed her stomach and slowed her heart. Then she followed the strand that poked into the wolf corner of her spirit, and let the connection go.

Nothing happened; she remained in the Overrealm.

Upset, she tried again, a bit more perfunctorily. Again, the response was nil. She remained in an elevated sphere.

Now her entire body was shaking violently.

Jiana exerted her entire will into severing that connection. A silvery laugh trickled back up at her from a little girl's mouth, a mouth filled with sharp teeth filed to a point.

Let—me—go! Jiana demanded.

Suddenly the connection loosed, and Jiana's spirit recoiled. She felt her spirit tangle in the broken, writhing umbilical.

Jiana fell, it seemed like half her own height. The impact of landing knocked her to one knee.

"Jiana? Are you alright?"

She stood slowly and opened her eyes again. The blue

was gone. Her eyes were normal, no longer seeing the Overrealm.

"Yeah," she said, "alright. Stumbled, s'all." She rubbed the feeling back into her hands. "Okay, m'lord. You ready? Mount up."

Taking a deep breath, Dilai climbed awkwardly into the saddle.

"You don't need the m'lord rot in private, Jiana. I'm still Dilai."

"Of course. My mistake," she smiled.

Cascade stirred restlessly, and turned around twice. But he made no effort to buck Dilai off his back.

The Lord sat rigidly atop the horse, holding the reins like a fishing pole.

"I always, that is, I nearly always travel by carriage. Actually." He seemed embarrassed by his lack of horse-manship.

Jiana smiled.

"You can afford to. Come on, Master. Let's get over the bridge. See what you can get for an uppity bitch."

"Put your clothes back on," he suggested.

2

They entered the Toolian camp, Dilai riding while Jiana trotted obediently behind. With every step she repeated silently in her stomach, *I can't leave, I can't go home, I can't turn around, he owns me.*

Soon she believed it. She felt her mind change, grow leaden, dull, and heavy, as if it were encased in hard metal. Her stomach grew weak with the weight of it.

Her head throbbed, aching from the back around the sides to her sinuses. She concentrated on the colors of day, dimming them to the greys of twilight and the shadows of night. She felt the hard road stub her toes and bruise her heels as she lumbered along, slave-like.

But her spirit rebelled. When she muted the colors and probed for the aches and pains, the wonderful smells of the world intruded, enticing her back to her wide, wild

ways in Bay Bay. When she stoppered her nose, her ears
heard the faint, faraway cries of fishmongers, flower-sellers,
and farmers hawking potatoes and pomegranates.

Jiana viciously hammered down every vestigial thought
or sense that held the faintest glimmer of light. But then
the Wolf Girl rose in indignation—or that area of Jiana's
mind that she chose to personify by Jianabel, if Toldo
Mondo spoke the truth.

I shan't be a slave! I simply shan't, and neither will you!

We have no choice, Jiana thought. *He owns us. We can't
get away; it would be wrong.*

That's not so, you're making it all up!

*We're trapped. It's too frightening out there. Let's pray
that he's nice to us, whoever buys us from Dilai.*

This is maddening!

*What are you, trying to make trouble? The nail that
stands up shall be hammered down.*

Jiana dearest, what are you doing?

Jianabel's frustration was understandable. In a dim,
unsunken corner of Jiana's stomach, she realized she was
being harsh and cold, not letting the frightened, little girl
in on what was happening.

But to do so would be to break continuity, and everything depended upon Jiana convincing *herself* that she
really *was* a slave. Pretending was not good enough: for
the lesson to hold meaning, the servitude had to be real.
Otherwise she proved nothing, except that she was a good
actor.

The demonstration ran deeper. She had to prove to
herself, and then to Radience, that a slave is never more
than one myth away from freedom.

Dilai halted, and Jiana reflexively dropped to her knees,
eyes downcast but ears pricked for a command.

She heard his leather cuirass creak. It was only for
show, and the Toolians would know that; it would not stop
a sword edge. But it was impressive as a badge of rank,
spun with goldenthread and frosted with white gold.

After a pause, Dilai spoke. He did not speak to anyone
in particular, rather to the air. Jiana guessed there was no

one of acceptable rank in the immediate vicinity, so he spoke as to a mixed group.

"Is there, ah, anyone to whom I could speak?" he asked.

Jiana heard two Horsemen mumble to themselves about an Overhorseman. Jiana felt a certain, mean touch of pride that her master so outranked them that they could not even speak face to face.

Footsteps crunched away, and after a few moments, two pairs returned.

Jiana sneaked a peek; one of the Horsemen had brought a superior. By sheer mischance, he had brought the self-same Overman that had beaten Radience earlier, and whom Jiana had stared down into submission.

Now she felt a shiver wash through her. What if he recognized her? What would he do? Would he beat her later, when no one was looking?

Worse—he might not even . . . She crushed the thought quickly, lest it show in her eyes.

She felt something pressing into the heel of her hand. It was a rock, flat and sharp-edged. When had she picked it up? She held it in a perfect throwing position, fingers curled around the smooth end, as though ready to sling it through the air and bury it in the Overman's forehead.

She shuddered, terrified at such a disloyal thought. This man could soon be her master! But listen: Dilai was speaking.

"Ah, good morning, exalted one."

"Good morning, magnificent Bay Bay lord."

"I see that the turns have treated you kindly, ladling wisdom and strength into your stomach while leaving hardly a wrinkle on your face or grey strand in your mane."

"Good morning, it is to marvel of your youthful strength and brick-a-bats."

There was a puzzled silence, as Dilai and Jiana both tried to imagine what the Toolian was trying to say. After a few beats, Dilai continued, presuming for the moment that whatever it was had been meant as a compliment.

"Sir, I leave by private transport this morning for the South, and I cannot take this fine horse on the ship. I have

heard from travelers far and near that the Toolians are the
greatest judges of horseflesh in all the lands that are not
under oceans."

Jiana watched through slitted eyelids. The Overman
walked slowly around Cascade, eyeing him with a calculating, gilt-edged glimmer.

"A magnificent friend, but you wish to depose of his
companiony?"

Dilai gestured vaguely at Cascade.

"I find I am less interested in the horse than in more,
hm, transportable goods."

"Coins."

"Coins or bills, if they are drawn on reputable banks."

"Coins. We do not use banks. There are no deserts in
the banks."

"Deserts in the . . . ? Ah, yes. But I thought your king
or Caliph was negotiating a deal with—" Dilai trailed off,
seeing the frozen, indignant look on the Toolian's face.
"Quite," continued Dilai. "Coins are the better, actually."

They began to haggle over the price. Jiana noted with
wry amusement that on two occasions, the Overman's lack
of ability with the tongue of the People led him to make a
disadvantageous leap in his offer. Lord Dilai clearly got
the better of the bargaining, except for the fact that Cascade was probably some sort of magical horse.

Finally, the moment of truth had arrived. Jiana pulled
at the hem of her plain but servicable frock, given her by
her master, as Dilai carefully held out for the last few
copper pennies that were the difference between the two
offers.

It was close enough for the Toolian to smell the deal,
but just beyond what he wanted to pay for a horse—*any*
horse. Dilai hemmed and hung, and cast about for some
way to sweeten the deal.

"Well, I just can't; it's still too low." He allowed his eyes
to light on Jiana. They narrowed, then brightened.

"Well, how about her?" he asked the Overman. "She
must be worth *something*, even to clean stables. She's
really quite good with horses, and this one is used to her."

"Her?" The Overman stared at Jiana, and she blushed. "Take things off."

"Take off your frock, Jiana," Dilai ordered.

Jiana looked pleadingly at her master, begging him with her eyes not to do this to her. She felt a terrible shame creeping up her entire body; but he was who he was.

Hands shaking, she took the ends of the frock and pulled it up, past her thighs and her crotch to her belly. There she froze.

"Jiana," Dilai said, in a reproving voice.

She took a deep breath, and raised the frock above her belly. The hardest part over, it took little more effort to pull it over her breasts and over her head. She stood, tiny and trembling, holding the frock behind her like a guilty, little girl hiding an outgrown rag doll.

The Overman walked around her, exactly as he had walked around the horse. Jiana's cheeks flushed red, and she was embarrassed to realize that other parts of her body were flushing as well.

The Overman completed his circuit, and fingered his dark-shadowed chin.

"She comes a slave?"

"She is."

The Toolian rubbed his palm against the stubble of his beard.

"There are no slaves to Bay Bay."

"Right-o." Dilai leaned in and nudged the Overman in his ribs. "No crime either. Haw haw!"

For a moment, the Overman looked puzzled; then he got it.

"Ah ah!" He accepted the explanation with little difficulty; the Bay Bay lord only told him what he had always believed anyway.

"Take your time," Dilai yawned, looking wistfully back across the bridge.

"Is okay," the Overman responded. "I will take, pay with horse and with slave. Stables you say?"

"She is good with the horses. Very good. Hate to let her go, but a deal is a deal."

"Is okay," the Overman added, definitively. He carefully counted out the money in Toolian gold and steel. Dilai counted it again, and the Overman did not seem insulted.

"Good-bye," said Dilai, his eyes misting. "I shall miss you, and I shall always remember." He rubbed Cascade's nuzzle, and Cascade tolerated the familiarity.

Then Dilai turned sadly, and began the stroll back into town.

Jiana became aware that the Overman was looking at her.

"You remind me of someone," he said in Tooltak; "someone of little consequence. Do you speak Language?"

Jiana hesitated, then nodded.

He looked at her face for a few moments more, tilting his head first one way then the other. Then he sniffed, and grunted.

"Stables, bitch," he ordered.

Jiana looked confused, then repeated, "Stables? Where—they are stables?"

The Overman pushed her in the direction of the stables, where Cascade had been boarded the previous day.

"Follow your nose, stupid," said the Overman. He watched her like a kite watches the dying, as she led the cooperative horse to the proper khayma along a somewhat meandering path, as though truly following her nose and not her memory.

3

The khayma that served as the stables was dark, and cooler than any of the others. Three slaves dutifully fanned the horses with palm fronds to keep them from overheating. The humans in the other khaymas fended for themselves.

Makes sense. Horses are more sensitive.

She blinked in the darkness. The only light came from the flap she still held open. The red glow from a portable forge painted everything inside the khayma lurid and bloody.

A burly man stood over the forge, hammer and tongs in

his hands. He had a scraggly beard, and a very un-Toolian hat. The hat was burned and blackened from the smoke.

"Another one, Curse," rumbled the Overman from behind Jiana. He pushed her none too gently into the khayma and stepped in after her, dropping the flap.

Curse grunted, and began to fan his forge with his hat. He stepped on a bellows, and the coals brightened.

"Collar?"

The Overman left her standing and bent down to a strongbox. He put his lips close to the lock and whispered.

His voice was practically a stage whisper. He spoke in the tongue of the Flower Empire, horribly accented:

> *Flick flack*
> *Click back*
> *Pop box*
> *Drop locks*

Jiana filed the spell away for future use.

The Overman tugged on the lock, and it pulled open reluctantly. *Probably doesn't like his accent,* she thought.

He removed a torque from the strongbox, and snapped the lock shut again.

"You," he barked, gesturing at Jiana. He did not look back at her.

She approached and kneeled, listlessly.

The smith took the torque with his tongs and held it in the fire until the ends glowed.

Tooqa! Are the bastards going to brand me? Am I really going through with this?

The Overman grabbed Jiana's neck and pushed her head down. She balled her right fist, and only barely managed to restrain herself from burying it to the wrist in the Overman's gut.

She could no longer see what they were doing.

Slow. Calm. Calm the breath, the soul will follow. Quiet. Peace. I cannot protest, I cannot get away, they own me, I am theirs. . . .

She felt a cold, wet rag laid across the back of her neck.

Then something—probably the torque—was passed around her neck. The ends were squeezed together, and Jiana heard the hissing scream of the white-hot metal touching the wet cloth.

They held her thus, immobile, for many heartbeats as the metal cooled. Then the Overman let go of her hair, and Curse pulled the rag out from under the torque.

She reached up to feel it; it was tight, immobile, now that it had cooled. It would take a strong man (or a very determined woman warrior) to pry it apart.

"Thanks," grunted the Overman. Curse ignored him; he was back at work on a skinning knife.

"You. Have a name?"

"Jiana," she answered. The Overman did not remember having heard it once before, from Dilai.

"Take your orders from me, then from him, then from the senior slave, Ysmal." He pointed at a black-haired, half-bearded, stupid-looking youngster inspecting nails in a corner of the khayma.

"How must I address the masters?"

"See this band?" He tapped a bronze band that circled his biceps. "Overman. I'm the slavemaster Overman. Curse is the stables Overman. There's the Overhorseman—fuck, ask Ysmal. I'm busy."

The Overman pushed her out of his way and walked towards the flap.

He paused, and turned back to her, staring at the bulge where her breasts lay under her frock.

He pulled at his long, dangling mustache, clearly debating with himself.

"Yeah, I'll come for you tonight. May as well."

Then he left without a backward glance.

Pleasing the horses was easy. Cascade seemed to understand that she had to make a good impression, and he quickly seized control of the horse community. Soon they were eating out of her hand, though each was a warhorse born and bred who would normally consider fingers a delicacy to supplement the oats.

Ysmal pretended to be amused by the way the horses

reacted to Jiana, but she caught a petulant pout on his lips and decided he might be trouble later.

He, too, seemed to hunger for her breasts. Three times he "accidentally" brushed against them while reaching for something on a shelf. Jiana pretended not to notice, but he was worse than Dida had been the first time they met.

The torque kept tingling. At first, she thought it was still hot. Then she decided it was just the unfamiliar tightness of a metal band about her throat.

After a long time, however, a third and more disturbing thought crossed in her stomach.

When she had a free moment, she closed her eyes, letting the core of magic glow like Curse's forge. She spurted a bit up her throat, through her head and face and into her eyes from behind.

She felt her consciousness rise slightly, not as high as the next sphere, just high enough to poke out of Reality Prime.

When she opened her eyes, the khayma looked the same as before. But there were two bright spots of blue: the torque around Ysmal's neck and the torque around the slave with the palm frond.

Jiana could not see her own neck; but she had no doubt of what she would see if she could.

Great. Just snakey.

She pulled her spirit back into her body without bothering to close her eyes. The shift was jarring, which was why shielding one's eyes was common practice.

Ah well. Knew it wouldn't be easy. Damn that Tunk!

There was little to do as the day passed. The Horsemen were so enamored of their animals that they performed the horse care personally, currying, combing, feeding and watering, inspecting their hooves, and putting them to bed.

She watched Ysmal and the other stable slaves and followed their lead, straightening up the khayma, oiling the saddles, and taking her turn fanning the horses. It was mindless work, giving her plenty of time to plan.

As the sun sank into a bloody sky, the Overman returned for her, as he had threatened.

He lowered his voice an octave and swelled his muscles.

"You will come with me, bitch," he said, trying his best to growl the words.

She trotted along obediently, already preparing her stomach for the spell. She had had most of the day to plan it.

Jiana kindled the power within her like an inverted fire. The base of the power began at the crown of her head, the flames fed by the waning sun. The tip of the flame ended at her crotch; her master in the Flower Empire had always spoken of a woman's vagina as the focal node of her spiritual power, so surely it was the point of her magic, as well.

Jiana remembered.

She remembered sunny days back in White Falls, long before the Wolf Time. She was a child, a little girl playing with the other little girls and boys.

No swords back then. She had a knife, a knife that years later she would pull out of her father after he—

Control. Control the mind. Own the thoughts.

The night was a party, a festival for the entire village. Lanterns danced and bobbed on the river like drunken flutterfires. The barges poled back and forth, from White Falls to Tojitown, their sister city in the adjacent parish (really the same city, but that was another tale long in the pulling).

She carried a great, blown-up pig's bladder, as did all the kids. They bopped each other, playing soldier, and the boys all complained that Jianabelana was too, too rough.

The Overman spun her around violently. A queer light shone in his eyes, as if they reflected those bobbing torches from two hundred leagues behind and a thousand, thousand, years before.

"Drop those clothes, you piece of shit," he ordered. Not giving her a chance, her ripped open her frock, ruining it.

She stood before him, naked and trembling. She futilely tried to cover her belly from his gaze.

. . . *She relaxed her stance, reached out, and tore open his throat with a simple, practiced thrust* [no, all a lie . . .] of her rigid, knife-like fingers.

Control. You are a slave. He can do what he will, and you have no power to stop him.

I have one power.

Yes, that you have. But for today and tomorrow, there is no blood dripping from your hands.

An unwiped trickle of drool leaked from the corner of his lips. He tried to smile, but instead grimaced hideously. His teeth had all rotted away but two [liar liar! you peer into his heart!].

"I know what you want," he breathed, in a sickening attempt at romance.

Jiana felt a cold, ice-knife of fear slide up through her bowels into her stomach. Her heart raced, and she began to hyperventilate.

Good. Better. Panic, just the ticket. You have utter control, and you are a frightened, hysterical, powerless slave.

Tamikami taunted her once too often, that picnic day back in White Falls, saying she had an unnatural yearning for her sister.

She wound up for a super blow with the bladder, cut underneath his pitiful attempt to parry (a frosty, snakey bitch even back then at age six), and walloped him under the jaw so hard they needed a bucketful to bring him 'round-about.

But her bladder caught on his tooth and punctured.

Jiana could see the bulge in the Overman's crotch even before he dropped his silk pantaloons. His penis was massive, gigantic. This surprised her; the way he was acting, she expected a pecker the size of a *tulee* twig.

It was pulsing now, as she blanched backwards. It grew redder and thicker even as she grew whiter and more faint.

It strained towards her, demanding attention, demanding a victim. A drop of clear liquid formed at the tip, but whether it was semen or urine, Jiana could not tell. Not that she cared.

Slowly, the bladder deflated. With every breath of Jianabelana, the balloon exhaled, wheezing and dying as she watched.

She pushed the power out of her, contracting her womb and vagina as if giving birth.

The bladder deflated, life-air leaking out with every heartbeat.

The Overman's penis began to droop and sag. It thumped against his thighs, and he suddenly noticed the betrayal.

He clutched at it, yanking on it furiously.

The bladder hung limply from Jianabelana's stick, as she sadly realized that it had given its life for that satisfying, orgasmic boffing of Tamikami's jaw. She shrugged resignedly.

In a moment, the Overman was savagely masturbating a flaccid piece of flesh. Jiana's attack was specifically against his sexual prowess, but the spell had a deeper current that Jiana felt stir *beneath* Reality Prime.

It struck to the heart of his manhood, as he saw it. A simple deflation, useless against a self-possessed man or woman who was not puffed up with himself.

But devastating against the Overman. With a roar of anger, frustration, and humiliation, he dropped his member and grabbed Jiana's shoulders instead, throwing her to the ground.

She knelt there, sobbing into her hands most convincingly.

Weak-willed bastard. Hardly a fucking challenge. Like fencing drunks in the Squatting Dog.

Own the thoughts . . . you are a slave, grateful for the reprieve offered by the Almighty Lords of the Sand.

The Overman took a step towards her, and tripped on his own pantaloons, which coiled around his ankles like a serpent. He fell heavily to his knees. His penis dangled like a worm on a fishing hook.

"Get out!" he shouted. But his tone was one of desperation and pleading.

Jiana did not wait for a second invitation. She leaped to her feet and dashed naked across the compound to the servants' khayma, not caring who might be watching.

She passed the night uneasily in the company of the other non-household female slaves.

Shortly before dawn, he came again. But he passed her by without so much as a glance. He grabbed another woman, a Toolian (as were all but a few). She went quietly, and the

Overman gave no outward sign of the previous night's failure.

But the fear would grow in his stomach, Jiana knew. It would grow and grow, choking off the fine edge of his brutal entertainment. Eventually, he would work himself into confronting her again.

Jiana grimned, and turned her face to the ground to hide her mirth. Next time, she would have moons, not hours, to prepare herself.

The sun rose, and a hairy woman burst into the slaves' khayma, brushed aside the silk curtains and chattered loudly with each woman as she stumbled bleary-eyed to her feet. Rethe, she called herself; she was the slave Voice (*tol*).

Rethe stood in the middle of the marked-off chamber—really just a corner of the slaves' khayma devoted to non-household females—and began reeling off an exaggerated, hilarious account of the previous day's events. The tales brought the girls up to date and warned them who might be hung over and brutal that morning.

Jiana knelt, like the rest of them, and listened and laughed: Two of the tribe had dueled drunkenly on the North Bridge of Bay Bay; they missed each other but not the water. The five wives of the Listmaster who had steadfastly proclaimed their purity for three weeks were one and all stricken with a strange malady—one that required a dozen douchings with alkali water.

The scene was comfortable and familiar. Jiana recognized Rethe at once.

She was the platoon sergeant.

Jiana's duties were light. al'Sophiate owned slaves for status, not so much for work. Even though there was a large encampment of the Caliph's Elect less than two leagues away, eight out of ten of the slaves were here with him. Where the Caliph went, so went the staff, and be hanged to the wives and children left behind.

Jiana bumped into Radience twice during the day. Neither time did the girl recognize her. Finally, Jiana decided to shake Radience awake.

During a lengthy break in horse business, Jiana approached the young girl diffidently.

"Little one," she began, noticing that Radience was on the verge of sobbing, "what makes you sad on a day when the clouds shield your head from the sun?"

"Oh, leave me alone, Short," the girl snapped. "You must be new, else you would know I am a servant of the kitchen, and should be addressed as mistress. And I'm not sad, and it's none of you business why anyway!"

"Mistress, you must have a reason. Young pups don't weep at the woes of the world."

"I'm waiting for someone. Go 'way and shovel some shit!"

"For whom do you wait?"

"For a liar who said she'd be here, and tomorrow's morrow was soon enough, but she said it day before yesterday."

"The sun has barely crept past midday, which you could tell more easily if the clouds were not in the way."

"She's not coming." Radience spoke decisively, but she unconsciously wriggled her arm inside her tunic, hiding again.

Jiana watched her, enjoying the moment. Then she sat down beside the slave girl.

"Why don't *you* find *her*?" Jiana asked.

"Ha. Ha."

They sat on a rock, and Radience seemed to have found the only flat spot. Jiana squirmed, but parts of the rock kept jabbing her.

"I see a bridge," Jiana said, speaking so low that Radience cocked an ear automatically. "The bridge is but a hundred steps, and no one is near enough to stop you."

"What's across the bridge?"

"Well the point is, you do not know, do you?"

"Yeah. Too bad."

Jiana pursed her lips to keep from smiling.

How the hell can I make it any plainer?

"I see a city. Seventy thousand people. Mazes and rabbit warrens, holes where even the Prince's Guard never ventures. They have no slaves there, Mistress. People wouldn't stand for 'em."

Radience gingerly touched her collar and sighed.

"They don't know how lucky they are, Short."

Snakeshit, do I have to bean her on the head and DRAG her across the river?

"Mistress, if you got up off this rock and strolled across the bridge, you could lose yourself before the less moon rose."

The girl's breathing became rapid and shallow. Jiana's sensitive ears could even hear her heart rabbiting.

The warrior *(slave, I'm a slave now)* snuck a glance at Radience's face. The girl stared at the bridge as if it had turned into an arching dragon. Her skin was white. If Jiana touched it, she knew it would be clammy.

Acute panic attack, Jiana diagnosed. The symptoms were familiar: in the field, they called it "contact shock" or "recruit fever."

"I—I have to go-go. . . ." Radience stood too fast, turned about, and almost fell down from dizziness. She shook her head and hurried back towards the Caliph's khayma. She tucked the other arm inside her tunic as she strode.

Jiana sat for a long time, looking at the Drilling Bridge. Something was blocking the girl; one part of her stomach would not allow the other part to realize who Jiana was.

Damn. This might be a long posting. Damn that Tunk! Why didn't that cockroach pass out before telling people about their fates?

When the shadows began to creep visibly, she stood and walked back to the stables. She would be busy all afternoon, checking shoes and searching for lameness.

Hal'Addad bin Kerat bin El al'Sophiate had concluded his business with the Bank of Bay Bay; he wanted to go home. Tomorrow the Elect would leave on the long march south to Tool and the oasis at Deh Bid.

4

Jiana's eyes popped open, and she sat up. It was nearly dawn, and her heart pounded exactly as it used to when she was in basic training.

She wrapped her arms around her; the air was still chill, and her blankets were wet with dew. She looked east; the tip of the sun was burning a hole through the clouds.

Footsteps. Rethe approached in the dark, wrapped in a woolen robe. She noticed Jiana awake, and smiled. She put two fingers to her lips in a conspiracy of silence.

Rethe ghosted into the circle of female slaves, carefully picking up her robe and skirting the embers of the fire. The slave Voice quietly picked up two iron pots, and Jiana put her fingers into her own ears.

"HAAAAA!" screamed Rethe, and an instant later hurled the pots into a huge pile of cooking gear. The rest of the slaves jumped to their feet, shattered dreams falling off and onto the ground as they lurched in circles, trying to find true north. They stared in shocked silence at Rethe.

"Good morning," she said, almost too softly to be heard. She nonchalantly put a pot of water on the fire and fed the flames.

They would have awakened soon anyway, as the camp came alive. After the Horsemen and the animals and the tradesmen and hawkers bestirred themselves, there was more noise in the Caliph's company than in a thousand pots clanging into an ocean of flatware.

Jiana shook her head, wondering if any Toolian ever talked to anyone closer than a dozen paces, or conversed at less than a shout.

She began to smell food being cooked, though the term *food* might be a charity. The most common breakfast was a sour mush made from rye flour, goat's milk, *tadahchi* root, and spices—mixed and beaten, baked in a portable oven, then fried in animal fat. *Tazh'na*, they called it, "it falls from heaven." Occasionally, it would be folded around dried meat or vegetables, almost like an omelet (Toolians, she noticed, did not seem to have discovered eggs).

Well it's not as bad as rations in Warki's army, or the gravy-soup of the Southers, she lied, choking down a healthy portion. Jiana watched Rethe and saw the woman grimace as she ate her *tazh'na*.

"Do not you like?" Jiana asked, speaking in broken Tooltak.

The slave Voice considered for a moment, pursing her lips.

"I would rather crawl on my hands and knees through monkey vomit," she said reflectively. Then both of them laughed, spraying *tazh'na* onto Kyaddi, staining the jacket she was mending.

Jiana passed Radience twice in the morning, and still the girl did not recognize her. In fact, she avoided Jiana, looking uncomfortable. The third time, Jiana stopped her with an upraised hand.

"Pardon, mistress," the warrior said *[slave! I'm a slave, I can't leave, I can't . . .]*, "but where should this go?" She held aloft the Horseman's jacket that Kyaddi had mended.

Radience put down the bucket of water she carried in her good hand and studied the jacket.

"It belongs to Akadr, son of the Overman of slaves," she said in a haughty voice.

Jiana stared into her eyes. At first, Radience looked away, but she was drawn back by the force of Jiana's gaze.

"Listen to your heart, not your stomach. You know me."

"No . . . I don't—"

"Look at me. Look and forget your idle daydreams of rescue, of a warrior on a great horse plucking you from this world."

Again, Radience started hyperventilating with anxiety.

"It's no good, Radience," Jiana said. "I won't play your slave games."

"Oh, God," she sobbed, dropping her face into her right hand, "I prayed to the Seer for us to be . . ."

"Together? He seems to have answered your prayer."

Radience turned and ran, not looking back. Jiana watched, allowing a faint smile to cross her lips. The new game began.

There was more work in the morning than at any other time, except for the work of marching. Breakfast had to be prepared, plates and pots scrubbed, animals fed and prepared, khaymas struck, and then everything had to be packed onto the *jamals* and the mules—which by itself took an hour.

During this time, by custom the slaves went barefoot. By the time they were ready to march, Jiana's feet were angry and sore from stepping on thorns and sharp, subversive stones. She pulled her goat-leather shoes on with relief, and envied the slaves who had grown up running barefoot across the rocks and sand.

At last the company of Elect was ready to travel. The Caliph had climbed upon his great *jamal* and given his blessing to the journey. Then the Captain of the Horse stood in his saddle and raised his fist. With this signal, the Horsemen started forward, and thus started the entire group, about three hundred freemen and one hundred and fifty slaves. The long day's march had begun.

Far away to Jiana's right, between two grey-green hills, she caught a glimpse of the sea. It was a brilliant blue in the clear light, a jeweled notch cut into the verdant woods south of Bay Bay.

The Great South Road led straight as far as Jiana could see, a legacy from the Eagles, who could never tolerate a curve. It was considerably wider and flatter behind the Elect than ahead of them, pounded by nearly a thousand feet and four hundred hooves.

The day crawled along with the fits and starts, detours and sidetrips like a Briar telling a tale. Jiana's legs and back ached from the long march and from carrying a heavy trunk.

When the sun finally sank seaward and the Captain called the evening's halt, Jiana was so exhausted that she curled like a baby on the ground for a lingering moment, seeking for her center.

Days to come, days to—

She watched her colleagues. They all collapsed. Some sat, some squatted, drawing in the dirt with a stick. No one spoke, no one but Jiana looked at the others. Radience was nowhere to be seen; Jiana had seen her once during the march, but only from afar. She did not look well.

Lying on the ground, she listened to the crickets chirp. The noise was getting louder.

Soon it'll be time to cook and—eat—again, Jiana thought, feeling queasy.

When the sky was fully dark, the older slaves would stir first. They wandered the compound, kicking some of the younger men to rouse them. The women were left to police themselves, but they did not lie idle when the men arose. If they did, Rethe made them regret their indiscretion.

As the sun fell into the ocean, Rethe sat cross-legged, staring at the bloody sky. The air grew chill; the salty night-breeze blew across the encampment. The crickets chirped, and when the noise reached a certain threshold, Rethe unwound herself and rose in a fluid motion.

At that signal, the women in her group, Jiana included, pulled themselves to their feet and began to mix batter and cut strips of dried tortoise meat.

They cooked only for themselves and the other slaves. The household slaves cooked for the Horsemen, and the rest of the Elect cooked their own meals.

The horses and *jamals* ate better than any of the men or women in the khayma, which made sense, Jiana realized, in a community so dependent upon its animals.

The Horsemen dismounted and walked their horses more than half the time. This was less important in the Water Kingdom than in hellish Tool, but the khayma's habits had been ground into them by burning sand and dry, firey air.

Occasionally the men brought down an antelope, which they (incorrectly) called *far gul*, but usually they brought no better than apples and bloodberrys, neither of which ran in terror at the sight of five hundred men and women with a hundred horses, a dozen *jamals*, and an unknown number of mules and goats.

Jiana's work was hard, but not relentless. Except for the Overman, al'Sophiate's men treated her with respect (as a slave, to be sure). Rethe the slave Voice was easy, and she knew a thousand and one khayma stories. The older women enjoyed listening, too. They said the stories grew in subtle ways every time she told them, a charge Rethe hotly denied with badly-hidden pride of authorship.

The next day, Radience waited for Jiana outside the stables khayma. She still looked angry, and acted betrayed, but she no longer had to fight a panic reaction whenever she saw Jiana.

Jiana saw the girl before she finished her chores, but she made no sign. When she made sure Cascade was well cared for, she leaned close and whispered into his ear.

"Now what? How do I break her out of this walking nightmare?"

She listened carefully, but all he did was snort and nuzzle her. Instead, a thought grew in her own stomach, almost like an answering question: *how did you get the goose out of the bottle?* The question was familiar, but she could not remember where she had heard it. In any case, she had no idea what it meant.

"But it's time, I know," she said. She snuck a quick look at Ysmal; for once, he was not watching her. His thoughts were full of the inventory he was conducting.

Jiana reached up and deftly unbuckled Wave from around Cascade's neck. Turning her back to Ysmal (thus facing Radience), she buckled the belt-like sword around her own waist. The worn, leather sheathe looked exactly like a belt anyway—the sort of belt that a Horseman might well give to a particularly pleasing slave.

I bet I know what they'll think I did to please him, she thought. She found a horse collar, a real one, and buckled it around Cascade's neck where Wave had been. Ysmal was still engrossed in adding up figures; he had seen nothing.

But Radience saw. She watched Jiana, her jaw clenched and her left arm hidden behind her body. Jiana stepped out of the darkness of the khayma into the sunlight.

"Free the stomach," Jiana said, "and the arse cannot help but follow."

"You mock us," accused Radience.

"Nope. Just you. Because you alone *know* who the master is."

"Which master?"

"There's only one; the one who makes the grass green and the sky blue. The one who enslaves you."

"The Lord of the Winds?"

"If you like."

"But what do *you* like? What do *you* mean? Come back here!"

Jiana continued on past the slave girl, who turned angrily away and ran towards the kitchen khayma.

Jiana had a hard time adjusting to being in an army again; there was nowhere she could go for quiet contemplation. A friend was sure to pop up and want to talk forever.

So different from the aloneness last time. No sweet cherry kids to share a haystack. Unfinished project. Damn that girl, her arm is more of a choke chain than the collar.

Radience was a hard case; she wavered, a mirage across the sands. They met and talked several times every day. They plotted and planned escape, then Radience worried about friends she would leave behind.

She had no will. She waited, and waited again for something to "free her."

Jiana stalked her as she would stalk a kill, edging closer to the wary deer who would scent the huntress and shy away. Once, she stood behind Radience as the girl was preparing the pots of *kaf* coffee for the Horsemen's breakfast.

"Put pepper in it," Jiana suggested.

"*Pepper?*"

Jiana handed her the box of spice.

"But that would ruin it! They'd choke! And besides, it's as dear as gold, I can't just waste it on—"

"On your owners?" Jiana left while Radience was still sputtering and groping for a crushing retort.

On another day, Jiana tempted Radience to cut part way through the cinch strap of the Overman's horse. She even put a sharp knife into the girl's hand, but Radience was too afraid, and she hid the knife under a pile of uncured hides.

For her own part, Jiana pushed the limits of the iron collar, pressing to the edge of the camp, feeling the bewitchment close tight around her throat. She strayed farther into the black each night, resisting harder and tighter restraint.

She discovered that tilting her head forward and clenching her throat muscles allowed her to still breathe, even when the magical collar was tight enough to make her faint and dizzy and turn her face bright red.

I can break it for you, sister mine, cooed the voice in her stomach.

I know you can. But I won't let you. Radience has no magic to spring her shackles; it's a lie if I use mine.

The days were long, but they were not lonely. She enjoyed the other women. There was a dreadful sameness to the food, especially for a city-girl, used to variety. But she could tolerate it without trouble because of her soldiering days.

It became easier to cope, day by day. They were nice people, the other slaves. Jiana liked them, especially Rethe.

Days, days go past . . .

Every day it was a bit easier to contemplate one more day. Without consciously noticing, Jiana fell into the rhythm of being a slave.

It was a secure and quiet life, a time when she did not have to *think*, when she *could not* simply stop and think. She awoke when she was told, did her chores, dribbled away her free time, gossipped with the other slaves. It was comforting to always know what she would do tomorrow, the next day, and the next.

Even the sameness of the food began to comfort her: there was not even the need to make *that* decision.

The lush forests were beginning to give way to flatter vegetation, braken and scrub. Mountains rose on her left, towards the rising sun, and the sea had fled from her view. The terrain was hilly, and the road rose and fell, rather than violate the straight-line the Eagle army had set for it by deviating around the mounds.

The less moon passed through her cycle once, and the Elect marched alongside a high cliff. Jiana spotted caves halfway up its face. Looking sharp, she saw what almost looked like stairs, cut into the rock, leading up to the caves.

She squinted against the bright sky. Had she been alone, she would have liked to climb up and investigate. As it was, she probably could have gotten permission from Rethe. But it was so much work, so much to *think* about. She turned her face back to the road ahead.

The collar began to loosen, day by day. It felt more natural. Eventually, even Jianabel grew silent.

The days began at dawn, and they were not particularly hard. She had worked much harder as a sergeant. The mass arose with the sun, Rethe performing her platoon sergeant act.

The Elect had finally run out of pre-baked tazh'na to fry, and rather than stop for a day and make more, they bought food from the local villages.

Thereafter, they breakfasted on fruit, mellon balls, rolled oats, hot mash, toasted bread, butter, and jam (excitingly different from county to barony to principality), dried tortoise, game bird, or game animal (as appropriate), occasional fish (salty *shortonies* or chewy *skeeniks*), and for desert, candied apples, dates, and *khalkas*.

Al'Sophiate did not drive them hard. They followed an easy, eight mile per day pace. The women and kids had no trouble on the journey south to Tool.

With each passing day, the Overman began to watch Jiana with a greater hunger; for her part, she reviewed in her mind the spells she had learned or developed.

But a bigger problem was beginning to develop. The Doorian she fought in the last bout of the physical saw her and dimly remembered having seen her somewhere else, looking different. Being a Doorian, and suspicious by nature of his culture, he took to shadowing her, spying on her, and scratching his bright orange, pumpkin-shaped head.

He never really saw me, she told herself. *I was masked, and now I dress as a slave.* But she worried nonetheless. Clearly there was something about her that he recognized . . . her gait? Or did he remember arresting her two turns ago? He did not have her long; when she escaped, his thoughts were occupied with other agonies.

Eventually I'll have to take care of the problem, she thought, but the matter was not yet acute.

Cascade played his part well. When they were alone, he would nuzzle Jiana and eat treats from her hand. When Curse or Ysmal or any one else entered, the horse acted stupid and four-legged.

Jiana kept up the regular visits to Cascade.

Another less moon passed, and Jiana began to feel a strange disquiet invading her contented stomach. Radience was as much a slave as ever, and now Jiana could feel herself slipping into the quiet time. Who was winning, sleep or wakefulness?

One morning she awoke long before dawn. Her heart raced and she could not catch her breath.

She sat up, and pulled her covers around her, staring at the fog rolling across the ground, clinging to every rock and tree. It mirrored the fog in her stomach.

Beads of sweat rolled down her forehead, but she could not remember what had panicked her so. Was it a dream?

Bits and pieces of the dream drifted into her stomach: she was eating . . . there was an aliveness, not the good aliveness of the earth or a tree, but an unnatural, malevolent animation that tore at her soul.

Once she had fallen into a trench during a ride-through at the end of a campaign. A Torrak monk was in the trench, and she found herself unexpectedly fighting a savage battle for her very survival in the midst of victory.

He was all over her. Wave had fallen in the mud somewhere. The combatants had rolled through the slime and Jiana managed to grab hold of a wooden tent stake. She wrapped her left arm tight around the soldier and drove the stake into his kidney from behind.

He died, screaming in agony. It took Jiana several minutes to extricate herself from his death-embrace.

She spotted Wave, and leaned across the corpse to pick up the sword. But when she had risen, she was tripped to the ground by the dead man, who had a grip on her ankle.

He had been dead, unquestionably. But Jiana had rocked him when she leaned across him, and it had shaken him alive for a moment, perhaps shaken some blood into his stomach, enough to revive him.

For an instant, he was alive again, though he never should have been. The dead lived, for an instant.

Jiana shivered in the pre-dawn chill. She pulled the blanket closer about her naked body, looking at the sleeping multitude around her. *Do they* all *live for instants in*

*death, like severed heads trying to bite their executioners
when they're plucked from the basket?*

Something else dead had come alive. She saw a piece of
it in her dream, though she now remembered nothing of
it.

A long forgotten voice whispered in her stomach. It was
Jianabel, cold and neglected, nearly dead from neglect.

Help me, she begged. *Don't let me die here, Momma,
don't let me die. . . .*

The voice faded at the end like a long-forgotten shout.

*How long has it been since I even pushed the edge of the
collar?*

She stood, dropping the blanket and opening her nude
body to the sharp, flinty winds and the clinging fog.

The fog shrouded the world and erased the *now* from
Jiana's sight. For the first time in moons, she closed down
her senses and listened only to her stomach. She remembered . . . the days and nights in Bay Bay, dueling on the
floating streets, slipping in the blood and laughing.

She remembered a kid, some kid—not Ysmal, but Dida.
She remembered Dilai, her own Dilai. Somebody else,
somebody who had helped her get the goose out of the
bottle: Toldo. Toldo Mondo, fat, atheistic priest. Sardonic
apostate.

What else? Why was she here?

Tunk. She remembered the Tunk, and the night in his
hutch. She remembered more: the road to Bay Din. But
this was the Great South Road, and Bay Din was leagues
and leagues behind!

She shook her head, not the road to *Bay Din*, but the
road to Bay Din, the hero's journey, magical quest.

Is that what she was doing, questing again? Questing
for . . .

"Freedom," she said aloud, and abruptly her own, private fog lifted. She touched her shaven head, and at last
she *remembered.*

Shit, shit, shit, she thought, *where have I been? Jianabel,
how could you let this happen? Where have you been?*

There was no response, and Jiana felt a chill of appre-
hension.

Jianabel? Wolf queen, where are those filed-down, pointy teeth? Hello?

She heard only silence in her stomach.

"Kid, you didn't die on me, did you?"

She closed her eyes and blotted out everything but the part of her stomach that had always been reserved for Jianabel. A faint "sound," an insect-like buzzing tingled at the edge of her consciousness.

It was something, something from Jianabel, or what was left of her. A response, so faint she almost mistook it for nothingness.

Concentrating on the words, she could barely make them out. They were the words of a long-ago god, killed by the very entity Jiana now sought: *I am who I am who I am who . . .*

Jianabel!

I am who . . . who . . . who calls?

Come back.

Come back come who come back come dum sum tum bum . . .

Jianabel, your place is here.

Come here.

Yes, come here. Come back to me. Come back to your place.

My place?

Yes. Your place is here. I've grown used to you.

I am dead.

No, you're still alive. I love you, my sister.

I didn't die. I live?

Who talks?

I talk. I always talk.

Who talks?

Now you know very well who talks, silly Jiana.

Jiana listened suspiciously; the words were true Jianabel, daughter of the Wolf Time. But the tone was hesitant, uncertain. But at least that part of herself was back, though she did not know why, Jiana understood that it was very important.

But what was that dream? Something dreadfully important was in it.

Jiana gradually came fully awake and found herself staring across the compound, at the circle of household slaves. One of them was Radience, but Jiana could not tell which while they were all wrapped in their sleeping cocoons.

She rubbed her hand across her head, and was pleased to discover that the baldness felt uncomfortable again. For several weeks, it had felt normal.

In the dream, she stood in a deep place. All around her was the ice. The river is frozen over, she thought, but in front of her—

Skating, lines in the ice—no, don't! it's too—

Falls, she falls through . . .

No she can't be dead my sister my friend my . . . my sister she can't be—

But I'll bring her back I must bring . . .

. . . and down her throat, squiggling, wiggling, squirming, the living things as she swallows and they crawl about, the pieces of meat, of potato, scream in agony as they hit the acid in her . . .

Jiana ground her fists over her eyes and shook her head. *Dammit, no! just a dream. She's dead; died twenty-five turns ago. Not coming back to—whatever.*

Jiana stood and hurried over to her own gang. Rethe would show up momentarily to tell them yesterday's rundown.

The troop was more than half way to Tool, and Jiana had done virtually nothing to wake Radience up. It was time to throw gentility, politeness, and patience to the Lord of the Winds (or was that exactly what "they" wanted her to do?). Jiana would have to shock the girl awake, and she could think of only one way to do so.

Stay with me, Jianabel. Don't leave me. Without you I wouldn't even need this collar; I'd be slave to the earth and the blood.

The Wolf Girl did not answer, but Jiana felt her presence spread like warm manure through her body.

5

Jiana waited until the sun set. Then she pressed through the thick of the throng, pushing west until the torque began to tighten. She walked back north along their path until she found Radience.

The girl had taken to looking north towards Bay Bay each night with a wistful longing, as if she had left something precious behind.

Jiana watched silently for a time, hands in her tunic where the valley wind did not blow.

"Still waiting?"

Radience turned and scowled.

"Leave me alone, horsegirl."

"The less moon has nearly cycled twice. You are still waiting for the one who said she'd come that day?"

"What do you know about it? You aren't her. You curry horses and shovel crap! Go away before I call your *tol* hag."

Jiana smiled. Rethe would not take kindly to being called a hag, not by a girl as young as Ray.

"What's so bad about shoveling shit? You keep returning to it."

Exasperated, Radience waived her hands dismissively and stalked back towards the camp.

"You've ruined a nice evening, Short. Thank you ever so much. I'm going in, I have *real* work to do."

Jiana let her get a shout away. Then she added in a strong voice, "Maybe she's waiting for somebody *worth* freeing."

Radience ran back down the hill towards the khayma, wiping her eyes with her good arm.

Jiana watched until the girl vanished in the crowd. Then she followed her into the camp, veered left, and entered the stables khayma. Cascade waited for her; if a horse could smile nastily, he was doing it.

Spreading the holiday cheer again, eh Jiana?

"Damn her, she doesn't know! She doesn't know how short a leash she's on. It's time to show her."

"What will she think when they reel it in? When master and slave snarl at each other across the abyss?"

Jiana looked Cascade in his big, brown eyes. For a long beat, she held his gaze, but it was Jiana who broke first.

She walked out of the khayma, embarrassed, imagining she could hear his iron chuckle behind her back.

The slaves' sisterhood was a society of behind-the-hand whispers. "An hour-old secret" was an expression that meant a thing known to all.

Jiana overcame her natural revulsion for tattle-tales and began to listen and record each little item overheard. She kept a diary of secrets, and religiously copied the day's gossip into it each night.

After three nights, Jiana decided she was ready to perform her first "demonstration."

Think they actually like you, trust you, girl? Surprise!

When the sun had long set and the Horsemen were bedding for the night, Jiana walked into the household khayma, quiet as a breeze, and woke Radience by placing a hand over the girl's mouth.

Jiana gestured that Radience should come outside with her. The girl acquiesced, wearing a look that said this *had better be good.*

"What do you want?" she demanded. "*Some* of us must rise early to serve the Caliph of the Elect himself."

"You say that with such a note of pride."

Radience looked guilty for a moment; since her beating, Radience had spent every waking moment striving to be a good, little slave. Jiana was convinced that Radience's pathetic attempts to curry favor had sickened even her. She was bitter beneath her hauteur.

Damned normal not to want to get beaten, Jiana thought, *but you can't cut yourself that slack, can you?*

"Can I show you something?" Jiana asked, politely.

"If you must."

Jiana walked carelessly through the sleeping bodies, stepping over them and making no sound. Radience followed a bit clumsily, and occasionally stepped on a hand or kicked a shin. The sleepers stirred and mumbled curses, but they did not wake.

The warrior brushed nimbly between two smouldering fires, and Radience was forced to draw her blanket up off the ground and hop. *What in the wind's name does she want to show me?*

Jiana turned abruptly and approached a khayma. It took
Radience a moment to realize it was the hareem khayma.
Jiana dropped to her knees, then her stomach. She wriggled close to the canvas and ran her hand along the bottom
edge.

Suddenly, her hand passed right through the fabric.
Gods, did she actually cut a slit into the hareem khayma?
Radience wondered in amazement. She shook her head
sadly; the woman's reason had fled across the dunes.

"Come in," she said to Radience. "The water's fine."
Radience scowled. What did water have to do with anything?

The slave girl followed Jiana, squirming under the heavy
canvas wall, through the slit and into the khayma, wondering how she had let *that woman* talk her into this. The
heavy fabric scraped across her back, which ached in memory of the last beating she had received.

The hareem khayma was not for the likes of Radience,
except when the Overman felt compelled to whip her with
one or the other of his rods. Among other reasons, the
hareem slaves kept an iron-bound jewelry box, out of
which they dressed in the evening. Half the box alone
could ransom the three Caliphs of Sand River. It was
Ruhol the Eunuch's primary job to guard the jewelry box.

And guard it he apparently did, for he stood in the
doorway at that very moment, holding open the flap and
staring protectively at the box.

Radience held her breath; her heart felt like it stopped.
Friends or no, trust or not, if Ruhol found her thus,
sneaking into the hareem in deadest night through a slit
into the jewelroom, he would kill her, probably without
thought or regret.

Radience looked at Jiana, who ludicrously held two fingers over her lips in a silent "no talking" symbol—as if
they had planned to!

How long they lay thus, watching Ruhol watch the box,
Radience could not begin to guess. Her heart was beating
so rapidly that it was no good judge of time.

Then at once, Ruhol moved. He walked decisively to
the box, and pulled on the great, Bay Din lock. He held it

in his massive hand for a moment. Then incredibly, he
fished into his groin-wraps, produced a key, and opened
the lock.

Ruhol opened up the box, and gazed speculatively inside.
Conducting inventory? Now, in the black of night?
Radience's mouth was dry as sand, and she licked her lips.
Even that faint sound frightened her.

Ruhol reached inside the chest and casually removed a
pearl. It was the size of one of his missing testicles. He
looked at it in the light of the less moon, filtering through
the smoke holes in the top of the khayma. He placed it
carefully inside his groin cloth.

Ruhol closed and locked the safe. He backed away from
it, a speculative but satisfied smile on his lips.

Then he turned and exited the way he had entered.

"Seen enough?" Jiana asked in a normal, conversational
tone as soon as Ruhol had left.

Radience stared at the still-swaying flap, stricken.

"Let's go get some sleep, little one." Jiana took Radience
by the arm and turned her back towards the slit in the
canvas side.

Radience allowed herself to be led, too upset to argue or
resist. She crawled out of the khayma and stood shakily.

Ruhol the betrayer! Radience was overwhelmed by shame
and sadness. Was this the way the eunuch repaid so many
years of kindness? What had the Caliph ever done to *him?*

Radience walked slowly back to her own territory. Jiana
stayed behind her, but luckily kept her silence and allowed Radience time to think.

Could she betray such a friend, a man who even stood
up to the Overman for her? Could she herself betray the
Caliph by *not* reporting Ruhol?

She was utterly confused, not knowing which way to
turn. *Was that really me, holding the dagger over the
divine Caliph's chest and preparing to thrust it into his
heart? Dream or no, what evil lies in my own heart that I
long to slay my master . . . yet consider denouncing my
only friend to the Chopper?*

It was senseless. As masters went, Hal'Addad al'Sophiate

was a saint. Even with an occasional Giathudin in his
retinue, life with the Lord was ease and comfort itself
compared to the hundreds of sand-poor, waterless farmers
scraping a miserable existence out of the clay and the mud
and revelling in their self-styled "freedom."

There is simply no question, she thought as Jiana left
her off near the household Khayma. *I cannot forget loyalty
to my Lord!* But neither could she forget all the little
things Ruhol had done for her during her first days among
the Elect.

He snuck food to her from the kitchens when her first
master, a young, hotheaded Horseman, sent her to the
stocks for falling asleep while washing. He interceded
subtlely with the Overman during many a beating, distracting Giathudin from forcing himself upon her many of
the times he tried.

He worked with her bad arm, strengthening it with
lifting and pulling exercises. He once passed along a di-
aphanous gown that he said the girls had gotten tired of;
now Radience was sure it was actually stolen from them.

There is no question. I cannot betray my friend!

Radience wrapped her arms around her body, good arm
on the outside. *And thus do I enter rebellion,* she thought.

She waited for the thunderclap, but the sky remained
clear. Try as she might, Radience could not force herself
to feel guilt at her monstrous act of betrayal. The dark said
nothing.

Chapter IV:

Rebel rabble
(stepping on the same piece twice)

In the morning, Radience performed her customary duties with little heart. She felt distant, pulled out of herself, as alien as the *bas reliefs* found on the temple walls of the City of Black.

She shuddered, remembering those inhuman depictions of perversions and atrocities that she saw in reproduction in the Caliph's sleeping chamber.

Am I metamorphosing into one of those? Is that why I feel so all-over queer? Radience grunted in annoyance at her wind-blown imagination and concentrated on balancing the breakfast tray in her good hand.

But how else to explain my lack of decisiveness about Ruhol? Surely a man would cast his darts on one side or the other! But I kneel like a jamal *and turn my face from the sun.*

She wandered the khayma like a zombie, handing out sweatmeats and flatbread in a daze. Overman of Horses received water in his *kaf*. She almost served *an egg* to Giathudin, who would think she was trying to poison him! He was very traditional; on all of their perigrinations, Giathudin positively refused to go native.

As it was he caught her hand as she reached for his water glass. She kept her eyes on his hairy knuckles, though she felt his black scowl through her forehead. He pulled her hand towards his mouth.

His son Akadr spoke up.

"Father!"

Giathudin stared at him.

"What?" the Overman asked, sounding annoyed at the interruption.

"One of the hareem girls is missing a great pearl."

"What? What the hell do *I* care if the hareem girls—"

"It was taken from the hareem jewelry box."

The Overman dropped Radience's hand.

"Stolen?"

"There is no other explanation." Akadr glanced at Radience and gestured with his eyes that she better move quickly down the line. She faded backwards to the next Horseman.

"Fucking cunts," complained the Overman, swilling his winelaced coffee. He rose and allowed Akadr to lead him out of the khayma.

Radience rubbed the circulation back into her wrist. His finger imprints would fade; but what of this feeling that gripped her, this "must/cannot" dilemma?

One of the Horsemen farted, and soon they all took up the challenge, laughing and outdoing each other. Radience left for the kitchen as quickly as her duties allowed.

Odd, she thought, that such a bastard could have a beautiful, fair son who treated the slaves with respect and courtesy.

When breakfast ended, Radience walked in trepidation towards the stables. The horseslaves were striking the khayma as she approached.

She found Jiana inside, disassembling Curse's forge and packing it in a pair of *jamal* bags.

Radience stood for many long moments, watching Jiana from behind. *She knows I'm here*, she thought. *Damn if I'm going to make the first move.*

At last Jiana finished, pulled tight the strap, then turned and faced her.

"Pleasant night?" the woman inquired, innocently enough.

"I don't like your tone," said Radience.

"What tone would you prefer?"

The slave girl glared, unable to think of a devastating response.

"Alright, I admit it. I don't know what to do about Ruhol. He's a friend, he's almost my . . ." She almost said "father," but she caught herself.

Jiana responded in a low, sing-song chant in High-Tooltak, the dialect of the Rime:

> *This desert wide;*
> *Build bars of sand, to sunder hand*
> *From hands allied.*"

Radience was sure it was a quote, but she could not for her life remember hearing any verses like that in the Word or the Commentaries.

"What is the hand you sunder?" she demanded.

Jiana made a fist and extended her arm, palm towards Radience. The girl winced when she realized it was Jiana's left arm.

"My hand is not sundered! I don't use it only because I don't *like* to!"

Jiana smiled.

"I did not refer to a hand but to a leg," retorted the warrior, returning the obvious lie. "So who owns us?"

"We are the humble servants of Hal'Addad bin Kerat bin El al'Sophiate, Lord of the Wind and the Five Sands, Prince of the Water, Caliph to the Elect from Qomsheh to Yazd to the oasis at Deh Bid, Master of Arts and Letters, Satrap of Dokamaj Tool. Didn't Curse teach you your 'recites?' "

Jiana waited impassively while Radience recited the litany of titles. Radience realized how hollow the honorifics rang this time, though other times they filled her bowels with awe, or at least cold fear.

"So who owns the tides?"

"The *tides?* Ocean tides? What are you talking about?"

"Suppose the Lord of the Wind ordered the ebb tide to recede again."

"That's ridiculous. The tide moves the same way all the time. It has a—a—"

"Destiny?" suggested the warrior.

"Call it a destiny. Sure."

"Suppose I come and go as the tides, following my own destiny. Who owns me then?"

Radience opened her mouth to speak, then realized she had no words. She closed her mouth and stepped back a pace. She absently tugged at her tunic sleeve, pulling it farther over her left arm, while trying to find the words that had dropped from her heart to the ground somewhere.

"You can't just not work," she insisted at last. "They'd grab you and *make* you work. The Overman would grab you."

"I am free," Jiana said in a low, unemotional voice. "I only work if I choose."

She turned and walked slowly to the coals dumped from Curse's forge. They still glowed a dull red. The two women were alone in the khayma.

Jiana reached her hand down into the bowl and picked up a lump of grey coal. She held it in her hand for a moment. Veins bulged at her temples, but her face remained unperturbed. No rictus of agony curled her lip.

Then she dropped the coal. It struck the leg of the forge as it fell, bursting open like a lava egg, exposing the red-glow interior, hot as a salt bed with the sun overhead.

Jiana clenched her left fist, cradling the whole arm with her other arm. She looked Radience in the eye and smiled, as if sharing a secret. Then she lowered her eyes again.

"Jiana!" cried Radience. The slave girl's knees were limp rags; she caught hold of a supporting pole to hold herself upright.

"Now let them tell me to work," the warrior whispered. She looked up again. Radience could see no pain in the woman's eyes, but the pupils were mere pinpricks.

"Radience . . . can you pick it up?"

The slave stared at the ugly, red coal. Her heart raced,

and her own breathing became as ragged as Jiana's. She
knelt slowly, stretching forth her hand towards the grey
and red lump.

Sands and windblinds, why am I doing this? Radience
was horrified, but her hand seemed to have its own volition.

Jiana watched her eyes intently.

"Soon your fingers will touch," she whispered. "Look
forward to the charred flesh, the smell of burning meat.
But I'll hold the pain from you. You won't feel it."

Radience's hand stopped just a knuckle's width above
the coal. She could feel the heat, blistering even at that
distance.

"Don't you believe me?" Jiana asked.

"Yes. Yes, I . . ." Radience trailed off, her hand began
to tremble. A part of her trusted Jiana implicitly—so what
if she'd only known her a day, a couple moons! Another part
recoiled in horror at the thought of what Jiana proposed.

The two parts fought violently, causing the tremors in
her outstretched hand.

"Are you free enough?" asked the warrior, matter-of-
factly.

"I—I *can't!*"

Jiana chuckled indulgently.

"Leave it, slave. Leave it for Curse. He has tongs."

The warrior rose to her feet and strode off. She held her
blackened left hand steady at her side.

"Come to me when you can pick up the coal, or walk
across a bridge," she called over her shoulder.

When Jiana left, Radience found a seat and sat down.
She blinked, surprised at finding tiny tears in her eyes.

*How long since I last cried? Too long. Back when Mara
died. . . .*

Mara?

Radience gasped, and jumped to her feet. Mara!

Memories flooded back that had been dammed, dammed
for thirteen turns.

The riders had come when Radience was only four.
They took Radience and her brother, raped her mother,

and killed her big brother Mara out of hand (he was weak from the bowlegs disease).

Stunned, the girl sank back into her seat.

Turns, turns . . . how could I forget? Mara, how could I forget you?

The pictures returned, pent up for thirteen turns. Radience sat with her head bowed and her eyes moist. But she did not cry.

They killed him. They *bruted* him. And they did it again, again in her stomach. They set her nine-turn-old brother on fire.

"I love you, Mara." Radience ran the words together into a single word, a mantra, a signet.

For a long, long time she strained her thoughts. Then she leaned forward and fought her gorge back down her throat.

I can't even remember my real name!

She sat thus, hunched over, until the sky turned purple and it was time to run light the lanterns.

2

By the time Jiana reached the medicine tent, she too was trembling from the strain of holding the pain shield.

She had dreamed up the spell two turns ago. Simply put, there had to be some tube or line that connected all parts of the body to the stomach, else how could one feel pain? Once that much had occurred to her, she immediately thought of a magical clamp, holding shut this tube and preventing the pain from traveling down it. No flow, no pain.

Of course, she understood the danger: the pain flow could build up enormous pressure if she held it back too long. What would happen if it burst, spreading the pain fluid all over her body? That was a thought upon which she refused to dwell.

Of course, the next problem was how to dispose of the pain fluid that was even now straining at the clamp. Sweat stood out on her brow. She felt as if she had drunk two pots of tea, but were forbidden from relieving herself for two days.

She pushed into the medicine khayma, gritting her teeth (which ached). She looked quickly around the khayma.

There was only one patient, a Horseman who had been caught beneath his horse. His ribs were crushed, and his lung was punctured; he would die before the next sunrise.

But in the meantime, he was in agony, holding a pillow over his face and whimpering quietly. As Jiana watched, he went into a fit of coughing, choking on his own blood. He recovered, and continued to breath, gurgling with every exhalation.

Rethe had told them about Rakashti's accident in her regular segment that morning, though she did so soberly: Rakashti's face went slack, and he began to convulse in the saddle. He yanked on the reins during his seizure, and the confused horse tried to follow his commands. It stumbled over a rock, fell on top of Rakashti, and crushed him. The horse was tried and acquitted, and given to Rakashti's eldest son.

Jiana felt guilt begin to well up within her, but she fought it down. *He'll be dead soon anyway. I have to live.*

She ground her teeth. Was this not exactly the sort of choice she loathed when Alanai, Prince of Bay Bay made it? She closed her eyes, and smiled without mirth.

With every step, I force myself down the same path as all the thousand and one demons of arrogance. What next, do I crown myself Queen of Reality Prime?

But the dam was about to break, and Jiana was no use to herself or Radience screaming in a tent as the full agony of charred flesh washed through her.

Straining to keep her sense of pain clamped tight, she strode forward and pressed her hands around his crushed and bloody chest. She let her eyes glaze over, and focused her Oversphere sight on her hand, and on the bulging cable of pain that threatened to explode at any moment.

She visioned a short, curling tube beginning from the

other side of the clamp, curving up and around her hand
and out her fingertips into the Toolian's chest.

*May Tooqa, the dead, non-existent Nameless Serpentine
forgive me now*, she prayed. Taking a deep breath, she
released the magical clamp.

The breath caught in the Horseman's throat for a startled
moment. Then he began to scream uncontrollably.

No one came. His injury had been so queer that many
Horsemen thought he was possessed; they would not be in
the khayma with him as he died, lest the *daeva* leap from
his body to theirs.

As soon as the fluid flow ebbed, Jiana visioned a healing
white light, glowing about her burned hand. She visioned
the skin smooth and pink, like a baby's hands; then she
saw her palm roughly calloused, hard and whole as it had
been a few moments before.

Her head began to throb, the blood pounding in her
temples like a shinbone beating a funeral drum. But when
she let the Oversphere slip slowly from her view, falling
back down into her body, the white light had done its
work.

Her hand was not perfectly healed; but it was well on
the road. At least the ache was dull and bearable.

*It works . . . wonder if it would be as easy to brush off
a wound struck in anger as an injury done for effect?*

Her hand still felt peculiar, and the burn was still clearly
visible. It would be several days before she could use her
hand to full effect. Jiana would have no trouble getting her
day off.

She returned to the stables khayma. One of the poles
had broken, and Ysmal and another slave were sliding a
replacement pole into the slot.

Jiana lowered her eyes to not encourage unwanted attention and tried to scuttle past.

"Hsst!"

She stopped, and deferentially looked up at Ysmal, worried at what he might have in mind. He motioned her
closer, and she obeyed.

"The Overman's in there, and he's really pissed about something. Walk soft."

"Thanks," she said, genuinely. She ghosted forward and through the doorflap. She made it halfway to her station when Curse spotted her.

"Jiana! Here."

She approached slowly, wondering what she might have done. The Overman watched her approach as if she were a hound that had urinated on his leg. When she drew near, he spoke in a very quiet, matter-of-fact voice.

"I am seriously considering having you killed, you bitch."

Her heart began to pound with the speed of dancing drums, and she fell to her knees.

"Please lord, what did I have to done?" she cried. *You're terrified. You're a cringing slave who barely even speaks Tooltak.*

"An item worth more than the lot of you has vanished, and I am certain that a slave has betrayed me by stealing it. And now Curse tells me you have left your post repeatedly in the past few weeks. Tell my why I should not play safe by having you quartered?"

Curse coughed and shuffled back. Jiana wondered if he really had said anything about her, or whether Giathudin made the story up.

"I have steal nothing, o great horse! I have *never* steal nothing!"

"Well," said the Overman, a note of expectation creeping into his voice, "I guess we'll find out, won't we? Come."

He seized her ear and strode out of the khayma and into the compound. He looked around speculatively. Then he led her away towards the household khayma.

They walked around the back and pushed through the doorflap. Jiana recognized the same room where the Overman had beaten Radience.

They stopped just inside the room. Jiana wrapped her arms around her body and tried to shrink smaller, hoping the Overman would feel pity, but he was having none of it.

He pushed her towards the center of the room. "Strip," he commanded, "Everything." Just then, Ruhol entered with the flail.

Can I really do this? Can I let those bastards—

Yes, you can really do it. Jiana stiffened. It was the voice she kept imagining for Cascade. Did *every* part of her stomach have its own volition now?

Jiana began to tremble; she pulled off her clothes, letting them fall to the ground. She was careful to drop her tunic so that it covered her "belt." Probably, neither Giathudin nor Ruhol could tell that it was actually Wave, but it was too dangerous to take chances.

"Keep track for me, she-man," said the Overman. He stood quietly for a moment, calming himself. He was determined not to repeat his earlier mistake with Radience.

He smiled sadistically at her, pointed his finger and moved it in a circle. Understanding, she slowly turned her back to him, sobbing already though he had not yet touched her.

The flail swished through the air a few times, then grew silent.

"Oh, I'm not really going to do anything," said the Overman. He laughed. "I just wanted to make sure of your loyalties. Put your clothes back on."

She stood frozen for a moment, wondering if it were a trick. Then she slowly stooped and picked up her tunic. She had just stood up again when the first blow fell.

Somehow her body knew it was coming, though it did not inform her stomach. She turned just slightly enough that the part of the flail that struck was a hand's-width above the tip, sparing her the worst of the blow.

"One, your terror," counted the eunuch. It was a late count. Apparently even he had been fooled.

For a moment, Jiana's back was numb. Then the pain began. It felt like a rope burn.

The flail swished again, and this time Ruhol counted just before the blow fell, giving Jiana a bit of warning.

"Two, your terror. Three, your terror."

The pain was savage, and Jiana felt her mask of slavery

slipping. She did not care. She began to breath (*in-hold-out*) as she had learned in the Flower Empire a dozen turns before. She tried to blank her mind.

"Eight, your terror." They paused, and Jiana allowed herself to collapse slowly to her knees.

Damn it girl, you better get back into character or they're going to sweat it. Slave . . . you're a beaten slave, you're in agony!

No! cried Jianabel. *What are you doing? Kill him! Don't let him do it to us!*

Jiana began to moan. She wrapped her arms around her stomach and leaned forward until her forehead rested against the canvas floor. She sobbed as convincingly as she could, and was startled to discover that what came out of her throat was more of a laugh than a sob. She hoped he would not be able to tell the difference.

The counts, the counts are so appropriate! He's so full of terror, of anguish! What is he so afraid of, dying? Living?

"St-stand up," ordered the Overman. Now that Jiana had penetrated the mask of pain, she could plainly hear the tremble behind his authoritarian voice.

She felt hands gently pulling at her elbows. As Ruhol lifted her to her feet, he whispered in her ear, "I thank the Overman for this correction."

She stood and parroted the *pro-forma* response, forcibly squashing a giggle that threatened to rise from her stomach.

The pain was severe, but swords and arrows had cut her far worse in her long, short life.

Giathudin struck the first blow of the second set with no preliminary loop through the air. He used no finesse, trying to muscle it in.

The flail staggered her, but it was far less painful than the cunningly snapped blows.

"One, your anguish," essayed the eunuch.

"You are wrong, half-man."

"One, your terror," amended Ruhol.

The next seven blows were progressively more angry, more brutal. The third blow knocked Jiana from her feet.

The fourth landed before she could even stand up again. For the last four, she lay on the canvas, covering her face with her arms to prevent an accidental injury to her eyes.

The Overman screamed something at her with the seventh blow, but he was in such an inarticulate rage that Jiana could not understand him, save for the phrase "all you bitches."

After the eighth terror, Jiana reflected that far from anguish she was more in a state of detachment.

I wonder if his blows have driven me up into the Oversphere? she thought, looking down at her cut and bloody body, curled into a ball on the khayma floor. Giathudin turned away and walked into a corner. His face was white, and he stared at the hand that held the flail. He pulled at his mustache. His breathing was rapid and shallow.

The eunuch picked up a pail of cloudy water and cast it over Jiana's body.

Time to return, she thought with reluctance. She enjoyed the high view.

Jiana fell back into herself and struggled to her hands and knees. At that moment, the salt-pain hit and she disassociated again. But this time, through the agony she visioned a set of silken cords through which she could manipulate her limbs. She pulled on the appropriate cables and her body rose shakily to its feet.

How quickly your own game comes back around, laughed the horse-voice in her stomach.

Shut shut shut shut up!

The Overman had regained control of his anger again. He swirled the flail in a complicated, double-looping dance and snapped it across her body's shoulders. From far below, as an echo from the bottom of a well, she felt the touch.

"One, your anguish."

The Overman stopped and looked at Ruhol a long moment.

"One—your *terror*," the eunuch amended, reluctantly.

Giathudin returned to his task. Just as he reached three

terrors, Jiana became aware of another presence in the room.

It was al'Sophiate himself. He entered silently, and stood behind the Overman, watching the exhibition.

Giathudin swung the flail up over his head again, but the Caliph's hand darted out and caught the shaft, just below the point where it split into five snakes. The Overman tugged at his end for a moment. Then he dropped the flail, gasping and turning around, hand on his knife.

Giathudin stared at his lord for several beats, his face blanching. Al'Sophiate looked curiously at the bloody tips of the flail, then at Jiana's body. He turned his gaze back on the Overman and raised his eyebrows.

"She—" began the Overman of slaves, then he stopped, realizing that he had not even taken the precaution of thinking up a plausible charge. "She . . . I believe it was she who stole the pearl, Most High."

"Oh?" said Hal'Addad, his voice a silk cloth hiding a sharp dagger, "and why exactly do you think that?"

The Overman merely stared.

"I have heard whispers of your cruelty; now I see they were not stories. Please remove your presence from my home. Leave your armband with the eunuch." The ex-Overman said nothing; he stood unblinking, his mouth open slightly.

Hal'Addad looked curiously at Jiana.

"What is wrong with her?"

"She has gone away," said Ruhol.

Pretty perceptive, Jiana admitted.

"Will she—come back?"

"I do not know, Most High."

"Well, sit her in a corner where she won't get in anybody's way. And if she does come back, let her rest a few days. Horseman, what *are* you staring at?"

"But—nothing."

The Caliph scowled.

"I mean I'm not staring, Most High. I mean. . . ."

"You have been *found out*, Horseman Giathudin. You have been caught. Now everybody knows what you are."

The Horseman grabbed his penis reflectively. He seemed to be having trouble catching a breath. Al'Sophiate turned and passed back through the doorflap.

"I think I shall give your job to Akadr, your son," he called back over his shoulder. Giathudin whimpered like a little boy with wormrot in his stomach. As soon as the Caliph had left, Horseman Giathudin fled from the khayma, still clutching the crotch of his robe.

Ruhol took Jiana's shoulders gently; he seemed concerned, but in a distant way. Jiana reeled in her silken cords and pulled herself back into her body.

She braced herself as she fell the final fingerwidth; but the pain was no more than a dull, burning throb. The ripped flesh of her back looked worse than it felt.

Still, she staggered and clutched at the eunuch for support. He pulled her back to her feet, and began slowly walking her towards the doorflap.

"Easy. Calm. Quietly. It's over. He won't hurt you anymore. Calmly. How did you burn your hand? Never mind." He led her to the hospital khayma, cutting off the objections of the surgeon.

Rakashti was gone. He had probably died. Jiana felt better; perhaps she had done good, despite the lowness of her intention.

"Take her to the horse doctor."

"Fix her up, Eshmun, or I shall tell the new Overman of Slaves about your desecration of Horseman Ibrahm's drunken daughter."

Eshmun stopped protesting and angrily drew Jiana across one of the tables. He poured a salve into her wounds, and pressed cool leaves against them.

"The *new* Overman?" he asked.

"Akadr," said the eunuch. Then he turned and departed circumspectly, without recounting the events that had transpired in the household khayma.

3

As soon as Ruhol was safely out of earshot, Eshmun had his two assistants pick her up by an arm apiece and lug her over to the doctor of horses. Jiana might have protested; she was more lucid than she let on. But she thought it was an advantage. The horse doctor had more empathy.

"Don't usually get ones that talk," he explained, dressing her wounds more carefully than had Eshmun.

"Not usually?"

"Well, I do recall, yes, it was fifteen turns ago that I doctored a horse that not only talked . . . or was it twenty? Recall one twenty-five turns ago that not only talked, he had wings sprouting from his back. Or perhaps more specifically his shoulders, front shoulders."

"Wings?"

She listened, occasionally gasping or "I'll-being" as the story warranted. She lay on her stomach, blocking out the pain as best as she could.

You let events overtake you. Teacher would be pissed.

Another sharp pain ripped through her back, and she bit off a cry.

I know. Paying for it, too.

The problem was that the pain itself was so distracting she could not still her stomach and conjure. In a score of fighting turns, as far back as White Falls, she had taught herself to feel the pain, to swallow it, and vomit forth a berserker rage. When the pain was great, the new teaching to *release* the pain evaporated from the surface of yesterday, leaving the jagged edge of sensuousness.

Sensuousness was a barrier to magic. Magic wanted detachment, aloofness, and imperturbability. Jiana was caught by her own nature.

So what is your game today? Jiana could not tell if the voice in her stomach was her own, the Wolf Girl's, or Cascade's.

She lay on her stomach, on her own mat on her own piece of floor. Her sense of touch was heightened; every haystem was a needle, every pebble a knife point. The hay stank of horseflesh, a smell she had never liked and never gotten used to, despite all her campaigns.

So what's this game? This game of "wait." This game of slave . . .

*But it's so blessedly comfortable! I'm in school again.
I'm making mischief, not taking scalps. I'm outrageous,
but I commit no outrages. It's restful, wishful. I like it this
way. Who am I to tell Radience she can't fall out when I
jumped out myself? Maybe I have no right anyway.*

How long she lay thus, Jiana could not tell. After a time
it was dark. She lay quietly, listening to the whinnies of
the sick horses and the occasional clang of a neck-bell
when the goat moved in its sleep.

She felt herself drift into sleep. Bizarre thoughts and
images flashed through her stomach. Her last thought
before stepping through the dream door, *so peaceful, so at
peace.*

*—all livingalive, all touching, squirming beneath her
hands in her mouth down her throat . . . deadliving,
deadalive, coming back, reanimate, all her, all Jianabelana . . .*

*stands He, declaiming "three times three times three
times" and evermore, black skin, rotting skin away from
bone and tooth peeling back like a rotted peach sickly
sweet, but livingalive from before all that is and all that
was and "you know who I am, your player"*

*stands He, arms outstretched outreaching reaching out
to clutch and grab and pull at the deadliving things three
times three*

*Living things, squirming things, things that wriggle and
quiver and quail and hurt and anguish, deadliving things,
all touched by the He and the She*

rages She

three times three

On the crisp blue field of grass beneath the lowering
green sky, Jiana sat, arms wrapped around her knees. She
trembled with a nameless dread.

"Something I ate, no doubt," she said.

A hand touched her brow.

"Oh, Jianabel," she cried, looking up into the wolf eyes
and filed teeth, "was it just a dream, sure?"

"Well, everything is just a dream, I dare say."

Jiana stood, feeling foolish at her hystrionics.

"I shouldn't be crying. Sets a bad example for the men."

"That's the spirit. Buck up, is what I always say!"

"This isn't White Falls," Jiana said, looking about dubiously at the blue grass and the green sky.

But in The Dream, it *is* White Falls. Winter, and the river is frozen over. Children skate, Jiana skates, and *she* is with Jiana her sister. The dream, so many nights to dream it now!

Jiana shook her head and the Wolf Girl returned. "Something troubles your eyes, your eyes," observed Jianabel.

"Is this still in the dream?" asked Jiana. "Which dream?"

"They're all dreams until we wake, sister dear."

Jiana crouched on the cold ground, wrapped arms around her body. The cold was within her, not in the ground. "I've seen this dream every night," she whispered (afraid to be heard).

"Then it comes from deep within, sis. Let it out, lest it break out in the nominal sleep of waking!" Taking breaths deep and wide, Jiana faced the fear and took the dream within her stomach.

Children skating, *She* is skating. *They ask me, but no, I'm afraid*, thinks the warrior (now only seven). *Scaredy scaredy! they cry. They'd not say it if I were out there to get my hands around! But it's too warm, the ice is too thin, has to be too . . .*

Jiana sees the skate marks, tracks clear as clear ice. Black-bundled kids skate, fat happy and unobserving, identical black tressed heads whipping and bobbing in mock-combat on the ice.

Tracks clear as clear ice; they spread wide as the sky and through them the grey river peeks. Breaks! They fall . . . *she's falling!*

Little girls scream, falling to the ice in panic instead of grabbing *Her*, let *Her* fall right through the ice into the river. Jiana forgets the thin ice, runs crawls (scaredy rat!) slides on her belly, reaches for *Her*. Up she heaves onto the ice, shivering in cold that numbs and dims. But *She's . . . too . . . heavy. . . .*

Turning her eyes from the sight, Jiana looks again upon Jianabel, unconfesses. "I didn't kill her," she says. "I did not kill my sister. *They* did, the kids that were there yet did *nothing!* At least I fucking tried."

"Poor Jiana, it was your task. Because you tried, you took the weight, and now you'll never throw it off. She drags on you even now, doesn't she? Pulls you down under the ice?"

Shakes her head, becomes young again. Jiana grabs for the hands, seizes *Her* mittens, pulls and pulls but Taidora

slips
        from grasping
          hands . . .

The world grows silent, voices drop away as Jiana looks. Stricken. Holding empty mittens in her hands as Taidora sinks.

Under the ice. Through the ice. Through the clear ice, clear as a cloudy sky, Jiana (now Jianabelana) sees Taidora's horror-stricken face. Taidora is still alive, under the ice; yet she knows she's dead.

The girl grips the rough underside of the ice for a moment, a heartbeat flicker. Reaches out to touch her sister on the other side of the ice-wall. Taidora looks so *betrayed;* accuses Jiana: her friend, her sister, her—(no that last is not a word she can think, not even now)—her friend.

Why? why can't we die together? *Will you come if I call?*

The current carries her away. Carries her off to glub and blub. Taidora does not call Jiana.

But *would* Jiana have answered?

The dream faded, and Jiana stood again before Jianabel. The wolfish queen pointed silently to the two columns on either side of her, one alabaster white, the other ebony black.

"Which is rising, hodge or podge?"

"Neither," answered Jiana, weeping; "they're in balance."

"Remember that in your darkest hour." Jianabel smiled, exposed row upon row of sharpened teeth, like skeeniks in Bay Bay harbor. "But you've seen nothing of Toq the Boy Frock . . . when does he come along?"

"You bitch, I'm trying to forget!" The green grass shimmered, the blue sky yawned wide. *Were they that way before?* thought Jiana. *I make my own books, turning pages with every step. No, this next part never happened, Toq retches into my stomach!* But the memory-wind did not listen, it droned on unstoppable:

Now is later; Jiana lies on the ice, still as unblown snow.

Her friends run home, scream to their mamas and poppas, but little Jiana lays on her frozen belly, eyes closed, seeing Taidora's final face. *Would you? Would you have come? Had I called?*

Please Tooqa, most perfect most slithering power, please God, by the Nameless Serpentine, oh please give me the power to bring her back! It is the wish of a child, unremembering the wheel of death and life, unknowing that "gone" is just "turned a corner." *I want the* lifepower, *damn your slitted eyes! Let me reach through the ice and pull . . . her . . . out!*

And in The Dream—but not in life—it is done. Jiana is granted grace. The power, the Jianabel power cascades into her like a waterfall into a deep pool. All she touches reawakens, if ever once alive. All that she touches shall come alive!

Jiana first learns of her power walking home. Finds a baby mouse, crushed by a horse's hoof. "Poor thing," she coos, licking her lips. *Not me,* thinks the older warrior, *not my words! Toq speaks filth through my mouth.* She-the-girl touches the mouse and a lifespark flicks from her finger, ignites the creature into "life."

It is a dubious twist of life. The mouse scampers wildly, unseeing unthinking, gibbering not in mousetalk but as senseless as an avalanche. It bites her, bites a rock, runs away possessed by furies.

"The flimsiest sort of metaphor!" declares Jianabel.

"Think I don't know that? The bastard positively lives for cheap metaphors! I know who the mouse is, and I know how I touched his life." Jiana covered face with hands. "It doesn't make it any easier, sister. The sick little puke is right about Dida. How can I *not* feel guilt?"

"Continue. The dream presses upon your stomach like wormrot."

Jiana opened her eyes. "Is that a door I see between the pillars? Open the locks, I want to pass through!"

"A Father Door . . . *pair o'doors*, actually. But you're not ready yet. You can't swim across the gate while your stomach is still full. Might get cramps!"

"You want it all?"

"On a plate," said the wolf bitch, baring her canines.

Jiana runs home, excited. The lifepower! It burns within her hands.

She touches the door on the way in and gods! leaves sprout, roots writhe. She runs inside, waits upon Mamma. Cut the carrots, slice the beets, Mamma says, and Jianabelana obeys, good little girl she.

But when she takes up the roots they squirm in her hand, sprout a thousand thousand tiny root hairs, wiggle and pulse; startled, she drops them to the dirt floor!

And where is Taidora? Has Toq forgotten her, sunk under the ice? Where is my sister?

The worst is yet to come. The meat: at dinner, she is careful *not* to touch with her hands. Fearful of the horror, she uses her knife. But within her mouth, down her throat—the meat, too, comes *alive*, alive.

Squirms. Writhes. Tries to flee. Chooses wrong (not a potato, so it has no eyes) and flees straight down her gullet. Bites of flesh in agony roll around stomach, stir up memories a million turns old!

Jiana vomits half chewed hunks of stew. They hump and slither across the table. She jumps to her feet screaming, falls forward and (*oh Tooqa not . . .*) it is her father who catches her.

He pulls her close, gentle arms wrapped around her. Jiana's hands press against his chest. . . .

Touches the horrible power to his heart. His chest bursts apart—the organ flees, escapes the dark sepulchre of bone and muscle. Blood geysers like Taidora's splash through the ice.

He dies. Jiana falls to her knees drips blood (his blood) from her red-stained hands. One thought, one horrid Toq-thought bursts through her numb stomach:

Cut them! off! Cut your hands off!

She stands. Calmly plucks knife from the table. She feels nothing; now is the time. She lays the blade across her wrist, feels the wood handle sprout leaves. Without a care or concern, she saws rapidly straight through the agony.

Halfway through: blood is pouring across the table and floor. It pools, and the pools roll about vainly seeking arteries and veins, the only world they know. Nearly through: the hand convulses, flops about like a beached fish.

It is severed. Hand drops, falls to table, scrabbles like a pulpy flesh-spider. She chops again, chops and chops and chops herself into the tiniest scraps, bits, and jiana pieces.

But they live, all they live, live they all do . . . forever. And ever.

Eyes still see, see Toq rising from the face from the lake, the heart from the chest, the hand from the arm. He opens a mouth wide as the green sky, words tumble out, knuckles from the boneyard:

Whence! screams the Talk, whence I curse you, for She was your sister, your (lover) friend. She beats her fists against the ice, and you stand accused, you are death in lice!

Dice! crows the Coq, dice cursed, for He was your father, your (lover) teacher. He falls to the ground *clutchit an' grabbit* and evidence is given, you are deaf without lies!

Spice! caws the Hoq, for Whoresy Blestfamy Unfamly culling doon the snake of wrybearth unto your quaiverung hoands! Tree Tines and you are *guilty*, greys Groq; thus three, three, *three times* shall I cross, my shuddow to cross, my shadow to crease your life! Three, the number of Toq, before another age is added to Jiana.

Three times . . .

There she WAKES—screaming into the black night of Jianabel's soul, quivering like a drop of dew on a bird-shaken branch. "The dream, the dream! He touched my heart," said Jiana. "I am full of fear. No feeling for a warrior!"

"He's touched deeper than your heart, sister." Jianabel looked down, unable to meet the warrior's eyes. "He's touched the thread of your life in the woof to come."

"A curse. I've never been accursed. Three times, before what? My next birthday? Why three instead of two or five?"

"Three is the number of all the conquering hero-king pirate gods. Watch." Jianabel held her hand up, palm towards Jiana. Her first three fingers were extended. As Jiana watched curiously, Jianabel curled her first and third fingers down to half mast, leaving the middle finger extended.

"It's all contained within this sacred sign, sister mine. But that's not here"—she pointed at Hodge—"and neither is it there." She pointed at Podge. "The reading is simple. Before your next birthday, Toq will blot your life three times."

"I know," Jiana admitted. "I fight the memory. Does un-remembered prophecy fail?"

Jianabel shrugged. "Alas, I think you're going to find out."

"It scares the shit out of me," said Jiana, trembling. "If *you* are but one part of me, then so too is Toq—and how can I hide from myself? Anyway, that's the dream." The turquoise sky faded seamlessly into the grass. Jiana could see no horizon.

"And quite a dream it is, sister mine. I've taught you well!"

"Why is Toq so pissed anyway?"

Jianabel rolled her eyes.

"Don't be stupid. For the *other* dream, the World's Dream, of course!"

"For *that?*" Jiana cried. "He's still on about that?"

"You defied him. He played you, and you turned about and played *him*. He's not used to being used. If the game rules permitted, he would wipe your existence from all nine hundred million spheres—but of course, they *don't* permit. Which is lucky for Toq."

"For Toq! What of me?"

"It would be his sin, not yours."

"But *my* existence that would be terminated!"

"Hah! Ever wonder why they say the weight of your sins shall drag you under like blood turned to stone? It's mechanical. When you drop a rock it falls not because it *likes* falling, but because unsupported things fall down."

"Toldo never believed in the last judgment preached by the Eagle Priests."

"If you dropped him over a cliff, would he believe in falling?"

Jiana chuckled at the thought of the roly-poly priest tumbling end over end over an endless cliff.

"Wouldn't matter what he believed, beast. He'd fall because it was falling time."

"Which is rising?" Jianabel asked, pointing at the Hodge and Podge columns again. Jiana stared, rubbing her eyes. One of them *was* getting bigger!

"It's Podge! The white one is rising, sure as snakes."

"That's Toq, the ultimate little-boy adolescent and his election. Am I moving too fast for you? Toq always appears in white. You dress in black, but your skin beneath is pale white. The Podge rose strong within you, and you became a warrior; but it's still covered by the black Hodge of your femaleness, which you think holds you back. Now I *know* I'm going too fast; I can see your eyes spinning!"

"Look, this is all very interesting, I guess, but all I want is a way to protect myself from Toq."

"Why not just say no?"

"What?"

"Toq won't blot your life, or whatever the silly calls it. He can't; it's not part of the rules. You'll do all that work yourself. So when each of the three times come, just don't do it!"

"How will I know what choice to make to not blot my life?"

"Wake up."

"Is this all a dream? Oh, of course it is, 'cause I can see you. You're just a part of me, even if you do talk."

"That's *not* what I meant, sister. I meant wake up from the dream of life. Quit this world. Quit the next world. Quit quitting."

"But I know different," insisted Jiana.

"Everything you know is wrong."

"Damn you, I had it all figured out! You *are* just another part of me, and I take responsibility for what you do and want to do!"

"I allowed you to come to a false conclusion, sis. You needed its implications at that time. You can face the truth now, Jiana. Toldo was wrong . . . I am not a part of you."

Jiana shut her eyes tightly and clapped her hands over her ears.

"I'm *going* to wake up now, I'm *going* to wake up now," she chanted. "I'm not listening to you, you figment!"

But her hands had holes right through them, through which Jianabel whispered into her ears.

"How do you know? Because a fat priest told you so? Because it's a convenient answer? I'm more powerful than you can possibly imagine, silly Jiana. I created this world and all the spheres! I made the grass green. Who are *you* to box me inside your tiny stomach?"

Jiana ran across the bright blue grass, fleeing the Other. The blades sliced at the soles of her feet like razors, and green blood dripped mocking from the sky.

A night wind blew, calling "fool, foool! ghooul . . . cruuel . . ."

"Please," Jiana begged, falling to her knees in the brittle blue blades, "I want to wake up now."

"You *can* wake up," Jianabel insisted firmly. Jiana looked up and saw the naked, alien being standing over her.

"You must wake up. You can't afford to sleep a moment longer. How long have you tarried, playing slave? How many easy roads have you taken on this quest? Why did you turn away from that slave girl, as you turned finally away from Dida? You're asleep!"

"But I have to! I have to get inside her stomach to show her freedom."

Jianabel waited silently. Anxiety crept into Jiana's heart. What did the wolf want from her?

"You've lost the path, sister," said Jianabel quietly.

"No."

"You tried a shortcut through the lotus fields. That was silly, Jiana. Now you're asleep and might never wake up again."

"No! I took no shortcuts. I did it by the book this time. Not like last time."

"Can you *really* pick up a burning coal, Jiana?"

Jiana's hand burst into flames. She bit back a scream before it rose through her throat. She clenched her hand into a fist, thought *not real not happening bitch is in my stomach stirring up agonies*.

"Stop slobbering!" Jianabel demanded. She stamped her foot and shattered a footprint into the grass. "You can wake *yourself*. Just walk through that door, the Father Door." Jianabel looked through Jiana, through Hodge and Podge—left and right sides of a doorway leading into a tiny, one-room building.

Now how could I have missed that before? Jiana thought as the pain ebbed. Sure and sure, a sign upon it read FATHER DOOR.

Jianabel whispered, sharing conspiracy, "Actually, it's a pair o'doors, a purse evil."

A chill breeze shaved Jiana's head. Tonight of all nights, she felt life's old pull, taffy hands sticking her soul back along the path, away from the Father Door, back to Daddy's door.

"I'm afraid," she admitted, did not like the word's taste.

The harrow wench touched her back and arm gently, put lips next to Jiana's ear.

"You ask the girl to step through *her* door. But you wouldn't even pick up a coal. What's through the Father Door? Frightness, madness, coldness, and loss. What's through the door is what you *bring* to the Father Door, Jiana."

Jiana looked back at her sister-plus. The girl's face had lost its customary smirk, carry-tale curl of cruelty. "You've walked through that door," Jiana declared.

"No," Jianabel shook her head. "I walked through my *own* Father Door. A bloody lot of them." For an instant, her eyes hollowed, stared into terrors beyond the edge of Jiana's night. Then she smiled, mask intact again.

Terror she had never felt before gripped Jiana. More than any arguments, this persuaded her to action. "Fuck it. Through the Father Door, frights and all!" To herself: *I cannot cannot cannot stand this indecision! Whatever hell's behind the door, at least the hemhawing will be gone. Please. . . .*

She began to walk, but she had barely taken five steps when Jianabel called to her. "O, sister, you must trust in the Master to provide; you cannot do for yourself. Matches and tinder must stay behind."

"But how will I ward away the cold?"

"You must look within; all fire comes from within."

Reluctantly, Jiana removed her tinderbox and matches and laid them on the grass like offerings to Mulak of Fire. She resumed her steps, but took only three more when the Other spoke out again. "O sister, the clothes too must stay."

"But, Jianabel! I need them for disguise, to enter the slave's world!"

"They must stay for that very reason. Silly, modesty like lust is a false mask to cover naked truth! Whatever you feel, feel with your own skin!"

Jiana undid her belt and dropped to the ground. The tunic and pantaloons followed, leaving only her sword. The wind made her shiver. Modesty? She burned to cover herself! Never before had she felt so vulnerable. Jiana forced her hands down, refused to feel eyes burning into her breasts, thighs, warm black hair, ankles.

She started again for the Father Door, trepidation turning to excitement to arousal to fear. She managed but two baby-steps before Jianabel called her to halt.

"Wave," added Jianabel, mournfully.

"My *sword?* How can I leave my sword? Wave has been with me since I don't know when. She's the final point in any argument!"

"Your stomach is sometimes full, sometimes empty. But it's your own. Your sword is bought, a hunk of steel."

Jiana touched Wave, stroked her. "Loved one. I will be back for you." She kissed the hilt, long and slow like a lover. "Don't listen to her; your soul is just sharper than most."

She laid Wave upon the blue sward and took the final step unmolested, reached the door itself. Jianabel's voice was faint with distance.

"Sandals, too, sis. Turtles all the way down."

"I'll be frightened without them," she said, more to herself than to Jianabel.

The girl answered just the same. "Depend only upon your own valor, not the happy accident of your magic. Oh, please kick them off! Don't stop now!"

Reluctantly, Jiana stepped out of first one then the other. Holding only herself, she was ready to enter the chapel.

"I'll wait for you," said Jianabel, concern and worry edging her voice. "I'll see you if you pass through. Do what you must, that's all. Always follow love, but do what you must. Can't go back though—it's a one-way door!"

Jiana gritted her teeth and did not look back. The chapel was unbroken grey stone framed by the Hodge and Podge pillars. Two doors, one said "FATHER," the other "DOOR." She grabbed the enormous, round latches with both hands and yanked them open.

Silence reigned. Rough canvas pressed against the soles of her bare feet. She heard only the rasp of her own ragged breath. *They're not even sure it is a door!* tittered the mice.

Jiana walked a long corridor, pulpy walls closing around her until she had to squirm through on her belly. She pushed through a sphincter into a great, red pentagon. Hot sweat dripped down her body.

She stood in confusion. Then light dawned; *the Empire khayma*, she thought, skin flushed. Three score dead Horsemen surrounded her, and she dared not move. She blinked. Pieces of sleep still lurked in her eyelids.

If I move I shall frighten them to life! She heard a dull strumming, like a great water-engine churning out the sea. *If it's the Empire khayma, one side leads to the inner sanctum of al'Sophiate, one leads to the desert. The other three sides lead to sleeping rooms, where dream the Overmen. But what is my task? Which door is the next Father Door?*

There was no clue which orifice led out, so she tried the closest one. Jiana groped in darkness, found warm wet that tasted of Sister Taidora's Secret. She pushed the rest of her body through. Blood scraped off the walls, coating her like a naughty hand on moon-day.

Jiana guessed wrong. The fleshflap lead to a triangular sleeping chamber. A man lay on the mat and shivered from cold premonition.

She heard a hacking cough. One of the Horsemen choked on something, probably his own spittle. He coughed his windpipe clear, but Jiana heard his neighbors stir on their mats. Any moment they would sit up and cook the poor blighter.

Frantic, Jiana yanked shut the flap and scurried to bedside. She crouched in a tiny woom. Curled on the mat was a tiny, transparent baby. On its back, it floccillated ceilingwards.

Who is he? Cute enough kid. Sweet he was. *A Kidder, she thought, Must be Akidder.* He was surely not his father Gi'a'thuddin'!

4

Hot still tent air stifled her. She sweated, watching the baby, boy, manling lying in his drenched bed awaiting fate. *Too many easy roads on this quest,* she thought. Frightening images of throats and coats, hearts and tarts danced before her eyes.

A familiar smell pulled her head aside. Toldo Mondo leaned close, a sun in his eye. Looked he did straight through her heart. He was not there sure, but he loomed large in her stomach. "There are always easy roads, Jianabelladonna, but some easy roads are true never the nevertheless."

"Take him," counseled the Evil Tampertress. "He owns you, he groans you, and now again he *bones* you!"

More voices uninvited in her stomach's ear. "-No! 'Tis father, 'tis Guy Hath a Dream!"

"Lick father," said Toldo . . .

"Lock son!" finished triumphant Jianabel.

Jiana looked down. A helpless infant, sucking on a foot. "Go on, it's only a dream! Matters not what I do."

A dream, a gleam, a scream! laughed the little girl, filing sharpness into pointy teeth. Jianabel stood beside Jiana in the dark, but Jiana stood alone. Was it Jianabel, or just the left of Jiana's right? Jiana cringed, covered breasts and belly.

Hands touched her from behind, a poke between her thighs: a naked Toldo, fat belly pressing her buttocks as he pulled him into her.

"Just blow, just blow it, just blow it up. . . ."

A long snakey umbilical cord (the Nameless Serpentine agrin) entwined out of the bay-bay-baby's belly, curled and twisted into phantastical knots of matter, essence, spirit, and stomach. The cord terminated in a nozzle like the tied-end of Jianabelana's pig-bladder.

Dilai, too, appeared before her. Long, slanky-black hair flipped from his eyes, half-lidded pale skin flushed with

excritement. He inhaled to speak. The air whooshed into
his lungs and he puffed into a bloat-ball. Dangling two
arms, three legs like fruit from a tree, he floated to the top
of the khayma, squeezed through the smoke hole and was
gone, wordless.

Jiana was alone. Again, at last, she looked upon the
birthcord, fingered it gently. Flecks of watery blood dripped
from the end. The child looked into Jiana's untrustingworthy
eyes.

"T-teeth!" stuttered Akadr, shivering in nightmare, "her
teeth, they're filed to a . . ."

Dilai my only love, you showed me the way, Jiana said
aloud in her stomach. Long-lovingly she brought the end
up, up to her lips, closed eyes, inhaled godbreath from the
babe into her mouth.

He collapsed inward. His frightened eyes opened wide,
scream-cry cut off in mid-wail as belly, then chest flattened as a toad beneath a cartwheel.

She heard a pop and one fat arm curled, followed by a
chubby leg. His skin folded, crumbled like discarded parchment as the last enthusiasm was sucked from his tiny body
into Jiana's gut.

Skin, all that was left. She had sucked the baby dry.
Overcome with remorse and guilt, she spit out drops of
baby and fell to her knees, cried "Tooqa, Tooqa, will *no
one* help the widow-maker's son?"

Drained, she sobbed. She wished for Jianabel, Toldo,
but most of all for Wave. *I know what you did, you
bitch! Worse than blood-sucker, a soul-drinker you
made me!*

She stood in a rivulet of blood, swamp of excrement.
War-buddies floated in soupy liquid, buried for compost.
Blood poured from her mouth, vagina—birth and death
linked in blood pudding.

Blood the suckrament, droned Toldo Mondo, shadowed
across her, hulked like a Skinpriest. "Blood on her
fourheads, Sign of the Snake! With this blood I do cum
firm, the knife rises and falls, whackity-whackity!"

Knife guts. Blood redeems. Jiana answers, completes the ritual: *fill the plates for feeders, fooders, suckers of humors!*

Her teeth felt funny. She touched them . . . marching around her mouth, mouth full of beetles, each filed to a Jianabel point. "Oh, gods, I'm a dead woman," she sobbed to the khayma wall. She cried tiny red rivulets down her nude belly, across battle-scarred thighs.

She pressed out her hands. Fingers sliced through the meat (*no, it's just a canvas wall!*), razor through a tight drum. She stepped through the gash, and spoke to the Wolf Within: "Sisters under the skin now, my heart. Brothers across the blood, my flesh. Murther and further, priceless and prancelust. I hate you."

I love *you.*

I love you, too, slobbed Jiana. Ashamed of her nakedness, she ran across the chipped blue ground to the water trough. The moons stared, uneven eyes watched from the depths. Jiana washed the blood from her skin.

It spread across the still water. Stained the five wooden sides. Dream-Akadr spiraled in the waking horse trough, candy red in sleep.

5

News of the shocking death spread outward from the household khayma like waves spreading across a still-water lake, touching every shore, after a great stone had fallen. Wives jumped up from their tables, and their slaves spilled the food. Chests and buckets overturned, and the Elect of al'Sophiate staggered as if physically struck. A cart fell upon its side, overturned by wave or heavy wind.

Everywhere, slaves, herders, Horsemen, and Overmen ran wildly like headless fowl, yelling the news that everyone already knew: Akadr was slain, yet *not a mark upon him found!*

Jiana woke from her bricker dream. She sat up in her sleeping roll, horrible images pushing against her eyelids until she thought they would burst apart.

She was sweating, though it was not hot, and her muscles ached. Her hands were cramped, as if they had clutched something hard and round all night, but she was rolled in her blankets, and nothing to be found. The sun had not yet cleared the eastern mountains, and the early morning chill made her shiver in her damp blankets.

"Akadr has been slain, yet not a mark upon him!"

Jiana felt a cold river trickle up and down her spine. *Was that me? Was that him? Did I slay him in a dream, in a trance? Or just a horrible, horrible coincidence?*

"But how was he found?"

Lips drawn back in rictus shrinking at the last from horrors unimaginable hexed to death witches and demons and daevas summoned from the blackest pits by—by a slave!

This inference was drawn within moments. No one knew who drew it first. Only slaves and Horsemen had access to the Empire khayma, and no Horseman (they said) would have attacked an unarmed man in his dreams, let alone call up a *daeva*.

By midmorning, the clampdown began. A slave who wandered off to sneak a nap was caught and beaten. Kyaddi, a member of Rethe's group, was kicked by a Horseman because she forgot to bring him a bucket of water for his horse. When she fell, he kicked her again.

The incidents themselves were not unheard of, but the men who perpetrated them had been gentle and lenient the day before. The Horsemen withdrew among themselves, shunning the company of the other members of the Caliph's Elect, herders and craftsmen with whom they had enjoyed an easy camaraderie for turns.

By noon, the clampdown became official. Slaves were forbidden to initiate conversation with freemen. Slaves were to be constantly supervised by Overmen and trustees such as Rethe. All but the household slaves were to be chained at night; those who worked in the household khayma would not be chained, but they would be guarded.

Jiana put down the saddle she was polishing and repolishing, wiped her forehead, and said, "I need break, damn it!"

Rethe pulled at her lip, looking back over her shoulder, looking for a noise she had imagined.

"Don't cuss at me. I'm doing what I can, Jiana. Kyaddi hasn't stopped crying since that oaf booted her."

"I'm not Kyaddi. I not cry. I need to the break, yes?"

"What if Curse or Ysmal needs a horse shod, or something?"

"The sun is high!"

"Damn you, Kyaddi's only dress was ruined!"

Jiana just waited impassively, watching Rethe. The woman pulled at her lip again, worrying at a cold sore that was trying to scab over. Finally, swearing unintelligibly, she picked up a bucket and a pair of stirrups and handed them to Jiana.

"Here. They'll all think you're on some crazy errand and leave you alone. Back *long* before nightfall, yes?"

Jiana nodded, and left in search of Radience.

She found the girl scrubbing a roll of canvas, tears streaking her face.

"Hello, Radience."

"You, too." Radience scowled at Jiana, looking speculative.

"How are you making out?"

"I got slapped for laughing."

"Dear me. Really treating you like a slave, hm?"

Radience sucked in a sudden breath, and her face paled.

"Did you—was it *you?*"

"Does it make a difference? For all I know, *you* might have done it; you *live* here." She nodded at the khayma, in whose shadow they crouched. "Matters not. We're all treated like murderers now. Remember this well, kid. To the master, every slave is a spy."

"No! It wasn't like that! Things were fine before. . . ."

"Were they! Could you have walked over that bridge in Bay Bay?"

Radience said nothing. She scrubbed the canvas so vigorously she lost control of the horsehair brush, and it flew through the air.

That night, Jiana waited until the other slaves had fallen asleep. Then she waited while the great moon rose into a dark cloud, excruciatingly slowly. At last the compound was dark.

She leaned over her shackle, letting her stomach drift. The words of the Overman tumbled out, almost without her thinking about them:

> *Flick flack*
> *Click back*
> *Pop box*
> *Drop locks*

With an alarming creak, the lock fell open. Jiana gingerly disengaged the chains and slipped her hands free.

She ghosted through the compound, letting her eyes drift, deliberately holding her stomach empty, seeking an outlet for mischief.

Jiana smiled, spying a mini-khayma, more like a tent, which contained the horse's feed for the next few days. She spotted the nearest torch, and scanned the route there and back again for Horsemen.

Jiana dithered, wondering whether she should use her magic. It would be so easy! She could simply walk up to the torch and fetch it back. Better yet, she could probably conjure up a fire in the tent without resorting to the torch at all.

But she felt a strong presentiment that it would be some sort of violation of the rules. *Rules? What rules?* But deep within she knew that there *were* rules that pulled her back and forth, as the tides were pulled in and out, as a stone and a stick in water were pulled in opposite directions.

Taking a deep breath, Jiana stepped from behind the household khayma into the shadows of the night. She stilled her pulse, and made herself feel confidence. *In fear, the shadows are blacker; they will not see me!*

She walked steadily, the cold stones of the clearing burning her feet like lumps of coal. A breeze blew iceknives through her, and she shivered, both with the cold and with anticipation.

As she walked, she bowed her head and tried to touch

the pulse of Reality Prime. *Every sphere has a beat*, she thought. *If I walk through the ebb tides, I can slip under their attention.*

The great moon rose past its concealing cloud, and Jiana found herself, naked and exposed, standing in the middle of a well-lit clearing. She was equally far from the storage tent and the safety of the khaymas.

She did not stop; she continued walking, eyes half-shut, listening for any change in the beat which would indicate that someone had taken notice. At last, she reached the torch. No one had seen.

She plucked it from its holder and continued towards the tent without missing a step.

Once inside, she kicked the grain to stir it up. It puffed up into a cloud of chaff, and Jiana nearly choked on it. She threw the torch into the middle of the pile, and ducked out of the tent again.

The sudden, bloody dawn roused the entire encampment. Horsemen bolted from their khayma in panic, half-dressed or naked. Herders and tailors, tentmakers and candledippers, rangers and priests, all streamed into the main compound clutching buckets, pots, or waterskins.

In the confusion, Jiana slipped back to her group. No one noticed; they were too busy yelling and pointing at the fire.

The children cried, and the women held veils across their faces and wailed. The men ran to one side of the Elect and asked who could have done such a thing; then they ran to the other side and demanded that the culprit surrender himself.

Some of the Horsemen became enraged when they saw that the loss was total. They charged the mass of chained slaves and began beating and kicking them indiscriminately. The slaves cried out for protection, but for a long time no one came to their aid.

Jiana curled into a tight ball, guarding her head and belly, and incidentally covering the fact that her own shackle was unlocked. She was kicked twice, both times in the side but with insufficient force to break a rib.

Eventually, al'Sophiate himself stepped into the fire-light. His sleeping robe was wrapped around him, but he wore his *ha'ik* headdress of religious office. The Elect grew silent, even the Horsemen.

"There are *daevas* among us," he said, speaking as Caliph. "No mortal man could have committed both these atrocities, the slaying and the conflagration, not under the watching eyes of Horsemen and Elect.

"We must root out these *daevas*, which certainly have taken residence in one of the Elect, or a slave. We must drive the devils out of this poor unfortunate, lest he die and be denied the Paradise which the Seer has promised."

Al'Sophiate looked into the flames for a moment. They were beginning to die down, but it would be full daylight before the fire was burned to embers. He turned and walked back to his own khayma.

When he had gone, the Overmen called the Horsemen together to confer. Jiana continued working at the tongue of her shackle, which stubbornly refused to latch.

Damn, can't be caught with this thing open . . . Jiana wished for oil, but none materialized. The Horsemen returned to the firelight, spread out and began to collect slaves, herding them into the slave's khayma.

Horseman Giathudin appeared with Rethe and Ysmal. The two slave Voices pointed out their own charges, and the once-Overman unlocked their ankles and pushed each to her respective Voice.

Giathudin paused as he saw her. His lip curled, and Jiana braced herself for whatever he might do to her.

She kept squeezing the lock shut, hoping he would think she was only nursing a sore ankle that was unused to a shackle. He reached her in three strides, and deliberately stepped upon her leg with his full weight.

"So, what filth is this? Got a devil inside you, you little, foreign-born cunt? I think not; I think you're just a murderous, disloyal, traitorous bitch." He ground his foot into Jiana's shin. She gritted her teeth and refused to cry out;

her days of playing the cowering slave ended in that moment, she decided.

Rethe was at Giathudin's side instantly, her clenched fists resting on her hips.

"I am *certain* you don't mean to be damaging property of the *Caliph of the Elect*, do you?" Her voice had a warning tone to it, and Giathudin looked at her sharply.

"*What did you say?*" he demanded, his voice cracking in falsetto.

Rethe stepped close to Giathudin and spoke so softly that Jiana could barely hear her voice, close as she was. Yet it was full of menace.

"I mean, you horseturd, that if you don't take your fucking foot off my girl I'll cut your balls off . . . my Lord *Horseman.*"

Giathudin stared at Rethe; Jiana could not tell whether he was enraged or terrified. The slave Voice continued.

"Remember, *Horseman* Giathudin: *I know where you buried the bones of Mansur bin Ibrahim.*"

Giathudin shrank back a step into the darkness, but Jiana could smell the sweat of fear coming from the former Overman.

Throughout this exchange, Ysmal had stood back in deference to Rethe's superior rank. He stepped forward as Giathudin withdrew.

Rethe squatted near Jiana.

"You alright, Jiana?" Jiana nodded. Rethe gently moved the warrior's hands away from the shackle and inserted the key. Naturally it would not turn.

"Ysmal, get this thing unlocked," Rethe ordered. The boy approached. He took hold of the key in one hand, and Jiana's leg in the other.

Ysmal twisted as hard as he could. With a wrench, the key turned in the lock. Ysmal took hold of the tongue, using both hands this time, and pulled it free of the body of the lock. He gestured flamboyantly.

"Hm," mused Rethe, "toss that thing to the desert, or the bushes, I mean. Damn, we're going to run out of locks before this night is through!" She smiled at Jiana. "That's the fifth busted lock we've had tonight. Been so long since we used these! C'mon, tough it out . . . the clampdowns don't last forever."

"Have ever been through it one, your most self?" Jiana asked.

"Have I ever been through one myself? Well, yes, when the immortal Kerat bin El, father of al'Sophiate, was murdered in his sleep by an assassin sent by the Old Man in the Mountains. I was fifteen, so it was, um, three or four turns ago." She massaged Jiana's ankle a bit. "It gets better. Wait till they find the possessed one and drive the daevas out. Things'll get back to normal."

Rethe gently punched Jiana's shoulder and stood.

"Arms up, girl. See you in the morning for a head-count."

Jiana stood slowly, feigning stiffness. She watched Rethe's back as she approached the next slave. *I like her,* the warrior thought. *How, when I despised one slavemaster, can I feel affection for another?*

Because, Jiana dear, Rethe makes no claim to OWN you. She is as much a prisoner as are you.

So was Akadr, Jiana responded. *Was he bred or led any less than Rethe, or Radience, or me?*

You're growing, Jiana! Alright then, Akadr died not because he deserved punishment, but because it was necessary at that moment. While his father was Overman, Akadr could learn the uselessness of brutality. But when he inherited the job, he could learn only one thing: to become everything he despised in Giathudin.

Great. So now he's dead, and he won't learn anything.

He's still on the Wheel, silly! laughed the voice.

Jiana shrugged and plodded towards the slave khayma, her ears burning. Jianabel was right, of course.

You can always learn something.

Chapter V:

Stands the sands and cracks the Teeth, Freedom in a cell

1

Radience sat in a corner of the household khayma, her knees drawn up and her good arm locked around them. *I'm not going to cry,* she promised, and kept her word. She had been sitting thus ever since serving supper to the Horsemen.

It would not be long until the new Overman of Slaves, Hakkim al'Kug (the Ghoul), cousin of Giathudin, came by to lock her up with the rest of the slaves for the night.

I will not cry. I won't give her the satisfaction.

Days had passed since the death of Akadr, and Radience was more convinced than ever that Jiana had something to do with his death. And who had set the store-tent on fire the next night? Who had loosed the horses, who had spilled the goat's milk?

The outrages continued every night, despite a dozen Horsemen and a hundred of the Elect, one hundred and twelve pairs of eyes watching every slave, every man and woman, each child—even watching the other Horsemen. The outrages continued, always in a different place, another trick that no one had thought to guard against.

It could not be Jiana. It could not be, for she was

153

watched night and day! Horseman Giathudin was utterly
convinced that she had given herself to the *daevas*, and he
maintained constant guard.

Yet the outrages continued, and the watchmen swore by
the Seer that her body at least had not stirred from stars
to sunlight.

*Could it be her animus? Is she projecting a malign spirit
to hound and harry us?* But that theory did not explain all
of the accidents among the slaves, even among those of
the Faith, who were immune to magic.

Yadzr dragged a cookpot and caught a pole of the household khayma, pulling one side of it down in mid-meal.
Three cooks burned themselves and were out of work for
days, leaving the cooking to the Horsemen's wives (who
were terrible cooks). Slaves fell off horses. Slaves dropped
the food. They became suddenly stupid, following orders
to the letter that were obviously meant to be liberally
interpreted ("get rid of those extra horses," said al'Kug,
and Ysmal pulled off their bridles and drove them away).

Progress had been reduced to a crawl, and the Caliph
was in a fury. He ordered beatings, and the Horsemen
took the hint and turned brutal, pushing and kicking slaves
even when they did nothing wrong. But this did not cure
the problem; if anything, the accidents grew more spectac-
ular and much stupider. Little Dorsis from the East had to
be killed when Aghi spilled a pot of boiling oil on her.
Al'Kug grabbed for Dorsis, but he was a heartbeat too
slow, and in an instant she was writhing on the ground
and screaming so heart-rendingly that the Overman drew his
tulwar and cut her head off to spare her agony.

That night, Aghi hanged herself, and al'Sophiate was
poorer by two slaves.

It was two days since Aghi's death, and Radience sat in a
dark corner with her knees up, waiting for lockdown.
*What's happened to the world? It can't all be Jiana—how
could even such a witch as she make Aghi spill a pot of
boiling oil or make Ysmal loose a pair of horses? It's
insane!*

Radience reached up and tugged at her collar. Somehow, it seemed to be getting tighter, and she was having a harder time breathing. She was afraid to mention this to any of the other slaves.

Voices and feet sounded in the next chamber; it was al'Kug and a Horseman. Curse the smith accompanied them with the chains. They entered the sleeping chamber, and al'Kug said, "Let's make this fast, yes? Get back to our nice beds?" He folded his arms and stood in the doorflap, impatiently blowing air through his lips without whistling.

Curse took one side of the khayma, and the Horseman took Radience's side. She did not know him. He rushed through the khayma chamber, slapping shackles around each left ankle. When he came to Radience, he did not even look at her face.

Al'Kug began slapping his hands together.

"Come, come! Faster! Three more groups to do, and we're all tired, yes?" Curse and the Horseman ran back to the Overman, and without a backward glance they passed back through the doorflap.

Radience sat in the corner unmoving. Then she reached down and absently tugged at the shackle.

To her surprise, it popped open. The Horseman had not pushed it far enough to lock.

So what? Remember the collar? It holds you, and anyway, will you repay kindness with theft? You're valuable property!

Kindness? What kindness have they shown me recently? They took Aghi from me!

Aghi took herself. She killed herself. Are you going to be a quitter?

Radience slowly spread the anklet with her fingers and noiselessly slid her foot out. She waited unbreathing, listening for approaching footsteps (*she pulled it out! look everybody, she pulled it out right in front of us!*) but no one heard. She stood slowly in the darkness.

You're going to be in a lot of trouble, young lady. You better just sit right down and lock yourself in again.

Radience crept along the edge of the khayma wall, feeling for the slit. Only two other slaves knew of it. One of the cooks had cut it years ago to facilitate sneaking out to drink forbidden wine. Radience often used it to relieve herself during the night—*used to use it,* she thought.

Even Jiana did not know about *this* one.

Tonight it served a more sinister purpose. *They can't make me cry, the bastards; I'll give them something to wonder about!* Radience had a particular destination in mind, the Caliph's dressing chamber.

Radience crept on cat feet along the outer wall of the household khayma. The sky was overcast, and she had to feel her way in the blackness with her bare feet and her little hand on the canvas.

She passed first one of the main poles, then found the second. After waiting one hundred heartbeats, listening for approaching guards and nerving herself to the task, she shimmied up the pole. The hand pegs were spaced too far apart, for they were spaced for a normal man with a normal reach, not a girl with only one good arm. But Radience discovered that it was still easy, just as it had been when she used to play hide-me-find-me with Teenja (*no! don't think about . . . !*).

A flicker of anger warmed her tiny frame. What right had *that woman* to ruin Radience's life? What right had she to burn storetents and slit the throat of Overmen? and why did Radience keep wondering what Jiana would think, in spite of all attempts to drive *that woman* from her stomach?

So who really had the *daevas?* Did the possessed one know it, or were they hidden, like the pox for moons and moons after you contracted it? Could they be possessing Radience herself?

That thought paused her. What if she were the vessel for the evil *daevas,* would she know it? It might explain what she was doing now, climbing on tent poles in the middle of the night like a monkey.

Oh Lord of the Wind and the Five Sands, she thought, *I'm actually going to burn all of your clothes! Why? Why! I don't know why, that's why!*

The compulsion drove Radience on, and she climbed

the last few pegs until she was over the ventilation flap that led down into the dressing room. The girl lowered herself gently by her good arm, and carefully untied the knot with her left arm. The tiny fingers were ideal for tugging and pulling on the exact strand holding tight the whole, and in a moment she had the cord undone and the flap pulled back. Then she dropped lightly into the chamber.

Now what? The pungent smell of warpwood incense enveloped Radience, and she nearly choked. It was a wonder the Caliph could breathe. *He's scared,* she thought, distressed. *He's burning magical spells to ward off the daevas!*

The air was smokey with incense. Radience felt her way carefully, almost stumbling over an expensive, eastern rug. She listened intently, every nerve trembling, for the sound of the Tokogare statue that had come alive during her dream foray into the Caliph's apartments.

She approached the light, found the torch. Her ankle began to ache where the shackle had prisoned it.

No! cried the voice in her stomach. *How can you be so thankless and ingracious? You cannot even consider it, much less actually commit such a heinous crime!* But Radience was immune to the blandishments of the voice—no matter how disturbingly it mimicked the voice of Mother Lhana.

"She's dead and buried under turns of sand," whispered the slave girl, a lump rising in her throat. "She's buried with Teenja and Mara and my mother who was beaten while with child—with me!—and my arm was stunted like—like . . ."

The Caliph of Qomsheh, Yazd, and Deh Bid stirred in his sleep, and cried out in a sleepy voice of fear.

"Will *no one* help the . . . ?"

Radience froze; no one answered his plea.

How many times this trip has he cried out thus? she wondered, amazed at her own insolence. The Caliph of the Elect!

Soon he sighed and rolled over. For one hundred long heartbeats, and five more, she stood as still as a lizard on a dune. Her pulse pounded in her ear, loud enough that she worried it would wake the whole khayma. Then she moved with a grim determination.

Radience plucked the torch from its holder and stole to the great chest in the center of the dressing chamber. The chest was unlocked, for the only door led to the chamber of the Caliph himself.

The slave girl opened the chest, and took a deep breath. The incense that had almost choked her now seemed calming, friendly; it wrapped around her guts and comforted their trembles. Bouyed, she lovingly laid the oil-soaked brand in the center of the clothes, and watched until the ceremonial aba coat, with its vertical stripes of white and blue, singed and curled away from the fire. A musty, smokey smell mingled with the incense to produce a most unpleasant odor.

Radience rose, but the walls of the khayma had folded in upon her. They pulsed regularly, breathing or beating like a living thing. *I am in the belly of a great, hairy jamal that humps and lumps and whumps along the Five Sands, I am—*

She shook her head, but the dizziness continued. *Something in the air. Something in the incense in the peppercorns in the hairy, humpy thumpy jamal that—*

Suddenly panicked, terrified at what she had done (the flames cackle merrily in the chest *oh come Radience come dance about the laughy red spirits, give us, have us, daevas!*) she clutched at the pole the edge of the pole stickuppy a happy roof of the khayma-climb, lizard on a rafty pole, daffy hule, the hole in the roof of the khayma jamal . . .

Outside on the khayma roof, the cold air cut through her stomach like a sandstorm. Her thoughts cleared. The smoke curling up from the roof flap was sign that her fire (*her* fire!) was burning bright.

Frightened, she fumbled the flap closed, hung by her legs from the pole to tie the knot again (*simple lock-knot; anyone could do it,* she remembered).

As she slid down the pole, the alarm was sounded. *Fire! Death in al'Sophiate's chambers! Destruction in the khayma!*

Soon the whole of the Elect was aroused, and they ran thither and yon searching for *daevas*, elementals, djinns, or Arhatman himself. No one noticed a tiny slave girl, scuttling along the edge of the khayma, feeling for a slit that led back to chains and safety.

Radience slipped inside; no one saw her. She was invisible in the dark of frightened women and screaming infants in the slaves' quarters. Her shackle was where she had left it; she closed it around her ankle, and this time it clicked home, unheard in the din.

At last the alarm died down, for the fire had spread no farther than the Caliph's clothes-box. Al'Kug stormed through the slaves' quarters, tugging at chains and checking shackles. When he came to hers, she held her breath, but now it was truly locked tight.

The Horsemen stumbled off to sleep; it was just another night's outrage, and tomorrow's day would be long enough. They did not even complain or grouse. The men were too tired, too frightened. They secured the khayma with lips pressed tight, and fell back to their pallets. Tomorrow's light would be soon enough to investigate.

Radience lay unsleeping. She exulted. Her outrage! With *daevas* in the caravan, who would ever suspect a slave girl?

It was mine, she thought. *I showed them all! Ghosted in the middle of the dark, silent Yes as a spirit on the wind! Passed beneath their very eyes, strike a blow Yes for Aghi, for Teenja, for all of them, for mother. But was it daevas? Was it daevas infesting infecting possessing driving me to do what I knew was wrong? But I showed them gave them a mystery they'll never solve. . . .*

With a resounding *Yes!* still echoing round her ears, Radience finally drifted off into a happy, peaceful void, dancing the *daevas* to dawn.

2

Three times . . .
Three times . . .
Three times will I blot . . .

Stands he stretched arms like windmill slowly spreading widening evil stench little boy-god Toq laughing like a blowriver of dried leaves . . . "Three times! three times! three times! before falls your next birthing-day!"

And alive they came became within her around her because of her, deadalive never living beyond trapped forever. AAH!

Jiana sat bolt upright, staring into the face of Toq, pale alabaster skin, oil black hair, wild pink eyes. His arms were outstretched, and he laughed like dust from a tomb, like the rattling of bones, like a dried out drum splitting under the hot sun, like desert sand wearing a great colossus to a shapeless lump, like cracking parchment, like a river of desiccated scarab shells falling from a brass jar, laughed like the clutching feet of carion-kites, walking across shards of broken window.

The image faded, and she saw a moonsplash on the khayma wall. The wind spit desert under the doorflap. She lay all night staring at the desert dust swirling in the moonlight.

Morning brought a dry, hot wind from the east. As Jiana readied the horses and led them out of the stables khayma into the angry wind, she found herself sweating freely even before the morning meal. She and Cascade talked, passing the time. She spent as much time as she could with the horse, as Radience made herself scarce.

Jiana made no effort to force a meeting; Radience needed time to absorb, to incorporate the new reality.

No Horseman had yet ridden Cascade. For some reason, they passed him over, magnificent a beast as he was. Jiana wondered about this, but Cascade chose not to illuminate her.

The Horsemen reveled in the dusty weather; they were nearing Tool and they knew it. Moons had passed, the coast had floated past. The Elect had avoided towns and the townsmen had not been anxious to press contact.

The forests and undergrowth of Bay Bay had given way to lush grasses and farms as they traveled south. Once the caravan took a short cut farther inland, and they had

journeyed along the Great Southern Road past five days of
fruit trees. The merchants among the Elect traded spices
and jewels for apples, pomegranates, boosfruit, succulent
grapes and berries, aromatic cracker-flowers, and truck.
Peaches and paschmelons were dried and stored; they
would last far into Tool.

But the grasslands grew wild, and they ate wheat, corn,
and rice. Then the grass grew tall, the villages grew scarce,
and the Elect ate dried fruit and jerky. Scrub brush pushed
the lawn grass aside, and what remained was coarse and
razor-edged.

They had crossed the length of the Water Kingdom,
skirted the edge of Door, and were now near enough to
the Lizard Teeth Hills to see the clouds that overhung
their peaks. In just a few days they would cross the Teeth
and enter the Desert of Tool.

The caravan crested a hill overlooking a cliff that dropped
straight into the ocean, and Jiana looked west. Her heart
leaped as she saw, far across the water, three peaks partly
covered with water mist. They were all that was left of the
islands of Oort, once home of the largest temple of the
Eagle priests, and home in exile of the Sisters of the
Serpentine.

Jiana had once called herself a daughter of the Nameless
Serpentine, but all things pass.

The Oort Islands sank mysteriously four turns ago; Jiana
remembered it vividly. She killed a snake, and she lost
her faith.

"At least I made my mark," she said quietly, staring at
the stark, shattered peaks.

"Made what?" asked Rethe, unexpectedly behind her.

"I say, at least I made marker did," said Jiana hastily.
Rethe almost smiled, and Jiana wondered how deeply the
slave Voice saw. *She'd be a good shield-mate*, the warrior
thought. *Maybe she'll come with us when we go.*

The leagues drifted along like a raft on a lazy river, and
soon the cliff was far behind and the Oort Islands invisible
over the horizon. The Lizard Teeth drew measurably closer.

Jiana spent all her spare time poking at a peculiar,

spiney plant one day. Great needles stuck out of it in a protective bristle, but the plant itself was succulent. It bore a flower with a curious, applelike fruit that Rethe called a "spineapple."

But the spiney plants lost their charm when Jiana put her hand down into a patch of them. Her skin swelled up puffy and red, and Ysmal taught her how to chew a certain root into a pasty poultice and wrap her hand with it.

Leagues and days passed, now hot and sultry like driftwood floating in a dead, chigger-breeding pond. Trees returned, but not the friendly, climbable oaks and housewood of White Falls, and not the tall bloodwoods of Bay Bay. These trees were caricatures of life, twisted and stunted as though molded by Kiddikikitik, the Termite Queen. They bore no bark, just a leathery, fibrous skin of sharp needles. Queer creatures inhabited them; in one, Jiana saw a two-headed lizard. She turned away with a shudder and never told anyone.

Nasty, black wasps infested the camp. Rethe had Jiana and the other slaves in her group burned a foul, resinous, local plant. The smoke kept the wasps away.

"They seek out great spiders," said Rethe once, as they all huddled around a camp fire. Though the days were hot as a skillet, the nights were freezing cold. "When they find them, they sting them a dozen times, and the venom in their tails paralyzes the spiders."

"Do they eat them?" asked Anahita, looking fearfully over her shoulder for marauding wasps.

"No," said Rethe smugly, "once paralyzed, the wasps lay their eggs, a myriad and more, right in the body of the still-living spider. The eggs hatch, and the young emerge . . . *eating their way out.*"

The slaves groaned, and Makao, a young boy whose parents were captured far to the south, chucked a turnip at the slave Voice. Rethe caught it without looking and ate it with the rest of her stew.

Alone in the stables khayma, Jiana was crowded with friends. She observed a genial peace with Jianabel, and Cascade could almost talk to both of them. Jianabel loved horses, being still in some very small ways a little girl.

Jiana kept to these two friends as much as possible, to avoid falling back asleep.

The scrub grew scarce, and the spiney plants grew few. The sand heaped high in spots, and other stretches were as flat and cracked as unoiled leather left baking in the sun. Jiana scraped some dust and tasted it; it was salty and bitter.

The caravan had left the ocean to cut straight across the Zephyr Desert, in an area unclaimed by the Water Kingdom, Door, or Tool. No roads led across the Zephyr, but there were occasional towns, built around gold and silver mines and water wells.

The Elect passed through one such town, Tinker's Hang; it was deserted. "Place was a real riverbed of desert diggers when we came up," Rethe said, kicking a rolling weed from the empty, lifeless street. "I picked up a strange wine from that shop there. Called the Waters of Life. Couldn't hardly drink a single glass without choking, it had such a kick."

"Is not wine your religion frowning at?"

"Hm," Rethe rolled her eyes upward in an elaborate pretense of innocence. "And our Horsemen are all learned philosophers, men of peace and godliness who never take the Seer's name in anger or sample each others' wives. You can quit the 'dumb foreigner fresh off the *jamal*' act anytime you want, Jiana; I've heard you talking to that horse."

"Oh?" Jiana kept her face impassive, but she felt the flush that belied her nonchalance.

"You know not a single Horseman's been able to ride that beast."

"I hadn't noticed."

"Go fuck a *jamal*. You knew damn well that's a one-master horse, and so did your former owner, that limp-wristed, child-enticing Bay Bay sheriff who foisted him off on Giathudin. And the ex-Overman has it figured by now, too, so your old faggot master better move to his summer house over the mountains or he'll get a scimitar up his arse."

Jiana cocked her eyebrow.

"Such it is vehemence is so violent, my rug."

"I don't *like* you white-skinned sheep. Present company mostly excepted except when you're doing that jabbering act. What do you have against speaking in honest Tooltak?"

"How long to Deh Bid?"

"Week. Two. I'm not a navigator. I don't read maps."

Jiana smiled mysteriously and continued walking.

Days passed. The country grew more deserty, the outrages tapered off and finally ceased. The caravan had left its *daevas* behind in the grasslands. Jiana herself had committed fewer than a third of the mysterious attacks, for after the first few, Giathudin watched her like a vulture.

After some time, the security measures began to become as much of a nuisance to the Horsemen as to the slaves, and the collars were loosened a notch.

Rethe allowed Jiana to sleep at the edge of the caravan, far from the clutch of women, men, and bawling infants. Jiana generally woke before dawn to watch the rousing of the Elect.

First a trickle of women, rising for errands of nature or creeping back from inappropriate khaymas. Then the household slaves, staggering in the predawn darkness to throw breakfast together for the Horsemen.

As the sun cracked the eastern mountains, a spur of the Lizard's Teeth, Jiana saw a brief flash of green. The haze was tinged with red from a sandstorm a few days ride away.

The *jamal* leaders arrived at the roped compound in a group. They brushed the hideous beasts, who in turn did what they could to sever a hand or an unwary arm.

Jamals were the most foul-tempered beasts Jiana had ever seen. They stood more than thrice the height of a tall man, and carried two gigantic humps in their backs. They were covered with dense, matted, brown fur that reeked like tanning fluid. But their splay-hooves were unparalled for walking across the burning, shifting sands, and they rarely needed to stop for water.

Jamals **had** a mind of their own, however, and were

next to useless in a battle; thus, the Elect brought horses along as well.

The currying came to an abrupt end when the *jamals* began to spit at the slaves, who wiped the spittle off (taking the name of the Seer in anger) and trotted out the *jamal*-packs.

The slaves hung bright-woven blankets over the *jamals'* backs, and then strapped on heavy boxes, rolls, bags, sacks, chests, and even chairs, centering the load between the humps.

All this time, more and more of the tradesmen Elect crawled from their mats and lurched about the camp, feebly bleating for more and stronger *kaf*.

Men and women divided into separate groups, stripped down to linen breeks, and washed the night-sweats off their skin. Fires were started, one for each three or four individual family/tribe khaymas.

The women boiled oats and wheat from the Water Kingdom, fried thick pieces of *jhur*-mush bread, and heated great pots of thick, strong *kaf*, a cup of which (it was said) would wake a corpse, provided it was not too long dead. Each family had its own *kaf* recipe.

While the women cooked, the men stood around the khaymas, trying to convince themselves to begin striking them. By the time they finally began, there was so much shouting and cursing, screaming from the *jamals*, childish squealing and singing that only the dead could still sleep (those that had not drunk their *kaf*).

Jiana stood just outside the household khayma, listening to the Horsemen argue over whose turn it was to ride shadow. None of them liked the duty except Faisal, for the shadow riders were excluded from the gossiping, arguing, and playing *sheyeti* (Rethe offered to teach Jiana the game, and Jiana instantly beat her three times in a row, once in only twenty moves. The same game raged across the Flower Empire under another name).

The sun glinted off the silver and brass of the *jamal* bridles as they lumbered upright, rear feet first, then the front, complaining very vocally whenever the slaves touched them with the switches. The *jamal*-riders mounted while their brutes were still kneeling, of course. The rest of the Elect assembled into a great mob, somewhat longer than it was wide.

When the sun was fairly high, and an army would have long ago been underway, the Horsemen finally made their appearance and pushed to the head of the line, using their riding crops liberally on the Elect who were foolish enough to stand where a Horseman wanted to ride. At a suitably dramatic moment, al'Sophiate himself made an entrance.

He generally mounted his great, white stallion to lead the parade, but this time (perhaps being saddle-sore, Jiana thought) he called for his *jamal* litter. The latter boasted a cushioned, velvet seat and an umbrella.

When all was assembled, the huge nation-on-legs lurched ponderously forward towards the Lizard's Teeth. They would not stop, Jiana knew, until the sun was nearly touching the hazy mountains to the west. By then, Rethe predicted that they would be camped at the foot of the Teeth, ready to spend all the next day crossing into ancient Tool.

3

Radience poked her head outside the household khayma, looked carefully left and right to make sure Jiana was nowhere in sight. Then she made a dash for the (brand new) storage khayma.

Jiana bushwacked her as she dipped into a shallow gully, diving out of a bush and tackling the girl.

"I just can't talk now, Jiana," pleaded Radience from her position under the warrior. "I have to get a jar of salt for the soup."

"Who is the master that makes the sky blue, kid?"

"I don't know who makes the sky blue. There is only One God, and one Seer. Is it He?" Radience tried to move, but Jiana held her immobile without seeming to exert much pressure.

"Who is the slave?"

"Stop calling me that!" Radience demanded.

"Why?"

"It's mean. I didn't ask to be a slave, I was born to it."

"I thought you were captured when a little girl."

"Well maybe. I don't remember. I never thought about it much. Just let me up, ok? I have to get the salt."

Jiana twisted to an upright, comfortable position, but Radience was still prisoned on the ground.

"Who is the master who chained you every night while the Greater Moon cycled around the world?"

"The same one who chained *you*, the Caliph, al'Sophiate."

"You lie. I roamed free."

"*Well, so did I!*" the girl cried, and then gasped and clapped her hand over her mouth.

Radience could feel Jiana gloating.

"Which outrage did you commit?" asked the warrior.

Radience was silent a long time. Finally, she could contain herself no longer.

"I burned my lord's clothes. Burned them in his khayma, practically right in his own sleeping chamber, just one chamber away."

"Hah!" Jiana seemed to find that revelation the funniest she had ever heard, and she cackled like the Caliph's monkey for a long time.

"So are you not a slave after all?" she finally asked, when she could breathe again.

Radience writhed, and almost bucked Jiana off her back. The tormentor regained her balance, however, and Radience was still trapped.

"They just forgot to lock me, that's all," the girl snapped.

"How many times were you unlocked?"

"Why, just the one—" Radience stopped in mid-sentence. *How would you know how often you were unlocked?* demanded a stranger within her stomach. *How often did you try the locks?*

"I . . . I mean I don't . . ."

"So who is the master who chained you every night but one?"

Radience lay quietly, unable to respond. It was obvious that the old answer was not good enough, but her stomach stubbornly refused to disgorge a new one. She suddenly realized she was chewing on her thumb, which she had not done since Aghi coated it with pepper, eleven turns ago.

"I—I Just Don't Know!" she sobbed, and with that she convulsed and threw Jiana easily.

"Time to stand up, slave girl. Time to find the real gaoler. If you find him, you find the key." Then Jiana stepped out of the ditch, spent an elaborate moment smoothing her shaven head, and walked off imperiously, looking so much like an Overman that Radience hardly dared breathe.

Her skin so white—her muscles so hard . . . As Jiana walked away to the west, the sun shone through her gauzy slave's tunic, leaving little of her lithe body to Radience's imagination. The girl stared hungrily, waiting until the warrior faded into the sun's glare before standing up.

Radience looked left and right, trying to remember what she had set out to do. Then she thought of her misery, and her tears, and of Jiana kissing away those tears as Aghi used to do, and making everything wonderful (or at least less wretched), and then Radience abruptly remembered the salt. The memory made her frown; it was an intrusion into a wonderful waking dream that might have led . . .

She climbed out of the ditch, smoothed her shaven head, and set out firmly for the storage khayma.

4

The journey up the Teeth was arduous and fraught with tragedy; the Elect lost a Horseman, two tentmakers, a *jamal,* and a horse to careless feet and treacherous trails. The peaks loomed and the crevices yawned (*as teeth in an open mouth,* Jiana thought, *which explains the name, I guess).* Jiana found herself strangely attracted to the edge of the cliff.

She stepped along a crack, heel to toe, looking down a sheer drop of what looked like ten leagues, but was probably not even a quarter-league. *Drop a plumb line*, she thought, *and it would hang straight to the rocks below. So why am I dancing along the edge?*

The Lizard's Teeth were not very high. When Jiana had trekked from White Falls to Bay Bay, she had crossed peaks that dwarfed the Teeth, mountains with perpetual snow at their peaks and vast, faerieland ice-castles filling what should have been ravines.

But the Teeth struck such a sudden and discordant note between the flat plains to the north and the Toolian desert to the south that they seemed a monstrous affront.

Actually, the Elect could have avoided the Teeth by sticking closer to the coast, as Jiana did four turns before on her quest for the World's Dream. But the Oasis of Deh Bid was a hundred leagues inland, and al'Sophiate had no desire to cross the sand owned by hostile Satraps, Sultans, and Sheriffs.

A bit after midday, climbing hard, the caravan reached the summit. Jiana scanned the horizon, but still could not see even a piece of Tool. "You won't," laughed Rethe. "This may be the summit, but there is another peak to climb before the final descent."

"The sun will be low, but the trail down is wide and easy, and we'll probably continue 'til midnight. We'll stop in Tool itself, at the Yazd Station. Deh Bid is only half a day's walk south from there."

The pass was barely a cut, winding high through the mountains. It was narrow and precipitous and terrible, unpredictable winds gusted between the peaks. The mountains themselves were barren brown, with only the thinnest streaks of grey vegetation.

The walk down from the summit wearied the warrior, since she knew there was an equally hard climb still to come that afternoon. By the time the Elect began the second slope, she had lost all interest in courting the winds at the edge, and simply plodded along with the rest of the mob.

The wind howled mournfully as it searched through the passes, sounding like a young mother who had lost her child. The lonely sound made Jiana feel even colder. Aside from the wind, she heard only the marching boots. The Elect had ceased all talking, as if by mutual consent.

The dust from two thousand tramping feet was so thick that Jiana could see no farther than her arm. She tied a cloth about her head and pull the bottom part over her nose and mouth, else she would have suffocated before reaching the second peak.

The cold caught at her flesh, pulled it away from the bones. The wind was a surgeon's knife that had lain all day in a saltdrift.

She concentrated on one foot ahead of the other, up the steep, angry trail. The ground jumped up and slapped her soles with every step, and her knees ached. She drank only a mouthful of water.

All day the air was still and sullen, baking hot though it should have been cool, as high as they were. Jiana was furious, feeling robbed of her right to a refreshing mountain breeze.

At last she crested the final hill and looked down upon the wicked Toolian desert. It was not the wretched Tarn, far to the west. The sands stretched forever, but did not warp the world of Reality Prime.

Jiana stared at the long shadows fading into black, the ruby dunes and wine-red flats, dry waves frozen by a mad magician. The sight moved her; a lump hardened in her stomach, and she thought of a little boy who wanted to be a warrior, once.

He was taken from her in the Tarn. Her little boy, innocent boy, snatched by bad guys on black horses and turned into a vicious Soldier Boy.

Shit. Shed the memories; they're useless now. He's gone, twisted by the Bitch Queen who thought she was a master when she was still a slave. Dida's dead; that's someone else now. That's a whole 'nother desert.

She took a deep breath, one half of a sigh, and made her first, jarring step down from the Teeth and into the driftdunes.

The sun sank, growing wider and flatter as it melted

into the ground. It began to flicker towards the end, like a flame blown out by the wind. She watched, but saw no flash of green when the sun vanished.

There was little of the choking dust on the southern face of the mountains; instead, the trail was rocky and broken. Rethe was right; it was wide. It was so steep that every plodding drop-step shook Jiana's entire body like a hammer blow, centering on her heels.

She had to yawn several times to clear her ears on the way down. After an eternity of bruised heels, she watched first the greater, then the lesser moon poke over the horizon. The trail began to level off.

It also became sandier. She no longer landed on her heels like a sack of potatoes, but she struggled for each step against sinking and slipping feet. The sand was gritty, and the crunching, grinding noise of a thousand feet made her head ache and gave her the shakes.

Even eternity ends.

Jiana continued to yawn with weariness, even as they finished descending. She watched the sky stars wheel overhead. The crowd began to bunch up, and the thought dimly penetrated Jiana's head that those in front were probably slowing to look for a place to sleep.

Rethe caught her arm, and called the rest of the women together with three sharp whistles. They stood and waited as al'Kug approached from the Horsemen's circle.

"Intercourse the khaymas," he ordered when he pulled up alongside. "There are no winds and no weather, and we leave at daybreak. Sleep as you can." He rode off towards the circle of cooks to deliver the same message.

"Horseshit," retorted Rethe, when he had left. "Daybreak, my arse. They always say daybreak. Sometimes we leave at noon, sometimes midday. The Caliph will rise at daybreak, wander around clutching his sleeping robe around him, and complain about a pounding head. He'll confer with the Overmen, then shake his head and stumble back to his mat.

"The Overmen won't even wake anyone else up; they'll wander back to their fire and play cards until the sun has risen to there—" she pointed above the horizon—"then al'Sophiate will sit up on his mat, stretch, and the rest of us will follow suit. If you wake up with the sun, you can watch the show."

As Rethe and the other slaves arranged their mats, Jiana walked toward the stables, which tonight were nothing more than an overhanging cloth and a hitching rope. She needed to talk, and there was only one creature to whom she could.

"Going to be now or now at all." she told Cascade. "I struck a spark, but it's the girl's job to kindle the fire." The great moon was full, and she was aware that she was quite visible to any passing spy.

She still hides her arm, noted the pretender horse-voice in Jiana's stomach.

"Blames a lot on it. Don't know if that's a curse or blessing, but today, for me, that arm is a bitch."

The sounds from the camp began to die down, as the Elect prepared to sleep. They were very tired, and so was she.

Jiana touched Wave, debating whether to sneak away and sharpen the sword. She half-pulled the blade, and thumbed the edge. It was adequate, but would soon need care.

She heard a boot scrape on the ground. Turning quickly, she caught a brief glimpse of the Pumpkin-headed Doorian, watching her from behind a *jamal*. He ducked back behind the beast as soon as she spotted him. It was the first she had seen of him in two moons.

Jiana stared . . . could he have seen Wave? Would he remember the sword, and thus Jiana? She stared, trying to spot him again. The moons were bright; if he had looked, he would certainly have seen the glint of the sword as she flexed it.

He would remember the sword; he would remember whenever he had to pass water.

She saw him again as the *jamal* bent to investigate some vegetation. He watched her with an expression of triumphant vindication. As soon as he realized she saw him, too, he began to back away, keeping the *jamal* between himself and Jiana. Then he turned and hurried off.

No! Damn it, not now! Jiana started to berate herself, but cut the thoughts short. There was no time. The Doorian had to be stopped *tonight*, before he talked. Otherwise . . .

She hurried after him, ducking under the jaws of the *jamal*, which tried to bite her.

He moved fast for a man of his bulk; he looked back a couple of times, assuring himself that Jiana was following him. Then he headed straight for the Caliph's circle.

He paused at the edge and waited for her, a nasty, predatory smile on his lips. The light from the Caliph's torches washed out his face and made it appear sickly yellow. He smoothed his great, black, drooping mustache, and waited for Jiana to make the next move.

She was still much too far away to speak, unless she shouted. Instead, she held up her hand and rubbed her thumb and first two fingers together. The Pumpkin-head recognized the offer and grinned, exposing teeth that were dark with decay.

Sister, no! You can't be serious? How can you even imagine *he would keep his part of the bribe?*

I think he'll keep his mouth shut, Jiana thought.

He'll ruin everything! He'll bleed *you dry, and surely peach on you anyway!*

The Doorian looked significantly towards a sand dune, a hundred yards from the perimeter of the camp, that Jiana could barely see in the moonlight. *He doesn't want witnesses,* she thought. *Well, good, neither do I.*

The champion of the physical began to stroll into the night, towards the dune. After a few moments, Jiana followed. As she approached the low hill, she felt a familiar tightening of her collar. By the time she joined the Doorian, she was having trouble breathing.

"I know you," he said in Doorish, and spat on the ground, "Janina, woman fighter. Criminal. Arrested you."

"So. Anything grow back?"

He grinned wide; but Jiana could see that he was wound as taut as a wire-wrapped sword hilt.

"Your money no good. Not enough. You give certain favors *and* money, or I tell the Caliph who you are."

Jiana slowly shook her head and rested a hand on Wave. A colony of desert insects began to click and grin, sounding like the gears in the water clock in Bay Bay.

Pumpkin-head curled his lip and drew his own sword.

"I hope you had say no," he said, and lunged gleefully at Jiana.

She ducked and side-stepped, but the Doorian crossed back in a lightning combination. Jiana had to drop to a crouch, left fingertips on the sand, and roll away from his attack.

She drew Wave while rolling, and rose with it at the ready position, rigid and pointing at his heart, almost within thrust range. He made no attempt to call for help; it was a grudge match—he intended to pay her back for what she had stolen from him.

They fought in silence, broken only by their ragged breathing. The insects had gone silent.

Jiana was no longer performing, as she had during the physical; she concentrated on business . . . and this time, she used the weapon that had been forged for her alone.

The Doorian was unarmored, and that meant he was almost blindingly fast. He swung at Jiana's head, reversed in mid-blow and cut a gash down her arm. It was not deep, but it burned.

She turned with the blow, rotating in a complete circle to strike backhanded from the off-side. But he slipped the cut, and she only shaved a hand's length from his greasy hair.

Her foot slid in the deep, red sand, and the misstep saved her life. The Doorian stepped forward boldly, swinging his arms in a suicide blow that would have cut her in half had she stood her ground.

She fell to one knee—Wave, over-eager, struck out on its own, or so it seemed. It was a hard blow, but poorly aimed. It missed completely, and the jerk at the end caused the thin, flexible sword to twist in Jiana's grasp and fall flacid.

Before she could regain her feet or control over her blade, Pumpkin-head's hand darted out and grabbed the tip.

They each yanked in opposite directions. Blood poured down his arm . . . but he succeeded in pulling Wave from her clutching grasp.

Jiana was disarmed. The Doorian kicked savagely at her face with his iron-shod boots, and she threw herself backwards into the sand to avoid the blow.

"AAAAA—!" he gritted his teeth and choked back the scream, as the pain from his shredded hand penetrated his rage. He hurled Wave behind him, far away from Jiana. He pressed his lips together and held down another cry of pain.

He moved forward slowly, a juggernaut in agony. Two of his fingers were missing, and thick, red blood dripped from his hand in spurts. He raised his sword as he stalked her.

Jiana backpedaled on all fours, but she never took her eyes from the blood that pumped from his severed fingers.

A song sprang unbidden to her lips.

"Call, call, come out, come all,
Pour, gore, more and more!
Sprout and spout, come all, come out,
Spurt and spry—drip it dry—
Drip 'til you die!"

It was gibberish; it was made-up, and it was the best she could do with fingers torn by the hilt ripping out of her hand, gasping and barely able to breathe.

But—the blood *did* begin to flow, just a bit harder. She kept at it, her own pulse pounding in her temples, keeping rhythm with the chant.

"Dribble and puddle and spittle and bubble
And slash and splash and pour the gore
To band the sand from hand and gland . . ."

An image pushed through her stomach, and she latched onto it and visioned it: all the old wounds, all the cuts and tears and slices opening wide . . . all, including the terrible decapitation she had inflicted upon him.

His skin pulled back. He stopped in surprise as blood began to drip down his brow into his eyes, from an old wound, long since healed. He stopped, slapping at his body as dark stains appeared everywhere under his clothing.

One great, black stain appeared in his crotch.

Even the moons turned to blood, bathing the scene in a deep burgundy. Pumpkin-head staggered a step, clutching feebly at his groin. He stared at his legs, his belly, eyes wide with incredulity.

His skin began to turn grey as the blood drained out upon the sand, which stained even darker than normal. He looked at Jiana, imploring, and held out a hand to her, trying to speak. But all he could manage was a gurgle.

The Doorian gagged, and a cupfull of blood poured from his mouth.

The power blazed within Jiana, and she reached out her spirit and squeezed him like a beet. The juice flowed.

He sank to his knees, then slowly leaned forward until his forehead was touching the sand. He shivered violently, as if he lay in a snowdrift, not a sand dune. He breathed a long, unhappy sigh and stopped moving.

Jiana crawled forward and felt for a pulse. The flame within her stomach flickered and died; she had no reserves left.

But Pumpkin-head had no pulse. She took her hand away, trembling slightly; her fingers were sticky with his blood. But she still could not remember his real name.

The insects began to sing again.

For many minutes she sat, breathing as well as she could through the collar. When she felt a bit stronger, she rose to her knees and began pouring sand over his corpse.

It took a long time, for she had to stop often and catch her breath. But at last he was buried. Time and the winds would eventually return him to the world.

She searched shakily behind the dune, and recovered Wave. Then she returned to the camp.

The Elect were abed, dreaming of innocence and home. Jiana fell into her mat, rolled herself into a ball, and drifted into a torrid and dreamy sleep.

Wriggled and squirmed down her throat, death
to life coming alive within, down the hatch
through the latch, unalive, undead, un—!
"Threety-turd," warned Tiq the Boy Toq, black
as a leech and white as bone. " 'For the
three and thirty be coming, three blots for
teapots and FIRE shall be the thirst!" He
stretched his arms to hug her. He reeked of
a watery barrow.
Dead she wast. Dead she waste. In! Deed!

Jiana rose too quickly, dizzy and tired. The sun was
high, and the slave Voice nudged her in the ribs with a
foot.

"I'm awake," said Jiana, but Rethe was already waking
the next slave. It was daybreak.

Jiana stood. As Rethe had predicted, the *jamals* had not
yet been saddled or loaded. No one had yet missed the
Doorian.

5

Just before noon the caravan got under way on the last
leg to Deh Bid. They pushed through sand that grew ever
deeper, and Jiana's feet dug deeper with every step. She
quickly became exhausted.

How long until they realize Pumpkin-head is gone? Will
they go back and look, maybe find the body? She was
uncomfortably aware that even a half-hearted search of the
campsite would uncover the man.

After a long time of marching, she saw more Horsemen
than usual riding up and down the ranks, searching. Each
time the riders passed her, they looked angrier. Rethe was
called away by al'Kug, and when she returned she asked if
anyone had seen the Doorian leave during the night.

"Bastard's buggered off," she muttered. "He used us,
the barbarian pig. Probably whooping it up with the Sheriff of North Yazd, selling him all our weaknesses."

"Would he?" Jiana asked.

"I hate Doorians," said Rethe, "hate 'em even worse than pale 'northers." She shook her head, and Pumpkin-head was forgotten.

After a longer time, even the Horsemen dismissed his absence. Deh Bid had just been spotted, across the dry lake bed of Flezer Tujd.

The tents and buildings seemed to float in the air, sometimes rising and falling as the air currents fluctuated. They reflected in a false sea of murky nothingness. Even knowing it was a mirage, it looked as real as the buildings of Bay Bay, floating on the mud-black sea.

Tired as she was, Jiana forced her stomach to digest a plan of escape. The Oasis of Deh Bid was the obvious place to stage it. It was a gigantic city, ten thousand residents or more, and the oasis fed directly into the Nag Deh Jambajala river, the largest in Tool.

The Nag Deh Jambajala (Glittering Path of Barred Passage) ran due south for a hundred leagues, passing out of Tool entirely and through a piece of Door. There it passed through a rock escarpment and vanished into the colon of the Earth—hence the name. If it emerged later, no one knew where.

Jiana had always wanted to journey down the Jambajala; there was no better site from which to launch an escape than the Deh Bid Oasis . . . and that would be the final decision time for Radience. If she would not leave, then Jiana had failed and the experiment would be ended.

In disgrace or triumph, Jiana decided to ride the Jambajala within three days time.

The plan buoyed her spirits and infused her legs with new energy for the remaining leagues of desert sand. As they reached the out-tents of the oasis, Jiana pulled even with Rethe. The slave Voice pointed to each khayma and every building, telling Jiana who lived there and what they had done in the past several turns.

The permanent khaymas were much more colorful than the transportable variety used by nomadic tribes, such as the Elect of Hal'Addad bin Kerat bin El al'Sophiate. The families and tribes of Deh Bid vied with each other in startling colors, stripes, and yellow and green slogans written in High Tooltak. The words of the Seer were most common, but occasional wisdom from the Commentaries, the Agtashi Roll, and the Old Mountain Man crept onto even the most pious of khaymas.

The stone buildings were constructed from shaped rock fitted carefully without mud or mortar; they were never decorated, at least not officially. Unofficially, they were covered by dense scrawls of graffiti in various stages of crudity, promising heaven despite a hell of a good time, all for a fair price (no credit extended to "wanderers").

Deh Bid was a hive of angry bees, buzzing in a dozen dialects of Tooltak and twice that many foreign tongues. Tradesmen and customers argued over the price of silk and tangerines, haggled market exchange rates, and imposed impossible terms of payment. Even random encounters in the street turned into animated conversations, banter, brawls, and bickering.

The slaves were not spared; no two slaves could pass on a public street, it seemed, without passing along ancient wisdom accumulated at the last intersection. *Probably a law*, Jiana theorized.

The noise was welcome after the unnatural silence of the desert; the Elect rarely talked while they walked, probably due to the heat and the exertion.

As the caravan pressed deeper into Deh Bid, Jiana felt the torq around her neck tighten, making breathing somewhat more difficult.

"Don't worry, Jiana," soothed Rethe. "Curse will loosen the band once we pass through the center and reach the Caliph's palace."

"But why—"

"Oh, come on, don't be an ass! With all these people, how else can he keep track of what's his? There's the palace ahead—see the spires?—the Caliph liberated it from the usurper, Yshtamael al'Kug, no relation."

Jiana walked quietly beside the slave Voice, breathing as well as she could. *So it's Curse who controls the collar, not the Overman.* Had he built them himself? Jiana had assumed that they were forged by a mage, and that Curse only opened and closed them around young necks.

The crowd reluctantly parted as the Elect entered the city. Young children ran alongside and sang, and from all parts musicians gathered and played them along the streets. Clowns and jugglers danced about the caravan, performing and playing, and the Horsemen raised hands in triumph and delight. Firesparkers flared suddenly as they rounded a corner, and the mob grew to a lusty crowd.

The weird, wailing music of the nose-whistles, *tapbors*, nine-stringed *qetzars*, pipes, and what sounded like a hundred different drums, cymbals, horns, and finger-bells danced and sang the Elect onto the palace grounds.

As the last Horseman crossed the threshold, and the iron gates swung closed, slowly and majestically, the crowd let out a roar that drowned all previous noises. Then they moved on, laughing and chattering excitedly. Their Caliph was home safe again.

At once the neckband loosened, and Jiana inhaled deep, satisfying breaths of air. Once the gates were shut and the mob gone, the Caliph's own professional musicians took up where the others had left off; what they lacked in numbers they made up in virtuosity.

"You are free to wander," said Rethe to Jiana. "Just be back here before the sun sets. And don't be foolish." She reached out and gave Jiana's neckband a significant tug. "It works as well inside the gate as it does on the desert sands." Then the slave Voice strode off towards an onion-domed building, scratching the sides of her head and yawning.

She'll come, Jiana thought. *I feel a destiny.*

She sniffed and smelled roasting meat. Having nothing better to do, and being tired of dried goat strips and grainy bread, Jiana followed her nose around the left side of the compound.

She discovered the kitchen, and noticed Radience already inside, cooking. Jiana did not bother her, plenty of time before the Big Moment. *Strange how she's sitting off by herself in a corner*, the warrior thought. *Is she think-*

ing or brooding? Shaking her head, Jiana continued her wandering.

Rounding the side of the palace, Jiana saw several out-buildings. Two were clearly storehouses, for equipment and food. She saw an armory; the Horsemen gathered about it, exchanging warlike arms for more ceremonial and courtly accouterments: moon-curved scimitars and barbed tulwars, jeweled daggers and ebony wands of rank.

The fourth outlying building was a stables, full of horses. Cascade was being led into the building. *It's to there I shall be reporting, I bet,* she thought.

She approached the fifth and last building, the farthest out from the palace.

It was the only one with a guard. The soldier watched her as she approached, but he did not seem unduly alarmed. Jiana diffidently approached a pair of slaves working nearby.

"Your pardon," she asked in flawless Tooltak, "a thousand blessings upon such faithful retainers; what is that building? I am new to the Elect, and have never been graced to be present in this heavenly estate."

The two slaves waited politely until she had finished, then they bowed their heads and touched their fingertips to their foreheads. Jiana returned the salutation.

"Most intelligent and beautiful woman, daughter of the Seer, may your belly soon swell with a son. This building is a prison, which oddly enough has an inhabitant at present. An infidel is being held for a thousand and one days for an offense with which this lowly and humble servant is not familiar."

"Is it permitted to look into that window?"

"I have never been told it is not."

"God is great," said Jiana, "and we heed the words of his Seer. I thank you once for each day that I have lived."

"You are welcome twice for each such day, and all that is mine is thine." They touched their foreheads again, completing the dictates of politeness, and went back to fitting a wheel onto a cart and ignoring her.

Jiana padded softly up to the window. The guard watched

her a bit more narrowly, but did not move. Jiana looked inside.

It was dark and gloomy inside the cell. The prisoner ate well, as his bulk attested. Jiana blinked several times, and her eyes began to grow accustomed to the dim light. She cupped her hands on the sides of her face.

The man sat at a small table, writing in a bound volume with a quill pen. He had shaggy hair that fell to the middle of his back, and a full, black beard. Something about his mannerisms reminded her of someone she knew. She watched, fascinated, as the prisoner cleared his throat with a rumble, and spat into a brass spittoon with a resounding clang.

Jiana whistled appreciatively, and the giant heard her. He turned about to face the window, causing Jiana a moment of fright. He was huge!

But his face was gentle, nearly glowing with an inner serenity. His eyes told a story: he had chased the All to the ends of the earth, and had finally caught up with it.

Then at once his features rearranged; the beard fell away, the hair was pulled back; the smooth brow furrowed, and four turns fell away. Her mouth opened in the shock of recognition.

At the same moment, the giant smiled hugely, beard and all, and called out, *"Jiana Analena! Life is complete!"* His deep, rumbling voice shook the walls and rattled Jiana's skull.

"Toldo Mondo!" she gasped, gripping the bars of the window. "Toldo, you pig, it's you!"

And it was.

Chapter VI:

Ties that bind and burn,
Twisting in the still

1

Jiana walked at a normal pace past the barred window, carrying a bucket in her hand. The soldier's eyes were already glazed from the heat and the boredom, and he did not find the sight of a working slave so enthralling that it snapped him from his lethargy. Thus he missed seeing her toss a rolled up parchment paper ball into the gaol cell.

It would have mattered little if he had intercepted it; few foot-soldiers in Tool knew how to read the pictographs of the Flower Empire. And in any event, what harm could there be in a few quotations from the *Changing Leaves* of Tiu Tiu, a seven century old book of poetry and philosophy?

IT HAS BEEN ASKED HOW ONE GETS THE GOOSE OUT OF THE BOTTLE. THE CONSCIOUSNESS OF ONE GOOSE WILL FLOAT DOWNSTREAM, BASKING IN THE RIVER OF LIFE, THOUGH FOOLS SHALL LOOK THE OTHER WAY. A SOUL MAY HAVE SISTERS, BUT ANOTHER MAY JOURNEY ALONE. THE FOOL RIDES ABOUT TOWN LOOKING FOR HIS DONKEY, WHEN ALL THE TIME IT IS CARRYING HIM ON THIS ERRAND. THE SUN SETS NOT TWICE ON A WISE MAN AT THE SAME POINT OF LIFE.

Jiana hoped that Toldo would have enough common sense to understand what she meant: in two days time, she would escape down the Jambajala, with or without "sisters," Radience and Rethe. She would definitely be accompanied by a horse ("donkey"), however. The first sentence about the goose came from an old conundrum her master had given her, back in the Flower Empire. In this context, she asked Toldo for some good suggestions to break him out of the jug.

She continued on her route to the stables for a long talk with Cascade. His intelligence was astonishing. Any good warhorse could sense his master's moods and needs, but Cascade seemed to understand her words, as well.

"I don't know how to get out of this damned collar," she whispered in his ear, speaking in the language of the Water Kingdom, which was also the language of the eastern plains of her childhood. "I can arrange everything else—escape, stealing a raft, rigging a false trail north; done all that a hundred times in this or that campaign. What about Curse? If I kill him, does this thing fall off? Snakes and eggs, I *just don't know.*"

Avoid fighting him if you can, Jiana. He is powerful and sees many realms.

She turned to leave, but came to a halt at the shadow line, looking out into the sunlight from the darkened stables. *Did Cascade actually talk to me? Or did I just dream that I heard his voice in my stomach? Or am I just dreaming now, dreaming I'm awake?*

She slapped her cheek to drive away the loopy thoughts, and continued on her quest to find Radience.

The kitchen looked empty; Jiana closed her eyes and thought of all the tiny places she would crawl if she were trying to dig a hole and pull it in after her. She found Radience in a barrel in the storage cell.

The girl's eyes grew as wide as millstones when Jiana pulled the lid off her barrel and said, "Hi, kid; time to talk."

"How—oh never mind, Jiana. I really don't think I

ought to talk about anything, I'm kind of confused at the moment."

"Best time to talk. Unconfuse yourself."

"No, I think I just need to get off by myself for a while, get the old stomach churning . . ."

"No churning time, kid. Decision time. A slave is a girl waiting for somebody else to free her. Old sage named Zara said that, or at least people say he said it. But let me tell you about a goose in a bottle."

"I don't think I'm ready to hear about this."

"My master once called me into his meditation room and showed me a glass bottle with a fully-grown goose inside it. There was no seam, and the neck was way too small for the goose to pass."

"Yeah, and you were supposed to guess how the goose got into the bottle."

"I thought so; felt pretty big when I did. It isn't hard really to get the goose *into* the bottle."

"You could slip it into the bottle when it was a little goose—"

"Or gosling, as you might say."

"Or gosling, and feed it right through the neck until it grew up. Now could you please go away and let me think?"

"But when I triumphantly announced this solution, my master didn't even blink. He sat impassively until the thought bit me that I had only solved *half* the problem. The bigger question was how to get the goose *out of* the bottle."

Radience opened her mouth to say something; Jiana held her breath. The girl stopped herself, pursed her lips, and remained silent.

"Second thoughts are good," Jiana said. "The first impulse is always to say 'break the bottle.' But if that were an acceptable answer, there would be no puzzle. How do you get the goose out of the bottle without breaking the glass—or killing the bird?"

Radience looked up from the bottom of the barrel. She was intrigued, despite her resolve to ignore that woman.

"Don't think I don't know what you're talking about," she snapped. Radience was the goose in the bottle. Or maybe her crippled arm was the bottle. Or else her inner self was the bird, and the rest of the world was the bottle. Or was *she* the bottle, and something else inside her was the bird, something she was imprisoning in the bottle of her . . . ?

"Wait a minute," she said, climbing out of the barrel. Jiana watched her narrowly, but Radience could read nothing in that woman's gaze. *Damned infidel witch is playing master with me again!*

It was a stupid problem, but Radience could not get it out of her stomach. She wandered away, lost in thought; when she looked up again, Jiana was gone, so she could not even ask for a hint.

Yeah, I'll bet you got it right away. I'm so stupid. Crippled arm and slow stomach—boy, I'm a real fresh rain.

She thought of a number of silly ideas: heating the bottle and stretching the neck, greasing the insides; but none was a real solution, since it was not a problem in bottle-making or goose-manipulation . . . it was about prison and freedom.

Is my collar tighter? Radience tugged at the collar in sudden panic; it felt much tighter, cutting into her breath, squeezing in and in until her neck was a mere finger-width in diameter. But no, it was only a terrible fantasy. Still, her heart raced, and it was difficult to catch a breath. She felt an ache under her left arm. She rubbed her left chest; it felt as tight as the collar, like Curse had grabbed her in a great bear-hug and was squeezing the life out of her.

She sat down, catching her breath, and after a long, lingering, painful time, the feeling subsided. Her heart slowed, and she inhaled great draughts of air. Radience's forehead felt clammy, coated with sweat, and now the *inside* of her throat felt constricted.

Oh God, tell me what to do. Am I disloyal for burning the Caliph's clothes and not turning in Ruhol, or am I a masochist for submitting to beating after beating? One your terror, two your despair!

How does that damned goose get out of the bottle?

And how did he really *get into the bottle?* She lowered her head into her arms and thought about that new question for a while.

Jiana told me a lie. Sure, the goose was raised in the bottle, but that isn't the answer to that question, either, not if the goose is me or some part of me. How did that goose get into that *particular bottle, and how does it escape?*

2

Jiana walked past the barred window. As she passed, she stumbled and fell to one knee. She palmed the rolled up piece of parchment and pushed off back to her feet, all in one fluid motion.

It took all of her will power to resist looking at the paper until she returned to her space. There, she had to wait an additional eternity for two other girls to finish some trivial, interminable conversation about a cute young servant boy in the palace and what they would do to him when they caught him alone.

At last they left, stalking the unfortunate lad. The thought of the two elephasian behemoths prancing and preening disgusted Jiana as she unrolled the parchment page and struggled to decipher Toldo's ant-track writing. He wrote in the language of the Water Kingdom, his and Jiana's native tongue.

LO IT HAS BEEN BUT A TURNING OF THE SEASONS SINCE I WAS HAPPILY SEQUESTERED BY OUR MUTUAL FRIEND. KIND HAS HE BEEN TO ME, SHOOING AWAY UNWANTED VISITORS TO CREATE MAXIMAL INCENTIVE FOR CONCENTRATION UPON LIFE'S WORK, MY OWN PERSONAL AS IT WERE WORLD'S DREAM, DON'T YOU KNOW.

FRUITLESS QUESTIONS AND BOOTLESS ERRANDS FINALLY BLOSSOMED SOME SEASONS AGO WHEN I FOUND SO TO

SPEAK THAT WHICH I SOUGHT: TO WIT, I FOUND THE END
OF ENDS AND THE BEGINNINGS OF ALL, THE PANGENITOR
(ALL-FATHER) HIMSELF, THE STARRY MILK OF NUED, GOD-
DESS OF THE JAMBAJALA PEOPLE, THE ELIXIR OF LIFE, THE
MEDICINE OF METALS, THE FOOD OF THE GODS, NECTAR
AND AMBROSIA, THE FIRST MATTER. FOUND I, IN SHORT,
THE FATHER OF ALL RELIGIONS.

IT IS NOT A SPIRITUAL TRUTH, GREAT OR SMALL. IT IS NOT
THE WORDS OF A GOD. IT IS A TOADSTOOL, AND IT GROWS IN
DUNG.

I HAVE SEEN VISIONS AT LAST, O MIGHTY WARRIOR GOD-
DESS; I HAVE SEEN NOT THIS OR THAT DESCRIPTION OF THE
UNDERLYING SPHERE, READ NOT ONE OR ANOTHER AC-
COUNT; I HAVE FELT IT MYSELF, SEEN IT WITH THESE EYES,
TASTED IT WITH THIS TONGUE. I SAW THE LIGHT; I CAN
TELL YOU WHAT IT LOOKS LIKE. I HAVE MERGED. I AM GOD
NOW. I HAVE FOUND THE BACK DOOR INTO THE WONDROUS
VALLEY, FROM WHOSE FRONT DOOR WE ARE FOREVER
BARRED BY FIRE-DEMONS.

OH JIANA, MY FAITH IS AT ONCE COMPLETE AND SHATTERED.
I KNOW GOD TODAY—I KNOW MYSELF!—BUT I KNOW TOO
THAT IT ALL CAME FROM A HALF-DOZEN FOUL-TASTING
MUSHROOMS AND AN ELABORATE RITUAL TO COOK THEM. I
HAVE KNOWN WINGS AND FLIGHT, AND THE TERROR OF
THE STARRY SPACES. I KNEW THE ECSTASY OF ABANDON,
AND THE DESPAIR OF ABANDONMENT. I AM EXHILARATED
BY GOD BREATH BUT HUMBLED BY MY LITTLE PLACE AS
A SUB-DEFINED BIT OF AN ALL-ENCOMPASSING IMPLICATE
CRYSTAL.

FOR AN ENTIRE TURNING OF THE SEASONS I HAVE STRUG-
GLED WITH THE REVELATION, FOR WHAT I HAVE KNOWN IS
AS TRUE AND DESPERATE AS ANY GOSPEL OF THE EAGLE
HIMSELF. WHAT LITTLE COULD BE VERBALIZED I HAVE COM-
MITTED TO PARCHMENT, DISGORGING A BOOK, A THICK
LIBRUM, "TOLDO'S TOME" YOU MIGHT DUB IT.

AND ALL THIS TIME, THAT SANDY FELLOW HAS COOPER-
ATED BY GIVING ME UNLIMITED TIME TO SIT AND THINK IN
SOLITUDE AND QUILL AND INK TO AMUSE MYSELF WITH
FANTASIES OF BURNING THE WORLD WITH HOLY FIRE.

BUT YOU ARE RIGHT, OF COURSE—HOW COULD YOU NOT,
BEING AS STAR, AS AM I AND DIDA AND ALANAI AND EVERY-
ONE ELSE? AND I CAN NO LONGER IGNORE THE CROCODILE
IN THE WATER-CLOSET; IT IS SURELY TIME FOR THIS OLD
PRIEST WHO HAS BECOME GOD TO LEAVE THESE IVY-COVERED
WALLS.

I HAVE SEEN LIGHT, JIANA. WORDS CAN DESCRIBE BUT NOT
RECREATE. LET ME SHOW YOU! LIKE THE DOUR RESIDENTS
OF YOUR NEW RIVER AREA WOULD DEMAND. THOU ART
GODDESS; YOU HAVE NO POWER OR RIGHT BUT TO SERVE
YOUR OWN WILL. LET ME SHOW YOU! I MUST FIND MORE OF
THIS MAGIC, MORE TOADSTOOLS. I MUST SHOW YOU!

I HAVE DECIDED, JIANA ANALENA. IT IS TIME FOR THIS
TOLDO TO TAKE HIS LEAVE. SEE YOU ON THE MORROW'S
MORROW. TAKE ME FROM THIS BOTTLE JUST IN THE WAY
YOU WILL TAKE YOURSELF FROM YOUR OWN BOTTLE. PECK
US OUT. THE WINE CONTAINS THE CUP. I TRUST YOU AND
MY WILL.

YRS SINCERELY UNDER THE WING,
TOLDO MONDO

Jiana stared for a long time, rereading the note. Surely
she had just missed the strategies and suggestions?

"Thanks a lot, priest," she said at last, shaking her head
and frowning.

Planning the break was complicated by the fact that
Jiana could not leave the compound, or else the neck band
would tighten and the Overman would be alerted. She
knew the river was very deep and nearly a league wide at
this point, though it narrowed considerably downstream as
it split into many smaller rivers. The river was a trader's

dream, and at this season, shortly after the biannual flooding, it would be crowded with barges, boats, and rafts.

Stealing a solid raft large enough for four people and a horse should be easy. But how was she to lay a false trail northward while imprisoned on the palace grounds?

Jiana sat and watched during the day, whenever her horse duties were temporarily completed. The Caliph's palace grounds were marked by packed earth that was watered frequently to keep down the dust, an incredible luxury, even at an oasis. The great dome was made of cut stone, each piece set carefully into place and the entirety plastered over with dried mud and paint. It was one of the finest palaces Jiana had ever seen.

The grounds smelled of *jamals* and horses, and all their associated products. Her duties in the stables were not severe; she quickly got used to the smell, and to the thought of what she was raking and shoveling into piles. She discovered she could turn off the conscious part of her stomach and let the underbelly think unmolested.

At last, a plan occurred to her.

From the pouch Toldo threw her, Jiana poured out her few, meagre coins. The total amounted to six steel teeth—enough for barely twelve days lodging in Bay Bay, but a tiny fortune this far south. Then she went out and stood against the front gate, waiting for a washerwoman to pass.

The palace road was the major thoroughfare in Deh Bid, and it was not long before a fat, sweaty woman came stomping along, balancing an enormous basket full of robes and sheets on her head. The sun glinted off the shiney cobblestones of the road, and nearly washed out the woman in the glare.

"Most gracious and generous princess," Jiana called softly, just enough to catch the woman's ear, "may you live to see nine hundred turns, your most exalted majesty."

The woman stopped and stared suspiciously, scratching the wispy, black, mustache hairs on her lip. She finally grunted, acknowledging the greeting of the slave and indicating that she would not call the palace guards if Jiana continued. The washerwoman planted her fists on her ample hips and waited.

"My master, may his faith stand as a mighty palm tree in the wind, earnestly desires some information . . . might such an exalted person of such high rank as yourself oblige?" At this point, Jiana held up one of her precious serpent's teeth.

The woman squinted at the silver; steadying the load with one hand, she hesitantly approached close enough to stick out a puffy hand, scoured pink by the washing she had just finished.

Jiana placed the coin deferentially in the woman's hand, and it disappeared within an eyeblink into a fold of the woman's full-body robe.

"Er, I thinks I kin give you such information as I might possess," answered the awe-struck woman with an extreme low-caste accent, "or I might not depending on what it were your master were wanting to know."

"A thousand blessings from the Seer," said Jiana. The woman grunted and quickly made the sign of the sun. "What he most wishes to know is which road would be best to take *to the north* for a traveler weary of company, one who wishes to travel unmolested by passers-by."

"Well, as it be, the road truly has no name, for it were old when I were young and has now lost all custom to the new Road of White Poppies that the Sultan of Tonnut did had built a few turns ago. But you find it I might say by journeying up this road until you are even with the House of the Houris, there to turn upon your right front leg, pass between the House and a chicken-slaughterhouse. This path becomes it does an alley, which turns a trail and then a road, later down the pipe."

"Your kindness to one of the Elect surpasses even your beauty, o nobly-born. But is there an inn a day's ride or so up this old road?"

"I know of there be an inn, the Broken Verses."

"And does it pry and ask leading questions?"

"What not or whether the shopman pries into business

of his custom, I would have no way of knowing thus, for I have not frequented that said inn, not myself."

Jiana bowed deeply, touching her forehead with both hands and turning her hands up and outward.

"My master will be ecstatic with your aid, and enraptured by your poppy-like beauty. But his joy would be complete if you would promise never to reveal to a soul what information was requested here. Will you boost him into the Blessed Realm by making such a promise?"

It was all the woman could do to maintain a straight face.

"Oh, certainly do I, I do. Not a word shall I breathe says I of this scandal to anyone, nay not even my sister." She made the sign of the sun again, and then sped off, making magnificent headway back in the direction she came, towards the main oasis.

Spread it, false one, Jiana thought, smiling, *flap it up and down, all over Deh Bid!*

Jiana left the gate, and began to slowly walk along the outer wall, checking for structural weaknesses or low spots that could be climbed or leaped. By the time she had completed exactly half the circuit, the front gate at which she had stood was now crowded with washerwomen, all talking to the soldiers in great excitement.

3

That evening, Jiana rushed through her stables chores and slipped out into the darkness; she intended a dry run of the next night's escape.

She waited in the shadows until the Horseman appeared with the keys to Toldo's cell. He was followed by a servant, carrying the priest's supper. It was a leg of lamb; the Caliph fed his important prisoners better than his slaves.

Jiana stalked the pair until they reached the gaol. Then the warrior hid and observed their ritual. Prison guards are rigid and invariant souls, Jiana had found; this one proved no exception. He walked through his opening and closing routine as if entranced, every movement precise and calculated.

The soldier waited outside, while the Horseman and the servant entered with the lamb. Jiana counted slowly—one hippopotamus, two hippopotamus . . . One hundred and twenty-five hippopotamuses before they reemerged, plenty of time for her to have cold-cocked the soldier. She could pick up the man's spear and swing it butt first into the Horseman's gut as he emerged. Quick, and nobody killed.

When the Horseman finished locking up, he and his servant returned to the main building. Jiana strolled briskly toward the stables. No one interfered; they were all at the Feast of the Lamp Oil Jars, which continued the next evening.

" 'Lo, Cascade," she whispered, stroking the horse's nose with her fingers, "tomorrow eve. Be ready."

Jiana returned to the slaves' chambers. Rethe stopped talking for a moment and looked suspiciously at the warrior as she entered; then the slave Voice resumed her lecture to the four new slaves acquired while she was up north. The single glance told Jiana all she needed to know: Rethe was annoyed but not angry; she assumed Jiana was out sniffing for food, love, or gossip.

Jiana laid on her sleeping mat, but too many visions bewitched her stomach to permit sleep. So many things to go wrong, even with as simple a plan as this. *Suppose the soldier forgets to feed Toldo? Suppose other Horsemen skip the feast and tag along? What if there are no rafts, what if the washerwoman didn't tell all her friends about the slave escaping to the north?*

What if they're smarter or luckier than they look?

Then you'll die, said a quiet, familiar voice. *Down to honorable defeat. Did you expect to live forever?*

Now that you mention it—yes, I did. I don't want to die just yet . . . I have unfinished business.

Jiana could almost hear the eerie chuckle of the once-a-time Tormentor, now more a part, more apart than ever.

Radience will either liberate herself, or she won't. You

*showed her freedom; now she's free to reject it if she
wants. Your business is through.*

*I didn't mean Radience; I meant the kid, Dida. I have
no intention of leaving this life with such a mess behind.*

Before I go, I'll find a way to call him back.

4

Grey dawn flickered dimly and retreated. Red sky, the
sand was gold, perhaps blood-drops fallen from wars in
heaven. Jiana shivered, finding herself naked and alone on
the desert, face down in the sand.

She tasted it; Tool was salt and bitter. Tool was tears
and blood. She woke more fully, and she was on a floor,
her face lying in sand blown through the window.

She was nude, still hairless, still a slave. Her blankets
were far away, and only one other slave was awake (Mugn
was outside, retching; she was pregnant by a soldier).

Jiana stood slowly to avoid dizziness. The bitter cold of
autumn in the desert made her nipples stand up, but she
refused to wrap her arms around her body. She stood still,
accepting the cold, letting it pass through her as she used
to do in the snows of the Flower Empire. The cold brought
memories. The cold ignited the icy pride of a warrior in
Jiana's gut.

*I spit molten iron and piss fire. Cut me open and find a
snake in my belly. I have no blood, left it on a thousand
fields from here to the Islands of the Sun. Fists are
rocks, arms are banded steel, my teeth are filed to points
the better to chew your balls off. I have no mercy; I'll kill
a baby for shits and grins. I am relentless. I died so long
ago my body rotted away to nothing leaving a stone statue
instead. I've eaten human flesh because it turned my stomach, and nothing is allowed to defeat me. I care nothing
for you. You have no soul, you're a piece of meat for me to
carve. I will cut you open and suck the shit out of your
bowels because I like it.*

Jiana smiled. It was time to stop shaving off her crest.

The sun finally broke fully over the eastern mountains,

but Jiana had been up for a long time. She performed her duties with joy, knowing it was the last time—come what may.

She watched Radience carefully, but it was not until noon that the slave girl found herself alone. Before Radience could scurry off and avoid the encounter, Jiana stepped out of a shadow and seized the girl's arm.

"This is it," the warrior said, quietly and unemotionally. "I leave tonight, during the feast of the Lamp Oil Jars. I go south on a raft, with my horse and a couple of friends—and perhaps with a young freewoman."

Radience stared at Jiana; she tried to speak, but no sound escaped her throat. She caught hold of her collar with the fingers of her good hand, as if it were suddenly too tight to breathe. Her knuckles turned white with the pressure.

"I am leaving," Jiana continued, "and I will not allow these magical collars to stop me. I can remove mine, and I can remove yours. But I cannot liberate *you*.

"Only Radience can free Radience."

"Why—why did you *tell* me? What do I do—what can I do now, where is loyalty. . . ." The girl's face was white; all the blood drained from her cheeks into her body, as though she had been struck a mortal blow.

Jiana gently took Radience's hand; her fingers were chilly.

"You must decide—and this time, doing nothing *is* a decision. You can join me, betray me, or let me leave unhindered." The warrior stroked the slave's temple with her fingertips. "I hope to see you; I'll tarry at the guard-house, where my priest friend is being held." Jiana turned and walked back to the stables. She did not look back.

Jiana made no particular attempt to conceal her activities as she secured gear for the escape. The Elect of Tool were a true slave society: the slaves themselves acknowledged their own servitude. Escape was not unknown; but it was uncommon. Being both a slave and a woman, Jiana was as invisible as if she had chanted "Rikki Tikki Pay-the-bill."

She found a saddlesack for Cascade and filled it with useful provisions: a hemp rope, tinderbox, lamp oil, bandages and poultices, whetstone, boots and gloves that looked like they might fit, filched from an inattentive groom, a shiny metal mirror, good knife, a few days' worth of dried goat meat, and horse-feed for Cascade. For the rest, she depended upon her own abilities and the Jambajala.

Just as she was balancing the stuffed saddlesack on Cascade's back, Jiana felt a presence. She turned; Rethe, the slave Voice, stood watching.

"What the fuck do you think you're doing?"

"I'm leaving. You knew I would . . . you knew I was never a slave."

Rethe opened her mouth to speak; then she closed it again. She glared fire into Jiana's eyes, and the warrior returned the look. After a moment, the slave Voice began to blink; then she dropped her gaze.

"You win. You're no slave." She looked up again, angry. "So who the fuck are you? What do you want with me?"

"I want *you*. You're no slave either, Rethe!"

"I belong—"

"You belong to yourself. You're a fighter, a sergeant. Where's your sword? You were born here, weren't you?"

"Well. . . ."

"Come with me."

Rethe sucked in a breath and took a step back. Her brown eyes floated in white foam, and she fearfully looked over her shoulder. She was just beginning to realize that she was a sergeant, but Jiana was the captain.

Then she frowned and clenched her fists at her sides.

"Damn you, I'll *do* it! Fuck these bastards, fuck the Overman, fu-fuck the Caliph!" She grinned, looked back at the dome and extended two fingers. "That's my 'hell with you and fuck off' salute," she explained.

Jiana smiled. It was a grand day for an escape.

"Meet me back here during the feast . . . sister."

Rethe held out her hand, and Jiana touched her palm.

"During the feast," Jiana repeated.

Rethe turned and trotted back towards her quarters in the dome to gather the things she needed.

No one paid Jiana any attention as she led Cascade out of his stall; she was just another slave preparing a horse for her master. She made her way as near as she could to the guardhouse while still maintaining cover, and began the vigil for Radience.

Will she come?

Sure.

Will she come?

I don't know!

Will she peach on me?

Jianabel was silent. For her own part, Jiana blanked her mind whenever she caught herself imagining a tale told to Giathudin.

She watched the feasting hall, its onion dome surmounted by a hundred torches that made the gilded roof blaze with yellow fire. Shouts were raised, oaths taken, quests accepted, challenges cast, treacheries hatched, justice applied, marriages made.

The Feast of the Lamp Oil Jars was the most boisterous celebration allowed the Elect, the "*days between the seasons*," when alcohol was legal, for the feast existed outside Time entirely.

When dawn broke, it would break on a new turn. But last night's sunset was the fading fire of the old turn. Today fell between the two, and no man or woman of the Elect could be denied paradise for transgressions committed " 'tween turns" . . . or so taught the caliphs of the Old School.

Jiana wrapped her arms around herself; then she forced them to her sides and embraced the cold again, as she had done earlier. It was getting late, and the Horseman had not come with Toldo's supper.

Radience had not come either.

A strange chill passed through the warrior. *They've walked across my grave,* she thought. But she had felt a similar premonition other times in her life, times when death had brushed her by.

Feeling prickles on the back of her neck, Jiana turned suddenly. Her heart gave a wild leap; a white, translucent ghoul stared at the warrior from an arm's length away, its red eyes dripping filth, betrayal, and hunger.

Then Jiana's eyes focused, and it was only Radience, shivering before her under a cloak too thin and sheer for the weather.

"You come with silence," Jiana said, fully in control of her breath again.

Radience merely stared, her face betraying shame and guilt.

"Radience," Jiana asked, "what did you do?"

The girl looked down at the ground. The misery in her face was eloquent; it was punctuated by the slight rasp of steel drawn from a wooden scabbard. The faint sound came from a deep, black shadow.

"I didn't know what to do," the girl said. Her voice was tiny but unwavering. "I was confused. I thought of Ruhol, of the Caliph, of my—*loyalties*." Her tone was flat, until she spoke the last word with such disgust and loathing that it struck Jiana like a fist.

"You betrayed me."

"Yes."

"There are Horsemen in the blackness. They plan to kill me."

Radience looked up at Jiana again. Her eyes were calm with the peace of death; her lips were set with the acceptance of the end.

"They'll kill us both. I know what I did. It was stupid; I was weak. Now I'll die."

"You accept this?"

"Freely."

Jiana smiled; it was all she could do not to grin like a loon.

"Radience, *you are a free woman from this moment*. You took responsibility for your *own* action, your *own* decision."

"I'm not a slave?"

"No longer. Damn!" Jiana cried, oblivious of who might

hear. "I finally did it! I finally got *through* to you, I finally. . . ."

Like a bursting dam, the power exploded from her with the suddenness of birth after nine moons of labor.

A scream of joy and battle-lust began in Jiana's feet, rose through her legs, her vagina, her belly, her heart, and burst forth from her throat as a shout to wake the sleeping dead. She tore the cloak from her shoulders, and with the same fluid motion drew Wave and snapped her so straight and rigid that the blade almost tore itself from her hand. An audible crack reverberated from the stonework dome.

Some of the Horsemen panicked at the yell, scrambling out of the shadows and running back towards the great hall as if Arhatman himself were after them. But the bolder ones were startled forward from their hiding place, into the light of the blazing torches. Five Horsemen, swords but no armor, momentarily thrown off balance by Jiana's battle yell.

Radience whirled to face them, a pitiful dagger in her good hand. But Jiana was already moving, accelerating past the erstwhile slave at the speed of a striking shakersnake.

The first Horseman never had a chance. He stared curiously as Jiana snapped the whip-like sword in a short arc. She had already passed him when he tried to turn his head; it kept turning, and rolled off his body.

The second man at least raised his sword.

The third finally realized what was happening, and managed to parry two blows, giving the fourth and fifth enough time to turn and follow their smarter, faster compatriots who were already half way to the onion dome.

Jiana watched them run for a moment; then she turned back to Radience. The girl was staring open-mouthed at the three dissected corpses. She looked dazed, and had probably not even been able to follow the battle, so quickly was it over.

"No time," Jiana said. "We've got to break Toldo out of the brig. Damn, where the hell's Rethe? Move it!"

"Toldo?" asked Radience, dumbly. But the warrior was already sprinting towards the gaol.

The guard stepped outside when he heard the yell. When he saw the madwoman bearing down on him, having just cut down three of the Caliph's finest in as many heartbeats, he threw his spear far away and stood absolutely still with his hands over his head.

"On your face," Jiana commanded as she reached the locked door. The soldier obediently dropped to the ground, face first.

She yanked on the lock, but it was tight.

"What's happening?" rumbled a voice from within. "I heard yells . . . is that—who I think it is?"

"No keys!" cried Radience. Jiana glanced at the girl, and saw to her surprise that Radience was frisking the prone soldier.

"I know. Horseman carries them. Leave that sod alone, will you? Let's get this fucking door!"

She stilled her mind as best as she could and spoke quietly:

> *Flick flack*
> *Click back*
> *Pop box*
> *Drop locks*

Nothing happened; the lock remained fast. *Too fast stomach churning calm calm can't do anything when—*

Jiana felt a looming presence, and a cold nose nuzzled the back of her neck.

"Ow! Cascade, what the hell?" The horse snorted loudly in her ear. He seemed to be trying to push her away from the cell door.

"Sorry boy, forgot all about you . . ." Perplexed, Jiana let Cascade push her away. The horse turned, and delivered a vicious kick to the wooden door. On the second kick, some of the panels split and splintered. Inside, Jiana could hear Toldo bellowing something about an earthquake.

With the third kick, a flash of light blinded Jiana for a moment, and a thunderclap hit her so hard she dropped to one knee and clasped her ears. The door shattered, along with most of the wall. Cascade reared and screamed, baring his teeth ferociously.

Toldo climbed cautiously out of the hole, momentarily snagging his robe on the still-locked doorlatch, which now hung from a single shard of the jamb.

"How—how—" stammered Radience, staring at the horse. Jiana herself kept her eyes on the feasting hall, which had grown silent as a tomb.

"Jiana! I knew you would come through, pull the irons out of the fire, um, as it were!"

The warrior held up her hand for silence; she listened intently. She heard the whinny of another horse, back towards the hall.

"Let's get the fuck out of here," she said, quietly and unemotionally. Toldo sobered at once, and Radience stopped gibbering about Cascade. "I don't like this . . ." said Jiana.

A cock crowed, far away.

Then suddenly, the metal band around her neck contracted like a vise being screwed tight.

Her eyes felt like they were bulging, and she could feel the pressure building in her face and neck. She had been caught on an exhalation, and her lungs pumped frantically, begging for air.

The world contracted to a tunnel, filled with white sparkles and edged with absolute black.

5

Who is the goose?
I CAN'T BREATHE!
Who is the goose?
I CAN'T—
Listen to me. If you die now, you are dead in this life. You must calm yourself and listen, Jiana. You are trapped in a bottle, but you are not a goose.
I'm dying dying—
You have a long time before you die. Be still, stop crying. You have trapped yourself in a bottle, but you are not a goose. The bottle is yours. Remember how they put

you in it when you were little, fed you and taught you that the glass walls were unbreakable? But Jiana dearest, it is your own bottle.

Help me—I don't want to die. Not now!

I cannot free you. A goose is a woman waiting for somebody else to free her.

I'm not a slave. I'm free!

Then you are not in the bottle.

I can't breathe!

Then you are still in the bottle . . . you must break your own bonds. The goose

can leave

whenever it truly wills . . .

Jiana, the bottle is your own *bottle.*

The green sky and blue grass surrounded her; the master willed the colors to reverse, and the grass was green and the sky blue. *Who is the master? Who is the goose?* But Jiana on the field of green chooses, "I will not die on this field. I will not join the thousands buried beneath, bottles upon bottles, inside the outside."

A little girl, she must marry. *No, I will not.* Pulls the knife, kills the solstice goose now red in bridal finery. But was that she? Was that she?

Glass shatters, green and blue shards fly outward diamond sparkles, sharpness sound cuts of ruby blood. Goose flies free at last, goose is free there is no bottle.

Once I heard five blind men, and they had found an elphas. *They argued, was it a rope? was it a snake? was it a wall?*

Man the talker. Man the bottle-maker.

Held you too tight, put his hands and fingers where they should not have oughtn't to have gone, didn't he? Called upon me then, but was really you.

Then you are me.

Jiana, Jianabel, and Jianabelana sit on a cloud, float through green sky over blue grass. Talk and talk, left and right and two-hands-caught.

No. We are both of us "us." He could not hold the goose, could he? He grasped it tight, but it was water and flowed all cold and crystal clear through his peeping fingers and he felt glass walls pushing pressing him, folding him unto himself. Felt the sudden-glass bottle, and he wept for he had no Will left, the silly goose.

Damn his frozen feet. Couldn't I have loved my own father at least?

Jiana reached within. Within was a core of power.

What was the power? If she would ever understand, it would be now, now that the bottle squeezed ever tighter against the goose's weasand, crushing under force of Curse's collar.

Power simply Will manifest said the Tunk, for he was now here.

He is, ahem, essentially correct, rumbled the fat priest, but his mystic mumble-jumble is all jumbo mumbo and he doesn't get the point (as it were) across. Now look at these charts I have prepared, my dear.

He flashed them; they were indeed prepared.

But it's all Hodge and Podge! she cried in confusion, as metal slave band squeezed and squeezed like the neck of a bottle and severed her neck letting her head fall with a thump dump on the hump.

Maq held her in his arms. Kissed her, shaved her head, pulled down her pantaloons and put it in her like he had always wanted to ever since she was a little girl and he had used his finger, the dirty Maqfather.

Thought you'd did me, he cooed, but you wrong. See, Jiana? Your daddy again, back again you didn't do me that time. The little shit with the pointy teeth didn't do me and neither did you. Did you know the sky was green? Should I be worried about that?

And Jiana saw that indeed, it had all come to pass, so mote it be. And she wept, for the Master had a stomach of its own.

Come to focus. Your stomach is wandering. You must listen to me; I won't shut up, I just won't! You have but a few heartbeats left of life.

I love you.

Yes, yes, but let's get to the important things: this goose must leave this bottle NOW. *There is no second time. She needs your help.*

Radience? Is she a slave again?

"They're not even sure it is Radience," distracted the Maqfather. *Get out of my belly!* she cried, *you are not Maq and he is not my father.*

Radience, and you, too, silly goose, explained Jianabel.

But the strange little one is right, so to speak. Toldo cleared his throat noisily in her stomach. The figment of your stomach is right, so to speak. Listen, Jiana; I found my own bottle. Found it and it was gone! I know the path, I have the key.

"First," Toldo amplified, "there is a bottle."

Jianabel: "Then there is no bottle."

Dilai: "Then there is."

But, ah, the bottle is always and ever yours. No one can impose it upon you from, ahem, from the Outside, as it may be.

The little girl crosses the plains, the mountains. First there is a mountain, then there is no mountain. She comes to the Floating City they called it Bay Bay but she cannot stay.

She drifts south, north. She stows away on a schooner laden with spice, bound for the Flower Empire, is stolen by Pirates who call themselves Ti Ji Tul, the Firstmen, and teach her the language.

She marries.

Did you remember that, Jiana? Did you remember Ton Kikijin?

Did you remember your little girl?

"NO! Take it away, take that out of my stomach, take it—"

YES THEY TOOK HER.

I remember: remember the pain, so pain, so pain I can't move can't walk, can only sit and hold myself around the belly. Something was wrong. She was growing wrong inside me I can tell, can't they do anything, the Firstmen?

No, ride it out. You will live. Oh Tooqa the Nameless Serpentine take this egg from me, let her die I don't want to die!

(And the bottle grows thicker, every day another layer of glass trap the goose push away the world.)

So I tell myself it's just normal, that all the women feel it like this but I know it's shit, I know I'm dying she's killed me, I want her dead. But she's my daughter, I love her.

O Tooqa help me with this. Oh mother why didn't you tell me? No it's not like this there's something wrong, please my love Ton-Ton help me, call her, call the one you spoke of, take this egg away from me.

I just want to live. Is that a crime, oh gods I want the pain to stop, I want to die, I want to kill her, I want to live!

You let it go. You spend days dizzy and vomiting and every moment of every day of every week of every moon it's a dagger in my belly something ripping and tearing and all for her, ALL FOR HIM, never for me.

Soon I can't even get out of bed, just lie, just lie curled around the growing pain like a dead goose stuffed in a roasting pan and they eat me:

She eats me from within, he eats at me from without—be brave! strong! persevere! think! of your daughter! think of your son!

Oh Serp I hate him! I love him hate him and wish he would die go away let me end this horrible, I don't want anything else, just stop the pain! She isn't worth it! Aren't I worth it?

I'm weak. Don't know how I've lived through so much of this. Know she'll kill me as she comes out just like he killed me when he came in and I became a vessel. Ghoul eat my innards out come out all bloody with sharp teeth filed to a point swallowing the last of the afterbirth and grinning.

She looks at me with horrible, horrible metal eyes and

steel teeth, pull on the afterbitch. I unplug like air bladder
my blood pour out upon the table for her to lap up so
much milk never come out of my breasts. She suck me dry
women scream in terror she gnaws remains of my body
until nothing left.

But I live I don't know how.

I push through one more day, just one. Then one more.
I think of the sword, think of the Flower Empire. Think of
my father and the knife, think of the wedding that almost
was and the knife.

Think of the knife. Think too much of the knife. But I
make it through. First there is pain. Then there is no pain.

Then there is; she comes out oh Tooqa none too gently.
I don't know, my stomach had emptied of all that is me
through most of it. Remember pain unbearable, and grim
silence of women pulled her from me, what there was of
her.

Don't know what there was. Can't remember. Won't
remember. Yeah it was wrong, gods she was wrong.

I don't think she had a head. She had a head, but it was
all pushed in, and she didn't cry, the eyes were dull grey
metal, and was alive but wasn't a she.

It was meat.

The women bit the afterbirth off and I thought they
would give me the wrong one to eat, it was almost more a
child than she. Gave me the afterbirth, and I could barely
choke it down, my sweet, my daughter. Wanted them to
bury her, but I wanted her. I can't describe it any more
than that. It was another bottle, another wall of glass.

She was a goose. They cooked her. That night I slept, so
close between dead and alive that I wouldn't have given
anyone odds which it was, five gets you only five.

And when I woke still pale still bleeding, sun high, she
was gone. They took her in the long, cold night. I don't
know where.

They took my daughter. They took my husband.

Or he left.

No, never again, never saw him again. His family looked
at me, a stranger; who was I? why did I haunt them? Why

was there always blood dropping from my mouth, always hungry, always eyeing the children and feeling empty rumble in my stomach?

I don't dream during this part. I don't dream for a long time.

They wouldn't stop me; the look in my metal eyes was enough, and I get my sword and I leave and the Pirates take me on to the original destination, to the Flower Empire.

I learn there. Learn to forget.

Now I learn to remember.

Whose bottle is it?

This too is just a bottle. The little girl does not exist, neither the one that was me nor the one that I made.

Damn it, it *passes*; everything passes. It's all temporary. Only one thing is real, only the mountain.

And I really *know* that now.

To hell with Jianabel. To hell with Radience. Toldo is gone, Dilai is gone. There is no more Alanai, no more Lyonalai, no princes or Kings or governors, anywhere. Toq, who is he? Sleeping Tifniz, a bug in a dream. No slavemasters, no slaves, no masters except the one who makes the grass green and the sky blue. There is nothing. There is no peace, no motion, no silver, no gold. Candles don't burn, and the moons don't rise. The earth is round, the earth is flat, there is no earth.

There is a mountain. The mountain is ME.

Not Jiana, not the goose, not the bottle, no nothing but the all-seeing eye, three cornered lid reaching out to Inside, Outside, Otherside.

And the goose is out of the bottle; the goose can leave anytime it wills . . . for it is NEVER truly in the bottle at all. It's just a trick of the perspective.

And the goose is out.

There is no bottle.

There is no glass.

Nothing breaks.

Nothing is.

*   *   *

Congratulations, Jiana. You really are free. And I love you, too. Something wet touched

her cheek.

Jiana reached up a hand to brush the tear aside. Her breaths came easy, serene.

Fingers brushed her throat; she opened her eyes, and Toldo stared at her bare throat, his mouth open in an "Oh" of astonishment.

"It works!" he breathed, awestruck.

"Radience. . . ." Jiana sat up, reaching for the girl. She lay on the ground, her face purple with the lack of air. But the proper color was returning quickly, as the girl breathed more easily.

"I took—" Toldo began; but he paused, uncertain how to proceed. "I pulled you out of yourself, um, I mean I . . ."

She shook her head.

"No, priest. It was my bottle. Snakes, get the hell out of here. Horsemen probably coming. How long . . . ?"

"Just a few moments, Jiana. They're out of the feast hall and staging—can your horse carry us all?"

Jiana looked at Cascade; he looked at her, seeming to say *Anything's possible, but I doubt it, not with him.*

The decision was Jiana's.

"We can't really run; you know that. We stand and fight and maybe die as free women. But stand we will—*here*."

She stood painfully, staring curiously at the two metal collars, lying peacefully on the sand. They were unbroken.

"Help the kid up, will you? I have to find something to do about . . ." As she watched, the regrouped Horsemen began their charge across the compound, crying the battle-songs of the Soldiers of the Elect.

6

Jiana felt the core of power well up within her, even before she consciously thought of using her Jianabel-spells. She closed her eyes, and pushed her spirit up over the hump, enough to look over the courtyard and evaluate tactics.

She saw a hot essence push past her on an intercept path with the frightened but determined Horsemen. Jiana opened her eyes, and saw that the angry essence was Radience. The girl positioned herself with drawn dagger between Jiana and the Horsemen, not realizing that she would not even slow them down.

They would cut her where she stood; Jiana had no intention of allowing that to happen. *Invisibility,* she speculated.

No—won't work when you're the center of their attention. Not at your level of power.

Transport?

Ever practiced it, dear heart? Jiana, you have only a moment—do what you do best!

I'm a warrior.

Use it! Fight them!

Jiana became conscious of a great reluctance. Things were happening too fast, it was out of her control again. She spared a glance at Toldo: he seemed oddly serene, accepting of whatever might happen. It was not the way she remembered him; he had changed.

The Horsemen were more than halfway across the yard, formed into a cutting wedge. There was no more time.

Jiana expanded her stomach outward, out through the crystal spheres with such rapidity that she could barely see them as they blurred past. She sought—what did she seek?—she sought a tool, something hard and hot and fast to stop them like a stone wall rising out of the cobblestones.

(Three times . . .)

"Jianabel! Help me—"

"Who?" asked Toldo, his voice calm and unconcerned. "Are you still on about her?"

Sister, I wish I could. But you too have passed through the Father Door and entered the chapel. Find your own path . . . I have confidence, prettiest!

(Three times will I blot . . .)

"I thought you buried that delusion for once and all."

All the sound in the world ceased; the Horsemen slowed to a crawl, though their beasts still galloped. All the white in the world fell into Jiana's view, obscuring the rest of the mundane sphere. The warrior realized she was still in yet another chamber of the Pere Dur Chapel . . . as she would be for the rest of her existence.

No one gets—

Doors and doors, more doors than there were numbers in her mind, all opened from the chamber in which she stood. The room itself unfolded into an infinity of star points, each edge of a point containing yet another point, forever.

No one gets out—

The grass was green but the sky was blue beneath her feet and above her head—*and I know the master who makes it so,* she thought. A snake of magical power rose within her spine, and she knew then that she would surely die at the hands of a black-skinned woman from the steamy, southern jungles, and not trampled under horses ridden by raghead jamalmasters.

But no one gets out INTACT.

Another voice intruded itself, spouting errant nonsense merely to confuse and/or dissuade her from Trueness and Comprehension.

—Bull bollocks! it screamed, and Razorboys and bald-headed women copulate with goats while the horny king and butterball queen succeed and suck eggs in a never-everending gavotte of—

The words rolled inuendo and out the other; Jiana was in another space, her own space at last. Her own room in the Father Door. *Let me reign over my own world,* she thought. *Let me rain over mine enemies.* She felt her teeth with her tongue and was unastonished to find them all filed to very, very sharp points: she understood now, they were not needles, not daggers; they were the points of the starry chamber of the Father Door—points of decision.

Each point held a door, a path that she might take; each door held a world, the world written by the path just taken.

"What is magic? How does the goose get out of the bottle?" Toldo lectured. Not the Toldo who stood serene on the flagstones, awaiting what must be, but the Toldo of four turns past, created in Jiana's stomach when she first met him.

"How many Toldos are there?" she asked, afraid to listen. "Are we nothing but images in someone's stomach? Toldo yesterday, today, my guess of Toldo tomorrow?"

He continued doggedly. "Magic is just *vision*. A magician sees the points, peeks behind the doors, chooses the path. What is your need?"

"I need to kill that charging bunch of ragheads, you motherless priest! Need to rain death and fire to save one particular set of Toldo, Radience, and Jiana!"

"Then search well the doors," whispered the Toldo's fading ghost, "but mind, look far down their paths, lest you turn right when you should after all turn left, as it were. Sometimes the paths are hard to . . ."

He vanished with a pop, leaving only his stodgy pedagogy.

Jiana flung back all doors at once, and the goose was debottled again. Behind one she saw a roaring, crackling, merry dance of flames. *Yessir, that's the door for me, I can tell,* she declared, putting her foot down.

DEMON FEET! AND
RUBBER MEAT! AND
MOMMY'S TEAT! AND
POISON TREAT! AND—

"Shut up, Toq; you have no power over me today, not you or any other bottlegod. Three times, my ass! You're nothing, you're negligible now. . . . I found the road to the starry Chapel!"

The boy-god appeared, white today as the perpetual snows of the great, east mountains, save for the blood-red gash where his mouth should have been.

"I've got to *hand it to you*," he yielded, "but don't drop it!" He shed a bitter tear, wiping it away with the severed hand of a virgin.

And then Toq too vanished away, leaving behind only his mocks and his socks.

And they all vanished away, all the other doors that Jiana had not selected, leaving only their sins and their might-have-bins.

The fire was left in Jiana's hands; the fire had eyes, the fire had a name. The fire squirmed and writhed, a door full of worms, a handful of fiery worms that burned and murdered all that they touched. Where did they fall? They fell from the sky, like every doom.

Jiana rose from the cobblestones of the Caliph's courtyard; Toldo and Radience were staring curiously at her, the girl in a panic and Toldo preparing himself for death. The Horsemen were no closer than they were before time began, in the aeons before Jiana saw the starry room.

But long, looping strands of fire were beginning to tumble down from the sky. They squirmed in the air, and Jiana felt a most uncomfortable certainty that it was not the air currents that made them shimmy.

"Jiana . . ." Radience stared at the magus with a look frozen halfway between awe and loathing. Jiana glared back, unwilling to be judged by a seventeen turn ex-slave.

The first fireworm fell across al'Kug, who led the party, and his face contorted in sudden agony. His horse screamed and bucked, frantically trying to throw of the coiling flames that wrapped around its neck and back. The animal succeeded in throwing the Overman, but the fireworms coiled five times about it and held fast.

The worms attacked the other horses and Horsemen indiscriminately. In a beat, two beats, all of the men and beasts were rolling on the ground, crying out in shock and terror and a pain so deep that Jiana felt it herself, wrapping around her chest like a monstrous rope, squeezing the breath from her lungs and all thought from her stomach.

The fire fell. It fell thicker and faster now, more worms than Jiana could shake a snake at, clinging to whatever they touched and crawling along the ground when they missed.

Jiana pushed back towards the iron gate, never taking

her eyes from the spectacle, another fiery butchery from Jiana, Slayer of All.

"NO! This isn't what I meant! I didn't call you to . . ." Her voice trailed off into silence, and nausea crept up her throat as the power had crept up her spine earlier. *Look far down their paths,* Toldo had warned. The words rattled round and round her stomach, mocking her, and she heard the silvery laugh of Toq.

You did it, girl, she told herself. *You did it again. Congratulations! Isn't it wonderful how you saved the lives of Toldo and Radience, spending only five hundred others in the process?*

Five hundred deaths was probably an underestimate; Jiana watched in horrified fascination as the minaret of the feast-hall itself burst into flames, flames that consumed (she knew) more than flesh and hide, but thought and spirit as well. Flames called from a blackened limbo of ash and the Dead Past by Jiana Analena, Maggus Supreme.

Suddenly, Radience grabbed Jiana's arm.

"What is it? What—"

Jiana looked past Radience, and the world lurched beneath the warrior's feet. A figure had just run out of the dome; it was Rethe. She looked left and right at the confusion, then jumped as a fire worm fell in a loop around her feet.

"Look out!" screamed Radience from behind Jiana.

Rethe did not waste time looking; she leaped forward, over the writhing fire worm. Anahita and Kyaddi were not so lucky: they ran out of the onion dome as well; but when they saw the fire falling from the sky, they grabbed each other in fright and began to yell for help. A coil floated down and laid itself across them, gentle as a goose feather.

Rethe saw Jiana and began to run towards her. Jiana urged her on, wildly waving her arms.

Rethe was two-thirds of the way across the compound when she collided with Ysmal, who had bolted from the stables when they caught fire. Both of them fell heavily in a tangled heap.

Rethe stood, but Ysmal gripped her leg in terror.

"LET GO OF ME, YOU FATHERLESS—"

They were the last words Rethe spoke.

Jiana turned her face away as one, then another, then a third worm draped across the woman's body.

Jiana shuddered as she felt Rethe's spirit burn inside her body. The warrior did not know why she felt that one death above the others.

You were meant to, whispered Jianabel.

You did this!

It was your door. *Sister.*

Rethe was consumed, past skin, muscle, bones, and ashes. In the end, there was only a dark stain on the ground.

Jiana focused her eyes on Radience, anyone other than Rethe. The girl stared at Jiana, tear streaks running from her accusing eyes, her mouth set in hard lines.

"Are you? the Arhatman?" she asked, her voice a mere squeak.

"I'm Jiana. I spit on your Arhatman. Go to the gate, you stupid girl, before I burn off your good arm."

Radience turned and walked to the great entrance. Her steps were hollow and her movements wooden. She was a marionette, not frightened, only disgusted.

Toldo followed, watching Jiana carefully.

"What has happened to you in four turns?"

She shook her head. *Later,* she meant.

Cascade already stood waiting for them at the gate, as if he knew what they were going to do. The black iron of the gate itself was brightly lit by the hellish glare from behind them, and this time Jiana had no trouble using Curse's spell on the lock. The gate swung open, just enough for them all to squeeze out, including Cascade.

She pointed, and Toldo and the girl squeezed through. Jiana mounted Cascade first, then urged him through the gap.

A crowd was beginning to gather. Merchants and whores, rich and poor, all pushed closer and closer to the fence to watch the conflagration. A few of them shouted questions to Jiana in Tooltak, but she ignored them and they turned back to the fire, entranced by the dancing, singing flames.

As they watched, their eyes glowed; with a shudder, Jiana wondered whether it was just a reflection of the fire, or if their souls burned in some demonic linkage with the sacrifice. Some of the spectators licked their lips—in hunger?

As she passed through the gate, Jiana could not resist a final glance back.

The fire was nothing more than a shining orb now, bright as the sun, impossible to look at without squinting. In the center stood a figure: it was a little boy, silhouetted in black against the white heat, almost invisible. He spread his arms in ecstasy and threw back his head, and Jiana knew it was Toq.

She realized with a flush of anger that he had already begun his revenge. He had just blotted her life—the first time.

"Two more, you bastard," she whispered, "two more, then you're *mine*."

She turned Cascade about and followed the priest and the girl.

7

Between the Parts . . .

The great raft, almost a barge, drifted gently into the Nag Deh Jambajala as Jiana cut the last mooring line and Toldo worked the stern-oar. The raft was so large that even Cascade had room to wander a bit. Radience sat in the front, as far away from Jiana and Toldo as she could get without swimming.

The warrior and the priest watched the dying glow, far behind them in the center of Deh Bid.

"I think another house caught," said Toldo.

"It'll be the last. The worms are fed."

"Worms?"

"You didn't see the fire worms?"

"I saw only fire, falling from the sky."

Jiana closed her eyes and listened to the river waves lapping at the sides of the raft. They were still close enough to the shore to hear chirpkins, crying for lost loves and nutritious mites. Far away a frog croaked, and the sound was carried to Jiana by a trick of the wind.

"Have you found a faith, o fat-headed one?"

Toldo was a long time answering.

"I don't know," he said at last. "Faith I have found, but one faith? I don't know. I am not certain."

"You babbled something about—"

Toldo waved his hand dismissively, cutting her off in mid-sentence.

"Yes, yes, I was not very coherent, I realize. Let me tell you what exactly I have discovered, and how I came to accept such hospitality on the part of our late Caliph.

"I found a mushroom."

"Congratulations."

"But such a mushroom! It looks deadly enough: white stem, red cap, covered with yellow, diseased-looking spots; the cap is bigger than your hand."

"Just a guess," Jiana said, "it's hallucinogenic, right?"

"No, dear, I'm not quite as foolish as you seem to think. I have had such delusory plants and fungi before, and I know the difference between them and—divine revelation."

Jiana said nothing, but the skepticism must have shown on her face, because Toldo continued hastily.

"I was in the south, in one of their interminable jungles, looking for God. Instead I found the Hoor-Gundu, the 'white men,' who smear some sort of white paste all over their bodies. Or perhaps they're albinos.

"Their witch-man spoke Tooltak, and we got into a lively discussion of local politics, astronomy, and herbalism. Oh, did you know there's to be an eclipse next turn? Anyway, Jatjaka kept asking simple questions that I could not seem to answer, such as what you would see if you set two perfect mirrors face to face—I could not figure out how to see anything without getting my own fat head into the picture as well. One thing led to another thing, and he called for this mushroom to be prepared."

"What does it do?"

"I saw God, Jiana; I *was* God. I was everything, a part of the entire, infinite lattice of crystal spheres, a part but not just a piece—I was the whole lattice. I can't describe it."

"Wait, did you see a great star chamber, with doors leading everywhere?"

"Oh, no, I've been there dozens of times. That's just a metaphor for the soul-quest."

"Soul-quest? Looking for oneself?"

"Looking to *transcend* oneself. Your teachers in the Flower Empire probably used the goose-in-the-bottle game. Somebody makes an absolute mint selling those bottled geese.

"But what I saw when I drank that foul-tasting concoction is as far beyond the soul-quest as your magic is beyond the bazaar-tricks of a market-square mountebank. Jiana . . . I think it may be the basis of *every religion in this world.*"

Jiana leaned down and scooped a handful of the Jambajala into her mouth; it tasted slightly salty, probably from the alkali cliffs upriver from Deh Bid.

"A mushroom," she summarized, licking the salt from her palm, "caused the birth of every religion in the world. I think that witch-man scrambled your stomach, chum."

"You won't know until you try it," responded Toldo with unusual force. "It cannot be described, only recreated. In the moons after my enlightenment, I have meditated upon the visions, powers, philosophies, and especially the words of every great seer, messiah, prophet, and saint I have ever studied—hundreds of them. And I am convinced that every one of them at one time partook of this particular mushroom, or something similar in another land.

"Fact: they all became dissatisfied with their former lives. Fact: they all forsook civilization, or their familiar town, and headed out into the physical or cultural wilderness. Fact: each and every one vanished from view for a long, long time—moons, at a minimum, often turns.

"Fact: they all came back changed, filled with a cer-

tainty and a need to proselytize that I now know well.
Especially their words . . . they all use the *same* phrases,
the *same* types of metaphors: dying and being reborn,
seeing with new eyes, going to a place far away and seeing
monsters from the dreamworld—literally from their dreams.
But always, they returned with that evil certainty, and it
caused them to misinterpret it all, to see heaven as *over
there* and the current world as a world of *sin*.

"It's just a world of sleepwalkers, Jiana. I'm certain of
that . . . but I doubt my own certainty; I fight against it. I
know that certainty is just part of the vision induced by
the alchemy. But my skepticism no longer allows me my
religion of atheism.

"Jiana, I KNOW that heaven exists. I've seen it. I was
there! It's all in here." He tapped his stomach. "Paradise
is within us; we live in the summerland, but we have no
eyes.

"I told all this to the Caliph, and he found my speculations fascinating—until I extended my belief about the
origin of religion to his own religion, and suggested that
the Great Seer himself must have eaten some of this
mushroom stew. That's when he threw me in the hole.
But at least he left me quill and paper, to work on this."

Toldo patted his pack with satisfaction; it undoubtedly
contained the book he mentioned before.

Jiana stared at the water, reflecting the moons in a
straight line back toward the lights of Deh Bid, now far
behind them as they drifted in the current.

"You've gone all mystical on me."

"Jiana, *you weren't there.* You did not taste the experience, so to speak."

She shook her head, unwilling to accept his ravings.

Toldo chuckled.

"You will," he rumbled. "I brought out some of the
mushrooms. If I can just learn to prepare them correctly,
to duplicate what the witch-man did . . . Will you then
try, and see what I saw?"

"No," she answered, immediately. "Toldo, I haven't yet
even found my own soul. I've just embarked on the soul-

quest, remember? Snakes, I can't go out questing for
Reality Boundless! Besides—" she glanced over at Radience,
who was still staring backward toward her former life, not
forward downriver—"I have a responsibility, now. She's
like my child. I have to do *something* with her . . . something more than I did with the kid, Dida."

The name brought a sudden pain to Jiana's chest, as if
she had been pricked by an arrow. Cascade looked up
from the water and nickered sympathetically.

"I'll help you, Toldo. I think I'd like to become an
alchemist or an apothecary. Keep me away from people,
for a while. But don't expect me to risk my soul or my
stomach on your quest for total insanity."

She stood decisively and walked to the center of the
raft. There was a small hut there, with beds and food and
navigational charts.

Jiana stooped and entered the hut, lay down on one of
the beds, and instantly fell into a deep sleep. But in her
dreams, she was chased far and near by a thousand thousand thousand burning *daevas*, each wearing Rethe's face.

Chapter VII:

Vine wraps oak, but the flower blooms free

1

The raft drifted on the Jambajala, lazy as a two-claw courtesan on a cold and misty morning. Radience stood respectfully in the center, near the house; Jiana sat cross-legged in front of the girl, watching and waiting.

"Uh, Jiana Mistress?"

"Yes?"

Radience lapsed into embarassed silence.

"Jiana?"

"Still here," said the warrior.

"Well, what are we going to do?"

Jiana waited without responding.

"When are we going to eat?" the girl clarified.

Jiana shrugged.

"We have no food," she answered.

"Well, we have to eat!"

"I'm all ears. Suggest away."

Toldo chuckled. He was hunched over his manuscript, ostensibly rewriting a section that Jiana had heavily edited. But the warrior noticed that his quill had not touched parchment for some time.

Radience looked confused. She looked at Toldo, then back to Jiana.

"What happened to all that food you had?"

"What, in my saddle sack?"

"Yes, it wasn't great, but it's—"

"—gone, is what it is."

"Gone!"

Jiana nodded brightly.

"Where did it go?"

"Into the Jambajala, after passing through our digestive tracts."

Radience stormed away to the other side of the raft, pushing past Cascade, who eyed her hungrily. She sulked for a few moments, then sat at the edge of the raft and trailed her feet in the Jambajala.

"Jiana?"

"Haven't moved, o diminutive one."

"If we don't eat, won't we starve?"

"That's usually how it works. Radience, you never have considered this problem, have you? There's no one here to suddenly pop out with a roast, or a sack of *tazh'na*. If your stomach wants some food, it had better come alive and *think of something*."

Radience slowly sat down, resting her chin in her good hand. She looked at the trees on the bank; the Jambajala this far south was so deep, so slow and gentle, that it seemed to be standing still, while the leafy jungle itself moved upstream.

"We could pull to the edge—I mean the shore," ventured the girl.

"That's a start," agreed Jiana. She stood and took the tiller. Pushing it to the side, the raft began a lazy realignment. Thereafter, while Radience began packing loose items away and lashing them down, Jiana steered the raft shorewards with short pulls on the stern oars.

They landed and beached the raft. At Jiana's direction, Radience covered the raft with fronds and dirt.

Jiana spotted smoke curling up from over a hill. There were a number of snake-like coils, probably from a hundred cooking fires or so. They clambered up the hill and crouched at the top, watching.

The village was small and reminded Jiana of the tiny hamlets that by and large made up the population of the Flower Empire. The houses were made of mud-bricks, and looked quite substantial, and very old.

Toldo peered into every building, hoping to find a clerk's office, one that had maps. Jiana looked for an apothecary or an alchemist, where she could buy raw supplies to embark upon her new career. It would take some time to remember all that she had been taught, but she was certain that many of the potions and elixers she learned across the ocean were unknown in Tool, or even up north in the Water Kingdom.

Radience ran back and forth on the streets from house to house like a monkey in heat. She even forgot to hide her withered arm, and amazingly enough, none of the inhabitants even noticed it—the arm which in Radience's world was as big as an elphas and twice as ugly. (But she could not hide the horrid thought, the image of what Jiana had done back in . . .)

The citizens were too busy gaping and gawking at the three of them to notice anything as trivial as a crippled limb, especially not when their own beggars seemed to specialize in facial and spinal deformities that brought a queasy lump to Jiana's stomach, along with a pang of guilt.

She almost succumbed to temptation and tossed a coin to a man with a huge, bulbous, bladder-like goiter depending from his chin to his sternum, but she came to her senses and hurried on, money bag held securely in her left hand, the hilt of Wave in her right.

As more and more residents of the town ran out of their houses and pipe-rooms to stare, Radience grew shy and crowded close to Jiana and Toldo, less monkey-like than puppyish.

"Well, priest," said Jiana, "you've wandered this territory more than I. What now? Do they welcome us, arrest us, or eat us?"

"I suspect not the latter. I can't say about the former. They're not likely to have heard about the fire, or to care if they did."

Radience whispered to Jiana.

"They look so dirty!"

"Dirty! I'll bet nearly every one of them knows how to read. How many of the Elect could even read their own holy book?"

"Well, the priests always told us it was too holy for mortal eyes to look upon. Have . . . have *you* read the words of the Seer?" Her voice dropped in awe, or fear of a priest or caliph dropping suddenly from a rooftop to punish her for apostasy.

"One version, at least. It really didn't hold my interest. I like the Akamite faction better than you Pushugites, anyway."

"That's a heresy!"

"Well, the Akamites say that *you're* the heretics, so I guess you're even."

They walked in silence, trying to avoid staring back at the parade of children, old men, and women that followed silently behind the trio.

"Ah!" cried Toldo, pointing ahead, "recognize the stylized mortar and pestle? I think we have found our man the apothecary."

"Jiana . . . have you—investigated—many heresies?"

"Every one I could find. Would you buy a jacket without trying it on, or buy a goat without sampling the milk?"

Radience said nothing, but Jiana could see that the analogies had flown as high over her head as the Arch of Lillies in Bay Bay.

"You've never bought a jacket, or a goat, right?"

The girl shook her head.

"Radience, part of life is realizing that your talent, money, and especially your time in this life is very limited. You have to learn to *choose* between paths."

"But . . . suppose you had been brought up as a girl among the Akamite heretics. Would they tell you that Akamat was the true successor to the Seer, and that *Pushuga* was the Lord of the Mists of Evil, rather than the true faith that we are taught?"

"Probably. Or else, that Pushuga was well-intentioned but misinformed. I don't think they call him evil."

Radience thought for a long time, until they stood outside the house of the apothecary. It was large, and seemed well-stocked.

"Then how do I know, Jiana-Mistress, that it was not *I* that was lied to? How do I know the Akamites are not correct? How do I know I won't go to the Underdwell when I die? Jiana, you know I taught myself to read . . . will I go to the Underwell for *that*?"

Jiana kept a straight face. Radience's skepticism was growing moment by moment, now that it had been unleashed from the shackles of the One Right Way.

"You *will* go to the Underdwell," said Jiana, with a voice that was at once low and penetrating. "For so long as you look for laws outside yourself, you are *already* in the Underdwell, land of shit and no roses." Without waiting for a reply, Jiana pushed her way into the apothecary's. Toldo followed, and Radience, recovering, ducked nervously inside. The crowd did not follow.

Radience stood in the center of the shop, staring at hundreds of jars, some of them glass. The jars were full of powders and liquids, in all colors of the world and even some colors that had come from no rainbow, rock, or crystal.

Jiana wandered from jar to jar, reading the labels and occasionally scratching at the stubble that ran down the center of her scalp, where she had stopped shaving. *She looks more Jiana-like*, the girl thought.

As Radience watched her, she felt something funny in her stomach, except it was not in her stomach, exactly, but a little lower. She caught herself visioning, running her fingers through Jiana's thick, black hair—*well, it* will be *thick and black soon, anyway*. She imagined stroking the bare sides of Jiana's head, here bare neck, her *(fire raining down upon the Elect upon my family upon—)* naked shoulders and arms, her—

"There's a baby in that jar!" Radience screamed, recoiling in horror from the gruesome figure.

She stared, feeling nausea creeping up her throat, then she looked up to see Jiana, Toldo, and the proprietor staring in astonishment, as if she had just pulled her breasts out and waved them around.

"I'm going to be sick," she announced, staring at her feet.

"Turn around," ordered the apothecary in a voice of command. Radience obeyed instantly, out of habit.

"Do you see that large, brass container, tall as your waist, directly in front of you?"

"Yes, sir."

"It's a spittoon. Go stand next to it," he snapped, then he resumed his discussion with Toldo about maps and potions.

Radience shuffled forward until she stood over the brass jar. She contemplated its inside, and gagged a couple of times. But there was nothing in her stomach to abort.

After a last dry heave, she took a deep breath and wiped the sweat from her forehead and her upper lip. She turned slowly, and approached the dreaded apparition, determined not to disgrace her freedom again.

The large, glass jar was indeed full of baby.

The child was not quite fully developed. It had hands with webbed fingers, and its skin was almost translucent. It floated in a vile, yellow liquid, and was bloated like a river-corpse.

A most horrible fantasy pushed itself into Radience's stomach. *It's going to open its eyes,* she thought. *It's going to open them suddenly and look right at me, and I'll die!*

She could not tear her gaze away. After a time, the force of the vision faded and she could turn to the other jars.

Most of them in this section of the shop contained animals in various stages of development. She inspected them all, determined to taste the jacket and try on the milk.

One creature that frightened her even more than the child was a ghastly, two-headed snake, whose eyes *were* open. So was one of its mouths, and Jiana could look straight down its gullet. The snake was as long as she was

tall, and it was coiled into a complicated knot, like yarn
after a kitten had got at it.

Feeling weak and queasy again, Radience crept forward
to rejoin Jiana. She tried not to think of two-headed snakes
and babies.

She watched the warrior haggling out the price of her
pile of chemicals. It was a fascinating process: apparently,
the proprietor asked a price ridiculously high, and Jiana
offered one absurdly low. Then they slowly worked their
way towards each other.

Radience quickly added the two original prices together
and divided by two to get the average; in the end, they
agreed to a price that was several claws less than that, so
the girl decided Jiana was the winner.

All at once, a blinding realization swept through Radience,
as she watched Jiana count out the coins.

That's *what I'm destined to be*, she thought, a thrill
rattling her entire body. *I'm going to be a warrior!*

Again, she felt a wonderful compressing, just below her
stomach, as she thought of Jiana, sleek muscles naked to
the world. She silently inhaled as she stared at Jiana's
smooth, rounded face. Then she slowly let her breath out
as the compression ebbed from her body, to be replaced
by a delicious lassitude.

A warrior is strong, she thought, *free. Nothing bothers
a warrior. I could call fire from the sky and kill everyone I
know and wouldn't feel a thing! I can start being a warrior tomorrow morning, for I know just where Jiana keeps
the razor.*

Radience trailed along behind as Jiana and Toldo exited
the shop and headed back toward the raft, their mob of
curious stalking them without speaking. Apart from the
apothecary, not a single person in the entire town had
spoken a word to them.

2

Toldo sat cross-legged under the stars, as the raft gently
rose and fell with the waves—waves on a river! Jiana sat

across from him, a roll of sheepskin and a grease pencil
before her. Whenever he spoke, which was infrequent,
she wrote the words down exactly as they came out,
whether they made sense or not.

I killed them. I killed a thousand—

She buried the thought; now was not the time.

Jiana tried to include notes about Toldo's body language: Did he gesture, storm about, rage? Did he sit
quietly, a beatific smile plastered across his face? It was all
of Primary Import, the priest said before drinking the
mushroom juice. Jiana did her best.

Toldo Mondo leaned forward slightly, his eyes closed
and an intense scowl on his face.

"Un, the end," he whispered as Jiana scribbled furiously, "he always be, befowls the murk, roturns and turns
to the unconchurns of foowl stomachs and the smale of
fard."

He sat. He laid back. He got up and wandered about in
an apparently heated discussion with two dwarfs, in an
unknown language. Then the priest ran furiously around
the raft, chasing someone or something invisible, so in-
sanely that Jiana was terrified he would throw himself
overboard.

*You should be the one, not Toldo. Hey, is that Rethe
there, floating in the water? Is that Mugn and her baby,
burned like forgotten toast?*

*NO! Stop it right now. I am a warrior; thought bows to
my will. You will be silent . . . now is the wrong time.*

Toldo did not hurl himself into the Jambajala. When the
sky began to pale in the east and the half Great Moon was
directly overhead, he curled up and began to snore.

It was past noon before he awoke, and Jiana and Radience
had navigated the raft far down the Jambajala, passing
many towns that looked too well-developed, too civilized.

For a long time, Toldo sat in the hut, his eyes unfocused.
He was wrapped in an inner vision still, though conscious
enough, and Jiana decided not to disturb him until he
chose to speak.

Radience was acting strange. She smiled as if she had a

secret, a plan, and Jiana was worried. What unpredicted
nastiness would Radience perpetrate, in all innocence?
Maybe I shouldn't have seized this job with such abandon,
Jiana thought nervously. She held her face impassive,
giving the girl no handle for mischief.

Smaller rafts, boats, and skiffs hugged the river shore,
half a league distant. The desert had made way for grassy
plains and bracken; great herds of variant corndeer, mosk,
and unidentified hairy things taller than a horse stretched
farther than Jiana could see.

Cascade did not seem to mind the river voyage. He
stood quietly, alternately contemplating the left, then the
right shoreline.

Jiana watched him for long periods, becoming more and
more convinced that he was *not* simply a horse, not even a
well-trained one. There was an amused intelligence behind his black eyes, and a tolerance for the foibles of
two-legged things . . . especially for the only one he regularly allowed on his back.

He turned to look back at her and whinnied. Jiana
would have sworn he was laughing, but not in a very
friendly way.

When she spoke to him, she spoke softly, not wishing to
engage in lengthy explanations to Toldo and Radience.

He answered her, too. Jiana was still not sure whether
he *really* spoke to her in her stomach, or whether it was
yet another part of her own soul, which now seemed as
fragmented as the rest of her life.

Pieces: the Jianabel shard, the Wave crumble, the Dida
crack, the Dilai hole, the Toldo tunnel, the Radience
shaft. None of them fit; their shapes could not be combined into an integration. Now she added the Cascade spur.

Radience and Toldo, Rethe, the holocaust of a thousand,
Dida, Dida, Dida. Like a shattered looking glass, distorted
visions of Jianabelanna Analena mimicked as she searched
through the pieces. She saw only twisted visions with
phoney grins, grimaces, laughs, and tragedy-dances. *Tricks
of the light all, mirrors and smoke, smoke from a burning
citadel, a baking town, a redglow underdwell.*

I'm part of the sphere, Reality Prime and all the rest. But the sphere is part of me. We map to each other. Each person a little model of totality, a perfect model—containing ourselves, even.

She sat down beside the vacant priest, watching the chill sun struggle to burn through the clouds.

The raft gently rocked on the sullen Jambajala, and Jiana half-closed her eyes and nearly smile. *Nameless Serpentine. I actually like myself. Nearly.*

She felt Toldo stir beside her. His face was sallow, but he was clearly back in Reality Prime again.

"Find what you were looking for?" she asked, stifling a contented yawn. *Found you hanging from a gallows tree,* sneered an evil accuser. It was not Jianabel; the Wolf Girl would not have been so cold.

Toldo shook his head.

"I found interesting things, awe-full, to be precise. That much I remember, though most of the day—was it only one day?—is a blank."

"Half a day and one night."

"I did not find the union I sought."

"I'm sorry. I tried to follow your instructions preparing the mushrooms."

"You did; the color, the odor—everything was perfect. It tasted exactly so." He looked down at his bulging abdomen. "But there was no soul. I do not know what was missing, but I intend to recreate it. If necessary, I will get Jatjaka himself to show me how."

Jiana looked speculatively at the Jambajala River. Wide as it was, still as it was, it moved swiftly, as many smaller tributaries had joined them as they passed. On they drifted, on it carried them, on to . . . ?

"Toldo, does the Jambajala take us to—to that tribe, whoever they were?"

"The river flows through Hoor-Gundu territory; this river flows through everywhere and everywhen."

"Thanks."

"Mix some powders, Jiana. Has your split personality returned?"

"Jianabel never left; she just buried her feelings under thoughts and words. Toldo, I am less convinced every day that she's nothing more than a piece of my own stomach, projecting itself outward."

"So am I, Jiana."

"Toldo! It was *you* who told *me* that—"

"Well, I was wrong. I said many things, many of them right! But even Toldo Mondo falls upon his behind upon occasion, ah, as it were."

"You son of a bitch. I spent *four turns* trying to burn that needle-tooth bitch from my stomach, and now *you* say she may well be a demon after all!"

"I did not say that, exactly."

Jiana stood and stormed towards the hut, furious. Just then, Radience emerged, a triumphant grin on her face.

Jiana stopped dead, staring at the girl. Radience had shaved her head again . . . all except for a wide warrior's crest, such as Jiana wore.

Jiana felt her muscles freeze tight in anger. She spoke, her voice dripping like water from an icicle.

"That crest is earned, kid. Not given. Not taken."

"But—but that's what I want to be: a warrior."

"It's a cold road you've chosen. Think hard. Three times must I ask. Do you *really* think you know what the fuck you're doing?"

For a moment, Radience looked uncertain, then her own face hardened into a mirror of Jiana's.

"Yes, damn it. I'm going to be a warrior. Teach me!"

"Not until you answer the third time. I taught you what freedom means. *Now you will learn slavery again*—slavery at *my* word, on *my* terms.

"I will own you. I will use you. I'll slice that grin off your face with broken glass. I'll peel back your skin and piss on the raw, bloody flesh underneath it, and you won't say one fucking word unless I order it.

"This is no joke, Radience. No one ever has to know you refused. Get back in that hut and say nothing more to either of us for the rest of today's journey. I'm going to put you off at dusk. Make your own way, you piece of shit."

Radience had begun to tremble after the first five words. Now she was shaking, and tears ran down her cheeks.

"Fu-fu-fuck you!" she stammered, her face turning bright red. "I don't care whether you're willing to do it or not! I'm going to be a warrior, and if you won't teach me, I'll—I'll just find someone else who will!"

Jiana let the anger drain slowly from her body, starting with her feet and her calves, working upward through her thighs, hips, pelvis, stomach, chest, and finally her shoulders, neck, and face. She dissipated the balled-up emotion from the top of her head, and faced Radience with complete dispassion.

"I accept you. We begin when the sun rises. Go away."

Confused, Radience hesitated, and then turned to re-enter the building.

"Girl," snapped Jiana. Radience paused. Wordlessly, the warrior reached into her kit, pulled out her razor, and threw it at Radience's feet.

The girl gripped the doorjamb so hard her knuckles were white. She picked up the razor and returned to the darkness.

Toldo cleared his throat, the rumble sounding like distant thunder.

"What if she had not accepted it?"

"I'd have cut off one of her ears and driven her away."

"Ah, would you still?"

"I don't know. If she has that little self-discipline, Toldo, she'll never be a warrior. Better an ear tomorrow than her head six moons from now, when she meets some soldier-boy in Door, or something. In a word—yes, Toldo. I'd put her off at the next beach. And I'd cry for a few days, but then I'd swallow the anger like I've swallowed all the rest."

"You can do that?"

"Yes, Toldo. I can do that." *I can kill a thousand people with fire from the sky, you stupid bastard. Do you think I'd scruple to mutilate a slave girl?*

3

Radience dreamed, dreamed she did, dreamed about a little, green chap with curly slippers and a long, mossy beard, and—

The floor jumped up and slugged her in the face. She awoke with a start to the sound of an Overman screaming at her.

"—MIDDLE OF THE DAY! LAZY BITCH GOOD-FORNOTHING LAYABOUT GET YOUR ASS ON DECK! YOU HAVE EIGHT SECONDS LEFT! MOVE MOVE MOVE!"

The lamps! I must douse the lamps! I—

Memory flooded back. She was not a slave, the Voice was not the Overman. This was a raft, not the palace grounds of the Caliph of Deh Bid Oasis.

No, it was that crazy woman Jiana. Had to be. She was the one screaming, as if she thought Radience was a—was a . . .

A warrior! She jumped up and looked about desperately for her tunic. It was nowhere to be seen.

The Voice thundered from outside the hut:

"GET—ON—DECK!" The last word was bellowed with such violence that Radience forgot all about her clothing. She dashed out on the deck stark naked, her face white with shock. *The boat must be burning!* she thought.

The only things burning were Jiana's eyes. She looked for all the world as if she were exerting a Perfect Act of Will to avoid seizing Radience by her bare scalp and bony tailbone and pitching her into the river to sleep with the fishes.

Radience stared open-mouthed.

"On your face," said Jiana. Her voice was cold and quiet now, but the girl could hear the barely-lidded rage beneath it.

"My—my face?"

Jiana leaned close, her mouth so close to Radience's eyes that the warrior's teeth brushed the girl's eyelashes.

"ON . . . YOUR . . . FACE."

Jiana's breath smelled like a dead rodent. Shaking, Radience prostrated herself before the woman.

"You will keep your body rigid," Jiana commanded. "You will extend your arms, pressing your body up on your toes. You will do this on the count of 'up.' You will hold this position until the count of 'down,' at which time you will lower yourself to this same position. This is called a press-up. UP!"

"But . . . but my arm! I—"

"GET THEM BOTH RIGID OR THEY'LL BE THE SAME FREAKING LENGTH!"

For only an instant, Radience hesitated; she had seen the Horsemen exercising thus, but she had never done it herself.

Something blunt and heavy slammed into the deck next to the girl's face, startling a scream out of her. She was afraid to turn her head, to look, but from the corner of her eye, she saw it was Jiana's iron-banded boot. How close did Jiana come to splitting the timbers of the deck? Radience pushed the thought from her mind quickly.

Panicked, she pressed to the up position, and tried to hold it, teetering off-balance because of her short left arm.

"You are a piece of shit," Jiana whispered, her lips pressed against Radience's ear. "You are nothing. You are a pig, useless to yourself, useless to me. You are a slave. How many seconds did I say you had to get on deck?"

Radience tried to speak, but all that emerged from her throat was a frightened squawk.

"OPEN YOUR FUCKING THROAT AND SPIT IT OUT!" screamed the warrior, deafening the girl.

"EIGHT!" she responded, nearly as loud.

"How long did you take to get out here?"

Radience's arms were shaking uncontrollably now, and her middle sagged all the way to the deck. Her crippled arm caused her to be at a slant, which made her good arm ache.

"I don't—I don't—I didn't—"

"IT TOOK YOU AT LEAST FORTY SECONDS! LOOK!" Jiana shoved something in Radience's face. It was a time-piece, one that had a moving hand for the seconds. It had to have been the priest's; what would a warrior need with the time of day?

"What's forty minus eight?" Jiana demanded.

"Th-th-thirty-two!"

"Down, up."

Startled, Radience allowed herself to fall heavily to the deck. Then, she forced herself back up again by sheer willpower, crying. She barely made it.

"Oh fuck. I've lost count already. Too bad you weren't keeping track for me. You can quit any time you want. Down, up."

Radience fell to the deck, bruising her breasts. She pushed herself grimly upward again, relying entirely on her right arm.

"One!" she gasped.

"My name is ma'am. You will either begin or end every statement you make with that name. You will not do both; I will NOT tolerate a ma'am-sandwich. Come on, just say the two simple words 'I' and 'quit,' and I'll never bother you again. Down, up."

"Two! Two, ma'am!"

"Down, up. Down, up. Down, up. Use both arms, you aren't an amputee."

How she managed to continue, Radience could not say. She had no more tears; now it was sweat that ran down her nose to drip onto the deck. She gasped for breath.

"Fha . . . five . . . Ma'am. . . ."

"Down. Half-way up."

Incredulous, Radience complied as best as she could, desperately trying to hold a position half-way up from the deck. Her left arm was nearly rigid, and she found herself leaning on it, for a change.

"You understand the significance? I told you eight seconds, you decided forty was good enough. Now you will do one press-up for every second you *stole* from me. Do you understand?"

"Y-yes, ma'am," she gasped.

"Have you lost count yet?"

"No, ma'am!"

"Ready to drop the whole thing?"

"No, ma'am."

Once again, the crazy lady shoved her mouth right on top of Radience's ear. But this time, she whispered so gently that the girl almost dropped to the deck.

"It's easy. It's so easy. Just say 'I quit.' Say it once, I'll hear you no matter how quiet you are. Won't fuck with you again, not even a second longer. One problem—you can *never, never* take it back. Say it. Please, say it."

Radience said nothing. She gritted her teeth, trying to keep her back from humping like a *jamal*, trying to keep her breath steady and smooth—for she *had* been taught, taught by the best. She thought.

"Down, up. Down up down up down up down up down up down up down up . . ."

Twice, the girl collapsed on the deck. Each time, Jiana put her mouth against Radience's face and screamed her up again. At last, the girl whimpered a weak "thirty-two," and fell to the deck like a dead body.

"On your feet MOVE."

I have no energy. I can't move. I'm dead. I can't do this. She's a monster!

But miraculously, Radience was on her feet, dizzy and seeing flashes of white crawling across her field of vision, but upright.

"Now we can start our exercises," declared Jiana, "unless you'd like to go back to being Radience again. I'll put you off at a good town. I'll give you some food, and one of these maps. Your curly locks will grow back and you can do whatever the fuck you want with them, I'll never know."

Radience stood, listing to one side like a badly loaded barge on the Jambajala.

"Straighten up that spine keep your heels together toes turned outward forty-five degrees DON'T EYEBALL ME BITCH, keep your gaze on a spot about ten feet behind my head you call that a fucking forty-five degree angle? Do you?"

"I—"

"On your face."

Radience lowered herself to her knees. Somehow, Jiana hooked her foot under the girl's legs and pulled them out from under her with one quick movement. Radience fell heavily onto her belly.

"On your face means ON—YOUR—FACE. Up down up down up down up down up down up." Jiana waited for the girl to catch up, ending on an upstroke.

"You are not an 'I.' You will not use first person. You will not use second person. I am not a 'you'; I am a ma'am, or if you need to get into my pantaloons I'm 'the field captain.' You don't ask me 'would you like to give me a fast kick in the ass . . .' you ask 'would the field captain like to give this initiate a fast kick.' Got that? Down up."

She went down. She went up.

"On your feet."

Radience stood weakly.

"Nope. On your face again."

This time Radience fell to the deck so hard she bruised her left hip; but Jiana did *not* have time to sweep her feet out.

"On your feet move."

Radience jumped up, but hesitated a moment before assuming the position Jiana had just taught her.

"Nope. On your face . . . on your feet MOVE."

A flash of senseless anger swept through the girl's body. *What right does this slave have to order me around like that? Shit shit shit you bitch I'll—* In her stomach, she flew up off the deck in a low dive, catching Jiana right in the midrift, pushing her back, back, sheer surprise countering the woman's remarkable fighting ability. Jiana staggered backwards, unable to regain her balance, and at last plunged over the side of the raft, into the wide river.

Could she swim? The girl did not know. But it was just a fancy. She had not really pushed the warrior across the raft and into the Jambajala.

Radience was standing rigidly in a good approximation of the posture Jiana had just taught her. She had no memory of having stood. One moment she was on her face, crying; without any intervening time span, she was on her feet, spine straight, heels together, toes at more or less of a forty-five degree angle, eyes straight ahead focused on a spot on the opposite shore—which was considerably farther than ten feet behind Jiana's head, but the idea was there.

Jiana looked her up and down, like a butcher eyeing a cow before converting it into steaks and roasts.

"This is the first position. You will always assume this position when you speak to me. You will now refer to yourself as a warrior initiate. You will eat breakfast four minutes from now by this time-piece."

The woman turned and walked into the hut, leaving Radience shaking but oddly exhilarated. Warrior Initiate! It was actually happening!

The first day was a month, the second a turn, and still no sword had been put into her hand. Jiana never drew hers, and they did not even try to buy any on their next excursion into town.

The town trip was utterly different from the first one they made, before Radience was a Warrior Initiate. This time she was carefully instructed how to walk, where to stand, how to respond when a villager queried her queer behavior. She felt a twinge of embarassment, standing in the first position while Jiana pawed through the stock of a dealer in manuscripts, looking for something about the transmutation of base metal into gold.

Radience wondered what stupidity that fat priest had put into the field captain's head, anyway. Nobody believed in that alchemical gibberish! Not even Ysmal, the stable boy! But perhaps it was warrior stuff, and she would learn all about it, when she was a warrior.

Radience and Toldo had poled the raft against a strong current that pulled them back toward the center of the river—the priest called it a "riptide." Jiana stood behind Radience, telling her everything as if she had never been trained in the court of the Caliph of Deh Bid.

In a way it was like being trained all over again. Yet something was different. The mere fact that she could actually quit anytime she wanted placed an enormous weight on her shoulders. Whenever she caught herself railing (to herself) at the field captain's unfairness, an instant, insistent voice would whisper into her stomach, "well if you *really* think it's unfair . . ."

In the bookseller's shop, Radience broke first position slightly to see the title of a book, to reassure herself that she could still read, that she *was* a person. But the title was written in a heathen tongue, and she could not decipher it.

She caught the field captain glaring at her, and she snapped back to first position, aware that she would pay later for her slip.

Three times the girl had almost done it, almost said the magic words. She approached the field captain diffidently, and timidly spoke, "would the field captain—"

Yet each time, something stopped her; another voice whispered, this time saying "go ahead, quit after two days! you *are* a slave and nothing more, face the truth!"

With that thought in her stomach, she could not possibly spit out the words "I quit." Each time she finished with a lame excuse, a silly request, a dumb question. She was rewarded with increasingly savage "ST," strength-training sessions.

Or . . . or was the title really in Tooltak, and had she forgotten her own tongue? Radience was too worried to check.

Meals were like a vacation in the underdwell. It was the same each time: "Ready . . . SIT. Nope, on your feet. Ready . . . SIT! On your feet. Ready . . ." When she was finally allowed to sit, allowed to place her plate in front of her, allowed to dish out her food, take up her knife, and eat, she was so upset and angry at her own incompetence that she had no appetite whatsoever. It seemed a miracle that she ravenously cleaned her plate every time.

Radience did nothing correctly. At first it was just the social status; it hurt her not to be able to call Jiana by her name, and even more that the warrior seemed to have utterly forgotten *hers,* calling her "raindunce" more often

than not. Worse, the girl was not even accorded the status
of being an "I," a person, an entity. Referring to herself in
the third person was exacting a toll; she thought of herself
less and less as a human being, let alone a free woman.

She had worked so hard to free herself. Now none of
that work meant a thing to her. Only a single thought held
importance anymore: it was *still possible* that she might
someday be a warrior. A real warrior, not just a girl with a
sword. The field captain did not actually say so in that
many words—but somehow . . .

First, her self-status, then, her volition, finally, rational-
ity itself faded. Radience could not talk. Radience could
not think. Everything she thought she knew was wrong.
Everything she had carefully learned was worthless.

The Warrior Initiate realized that she could *almost* see
the title of the nearest book without breaking position;
almost, but not quite. The temptation was maddening.

Her words invariably came out all wrong. The field
captain was not imagining it, even Radience herself could
hear that the sayings and strategies she was supposed to
have learned were all jumbled. But there were so many of
them! And the field captain could stop her at any moment and demand to know what was Stage 5 in Hooruki
Tongtadure's Eight Stages of Armed Resistance.

Her tongue was no longer hers; it seemed a living thing,
speaking nonsense and shuffled strategies and rules, with
each mistake earning her another chance to kiss the deck.
Then abruptly, all emotional cues were removed.

Was the field captain angry? *Really* angry? Or just acting angry? When the girl did something right, there was
no praise, not the slightest hint that the field captain was
even pleased . . . just an instant order to perform the
next task.

Radience was utterly confused; it did not help that
she noticed very un-Initiate-like feelings toward the
warrior . . . feelings that spilled over into her dreams.
Could the field captain peek into her thoughts? If she did,
would she do to the Initiate—to *Radience*—what the Overman of Tithes had done to his wife when he caught her
with her own dressing lady?

Again, for the hundredth or the thousandth time, a terrible feeling of dread seized the Initiate, fear for her actual life. The field captain insisted upon describing some of the training that would eventually be given to the girl, and Radience could barely believe that she would survive. A whole girl, maybe—but a cripple? The strength tests, the survival trip, the rope walk!

A horrible thought turned her stomach sour, a thought that would not go away, no matter how deeply the girl tried to bury it. She really knew very little about the field captain. *What if she were truly insane?* What if she *did not* know what she was doing? Would the field captain stand over the Initiate's limp, dead body, stunned at the tragic accident? Or perhaps she would simply shrug and say "she was just a slave, after all."

Radience stood in the bookseller's shop, first position held rigidly, smelling the musty, breathy odor of ancient manuscripts. The old woman behind the counter watched them all sharply, as if expecting a scroll or two to slip into someone's sleeve. The priest had two books opened at once and was comparing passages.

Only the field captain was animate, stalking from one end of the stall to the other, flipping through piles of manuscripts looking for something in particular. Looking to turn lead into gold.

She's insane, whispered the liar. *She's chucked it. She's dropped the arrows from her bow. Her moneybag has a hole in the bottom. You're a dead girl!*

But a stronger thought pushed the doubts back, kept the girl going, kept the two magic words from passing her lips.

There is still *a chance! No matter how often you fail, no matter how fucked and tucked you are, Initiate Radience, YOU HAVE A CHANCE.*

She stood at first position, silently practicing the list of the Nine Perfect Masters of the Sword.

For that brief, magical moment, a great feeling of peace pervaded her body. Everything felt *right*.

Then the field captain spoke.

"Enough fun for now. Tomorrow we rip your *spirit* apart."
She hissed like a shakersnake.

4

Toldo lay on his side, his face red and sweaty. His
breathing was too fast, ragged as a slave's dress. Radience
knelt quietly beside him and felt his forehead.

The field captain was on the other side of the raft,
reading her alchemical texts. She had already ministered
to Toldo as much as she was able, and told Radience that
the priest was caught within himself—a phrase the girl
did not understand.

What Radience did understand was that there was nothing either of them could do for him; he would either find
his way out, or not, by himself.

She felt for the pulse in his throat, first with her right
hand, then her left. Inexplicably, she could feel more with
her left hand than she could with her good hand. She had
made many surprising discoveries about her differently-
abled arm.

Radience stroked the priest's face gently with her left
hand; the tiny, undeveloped fingers could feel every vein,
every slight twitch of a muscle, the faintest fluctuation in
skin temperature. It was the hand of a baby, weak and
uncoordinated, but as sensitive as the antenna of a
catercrawler. Her "good" hand was a bear-claw by com-
parison.

*Good? Bad? How come I never noticed before? Always
too busy, always hopping to light the lanterns and lug
bowls of candied dates and mungberries. Bastards. Or
was it just me? Just different, not good and bad. Jiana—
the field captain never pays any attention to it; maybe
that's the path, each one does what it can do. . . .*

Toldo coughed and blinked. His eyes focused. He looked
across the placid river, towards the shore—full jungle
now, not a trace of desert sand.

Radience stroked his head with her small hand; she
could almost feel some kind of healing power flowing

through her arm and into his head. If such a power existed, Toldo did not seem to notice.

After a time, he sat up and turned towards Radience. He scowled for a moment, then recognition illuminated his face.

"Ah, Radience," he rumbled, his voice phlegmy and liquid.

"Are you back?"

Curious. The Initiate could almost hear actual emotion in the field captain's voice.

Toldo nodded his massive, bovine head, then coughed again.

"Did you find what you were looking for?"

"No. So close, though."

They sat in silence for a long time. Radience counted two hundred heartbeats, and she wished she could look at the field captain's *timepiece*.

(Be still. Hold the image steady, whispered the field captain. Radience knelt in the second position, dutifully visioning the orange.

It's orange, she thought, orange and lumpy, not quite a ball, bulging a little on one side . . .

The rap caught her unexpectedly behind her ear. She yelped, but did not open her eyes.

Wandering, said the field captain. Grudgingly, the Initiate admitted to herself that she had been; she had been thinking about the orange, not visioning it.

She began again, visioning the orange. . . .)

Almost half a moon had passed, Jambajala-wards. Not once had the field captain slipped, not once had she broken character. Radience was beginning to wonder whether she was dreaming that Jiana was a field captain, or had dreamed that the field captain was ever just Jiana.

"Do you think you will? Find it?"

Toldo hesitated a moment; he did not like to talk about his failed attempts, not even to the field captain.

"I, ah, well, I don't know. I thought I would, that is, before I began I was sure it would not be too hard to recreate the experience. But now I don't . . . wait—"

Toldo spoke the last word tersely. His face whitened; he stood and walked quickly, brushing right past Cascade.

The horse watched him, almost intelligently. Toldo breathed raggedly for a few moments. Then he calmed, as if by an act of will. He shuddered and returned, resuming his speech as if he had not stopped.

"I'm frightened, little one. I don't know if I can ever find it again."

"Aren't we going to the people who did it to you in the first place?"

"We are. But will they consent to show me how to do it again, or will they want to keep their secrets?"

Toldo began to pace; then he abruptly turned and entered the hut. Something in his tone had bothered Radience. He had left something unsaid. She looked at the field captain, then at the blackness into which Toldo had vanished.

"I want you on the deck in five," said the field captain. Radience stood immediately and followed the priest inside.

"Toldo," she asked, even before her eyes could pick him out in the dark, "what do you *really* hope?"

For a moment, his eyes widened perceptibly and his lips pursed; he looked just like the Caliph's Tokogare, stone-like, even. Then he recovered his aplomb, but he seemed shaken.

"I—don't know, Radience. That is the truth, and it's damning me to failure after failure. I just don't know whether I'm hoping to succeed or fail.

"I seem courageous, do I not? All-knowing, benevolent and wise, the very picture of the Seeker of Truth, and damn me if I'm not every bit as worm-eaten with doubt as that warrior over there! Who am I fooling? You? Me?

"It's . . . I don't . . . O piercing one, why do you ask questions like that? Why am I answering you? I would not answer *her*, and I have known Jiana for four and a half turns."

"Well, maybe because you *haven't* known me for four and a half turns."

He shook his head, rumbling deep in the back of his throat.

"You have something, Radience. When you shed your slavehood, you gained a power besides the power to say yes and no. I suspect anybody will do what I just did."

Radience sat back, tucking her arm inside her tunic.

"I'm not so sure I like that idea. Anybody? They'll just tell me anything . . . ?"

"Don't be silly. Of course not. They'll tell you what's *important*, as I just did."

"How do you know? Excuse me, but you aren't exactly noted as a seer or necromancer!"

Toldo chuckled; he was fully in possession of himself once again. The curtain was closed.

"One of the side-effects of union with the cosmos, my dear. At times I, as it were, simply *know things.* Use it sparingly. It's a far greater gift than fast hands with a sword."

"I'm worried myself. I wonder if I'm really cut out of the warrior's cloth."

"Then quit. I believe the young lady you call 'field captain' has made it quite simple for you to do so."

Radience shook her head.

"I can't do that! It's not the quitting part. *Jamalspit,* I'd drop this game in a heartbeat if I really knew it wasn't for me. But how can I quit when I *still don't know* whether I'll make it? I have to tough it out, at least for another day. Maybe another moon."

"Radience, the best favor you could do yourself is to follow Jiana's lead. She may hurt you; she may cripple you. But she won't kill you, and in the long run, she'll strengthen you. Stay with the ringmaster, for now. You'll know very soon . . . and don't ask me how I know *that,* either!"

As the days passed, as a week and another rolled by, Radience discovered she could actually vision the orange for longer and longer periods of time. The slaps grew less frequent, the field captain withdrew into the background.

One day, the Initiate discovered that she had actually visioned the orange into existence. The vision persisted, even when she opened her eyes. For the rest of the day, the orange hovered wherever she looked, though always in the corner of her eye; it vanished if she looked directly at it.

Though she was quite frightened, she said nothing to the field captain. But the fear must have shown in her face, because Jiana led her in a body-calming exercise six times that day.

The warrior builds her own universe, said the field captain. And again: fear is failure, and brings failure upon.

Jiana stood next to Cascade, stroking his black nose. She watched the hut, hearing the priest's rumbling chuckle.

Must have just caught on to her power, she thought. It was a queer ability for the girl to develop; raised as a slave since she was a toddler, little more than a horse that could take orders. How could she have developed such a Wolf Power?

Jealous? asked Jianabel, snide as always.

Perhaps. But as usual, you cut the gem to expose the ugliest facet. Maybe I'm just worried that she'll have as hard a time controlling her "Jianabel" as I did controlling you.

You were the one who tried to kill me, dearest . . . or don't you remember?

Jiana smiled; much as she tried to hide them, the Wolfish Queen could not help baring her teeth, filed to a point.

How could I kill you? I only kill the innocent, remember? Anyway, you're not even a part of me.

I'm not even a part of this sphere, Jiana.

What? You're not?

The small human girl and the fat human man sat at one end of the raft, conversing in primitive grunts. The master human spied on them, arguing with a strange entity poking into this sphere from somewhere beyond.

She also rubbed her appendage against Cascade's nose, producing a pleasant sensation.

Cascade watched both scenes, one with each eye. He

was losing interest in eating the little human, now that the master human was teaching her to walk. But the fat one still posed a threat.

It got out of its cage once; it touched souls with the entire sphere, and with Cascade, too. Cascade did not like that; it was as dangerous as torches in a hayloft.

Once again, Cascade carefully peeled open the man's scalp, his cranium, his brain. The structure was very different than what Cascade was used to dissecting, but it was easy to trace a path. The thought structure that contained the key to *breaking out* was black, but it was surrounded by hot, white near misses. Surely an intelligent being would have remembered it by now!

Wanderings. Cascade narrowed his concentration, and rewrote one of the pathways, subtlely crossing it with another that ventured too near.

Humans were easy to confuse; they seldom analyzed their own brain function, and had no idea how to correct a cross-circuit even it they discovered one.

Cascade sensed perturbation, and pulled out of the fat one's mind too quickly to be detected. It was done.

Perhaps that would keep the animals as animals for a few more days. Foals who had just discovered "cosmic union" were more irritating than a stickthistle in the hoof.

The Initiate began to calm down. She found that even the physical part of her training proceeded more smoothly, the more she practiced visioning.

After a while, the field captain had her vision a glove, a horse, a castle . . . then a circle, a line, and finally a dimensionless point. Eventually, the field captain ordered her to vision Nothingness.

After her first attempt at that last exercise, Initiate Radience was so shaken that for the first time since the third day of training, she nearly spoke the magic mantra.

She had been successful; she had visioned Nothingness perfectly and terrified herself.

She struggled to hold down the words. Kneeling in second position, her face grave, she visioned it again and again, until finally it, too, lost its fear-hold over her stomach.

Fear is failure, she repeated to herself, and brings failure upon. . . .

5

Jiana clamped her teeth together as she carefully poured the Puff-Semen pollen from the envelope into the crucible, where it vanished at the surface of the bubbling, amber liquid. Her lip was swollen where she had bitten it three times so far, concentrating on the mixture.

If she poured the pollen too slowly, the mixture would be virtually inert. If she poured too quickly, the mixture was explosive. And she was shaking so violently from another horrific day as "field captain" that she might miss the crucible entirely and spill her seed on the deck.

Toldo was already beginning to hallucinate vividly from the *guurd* root, but enough of his mind remained yet that Jiana risked a question.

"Toldo—I haven't slept for four days. I'm terrified of this horrible dream I have, every night it seems."

"Dreams are the stuff that dreams are the stuff that dreams. What dreams? Dreams of fame and fourteen? Drams of fountain?"

"Here, it's ready. I dream of the ice, falling through the ice. No, wait . . . not me, it's my—my friend who falls through the ice. I want to bring her back to life, but . . ." Jiana shivered, unable to continue describing the horror of the Touch of Life, of eating meat and feeling it come alive and begin to squirm as it slides down her throat.

"So how do you know in a sense, as it were, that it was he he he who sent them you, I mean to you since you cannot remember? How does he send them? What is the physical mode of conveyance?"

Toldo suddenly propelled himself forward, causing the entire raft, enormous as it was, to shift slightly. Jiana heard Radience swear angrily, outside the hut on deck. The girl was on guard duty this night.

Toldo stared in horror at a spot on the floor. It was roughly circular, a discolored spot in the wood, and the priest's eyes were bolted to that spot as though it were dissolving even as they spoke, leaving nothing but a water-spout inside the hut.

Jiana blinked. The image had come suddenly into her stomach, as clear as the night sky: the funny spot in the wood rotting and dripping into the river, a great geyser of water pouring up through the hole.

Of course, it was absurd; the point of a raft is that it is lighter than water. Even with a hole cut in the bottom, the raft would not sink, and therefore no water would spray into the hut.

"Toldo," she asked, her eyes shifting into and out of focus, "what were you just thinking of, as you stared at that spot on the floor?"

"I saw it grow, grow into a father one, two, tree right there in our hoot."

At once Jiana felt very, very tired, but still, she did not dare sleep . . . not until she finished her *second* project for the night: a powder to make her sleep until midday without a single dream.

She heated the crucible over a candle-flame until the color changed, then she handed the tongs to the priest. At first he did not even see them, then he blinked back to Reality Prime and chugged down the third and final ingredient.

Jiana did not care whether it worked or not. The lack of sleep made her long for only one thing: a long, snake-like, dreamless sleep of the dead. She put away the alchemical text and unrolled the simple *Pharmacopia* of Tondo Tsunda. Her eyes and temples ached.

Toldo was quiet and placid. *I never liked alchemy,* Jiana thought, *not even back in the Flower Empire, though it was a nice break from stomach-numbing sword and spear practice. Maybe it's time, now that I think of it, time for Radience to . . .*

She held her breath as she ground the blue *sulka* crystals in the mortar; their odor was noxious enough to gag even her.

She looked up through the smoke hole. The less-moon was beginning to wax again. Soon they would have been on the Jambajala for a moon and a half.

The world slid past; they must have crossed into Door by now. There was no way to tell, however; the townies on the shore had no idea where the two distant kingdoms chose to draw the imaginary boundary line (nor did they care).

At least that fat priest isn't yowling, like last time. In fact, Toldo had been deathly quiet for some time. Jiana glanced over at him.

His face was ashen white, completely drained of blood; his eyes were open and unblinding. His mouth was open a crack, caught in a frozen half-smile.

Jiana stared, and the pestle dropped from her hand. Dreading what she might not feel, she slowly reached her hand over his motionless chest and laid her fingers across the right side of his great, bull neck.

Jiana felt no pulse at first, and her throat constricted as if she had swallowed poison. She closed her eyes, and forced herself to breathe slowly, rythmically, stilling her heart; her own pulse was pounding so hard it would obscure any faint pressure in Toldo's neck.

The first beat she discounted; she was keyed up for it, and could have visioned it. But the second beat was sure: weak and sporadic, but certain.

Toldo was alive—scarcely. Slowly, Jiana slid across the floor and put her ear against his mouth. She held herself thus, perfectly still, and lowered the focus of her hearing. Finally, she could hear the faint intake of air into his lungs. Alive he was, but spiritless.

"Tooqa, what have you done? Toldo! Damn you, come back here!" She raised her hand to strike his face, snap him out of his coma; but Jianabel stopped her.

No! Don't strike him—you'll kill him in that condition.
What do I do? What do I do? What's happened to him?
Sister, he is fled . . . or taken.

Again, Jiana's throat constricted, and this time her stomach began to burn as well.

But what can I do?

I don't know. Jiana, there may be nothing you can do.

Jiana sat back and looked at the priest. It was so quick, so unexpected. *Did I kill him?* she wondered.

You mixed the potions.

He told me to!

You mixed them.

Jiana pulled her knees up and wrapped her arms around them. Outside, the girl's feet crunched up and down on the deck. She no longer "walked silently with utmost humility," now Jiana and everyone else could hear her coming a league away.

I'll have to train her out of that.

You trained her into it. You told her to stop skulking like a slave and walk like a warrior.

Jiana stood, struggling for control.

"Fuck a snake, Toldo—I will *not* take the blame for your stupid death! I will *not* take the blame for this one. INITI-ATE!" she called, "fall in!"

Jiana barely had time to finish the order before the girl pushed into the hut. Her eyes flickered briefly to Toldo's body. For an instant, horror passed across the girl's face, then she took command again, and her features became rigid and immobile, along with the rest of her body, as she stood at the first position.

I'm still in shock, Jiana thought, for she felt no grief for Toldo—only pride that Radience did not break position, even in the presence of what seemed like the corpse of her friend.

"As you can see, Toldo has . . ." Jiana paused, and took another breath; her heart was beating wildly again. ". . . miscalculated. He is not dead; his pulse is faint, but detectable."

Radience did not break position, but there was a slight relaxation in relief.

"His spirit has been taken."

Again Radience tensed, this time moving slightly, but Jiana decided this was not the time for correction.

"I must go on a journey, Initiate. Into Toldo's dream

sphere. I might be able to find him and bring him back. I've done it before."

I did it for you once, Dida. Do you even remember now? Or are you so set in your swaggering ways that you can't remember the little boy who was lost under a million tons of mountain?

Something was wrong, something in the hut. Jiana looked at the floor. Waves were rolling outward from Toldo's body—waves in the solid wood like ripples from a stone dropped in the river. Jiana could see them, but she could not feel them, either with her feet or with her balance.

Radience noticed them, too; she broke position and stared down at the floor. Jiana saw the terror spread across her face, but only for a moment, then, the girl reasserted her will.

"*You are at first position, Initiate.*" Radience snapped her head up again.

"While I am gone, I will be as vulnerable as Toldo there. Do you understand me?"

"Yes, ma'am!"

"It is possible the priest has merely gotten lost. But let's not delude ourselves: he might have been stolen, too. If so, whoever stole him *won't want to give him back*—and may decide to fight.

"Initiate Radience, you will have to stand guard over us both, Toldo and me." Jiana stepped forward, her voice surprisingly soft. Instruction had ended for the moment.

"You must be clear about this. Until this emergency ends, we are not field captain and initiate; we are warriors, comrades at arms. Get out of first position and listen to me."

Radience relaxed and stood attentively. Gone was the submissiveness of her slave days, and gone was the rigid discipline of "the Initiate." Her eyes were determined, but calm; her lip did not tremble, and she did not stuff her arm inside her shirt.

It's the Warrior Heart, Jiana marveled, astonished as always to see the higher soul take charge from the Fool Killer.

"Draw your knife. Sit between us. Your vigil may be uneventful—but I don't like the look of those ripples. This thing may extend itself into this hut, and you must be ready."

"The Initiate will fight with honor," Radience swore, her voice hoarse. "If she must, she'll die for the fi—for you."

Jiana ignored the breech of protocol.

"I'd rather you *lived* for me, since you'll be guarding my body. Don't yield to fear. Radience, the fear of death is the beginning of slavery, and you are not a slave. You are not an animal. You are free, and you can freely choose to ignore your fear."

"Field Captain, how does . . . how do I fight this thing, if it comes?"

"With courage. Without cringing. Beyond that, I don't have a clue. Can you do it?"

Radience nodded solemnly, and drew her knife.

"I'll guard you both."

She settled down cross-legged between Jiana and Toldo, looking so serious that Jiana almost laughed. She stopped herself; the girl would not have understood.

Jiana laid down, folded her arms across her belly, and began building up her magical reservoir.

She stretched forth her consciousness, concentrating on her sense of balance; she felt Reality Prime shift slightly. Was it the Great Serpentine stirring? Had she made contact? Had he come back? But no, the balance was all wrong. Jiana did not know who made the earth shake, but it was no one who liked her.

The warrior brought vision into her expanded self, and found the spot where Toldo's body lay.

There was no soul-light whatsoever. Toldo was an empty vessel.

Oh, gods, she thought, and pushed her spirit towards his empty stomach, hoping to find a sepulchral finger pointing the way into the bowels of hell, towards whatever nameless Thing had stolen Toldo's soul, and now shook the earth.

Chapter VIII:

Within the pale, feathers fall like snow the square is circled.

Jiana breathed ritually, in-hold-out, pushing her consciousness outward. She let a song roll around and around her stomach, beating in time to her breath; her stomach tightened, and the queasy, fright-feeling of magic exploded through her:

> *Toll, toll the bell, pound it well,*
> *Sound the round sonorious bowl, toll,*
> *Toldo mold abode-o, no!*

Jiana melted into a round pool of warm blood, bones, and fluid, waves lapping at the great, white cliffs of the priest's rock-like slab of flesh. It was not solid but porous like chalk. Jiana seeped under the skin, into Toldo's stomach, seeking a trace of her friend.

Jiana awoke into herself. She saw a vast cathedral, the ceiling arching so far above her eyes that it was lost in the haze of distance. She pressed to her knees, breathing raggedly, and stared across the echoing room at an enormous Eagle altar, before which stood a shouting man.

He raved about the House Alanai, the all-seeing Eagle, and the sacred beak. No one heard except a pair of pigeons, who flapped noisily from one arch to another.

253

"—mad lust of a bloodline," argued the voice, "and such brigands and thieves present no statistics to back their claims, leading one to the inescapable concubine that these conclusions are, um, wild-eyed fanaticisms, half-trolls, and utterly without swifty and jam. And do they dispute? Fog, I say! Fog and rooster eggs! As it were . . ."

"I hope I'm not interrupting," Jiana said, before the man could launch into another lament. "I'm looking for Toldo Mondo."

"Foolish woman, I am he whom you seek."

"You're Toldo? I don't think so."

"Of course I am! Whiff this fiery smell! A brand for justice, that is what I am, so to speak! A flame for freedom! Smell the sulfurous stench of miscreants, roasting like hoosenuts in a vat of coals."

The preacher did resemble Toldo, in features and manners. He was round, clean-shaven, and wore a great, white robe. His voice roared like a wild bull.

"No," she said, "I think he left you behind a long time ago; years back, back when he thought he could save the world by preaching the word, when he first heard the call.

"But perhaps you can point the way he's gone, for it's *awfully* important that I find him again."

"Important? You are not important, and I have no time for your seekings. Be off with you, woman!"

Jiana drew back, raising her eyebrows in surprise. Had Toldo really been so intolerant in his youth?

The ersatz Toldo Mondo rotated ponderously, and rolled up the aisle of the empty church like a hoopsnake, shaking the floor like an *elphas*. Jiana turned her back on his retreating bulk and exited onto the crystal street.

The sun was low, judging from the long, red light, but she could not see it, no matter which way she turned. There were numerous buildings, silent and deserted.

So where the hell are you, priest? Which way should I go?

The street was made of millions of tiny crystals, like the sand at Kgung Tuo Beach, rough as a Toolian's beard.

Still crouching, she closed her eyes and sniffed. A faint, sour smell prickled in her nostrils. She recognized it, but could not bring an image forward in her stomach. It was probably some animalistic emotion flooding Toldo's empty body—fear, or sadness.

Water was falling; far ahead, she faintly heard it plop sullenly into a pool. Jiana followed the sound, having nowhere else to go.

The dead buildings absorbed all sound, and she ghosted like a multi-colored shadow between hulking, stone ware-houses and neat, identical mud-brick houses.

The architecture showed no creativity or adventurous-ness, just utilitarian boxiness, muted browns and pastel blues and greens. They were colors of the "higher spiritual values," yet weak and washed out.

Toldo's city was round, with roads like spokes from the cathedral at the hub. Jiana walked outward towards the water sound.

Streets grew narrower, buildings shorter and broken. She hiked through empty fields and vacant lots, stepping around unfilled holes in the crystalline street. Without the buildings to catch sound, her feet crunched in the grainy pieces of street.

At last she passed the last rim of houses and faced a sward of dead grass and sand. At the horizon was a faint, dark green line that could be the tree-line along a river.

The village was already fading, a half-remembered half-promise on the morrow. She continued, aimed for the trees.

As Jiana walked, eyes fixed firmly on the horizon, she tripped across something big and suspiciously square.

Cursing, she sat up, rubbing her shin. The culprit was a great, cubical rock of granite. Its surfaces were covered with chisel marks.

She kicked it hard, and was rewarded by a painfully throbbing heel in her right foot. But her kick turned the stone slightly, and she could see words carved into one face:

I Am Not Perfectly Square

"What a peculiar thing for a stone to declare," Jiana dreamed. She looked close and saw it did not lie; one face was slightly bigger than its opposite, barely enough to notice unless looking for it.

"It's a shame they rejected you," she added, still rubbing away the bruise on her shin. "There's something rather beautiful about you; maybe striking is a better word. I wouldn't mind putting you into a house or a temple myself."

Great, Jiana! Talking to a stone! In a dream!

Shaking her head and chuckling, she flexed her leg a few times and continued towards the tree-line. Somebody else's dream, to boot!

The trees approached much faster than they had a right to; every stride brought her ten strides closer. Soon she was close enough to see that the trees were unlike any she had ever seen before. They were tall and green as trees, but their trunks were made of flesh with coarse hairs growing out of them. They pulsed and shimmied with a regular bloodbeat.

High above her head, the first "leaves" began; they were actually stiff, green tongues. Tongue-piles littered the ground beneath the branches.

She wove her way through flesh-trees and tongue-piles, trying not to touch either one. They grew so dense near the river that she had to squeeze bodily through; it reminded her of trying to reach the bar at one of Dilai's parties.

Dilai! Where are you, Lord of the Scented Bedchamber? Jiana buried the thought under eaves and *crokuses*.

She burst through the last pair of trunks and almost fell in the dark river. The grey-brown stream was thick and clotted, pushing reluctantly between the sharp banks. Jiana recognized it immediately, both from sight and smell. She had smelled it every day for forty nights now: the Nag Deh Jambajala, dead and putrid.

The Jambajala flowed south; far downstream, Jiana remembered, was Jatjaka of the Hoor-Gundu, who first introduced Toldo to the abyss of hallucinations.

If anyone could find the priest, it would have to be the witch-man . . . which meant Jiana would have to find *him*.

At her feet waited a tiny skiff, half drawn up the bank.

2

Radience stood over the bodies as the raft gently pitched and yawed. She nervously paced, telling herself she was marching like a sentry.

The goose had flown; her stoppered bottle lay in repose, hands over face in the death-posture. Or was she truly dead?

For the third time, Radience bent and checked Jiana's pulse at the neck, as she had been taught. The body lived, but so had the body of Rant al'Quurn. It had lived for three moons without spirit before finally admitting death.

The raft lurched unexpectedly, and Radience stumbled to her knees. She rose and bolted out the door. The Jambajala flowed faster, white rapids and foamy threads glittering in the moonlight. The raft spun and dropped, throwing Radience to the deck again.

Cascade seemed to notice nothing unusual. He stood like a statue, unconcerned. Radience lay full-length against the planks, however, gripping the wood to keep from washing overboard.

The river roared; a deep, ominous roar that warned of approaching doom. She saw an edge; the mist cleared, and Radience froze at the sight of a huge fold in the Jambajala, grandfather of all waterfalls.

God punishes us for what we did at Deh Bid! she thought wildly. Entranced, Radience watched as the raft touched the lip of the fall, rotated gently over the edge, and tumbled into space.

She squeezed her eyes shut, waiting for the weightless moment, the wind, the smashing. Agony, or just an instant? She waited and waited, and after a moment opened her eyes.

The raft was not falling; it floated on a new river, just like the Jambajala but over the world's edge. Radience looked back and saw the fold: water rushed *up* from the real Jambajala and flopped over the edge into the new current. The moons crept visibly across the sky in the edgeworld.

She was not yet out of danger. Ahead, the edgeworld Jambajala was full of monstrous whirlpools that glowed hellish green. One spun directly in the raft's path.

Radience leapt towards the tiller. The raft had spun around backwards; she dipped the steering oar in the water and pushed it hard to port.

The great, wooden vessel rotated ponderously. Radience stared as they drifted closer and closer to the spout.

We're not going to clear, she thought, as the raft lurched and groaned, *Sorry, field captain, I really did try. . . .*

They fell into the spinning vortex, round and round, until Radience was so dizzy she could do nothing but grip the steering oar for life. Her last sight was the green-glowing water swallowing the racing moons.

Radience blinked uncomprehending. Then she leapt upright, clutching wildly for support.

The raft rolled slowly with her motion; after a moment, she realized it teetered precariously on a gigantic, needle-like spike that rose from perfectly dry ground.

The less moon was startlingly full; in the glare she saw that the raft balanced a hundred man-heights in the air, supported by a pinnacle of rock. She lay still against the gaping door of the hut, afraid to move lest the raft tumble to the white rocks below, killing them all.

She gingerly turned her head and looked inside the hut. The racing moons cast flickering images against the far wall. Cautiously, Radience slid towards Jiana's body. The deck tilted alarmingly, and she froze.

Radience stared again at the blotch of moonlight. It shimmied, formed into a face—Teenja's face, grimacing in pain and torment.

The head floated in the air, its face not as Radience remembered from three soft, stolen nights in the kitchen khayma, but as it looked *after* Giathudin had . . .

Why did you not you protect me? the apparition demanded silently. Radience turned away, breath caught in her throat, but the specter persisted at the edge of her vision. Then the girl felt Teenja's *breath*.

Radience stared not just at Teenja's face, but her entire body now—torn and water-logged, exactly as it looked when they drew it from the well. Behind, the Less Moon crossed the window, having waned to a sliver.

Teenja opened her mouth; as her lips parted, a stream of sandy water expelled from a throat long dead, eaten away by worms and diggers.

"Infinite God!" cried Radience, arms and legs losing all strength, "sinners we are, but where is Your mercy?"

Teenja reached forth white arms, one of which (the left arm) hung broken and limp from the elbow. Perhaps Teenja herself broke it as she threw herself down the well. She puckered her lips around broken teeth, begging a kiss. The raft barely rippled under the apparition.

Teenja groped with nerveless hands for her robes, sewn out of a winding sheet. Grinning with mindless excitement, she pulled the gown apart. Her breasts were white and pulpy, nipples black as coal-beetles. A smell of putrefaction gagged Radience and nearly overwhelmed her.

You've got to move, thought the girl, frantic, *just get up and MOVE!* But how, without plunging the raft from its unstable eyrie?

Teenja's jaw stretched impossibly wide, reminding Radience of a horrible sight she had seen as a child: one toad swallowing another of equal size, looking like a mutant toad with two sets of hind legs attached together, rolling and squirming along the ground.

A tiny voice spoke up from deep in her stomach. *It's not real, girl! It's an apparition, a visitation. . . . You're under attack—defend yourself and Jiana!*

"Damn you, Teenja, we buried you!" Radience felt warm love flowing through her, strong as the terror but completely different. The girl she had loved would never terrify her like this. It was a *daeva.* Radience turned her eyes away, blinking away the tears, afraid no longer.

Radience stood angrily, uncaring about the tilting raft. She slid towards the field captain as the raft skewed.

The *daeva* gnashed its teeth and dropped its mask. A

moist, yellow ghoul clutched at the girl now, knocking her
off balance.

Jiana's horse whinnied outside; Radience pinwheeled
her arms and cried out, "Cascade! For the love of God and
your master, balance me!"

After a clatter of hooves, the raft righted. Snarling like
a *daeva* herself, Radience advanced upon the Teenja demon.

The ghoul would not face her. Instead, it angrily stamped
its foot on the deck, splitting timbers with a groan. The
creature fell out the bottom of the raft, and the planks
slammed closed like a door.

Radience stared at the deck, feeling the loss of Teenja as
if for the first time, but unwilling to cry. *Still so jagged
and raw,* she thought bitterly.

3

The skiff was too small for Jiana to sit comfortably; it
balanced well, however, and she found she could kneel in
the center and pole her way into the current.

The Jambajala flowed sluggishly, thick with mud and
clotted with flotsam: matted, woven grass, gnarled, sallow
knuckles reaching up to clutch her pole and grope the tiny
boat.

Ahead she heard a white roar, faint at first. Jiana could
taste the sour smell of the Jambajala with every breath.
The sun shone red, but did not warm. Jiana cast a long,
orange shadow, and the Jambajala picked up red sparkles
that danced and mocked her.

The current picked up; the skiff began to bob. Jiana
used the pole to keep her balance, crouching low and
catching the sudden rolls with knees and hips. *Is the boat
growing larger?* she thought absurdly.

A fish jumped, and the warrior turned, startled. "A fish
in the Jambajala? This far south?"

It was bloated and misshapen, like a corpse left too long
in the ocean. It splashed and circled the skiff, eyeing
Jiana. Its mouth worked and intelligible words bubbled
out.

"Who—seek?"

Jiana arched her eyebrow. "An ambiguous question, to say the least. Do you mean by that, who do I seek? Or do you ask who seeks me?"

The fish swam lethargically, eyeing her with bulbous, unblinking orbs.

"I seek a witch-man called Jatjaka," Jiana continued, "of the Hoor-Gundu. He lives down this sluggish stream, but there's no way in six hells I'm going to get there at this rate."

The fish rotated onto its back its belly looking even more corpselike than the rest.

"I'm *not* climbing aboard you," Jiana declared, nervously.

"Throw line," it bubbled, mouth half submerged.

Jiana reached back and skinned her knuckles on a coiled rope; she lashed one end to the bow-ring, tied the other end into a field-noose, which she threw overboard.

The monster caught the loop in its mouth, clamping teeth like broken glass around the rope. It dived and began to swim.

The skiff picked up speed, and Jiana was thrown to the deck. She held onto the sides and stayed low as the scenery rushed past.

Trees grew dense and crept closer to the Jambajala; dangling creepers grasped at Jiana with suckers on their leaves. Soon, the river widened into marshland, algae-grown ponds, and backwaters.

She passed another Toldo Mondo on a rock, fishing. She flew by so fast, too fast! But he was young, innocent, and frightened by the howls of the beast. *Toldo in seminary school?* she wondered, *Toldo cutting class?* He was gone, far behind.

Not the Toldo she sought; Jiana let the fish pull her away without regrets. She cared nothing for this Toldo.

The river narrowed; the boat buffeted wildly. Jiana gritted her teeth against the queasiness.

Looming closer with a frightening speed was a great, unbroken cliff, into which the Nag Deh Jambajala disappeared. The fish showed no sign of slowing; if anything, he accelerated, and Jiana had to grip the sides with all her strength to avoid being blown overboard into the diseased river by the force of their wind.

As they closed, Jiana saw a black spot where the river touched the rock. It was an opening, ludicrously small. *How does all this bloody* water *get through?* she thought abstractly, afraid to picture what would happen to *her* when the ship struck the rock walls at such a speed.

The water roared and picked up speed. The crash of the current deafened Jiana, and she lost all sense of balance. She lay back in the boat as the world reeled and tilted wildly. Faintly, she imagined a horse whinnying.

She saw only flashes: rusty oar-lock, her own leg. Jiana resigned herself to death, closing her eyes and crossing both arms over her face. Her last thought was of Radience, riding a flaming horse and striking a mortal blow against a toad with no head.

The world boomed with the sound of splintering wood; all was blackness.

She woke still in the skiff, floating so placidly she thought it all had been a dream. But when she sat up, the little boat rocked. The fish pulled her slowly across a still lake, under a glittery sky.

The tunnel opening had been just barely wide enough to allow the skiff to scrape past; the oars and rudder were sheared off. She was in a cavern, cool and sterile. The only light came from the river itself, where floating fungus gave off a faint, greyish glow.

Jiana struggled up to a kneeling position and pried her fingers loose from the wooden sides of the skiff. Her eyes adjusted to the light, and she could make out the rocky walls, far in the distance.

She shivered with trepidation. *Who knows what lies in the stomach of that bloody priest? What next, death by ant-hilling?*

The Jambajala flowed under the continent like rainwater, seeped into the ground beneath the fields. *Where am I?* she wondered. *How many moons have passed? Is*

*Radience grown and gone, or still standing guard, hair
grown white and long, skin like wrinklefruit?*

She heard the sounds and burbles of the understream: a
splash as the underground stream squirmed through rock
ribs to wash against tiny cliffs, the *pak pak pak* of the fish
as it pulled her along the narrow tunnel, its leathery tail
slapping the water.

Unexpectedly, they rounded a curve and burst into
glorious light from uncountable blazing jewels and crystals. Light from another full moon filtered from the outside, and the crystals threw it about the chamber. *Why do
the moons wax and wane so?* she wondered.

The fish slowed and dropped the line. The skiff drifted
to a halt, and the warrior found herself becalmed in the
center of a gigantic, undergound lake whose sky was a
glittery sphere of facets.

The silence beat at Jiana's ears like hands slapped on
either side of her head. A triangular lump sat unmoving on
the far shore, the size and shape of a man. Jiana felt the
probe of an opened eye, studying her.

She reached for the stern oar before remembering that
it was sheared off in the collision with the tunnel mouth.
She rummaged with both hands and found a splintered
piece of wood, probably part of an oar-lock. It was clumsy,
but Jiana rowed towards the immobile lump.

It was a man, naked save for a loincloth. His long, wild
hair was white, his skin polished bone. He watched as she
scraped bottom, and pulled the boat up on shore.

Before she could thank her fish, it sank like a stone in
the water; she shrugged and turned back to the old man.

"Old man, I'm looking for someone. Big, fat priest of
the Eagle. Name's Toldo Mondo. If you are who I think
you are, you know him well."

"I know him," replied the old man. His cold voice
tightened her stomach.

"I need to find him."

"I can find him!"

Jiana decided to step cautiously, until she knew what

price would be required for the knowledge. "What do you require, in exchange for telling me how to find Toldo?"

Jatjaka opened his eyes quickly, and Jiana jumped. She had been under the strong impression that he had watched her from the moment the fish dragged her into the lake.

"I *know* you," he declared, baring his teeth, black against the white of his skin. "I know, yes yes! You hold powerful magic in your breath to smite my enemies, yes yes! Make them fall to the ground with fits and staggers!"

Off the deep end, Jiana thought. *Life hangs on a madman's whim!*

"Don't demand too much, little man. You'll piss me off."

"No no!" he cried, unhooking his legs and leaping to his feet. In Toldo's dream, he was astonishingly spry for a man of his evident age.

"No less! Yes, yes, give what I ask and I give what you seek, the whena-whereabouts of your priest! You must protect this one and guard him from attack, for all the rest of your days. My enemies impotent, their darts and spears to roll off like spittle! This I want, yes yes!"

"Ask not, I say again," Jiana cautioned, dropping her voice, "the getting isn't as good as the wanting."

Jatjaka stood to his tallest, still a head shorter than Jiana, and drew one leg up like a *tauni* bird. "That is my bargain," he declared with finality.

"Three times you asked. The deal is done. I'll secure you from these great enemies of yours, for the rest of my days."

"Your word?" Jatjaka asked, eagerly.

"Yes."

"Then I shall keep mine, and show you how to find your fat, pale priest, yes. Come."

Jatjaka lowered his leg and turned in one fluid motion. He set off at a rapid pace into the darkness.

"You promise too much, sister!" hissed a voice in Jiana's ear. The warrior turned quickly, but no one was there; only then did she recognize the speaker.

"So you're no longer content speaking through my stomach?"

"Silly! In here, *I'm as real as you* . . . Jiana dear." Jiana felt the Wolfish Queen smile nastily. "Don't fret; leave the old man to me when time comes to pay your debt."

Darkness enveloped Jiana as she followed the witchman. She looked back once: a pair of eyes watched mournfully from the lake. Then the fish sank into the ice-black waters again and disappeared.

4

Radience balanced gingerly over the field captain's body. There was something in the girl's hand, her small hand. She looked down and was startled to see her left fingers curled around the knife the field captain had given her.

My arm's grown considerably the past few weeks, she thought, *though it's still exactly the same size. It was so small before I became a warrior!*

She closed her eyes, forcing Teenja's image back down her throat by brute force.

"Who are you kidding?" she asked aloud, surprised at the bitterness in her own voice. "You're no warrior. Not yet. Maybe never."

She saw her faults clearly now, everything the field captain said and worse! Every time she tried to follow an order, she fell short. How could she suddenly be so incompetent? She had spent years learning how to follow orders!

In gaining freedom, did I lose loyalty? Maybe a slave was all that I was, and now I'm not me anymore.

Without warning, the floor fell from beneath her feet.

Down she fell for what seemed a hundred leagues. Radience drifted off the floor, floating in mid air. Jiana's body floated next to her. "Goodbye, most loved," she gasped. Then she slammed into the deck as a terrible crash deafened her.

Radience crawled painfully to her hands and knees and looked out the sagging door. They lay at the bottom of an

immense, raft-shaped hole; dirt poured down upon them
in a steady stream. Far above, the half Less Moon flickered briefly across the tiny opening, but was it growing or
shrinking?

She limped out onto the deck. Incredibly, Cascade
chewed his oats without a care. More dirt fell, directly on
Radience this time.

She brushed it off of her head, but before she could get
back inside, a particularly large clod slammed into her
back, knocking her down. She tried to rise, but a dozen
shovelfulls buried her legs.

For an instant the scene lurched: it was not dirt but
hundreds of packed, writhing bodies of the martyrs that
buried her.

*Oh holy God, she killed them, killed them all! Anahita
and Alyz and Bukta and Ejtaq-dal and the Caliph and the
Overmen and all of them!*

A horrible thought intruded into her grief: *you were as
much a part of their deaths as Jiana.*

No! I was only a slave, it was her! She's the one—

*You stopped being a slave the moment you took respon-
sibility for your own actions. Killer! You betrayed Jiana!*

I didn't mean to—

Witch. Blasphemer. You follow foreign gods!

No. Control the mind—I'm on post. . . . She blinked
and the bodies were gone, replaced by dirt again. Radience
clawed at the dirt, but the more she pushed aside, the
more poured onto her body, working under her eyelids
and grinding with every blink. She blew a great pile away
from her mouth and gasped for air.

A presence loomed over her. Giathudin grinned and
casually snapped the back of his hand across her face.
Radience bit her lip to keep from screaming her rage and
hatred at the bastard; he was one of the Elect, the Overman of Slaves.

A thousand temple bells rang in her ears, and her
stomach rolled. She could not lift an arm to defend herself. He grabbed her around her neck and grinned
crookedly.

She felt no fear, only silent loathing. She struggled to keep her expression neutral, to find the warrior's serenity.

He leaned his face next to hers and began to lick. Radience sobbed once, recovered control, and made no more sound.

Giathudin pushed his hand into the earth. He grunted animalistically as he dug for her body, slobbering over her face and wheezing.

Radience held her hatred tight; it inspissated into a great pyramid of angry brick rising sharp and jagged from the sands of helplessness. He found her legs, wormed his hand between them, and forced his finger inside her. Radience went *elsewhere*.

A room, canvas walls, rough floor beneath thick cloth. She was in the traveling khayma. The Caliph slept like the dead at her feet, open eyes staring blankly at the stars visible through the smoke-hole. The Less Moon was full again.

She held a knife in her hand, the field captain's knife. She held it point downward, touching the breast of the Caliph of the Elect, al'Sophiate. But on another level, the Overman groped between her legs—and on the deepest level, the *real* level, she was being slowly buried alive by the pouring sand, crouching over the field captain's body. Which was real?

She shook her head, and was standing over the Caliph again. Fury pulsed like an old burn; *this* was the man who subjugated her and *stole her life!*

I was four turns. I had a Ma, a baby brother, and once I even had a Da, but he's gone a long time now. You came, white horse and bloody Horsemen. Why did you need me?

Ma ran, but your bastards cut her down from behind, and you even tore Mara apart in front of me like dogs ripping a cornered rabbit and set him afire. You dragged my dead eyes to the red sands—despoiler! What did we know about what you and Da had between you? Did we care, by the Seer?

Today I pay you back, she exulted, squeezing the knife, preparing for the push that would send on its final journey the soul of Hal'Addad bin Kerat bin El al'Sophiate, Lord of the Wind and the Five Sands, Prince of the Water, Caliph of the Elect from Qomsheh to Yazd to the Oasis of Deh Bid, Master of the Arts and Letters, and Satrap of Dokamaj Tool.

She pushed down with all the force of her good right arm to puncture his cruel heart, but she missed! Her traitorous left hand, crippled and weak, pushed sideways suddenly to deflect the point from the Caliph's breast.

Shocked at such betrayal, Radience tried again; again treachery intervened: the stunted left arm that had so often brought the troubles of the world upon Radience's head knocked the death blow wide.

"Warrior!" cried a voice from within her own stomach, "do you strike in *anger?* Then you *are* a slave!"

She looked at his eyes; they stared into hers in terror, conscious and awake, pupils a pinprick. She saw a man, not the master; a harried man trying to finish a job generations old: preparing the world for the return of the Seer, the judging, Paradise or the Underdwell. What if the rotting sickness returned? What if goats died, water dried?

What if—what if it were all a lie, and death brought not holy communion but the black abyss?

All at once, Radience could not sustain her anger. Every painful throb from her right hand dissipated into laughter out her left.

"I never understood," she giggled. "You're nothing but a *jamal*-trader, boss of a tentmaking concern! Caliph and Satrap, just a pair of jobs you hold, a couple of crowns to wear! You wear your mask, like Jiana; she's just learned to take hers off once in a while."

Suddenly she remembered—Giathudin groping pathetically between her legs for her private soul! The Caliph faded, and again she was lying in the sand staring up at the Overman. But all her anger was gone, and she saw him too through new eyes: a little, ungrown boy, angry and frightened.

He jumped back like a guilty little boy caught with his

fingers in the jar of sweets. He looked at his hands as if he had never seen them before.

A wind rose, and it blew him apart like lost smoke. Radience was alone in the sand, drowning under the weight of it.

"Cascade!" she cried, "for the God of love and for my sake, pull me out!" Teeth gripped the back of her shirt. She smelled the horse's hot breath as he yanked her from the pile with a single tug.

Shivering, she tucked the knife back in her belt. There was no Caliph, no Giathudin. No Jiana, no Toldo, no monsters, no red rage. *Is there even a Radience? Maybe I'll go questing and find her some day.*

She sat cross-legged in the hut, looking at the two supine bodies, one empty and begging, the other pale as a ghost and straining.

"What do I feel for you? For Teenja? I'm supposed to feel it for men, not women. Is this the face of evil, or just another mask? I wish you could tell me.

"I wish I were a warrior already."

Fear and hatred, she thought, two attacks. *What will be third? Who is the enemy?*

5

"Yes yes yes, we must leave from under this place!" cried the witch-man. He seized her hand and dragged her away.

She was vaguely aware of a great journey down the Jambajala, mountains and jungles flying past, but Toldo's dream was short on the details of travel. In the next instant, Jiana found herself lying face down and naked in a mud-puddle, centuries and half the world away.

She choked on a mouthful of water, and knelt for a long time, coughing and trying to breathe. She stood, unsteady in the mud. The heat made her glad she wore only caked mud clothing. Jatjaka set off, and Jiana caught up with him.

The mud grew thicker and stickier, and it required an

effort for her to pull her feet out of their own footprints, making a sucking noise; it was the only sound save for the old man's labored breathing.

The iron sky pressed down upon her head, making it ache. Jiana heard a splash and a curse ahead of them. As they approached, she saw a man, mired in the mud up to his chest. He struggled to free himself.

"Please!" he begged, catching sight of them, "by the black god and white goddess, free me! Free me!"

Jatjaka ignored the man and his cries, and lurched past. Jiana shrugged. "Free yourself," she suggested, turning away from his lamentations.

It seemed like half a day before they finally left him behind, though it was surely less than an hour. No sooner was he past, when they came upon another, stuck up to his armpits. Then a third and fourth.

"Who are all these men?" she asked her guide. "Why don't they climb out?"

"I do not know why they do not, I have not passed this way before."

"What!" shouted Jiana indignantly. "You've never been this way? Then where the fuck are you leading me?"

"To the priest."

She took a slow, deep breath and counted backward from seventeen. Jatjaka pushed on, and Jiana slogged after him.

The weeping bodies grew thicker as they passed; it was a challenge to pick a path between them. All cried out to be rescued, to be freed. Jiana stoppered her ears and shut her heart against them.

But at last she and the witch-man halted, facing an ocean of writhing bodies with no trail to pick among them. Jiana stared, guilt building within her. The citadel of al'-Sophiate burned bright in her memory.

Jatjaka seemed clueless; he scratched his alabaster head, looking left and right. "We go that way; I am sure, yes yes! But how? That is a perplexment, to be utterly certain."

"I know how," she answered. "I know what Toldo wants

to teach us, but it's a false and hollow lesson. This time, you follow me."

She approached one of the bodies at the edge of the "sea." It was a woman who gazed unblinkingly at the sky, oblivious to their presence.

Jiana reached forth her foot and pushed the woman; she did not respond. Shaking her head, the warrior moved like a flash: she stepped upon the woman's ample stomach and balanced carefully, then stepped from her to the next body. Jatjaka clambered up behind her.

At first, they had to hop from belly to chest to back, as if crossing a river on stones. But after a short distance, the bodies were so tightly packed they could walk at a nearly normal rate, so long as they were careful not to step on an unstable face or leg.

Some of the prisoned souls cried out in pain or torment when trodden on, but most were sunk in apathy and did not notice the indignity. The air was thick with the odor of unwashed bodies; Jiana breathed through her mouth, trying not to gag.

In the distance, the warrior heard the low moan of wind through trees. It gained in intensity until it was all around them. At last she realized it was a collective moan of anguish from the millions of trapped people.

Toldo had once told her the theory of Descention, that humans were once animals. As if in confirmation, Jatjaka began singing a warbling, ritual song in his own language, forming a counterpoint to the moaning chords. Jiana wished either he or the damned souls would shut up, preferably both.

She saw a building far off in the distance. "Jatjaka, is that where Toldo is?"

The witch-man puckered, then stretched his lower lip nearly to his chin. "Maybe I am not quite sure. Maybe, yes, I have lost the trail . . . do you still remember your promise, yes?"

"I won't break my pledge."

Jatjaka scratched nervously, and looked back the way

they came. "Then yes," he said at last, "yes yes, it is from there that I feel the anguish of your worthless priest."

"His worth is none of your fucking business!" cried Jiana. "Be thankful you extracted a promise from me, little man. It's your damned magic potions that have so nearly murdered him!"

Jatjaka looked wounded. "The fat one did not fly from himself when *Jatjaka* brewed the Visioning! Did he drink the Visioning in the sacred clearing of Jawoongtor Yiltor? Did he paint symbols of safety and luck upon his face and hands? No no!"

"What use are your symbols and sacred clearings? It's a drug, nothing more! We brewed it together, and he drank it on a raft in the middle of the holy Nag Deh Jambajala. Isn't that good enough?"

"It would appear not, yes yes," said Jatjaka. "The symbols serve to settle the stomach and prepare the soul for the journey. The Jawoongtor Yiltor clearing was carefully chosen to present proper sights and sounds, smells and breezes that ensure a profitable and educational trip. So much have I learned at the Seer's University in Deh Bid, in the desert lands."

Jiana stood silent for a moment, stunned.

"*You* went to university?"

"Yes yes, did you think me uneducated? Where did your priest study herbism? Did he not know of the importance of the world outside and the world inside?"

"Well, I never heard him . . . I mean I don't think he talked much about—"

"He thought us savages, yes he did! Do not blame me for his foolish and rash experiments. No, no! Blame the priest for knowing little and caring less!"

Jiana turned angrily away. The witch-man had no right to give Toldo but a glimpse of the Serpent's lair without the power to find it again. Jiana set off towards the building again, mouth set in a grim line.

6

Can I still be a warrior with my head shaved bare?

Radience fingered her scalp, feeling the stubble so like a slave, so different—*it would all stop instantly, Jiana said—the* field captain *said—if I simply say "I quit." Probably even let me grow my hair back again.*

Come to that, she thought, *I could even shave my head as Jiana does, in the warrior's strip. Who would know I had no right?*

Radience rubbed her palm against the sandpapery rough-ness of her head, where the hair was growing back.

She heard a sound, and yanked her hand away guiltily. She peered around the cabin, but saw no one aside from herself and the two warm bodies, both still alive. The dirt had stopped falling.

"Damn, it's dark in here. . . ." She tried to remember where the field captain kept the lamp, then felt ashamed for being afraid of the dark.

"Damnit, Cascade's right outside. If there were intrud-ers, that horse would surely have screamed or whinnied or something. . . ." Radience rubbed her left hand, massag-ing out the aches and pains she had begun to feel lately.

No, something is wrong. I'm still under attack, but I don't know by whom . . . the same somebody who took Toldo's soul.

Again the noise like a foot, dragging on the deck out-side. *Not* a horse's hoof. "Better investigate," Radience told herself. Then, a bit louder, "I'm coming out on deck now. Here I come. Any *daevas* better be gone when I get there!"

She rose and pushed the cabin door open. The raft floated in the midst of void. And Cascade was gone.

Frantic, she ran to the back, then the front of the raft. She looked down and saw faintly-glowing hoofprints on the wood planks, leading to the edge of the raft.

Her eyes tracked the course, and she swallowed hard. She could see the glow of the footprints leading into the directionless abyss. They dimmed and faded as she watched.

Cascade—whoever or whatever he was—had deserted.

Radience turned abruptly and saw a blue glow coming from the half-open cabin door. She hesitated outside; again she heard the scrape of a foot, this time from inside the cabin.

She reached for the door, but her hand paused, trembling of its own accord. She tried to force it forward, gritting her teeth and *willing* it. It would not move.

Radience fell back a few steps, unable to stop herself. "This is stupid . . . I should be in there, damn you! Back to your post, soldier!"

Again she reached, but her hand froze as if confronting an invisible wall. "God, God, what have I let happen?" she cried, blinking at the salt tears in her eyes.

Mesmerized, she stared at the eerie blue light leaking from the door's edges; the sound was now a *clump clump* from one side of the cabin to the other. Abruptly she remembered that she was *not* one-handed.

She blanked her mind, as if preparing to meditate upon an orange. Careful to keep the intention out of her stomach, she darted her small hand out and pushed the door open.

A malevolent imp crouched in the center of the room, a ghastly little boy with skin white as pus from an infected wound, fingers black as ashes from a corpse, burned on the sands.

He slowly looked at her, mouth red as the Caliph's own wine, limbs twisted as a lightning-blasted Tarly tree.

The dwarf grinned wickedly, stood and stretched his arms; they truly stretched, wide as the sands, long as the mountains. He laughed like an iron-shod ship wrecking on the jagged rocks of the Worm's Teeth.

"You have met me at last, you useless, little cripple, Jiana's playtoy. I am Toq. Time for your birchin', you blasphemous urchin!"

Toq stood astride the bodies of Jiana and Toldo; both had been sliced open, neat and clean, their organs lovingly removed and arranged about them.

Radience stared numbly at Toq's handiwork. She gasped,

her first breath since entering hell. Toq's odor was as foul as gravesand gas, but Radience refused to gag; she glared at the godling.

She reached across with her left hand and drew her hunting knife without a word. Fear was gone; it lay on the ground with Love and Anger. The calm spirit infused her body, pumping strength and hardness into her heart, stomach, and muscles.

Her feet burned footprints into the wooden deck as she advanced upon Toq. The knife in her good, left hand glowed white with unbearable heat.

Toq stepped back, startled.

7

As Jiana and Jatjaka closed upon the castle, more and more of the bodies were apathetic, dead but not yet dead. The castle was obscured by clouds until they were quite close. Then she saw that it, too, was built of bodies. They writhed in rhythm so that the entire building pulsed like a living thing.

The sky was red, lit by an invisible, angry sun. The moons still crawled visibly across the sky, and the Less Moon had shrunk to a black penumbra again.

The smell of rot and decay over-powered Jatjaka, and he buried his face in his hands as he and Jiana crossed the bridge across the moat.

"Is he held prisoner here?" she asked.

"The priest? Yes yes, surely he must be."

"He's not one of these bodies, is he?"

Jatjaka did not answer, but Jiana knew the answer was negative even as she asked. "Who lives here?"

The witch-man shrugged angrily. His skin looked paler than normal, and he trembled. Jiana let him alone.

Inside, the bodies were crushed against an invisible wall, as if they had been packed against a thick glass pane by a wine-pressing screw. But there was no glass; Jiana could have reached out and touched a flattened face or deformed limb.

Incredibly, the bodies were alive, although pressed into less than a hand-span of thickness. They rolled their eyes and worked their jaws. She could not make out individual voices in the cacophany, but most begged and pleaded for death.

Passing through the walls, Jiana and Jatjaka discovered an interior courtyard surrounded by five walls. At the far end was a staircase which led up through massive, open doors to the main hall.

The courtyard ground was made of volcanic rock, marbled with veins of red. The pair crossed it and mounted the stairs. After several steps, Jiana realized the stairs were made of genitalia, stretched and pounded into place.

She quickly mounted the obscene steps to the upper floor. She entered the great hall and finally found Toldo Mondo. He sat at the cold end on a throne sculpted from a living heart as large as the hut on the raft.

There was no question this time; it was truly he. Jiana had never seen him so defeated and weighed down by calamity.

"Toldo," she called, "get up, you're being liberated. Again." He did not stir or notice her entrance. "Look, priest," she continued, "I can't stay in your stomach forever—get up and move! We've got to get out of here."

Jatjaka interrupted her.

"It is he, it is he, yes yes! I have kept my part of the deal, have I not?"

Jiana was surprised to see no chains or shackles upon the priest's arms or legs, no collar about his neck. She reached out to grab his sleeve, but his hand shot forth as quick as any warrior's and caught her wrist.

He laconically turned his bovine head towards Jiana. "Woman?" he guessed, eyes focusing. "Jiana? What dream is this?"

"Your dream, I would guess—leggo my arm!—through which I've journeyed to rescue you. Damn you, let go of my wrist!"

She yanked, but he held her with a grip of stone.

"But how could Jiana still be alive, a thousand turns after I met her? No matter; she will not thwart my plans."

"Toldo, are you feverish? I'm getting old, but my birthdays aren't measured in centuries! Come, let's get out before the castle lord returns."

"Are you truly Jiana? Or another demon, come to wrest the kingdoms of the world from my hands and prevent the Great Awakening?"

Jiana stared silently, digesting the question. Jatjaka tugged at her other arm. "Lady, I have given my all, and my all has brought you and me both safe and sound to this location. Now I wish to be paid . . . I can feel my enemies creeping upon me, even as I speak—I demand your protection, as you promised!"

"Shut up, you annoying speck of dust. Toldo, WAKE UP! You ate some mushrooms and drifted far, far away; now it's time to return. What kingdoms?"

"All the kingdoms of the earth, Jiana!" cried a familiar little boy's voice. Jiana spun about, her left arm now pinioned behind her by Toldo's motionless grip.

An ancient-eyed dwarf child stood in the hall's center. He had alabaster skin, obsidian fingers, and a blood-red mouth, as if he had just feasted.

"Toq," said Jiana, her lip curling in disgust.

"I made your fat priest friend an offer, and he has accepted. I once made you the same offer, but you foolishly refused, for which I am sure you berate yourself every waking moment."

"An offer?"

"Toldo's great awakening! I have allowed him his most desired opportunity: to grab the world by the scruff and shake it awake!"

Jiana tried to free her arm by twisting while she puzzled Toq's latest atrocity. "He plans to bring mushroom enlightenment to the world?"

"To all the kingdoms of the earth. They are all his, if he will but serve my thirst for knowledge."

"Knowledge! The last thing you so desperately thirsted after was the World's Dream, not knowledge!"

"Well, we rather put *that* little dream behind us, *didn't we?*" Toq's voice had a nasty edge, and his hair writhed like a thousand squirming worms. "But I adjust to circumstances, as you know. So does Toldo."

"*He* is one of my enemies!" exclaimed Jatjaka, hiding behind Jiana and pointing at Toq. "Protect me from him, yes yes! I insist!"

Jiana looked back at Toldo; rather than follow the conversation, his glazed eyes stared into the middle distance. She deftly unlatched her arm from his grip, and his hand settled slowly to his lap.

"What do you mean, bring a special wakening to the kingdoms of the earth?"

Toq gestured grandly at the walls; wherever his hand pointed, the packed bodies screamed in anguish, as if he had sliced them with a razor.

"Someday, all this will be his."

"A castle built of body-bricks and blood?"

"That is what *you* see. Your priest sees a different world."

"He sees an hallucination."

"Don't you? Why not? His hallucination comforts him more than yours does you, though I do admire it myself." Toq's eyes bored into Jiana's, and he drifted closer and closer to her. She could not shift her gaze.

"Come to me. Come to me, Jiana Analena; come as Toldo came. Come through the sacred mushroom. . . . I shall wait for you."

Blinking, she wrested her attention away from the boy-god.

"Don't hold your breath."

"You *will* come. I prophesy it, though I know not when. I am content to wait." He half-closed his eyes and let a half-smile play across half his face. In an instant, Toq was nothing more than twisted, black roots and a burned-out, hollow husk, burning clean through the earth into the Underdwell, leaving a furnace odor to fade slowly.

"This is really *most* unfair," complained Jatjaka. "Here I have led you to the priest that you sought, and you do not even acknowledge our bargain, or tell me how you are to protect me!"

"Leave me alone, I warn you!"

"I demand the protection you promised this instant, yes!"

Jiana felt the other move through her body like fever. She whirled, stepped forward, and spoke. The voice from her throat sounded like hers, but the words were Jianabel's. "You want to be *protected?* Forever safe from nasty, horrid enemies? *Let me take you under my wing!*"

Jiana felt her guts wrench to the sides. Her entire body split vertically. The split gaped like a maw, filled with thousands of tiny teeth, each filed to a needle-sharp point. A long, sticky tongue darted out and wrapped around Jatjaka, dragging him towards her.

The witch-man screamed and struggled but was pulled inside Jiana. The mouth slammed shut, and he screamed again—this time in agony as he felt the teeth.

Jianabel let go of Jiana's body, and the warrior fell to her knees, gasping. "He'll be safe *now,* the silly! I promise that none of his enemies will *dare* harm him where he is now!"

"You killed him!"

"Hardly such an easy fate. He's alive within you, sister mine, and I have him ever so secure in my arms. We shall have many long, pleasant conversations, I think. . . . he is my special dolly now, my new Krakshi!"

Jiana gagged and tried to ignore the fluttering, squirming sensations inside of her.

"Toldo, listen to me," she said, "a desert trip and four moons of slaving taught me you can only awaken yourself, no one else."

The priest shook his head slowly back and forth. He snorted; for a wild moment, Jiana thought he would paw the ground with his foot.

"All around them, but they would not see. Seers and sybils spoke, but they would not hear."

"What? Priest, wake up yourself!"

"It is now time," Toldo pontificated, "to *make them*

understand. Now it is time to thrust the secret right in their faces and beat them awake. Some may be hurt, some die. I am willing to, um, I say, to take that responsibility. As it were."

Toldo was lost in his own universe; words alone were not enough. Jiana squinted, forcing herself to see the walls as mere walls, the stair as a sequence of stone or wooden steps. *All the same, all hallucination.* She wrapped arms about her body, quieting a shudder.

A thousand, thousand flying insects invading Jiana's guts, battering her insides like moths crashing a lantern glass. *Toldo's dream. Is Radience nothing more than my dream?*

"Toldo," she said, "you can't wake them out of their dreams; I've tried. All you can do is wake yourself and hope the other poor bastards take the hint."

Her voice sounded cold and dead, and she choked on the taste of Jatjaka the witch-man, himself finally waking.

"Play your mushroom games," she continued, to Toldo, Jatjaka, Radience, Jianabel—anyone who cared to listen. "You might learn something to wake from your *own* walking nightmare—Tooqa knows Radience has helped me end mine."

Toldo jumped up, his eyes wide with wild purpose. He flapped his arms.

"AWAKE! I'LL *BLAST* THEM AWAKE, THE SLEEPING BASTARDS!"

Jiana laughed, and shook her head.

"I can't wake you up, but I can sure as shit keep you from sleepwalking—at least *this* time. I guess that qualifies as rescuing you, don't you think?"

She pressed her palms over her eyes and stoked the burning cord of magic that ran up her spine. She fanned it into an inferno, a fiery streak of pain *(one, your terror)* running up her back. She let it flood through her, feeling it, reveling in it *(two, your agony).*

She feared if she burned any hotter she would incinerate herself. She opened her eyes. *(Three, your despair!)*

Toldo was staring at her, his eyes wide with astonishment. His face was brightly lit, as if the fire were shining out of her skin with a brightness to match the heat. She focused her eyes on the priest, and visioned him at the center of a raging fireball.

Toldo opened his mouth, but no sound emerged. He twisted his legs and arms and fell from the heart-throne onto the floor.

First, his robe burned away. Then the outer layers of skin, the new, pink skin underneath. The muscles were exposed, bright red for an instant; they turned black and charred, leaving a veined skeleton enclosing internal organs.

The brittle bones broke, one by one; the organs resisted the heat as yet, though Jiana would have expected them to burn before the skeleton. Finally the skull itself burst with a great, loud *bang*, and all that was left was a pile of organs. They began to melt and liquify before Jiana's eyes.

"Come—OUT," she ordered, unable even to articulate a controlling cantrip. She burned with unchanneled power, unsubtle Will.

The world shimmered like a desert mirage. The walls screamed as they roasted. At last, the oily run off from the melted organs trickled blackly away, revealing a tiny, white, waxy figure at the center.

Jiana slowly cooled the fire within, feeling her consciousness ebb with the power. He had cost her; she understood dimly that she might not recover.

But the warrior spirit was strong within her this day, and she faced death feeling neither fear nor despair.

She was a furnace cooling towards shut-down, a flywheel coasting and slowing ever-so-slightly towards rest. After tense centuries of turns, Jiana realized to her surprise that the danger was past; the fire was controlled and she would live.

She crawled forward, slipping in her own sweat, and plucked the white-wax figurine from the ground.

She did not remember rising. She caught quick flashes of image as she staggered through the throne room, down the stairs, and out the door.

The castle was dead; every soul in every wall had been charred and burned. Even the sea of bodies outside was gone, replaced by a lava overflow. The substance still glowed red, but Jiana was not worried; the heat would be nothing compared to what she had just released.

Cradling the Toldo figurine, the warrior stumbled across the hot, red sea, timeless and nearly senseless. She noticed when she moved beyond the lava. She briefly noticed when she fell into the Nag Deh Jambajala. She looked up and saw the Less Moon full again, the fifth time she had seen it so in the dreamtime.

She waded through water that rose to her naked breasts. She held the figurine aloft, keeping it out of the water, an inner gnosis informing her that she dared not allow it to touch until she gained the birthing pool under the mountain, where she first had met Jatjaka and bid farewell to the Fish of Earthly Knowledge.

At last she stood in the pool, the Lake of Forget Nought, far under the measureless tons of rock. Stooping, she dipped the figurine in the waters. She dipped it again, and three more times again, making five times in all (once for each pregnant moon).

It grew heavier and thicker with every baptism until Jiana did not hold it so much as cradle it, letting it fall into the waters and hoisting it out again.

After the final dunking, it was not a figurine but Toldo Mondo himself who stood white and shaking before her, wearing the cold and cloaked with as much memory as a man can withstand.

"Please take me back," he begged.

8

"Jiana is dead," said the boy-creature, grinning nervously. Radience continued her advance, ignoring him.

"I tore her guts out, ho! and scattered them to the four winds." He giggled. "Except for part of her stomach; I *ate* that, don'tcha know."

He backed into a corner and stopped; Radience moved swiftly and thrust the knife at his chest. The blade broke, as it would if she had thrust it against the Caliph's statue, and Toq laughed with a musical tinkle.

"Can't catch me!" he sang, "I'm the gingerbread god!" He danced around the girl, cackling like an old woman's chicken.

Radience turned and advanced upon him, emotionless and relentless. Again, Toq backed away, this time gesturing her forward with both his hands, mocking her stern demeanor.

Radience paused, biting her lip. *This is stupid. What am I going to do, beat him with the broken hilt?*

"This is stupid," agreed Toq. "What are you going to do, beat me with the broken hilt? Suck my toes, pick my nose? Heigh-de-hose!"

Unthinking, Radience caught Toq in a flying tackle that brought both of them to the ground. For an instant, his hands were pinioned, and she seized his throat in a death-grip.

After a moment, she realized he was not struggling. He was looking at her with a bemused expression. She stared back, incredulous. It was hopeless!

"It's hopeless," he croaked. Radience rose into the air, and realized Toq lifted her by her belt. She maintained her grip, but he tossed her aside, and her hands were torn from his throat. She fell upside down in the corner, gripping two large hunks of bloody flesh.

Toq ignored the gaping neck wounds. He advanced upon Radience while she was still blinking and trying to focus her vision.

"It's hopeless," he said, squatting before her, hands on his knees. "It's like this, see: I'm a god, and you're a piece of lint. What do you think you can do to me?"

Radience lashed out with a left-handed punch at Toq's face, but a new mouth opened where his eye was, and it caught her fist in its toothless gums. He spoke through a mouth that opened over his other eye.

"Look at Jiana. Take a good, long look at your fuck-fantasy. Think you can do better than she?"

Radience stared at the second mouth in horror, barely

hearing Toq's words. She felt ill and struggled to pull her hand free.

The mouth opened and released the girl's fist. It vanished as soon as she withdrew her hand, leaving nothing but Toq's eye again.

"Oh yes. Oh yes. Yes, oh yes, yes oh, oh! I know *exactly* what you want to do with Jiana! I know the *real* reason you wait upon her, hand and foot!"

Now it was Radience who inched backward, until her back pressed against the corner. He leaned close, and she smelled decaying orchids on his breath. His face filled her entire field of vision.

"Do you want to *do it?*" he whispered, gesturing towards Jiana's body with his eyes. "I can put her back together again, you know."

Radience's gaze was dragged towards Jiana's body. No longer were the guts strewn about the room; it was whole, still pale in death, but unmarked.

Jiana's feet were small, calloused, her ankles slender; each calf comprised two thick, well-defined muscles. Soft, black hair sparsely coated Jiana's shins.

Her thighs were milky-white, thick with muscle, yet feminine. Higher, the hair was black and dense. Radience visioned her fingers stroking it, perhaps her tongue.

Jiana's hips were wide, her buttocks smooth and hard, white as the salt-sands at high noon. Her belly was strong, Radience knew, but not ribbed like sand dunes, like the boys of the Elect. It was a smooth, curvaceous slope through which the ribs bulged.

Her breasts were medium, larger than Radience's, but smaller than most of the women of the Elect. Smaller than Teenja's. The nipples were dark brown rather than pink like Radience's. Frozen in death, they neither rose nor fell.

Radience stretched her hand towards those breasts, desperately wanting to stroke them, feel them, kiss them. In her vision, her lips and tongue caressed the nipples, begging them to harden, but they lay still and cold.

Jiana's shoulders were broad, the muscles large and cut.

Strong enough to tear a tree from the ground, tear a stone apart; strong enough to tear Toq in half.

Her throat was white and soft, tendons distinct, a blue vein running down the side. Her face was round, cheeks hollow. Her nose was smaller than the women of the Elect, not as tiny as the northern women.

Radience blinked a tear from her eye; it interfered with visioning the hopeless love before her. *No hope. . . .*

Jiana's coal-black warrior's strip was thin, where Teenja's hair was thick and matted; soft, where Mugn's was a fistful of bristles. Jiana proudly bore a few grey strands in front like battle ribbons.

Most of all, Radience wanted to run her fingers through that soft, black hair and kiss Jiana's cold forehead. But more: she wanted Jiana to run *her* fingers through Radience's blonde, straight locks, soon as they grew back.

But it would not happen. It was hopeless. Jiana was dead.

Radience felt her lip trembling. She realized what Toq was doing. "I have no lust for her dead body," she said.

"Pity," said the boy-god, "if you had amused me, I might have spared your snotty, little life." She knew he lied.

He grinned so wide his face cracked, and reached forward to seize her by her throat and lift her to her knees.

Radience looked into Toq's pink eyes and ashen face, and knew she would die in a moment. There was nothing that could stop it, not in the hut of death, not out in the void. Hopeless—the end of a short, miserable life.

"There is nothing that can stop it," Toq said, so quietly his voice was barely audible over her own pulse in her temples. "You are at the end of your short, miserable, disgusting, bootlicking, perverted, beastial life."

Radience felt no fear, only peace.

Toq scowled, and a million black, bloated roaches erupted from his flesh. They scurried around eyes and nose and into his gaping mouth.

He held up his right hand, and long, sharp claws pushed

through the flesh of his fingertips. Blood dripped down his hand.

Why am I not afraid? she wondered. *Is this the warrior spirit at last?*

Toq drew his hand back, drawing out the moment. The roaches fell from his face to scurry across the deck, across Radience's feet. Still, she did not fear; she would die soon, anyway.

She looked deep into Toq's eyes and understood; she saw the wheel, saw his place and her own on it. And Radience saw in Toq's eyes release from the wheel. She saw how she could stop it, in death, and get off—if she kept her head and her resolve.

No hope, Radience thought, *but no desire; no cares.* She smiled, genuinely happy. "Good time to die!" she laughed, feeling a cool breeze blow through her body.

From nowhere, a lightning bolt tore through Toq, and the entire raft shuddered and nearly broke apart. The boy-god flew across the room, spinning wildly, and landed upside-down against a wall.

Cascade reared inside the cabin, screaming with battle-lust. Hoof by hoof, the horse advanced upon Toq. When the tiny, white god tried to rise, Cascade trampled him like a snake, tearing with his teeth and kicking repeatedly with hooves that burned their mark into Toq's flesh with every blow.

In a moment too brief, Toq was obliterated. There were no pieces left, just flattened, burned lumps of clay.

Cascade turned an eye to look at Radience. He watched her, unblinking, for a long time, then turned and walked back out of the cabin onto the deck, into the void, as unconcerned as if he had merely nibbled a few blades of grass.

Radience was still on her knees, where she had fallen when Toq dropped her. She tried to stand, but her legs would not hold her.

She crawled towards her charges. They were both alive, still lying as they last had been, still sleeping.

She slid her hand under Jiana's shirt and touched her

breast. It was warm. It rose and fell. The girl pulled her hand away quickly, before she could begin to feel . . . anything.

Light shone into the hut and burned away the void. It was the Seer's Moon, the Less Moon, the Mother of Introspection opening wide her eye for the fifth time since the raft flowed over the edge.

Exhausted, Radience fell across the two bodies, still protecting them. *I did it!* she exulted; *I guarded them, kept harm away. . . .*

Her eyes closed, and she knew nothing more.

In the quiet night, Radience dimly felt a flip, a flap, as her stomach rolled. The raft flowed over another Edge, flopped, flipped, and the world righted itself.

Radience smiled in her sleep, but knew nothing more.

Chapter IX:

Crucible of market reality prime,
moons in the half-shell

Jiana opened her eyes. She looked at the regular, wooden roof of the cave. She blinked, and it became the ceiling of the cabin, on the great raft.

When she inhaled, a sharp pain lanced up her back, as if she had rolled onto a knife. Wincing, she tried to sit up.

She fell back heavily, dizzy. "Wu—whu . . ." The words would not form on her parched lips, but someone understood and held a cup of water for her to drink. After swallowing some, she took a mouthful and rolled it around her tongue and lips until they responded to her commands again.

"Toldo?"

"In the flesh, ah, so to speak." His voice sounded deeper than usual, as if he, too, had risen recently with a mouth like the bottom of a bird-cage. He hawked and spat phlegm out the door of the hut, paced back and forth.

Underneath the creaking and groaning of the deckboards, Jiana heard the clopping of Cascade's hooves. In a corner, Radience snored loudly, a blanket tucked around her. She whimpered softly in her sleep.

"I found her fallen over us both, that hunting knife clutched in her hand and covered with dried blood. I don't think we had the only adventure, pale one."

"Her own blood?"

"Not human. Not horse, either."

This time Jiana succeeded in sitting up, but her back was lacerated with every breath. "Uk. Do we have any food? I forget."

"*Kaf.*"

"Better than sucking my own spit."

"You are so delicate, fair flower of maidenhood."

"No, my stomach gives me trouble whenever I think too much. Constant indigestion. Now my back hurts, too."

"I thought you warriors bore your travails without complaint?"

"Fuck no; we whine and bitch like old ladies. Should hear a barracks-room bitch-session someday: you'd swear we were a bunch of grandmothers with gout and rheumatism. Toldo—how do you feel?"

"Do you mean, am I still possessed by the megalomaniacal dreams of enlightening the entire world? No. But something did happen, some kind of awakening. To me, I mean."

"Did you find what you sought?"

Toldo paused in his perigrinations and stroked his beard. *He looks so different with that,* Jiana thought. *Cleanshaven, he looked hungry. Now he's full, and trying to digest.*

"Yes, partially; no, not completely."

Jiana chuckled. "Well, that about runs the line from left to right."

"I know what they mean when they say they've *seen the light.*"

"They who?"

He shrugged.

"You'll see it someday."

"That's what Toq said; someday I'll follow you on the journey you just took. Then I'll be his. Toq's."

"If you *truly* follow me, you'll be yours."

"So where are we? Not to change the subject."

Toldo moved to the opening and peered out at the countryside, drifting so slowly by.

"Um, Door. Yes, it must be Door. Might be Door, I mean."

Door, she thought. *Something important about Door. . . .*

"That's all? That's only, what, forty leagues from Deh Bid?"

"Well, we're *somewhere* in Door; I don't see the mountains, but we might still be anywhere in a three hundred league range. How far south do you think we've come?"

"You're the one with the maps, o great navigator. I don't even know for sure how long we've traveled. You tell me we're in Door. Now what?"

"Good a place as any to start, Door is. Let's beach the raft at the first town we find. Or perhaps the second."

There is something I must remember about Door, but my stomach is empty. I can't remember. Damn!

"Why? What do you plan to do? If you don't mind my asking."

"Set up shop."

Jiana stared in astonishment.

"Selling what? Enlightenment?"

"You bet, Jiana. I can't enlighten them, but I can certainly *show them* what waking life is like. Show anyone who wants to see, that is."

Jiana snorted, and struggled up onto her feet, wincing at the tearing pain *(four, your death).* She brushed at her tunic; it was encrusted with ancient sweat and grime.

"Well, I guess can sell love potions and undetectable poisons; maybe buy something nice to wear for a change."

Jiana looked down at Radience: the girl's face was older, her eyes less innocent, even while closed in fitful sleep. "You're going to make a hell of a warrior," she whispered. "Time to put a sword in your hand."

Radience practiced the sword dance the field captain taught, crazy though it seemed. Who ever heard of swinging a sword so excruciatingly slowly, almost as if underwater?

Whenever she tried to speed up a cut, the field captain caught her wrist and slowed her down even further. "Training your muscle memory," Jiana called it, but Radience felt silly, especially when Toldo watched.

The girl stumbled, seeing sparkles before her eyes. She

blinked. *Must be a late hit from that daeva,* she thought uneasily. She was grateful when the field captain decided it was a good time to stop the first day.

But why would she still not teach Radience to *fight* with the sword? The girl felt discouraged. *Am I that dense?*

Jiana sat bolt upright, her eyes wide. She clenched her teeth to hold back a scream. It was the dream again, back to haunt her: the dead, the living, a blurring of the lines; limbo, round and round again, three times; three times would Toq cast a shadow across her life before . . .

Shadowed me once yet, the killings at Deh Bid—No! Stop the thoughts, turn your stomach away! Can't look at that. Not yet.

She stood quietly to avoid waking Radience. The priest was already awake. She found him out on the deck, sitting cross-legged next to Cascade. Both he and the horse watched a great clump of lights approaching, far ahead.

Nine towns had they allowed to pass unexplored, except for brief food excursions in the first, sixth, and eighth. Toldo's money store was dangerously low, Jiana's exhausted long before.

Jiana silently approached the priest, but she must have made some little noise, for Toldo spoke immediately, "It could be Hak'sha."

"Seems big enough. I've never been there. But that's crazy; we can't be going that fast. That's at the south end of Door, almost at the land's end." She dubiously eyed the shore crawling past, slow as a Bay Bay merchant making change. "Unless . . . snakes, how the fuck long have we been shedding our skins out here?"

"I don't know; I remember nothing since I took that last batch of the Waking."

"I dreamed the Less Moon waxed and waned five times. I don't know how long we spent in that Summerland; I'm afraid to find out."

"Well, is that Hak'sha?"

"Don't know. Never been to Door."

Toldo raised his brows. "I thought you'd been *every where.*"

Jiana ignored the jibe. Door was the one country she avoided, so hot that northern visitors were rumored to occasionally burst into spontaneous flames. It was little and squalid, with wretched, poverty-stricken people; yet the people lived in the shadow of palaces and manses that dimmed those of the Flower Empire.

"If the people of that city ever stopped smoking their Hak'sha tobbacco, they'd rise up, butcher their princes, and move into those palaces."

"Perhaps, after smoking enough Hak'sha tobbacco," Toldo said cryptically, "they *already* live in those palaces."

"I hate this place. But there's something about it that I can't remember, and should."

"Oh? What can't you remember?"

"Nice try; I wish it were that easy! I can't dislodge it from last night's potatoes."

Jiana looked at the red glow in the East. "Well, time to kick the kid awake and play field captain. You saw her sword practices. Not bad, almost holds the sword correctly after one day! Took me a moon to learn that!"

She turned without waiting for a response. Toldo had not watched Radience practice; he was too preoccupied with the internal landscape.

Jiana ducked through the cabin door and found the girl already awake and washing herself. Radience's body was always lean, but it was less gaunt and more muscled than it ever had been. She noticed Jiana watching her, and became self-conscious, twisting slightly so that her left arm was out of sight behind her body.

Then she caught herself. She turned face front, seemingly unashamed either of her arm or her naked body, but the action was clearly forced.

No matter. What is staged today is habit tomorrow.

"Ma'am, will this initiate still begin actual combat training today, as the field captain promised?"

"Are you implying I'm a liar? On your face." Radience dropped, half smiling.

"Down up. Down up. Hey, Initiate Radience."

"Ma'am?"

"Is it true you studied healing while you were a slave in al'Sophiate's khayma? Down up."

"Yes, ma'am!"

"Down up. You mean they actually let you handle knives and needles and sharp things?"

"Yes, ma'am!"

"Down up. Remind me never to have an accident in Deh Bid."

"Aye, ma'am!"

"Down up. Down up. Hey, Initiate Radience, did they actually let you cut people up?"

"Sometimes, ma'am!"

"Down up. Snakes and Serpentine, did they also teach the cooks how to brew poisons? Down up."

"No, ma'am!" By this time, Radience was visibly laughing as she performed her press-ups.

"Down up. Down up. Down up. Keep going. Stop making that weird noise, or the Hak'sha Physicians' Union will quarantine you when we dock there."

"Aye, ma'am! Is this initiate to understand we're close to Hak'sha, ma'am?"

"Hey, Apprentice Radience. You got some business out in town?"

Radience stopped at an upstroke and looked up openmouthed at Jiana. "Did—did the field captain say *apprentice?*"

"As of this moment, Apprentice Sergeant at Arms Radience, you are allowed the privilege of using the first and second person in your speech. That means you can now say 'I' and 'you,' in case your little, walnut-sized stomach didn't quite catch that."

"Thank you, ma'am! Field Captain! Ma'am!"

"Down up."

"Aye, ma'am! Ma'am?"

"Now what? Down up."

"Are we in Hak'sha? Field Captain?"

"On your feet."

"Aye, ma'am!" Radience bounded up.

"Get your clothes and your shit and be out on deck in

fifteen seconds. Bring that deck pad we picked up yesterday. Better teach you a bit of fighting."

"Aye, ma'am!" Radience rushed into her clothing as Jiana strode around to the back of the raft to await her. She arrived a few seconds early with the straw-filled mat, and Jiana had her lay it out and wait in the middle.

"The first thing you are going to do is to learn how to punch.

"You think you already know how to punch. *Everybody* thinks he knows how to punch. You are going to learn by punching me. You will enjoy this exercise, but if you think this opportunity of yours to exact some revenge against me or will make me any easier on you in the future, Apprentice Radience, you are in for a big, fucking surprise."

Radience smiled, and tensed eagerly.

"Since I want you to still be able to walk and breathe and other such niceties, I won't punch you back. Yet." Jiana joined Radience on the mat.

"The first punch we will practice is a simple punch to the solar plexus. Right here." She gently poked Radience just below her sternum, hard enough to make the girl feel it, not hard enough to bruise her diaphragm.

"Punch."

After a moment, Radience wound her arm up and swung it at Jiana's belly, roughly in the correct place. Jiana stepped out of the way of the blow with no trouble.

"Watch me."

Very slowly, Jiana stepped back a touch out of range and simulated a straight, stepping punch from her hip to Radience's stomach, snapping her hips at the end.

"Stand like this; this is the fourth position. Now do what I just did," Jiana said, stepping back into range.

Again, Radience tried. She signalled the punch less obviously, but was still too slow by a wide margin.

Jiana worked with her through the entire morning, drilling her on the form. Then she changed the focus of the lesson. "Begin your reservoir exercise."

Radience started to sit down on the mat, but Jiana stopped her. "No. Stand in the fourth position and let the Power build along your spine."

For a moment, Radience looked confused, then comprehension dawned. She stood in the ready position before the punch and let her facial expression go blank.

Jiana squinted and opened her inner vision; she saw a faint glow of Power running through Radience's body like a sword blade.

"Now strike again, but let the force come from the Power, not from your own muscles. Follow the form; it is designed to work *with* the Power. Strike!"

Radience lashed out, but with her left hand, not the right that Jiana expected. Caught by surprise, Jiana was forced to actually block the blow, rather than step aside.

The impact made the warrior's arm tingle.

"Nice punch. Can you manage to *control* it a bit better next time?"

Radience stared, open mouthed.

"I'm sorry!"

"You're *what?*"

"I apologize for—"

Jiana swung her hand in a short, slapping arc, but instead of hitting Radience with her palm, Jiana curved her fingers and struck the girl with her fingertips in the jaw-muscle. Radience was staggered, though she did not cry out. She held the side of her face and worked her jaw, blinking rapidly.

"Do you expect *me* to apologize for *that?*"

"N-no, ma'am. No, Field Captain."

"Why not?"

Radience shook her head, trying to restore her balance.

"Because you are the field—"

"Snakeshit. Because I am a *warrior*, and that is what warriors do. Never apologize for acting like a warrior, unless you sincerely don't mean it."

"Unless I *don't* mean it?"

Jiana looked stern, imitating the manners of Tu Tsai, one of her old swordmasters.

"Civilians are strange," she said, "especially city lords. They call you awake in the middle of the night to put down a drunk on a rampage, then recoil in horror when

you decapitate the son of a bitch. They don't understand
the value of sleep."

"So in that case, a warrior says he's sorry for acting like
a warrior?"

"A warrior says anything they want to hear, so she can
get back to her mat. Time enough to slap some sense into
them in the morning. Now try that punch again . . . *right
handed*, this time."

2

The city approached. Soon it was close enough that
Radience could actually make out individual people at the
docks. She was quite excited; she had never been to a city
as big, as fabled, as adventurous as Hak'sha! The field
captain had even hinted at a certain bit of liberty, at least
in her company. Perhaps an *apprentice* could wander a
bit?

The entire center of legendary Hak'sha was fabled to be
a vast trading bazaar, tens of thousands of tents and stalls
selling—everything.

Radience closed her eyes and visioned it clearly: barrels
of wine, buckets of tar, odors of perfume, ghastlies of
potions; swords and armor, flying rugs, maps to mythic
lands, whole libraries of books! diaries of generals and
courtesans, philosophical speculations, astronometric descrip-
tographies, erotic fantasies, fried dates, mungberries,
sweetmeats, candies, gold and silver, jewels, sparkles of
ruby and emerald, hurgate, obsidian, great hunks of quartz
with trapped slivers of roachrock, gods and *daevas*, small-
creets, elphas-headed heirophants and Luminous Ones,
holy and profane all rolled together like spiral cakes into
one, great, sprawling, howling, bargaining, cheating, laughing, underdwell of a market: the Market of Hak'sha.

But the field captain directed Radience to pole the raft
to the shore long before they actually made port. Toldo
helped, but he was distracted, as usual, and the apprentice did most of the work.

The field captain gave her only a moment to rinse the

sweat off her chest and face before ordering her to pull the raft far enough ashore that it would not float away. Out of the water, it was heavier than Radience thought possible; it took the efforts of all three of them to shift it. Radience looked curiously at Cascade, then at the field captain, but the venomous look she received warned her away from making the obvious suggestion.

Later, as Toldo passed her he leaned down and whispered, "A good warhorse is worth ten soldiers. You don't waste him pulling ploughs or hauling loads."

They piled brush all around the raft.

"Ma'am," Radience asked, "is there no better way to conceal it? I can see it as plain as a castle wall."

"You'd be surprised; you already know it's there. In any case, I only care about hiding it from eyes on the river. If anyone stumbles across it on the shore, they're likely to see it no matter how well we camouflage the thing."

"Why from the river?"

"Because it's damned valuable—like Cascade. Any rag-ass river-snake that floated by and saw it would make off with it, sell it downriver. A farmer or a townie isn't likely to be going anyplace anyway."

"Where to now, ma'am? The market?"

"You haven't earned any liberty yet. You get one-half day in five."

"We've been on the river for—for I don't know how long, ma'am. Days? Moons?"

Jiana smiled nastily.

"Initiate time doesn't count. Pack the trash."

They hoisted their bundles and looped the straps around their shoulders. Toldo's was the heaviest, but he barely noticed the weight. Radience had the uncomfortable feeling that her own pack was the lightest.

The field captain did not mount Cascade; he walked unencumbered beside them. Every few moments, Radience caught the horse looking at her. It gave her a creepy feeling, which was immediately followed by embarrassment.

Darn him, he's just a damn horse! You're not a slave anymore.

* * *

Hak'sha was completely different from Radience's visionings, but just as wonderful. The houses were neither grand nor tall, the streets unbejeweled and the beggars unadorned.

But there were more people than the world contained, and the houses ran together like the stones on the beach of Triangle Bay. Pushing through the crowds reminded her of feeding time in the goat pens; she expected to push through the last of them at any moment, and find the rest of Hak'sha deserted—but it never happened. The mob was ubiquitous.

The smell of unwashed humanity was overwhelming; her heart raced and she kept worrying that they were crushing her, bearing in upon her like a million *daevas*, pawing and clutching. She pressed as close to Toldo and the field captain as she could and fought the terror.

An ugly face pushed close to the girl and screamed at her in a strange gibberish. She could not tell whether he was angry or anguished. Hands pulled at her clothing, tried to grab her wrists.

Two women, younger than Radience, threw themselves in front of the trio, crying and extending their dirty hands. The field captain slapped them aside without breaking her stride.

The lamentations of the beggars were so loud that Radience could not even hear herself shout. She choked on the smell, and put her mouth against the field captain's ear.

"What do they want? What do they want?" she cried.

"They want your blood," said Jiana; Radience could barely make out her words.

"Blood?"

"Food!"

"What?"

"I SAID FOOD! THEY WANT FOOD, CLOTHING, MONEY. THIS STUFF." Jiana showed her hand to Radience. She held two dull, iron eagleclaws, Toldo's entire horde; the lot would buy barely a night's lodging in a stables.

"Heeeeeeeeeeere, chick chick chick!" she called, and flung the coins away from them into the crowd.

With a single, tortured cry, the mob of beggars tore after the pitiful sum, trampling the weak and the crippled underfoot. While they screamed and fought like kites over a corpse, Jiana grabbed Radience's arm and ran the opposite direction, into a squat, ugly building that smelled of malt and disinfectant alcohol.

A burly man wearing his turban all wrong slammed the door, and the noise abated somewhat. Radience watched the door, convinced that the beggar's army would shortly batter it down, but they drifted away, those who could still move. Through a barred window, she saw two bodies in the street that did not look alive.

"Hey, Apprentice," said the field captain.

"Ma'am?"

"Welcome to civilization."

"Where is this? Ma'am?"

She was gone, dickering with a fat man who wore a leather apron.

A meaty finger thumped on Radience's shoulder. It was Toldo, who seemed a bit more awake to his environment.

"We are in what is called, in common parlance, an aleshop; to wit, it is called the Dangling Jamal."

"They sell alcohol here? To drink?"

"Ah, so I am told. As it were. Brewed into a malted beverage, I believe."

"Are we going to . . . drink this beverage?"

"They also sell rooms, or rather, let them for a daily rate, payable several days in advance. And unless you restrict yourself to water, then yes, you will be drinking this beverage. Are you devout?"

"No. I'm a soldier, or an apprentice, anyway." She looked back over her shoulder; the Seer was *very* strict about alcohol. Still, she knew what was often in the *kaf* that the Horsemen drank, and they had not been struck deaf and blind, as the priests warned.

"No," she said with firmness, "I'm not devout. I'll try the alcohol."

"Ale."

"The ale."

"Good. You'll probably hate it."

"Thanks."

"Mention it not, o diminutive one."

Her mouth was very dry. *Maybe I need some of that ale now. Oh Sand Lords, I hope not!* The chore did not hold the slightest appeal.

She looked around the smoke-choked room. The only light came from the windows set high in the walls; sunlight dripped down onto the floor, catching sparkles from a dust cloud that looked worse than the one tramped up by the feet of the Elect. . . .

A rush of emotion seized her throat; she gripped a nearby table to stop herself from falling.

Dead! They're all dead! Ysmal and Mugn and—and—

She fought the horror down; "no," she whispered, uncaring who heard; "they just went around again . . . we did them a f-favor . . . it was an accident. . . ."

The words rang hollow, but they worked. Radience was able to forget again for a time. She opened her eyes.

A young boy and his girl sat at the table, staring at the Radience apparition. They rose, took their drinks, and vacated across the room. Shrugging, Radience sat down and waited for Toldo and Jiana.

3

They took rooms at the inn, though Jiana still marveled that she convinced the hosteler to let them stay on credit.

For several weeks, Jiana drilled Radience in boxing skills; she tired to ignore Toldo in the other room experimenting with powders, philters, potions, and effluences. She also kept the other thought buried. Never in a life of horror had she killed a *thousand* men, women, and children—*no, not yet. Not today.*

Sales were brisk; what Toldo developed, Jiana manufactured, and the market eagerly sought. But she was continually haunted by the certainty that one day their luck would turn, and one of the compounds would prove fatal.

Radience tried a combination of punches that startled Jiana with their complexity. Radience left herself off-balance, but it was a well-planned attack.

"Try it again," Jiana ordered.

Radience had to think for a moment, remembering her own moves. Jiana allowed her to execute the combination four more times before stepping in and pushing Radience gently on her coccyx. The girl fell backward, but scrambled to her feet.

Watching Radience, Jiana felt the same tight feeling in her stomach that she felt when Toldo tried a new potion. Toldo was out of control. Radience was out of control. Jiana could not hold her on the bare path—she would drift, fall, *just like Dida. . . .*

"Damn you, *pay* attention!" Jiana reached out and center-punched Radience, harder than she intended.

"Get up. Body punches, twenty-five. One! Two!" With every count, Jiana punched savagely at the girl's chest. Radience stepped forward, along a diagonal path, which moved her just far enough off-line that the punches missed.

"Ma'am?" the girl asked when the count finished. She was out of breath; stamina would come. "We fight with fists, but we only dance with the sword. When do we *fight* with the sword?"

"When I cannot do this," Jiana said, casually driving a hook into the girl's side, just hard enough to ache. Too late, Radience tried to block and swiped empty air.

"Break for lunch. Work on the *Six Spurs*. Apprentice, dis-*missed.*" Radience saluted, and crossed the hall to her own room.

Jiana rubbed her scalp; time to shave again.

Toldo's head was tipped back, eyes shut. His skin had grown sallow, and he had ugly, black bags under both eyes. He spent more and more time every day lost in his inner worlds, sampling the dark alleys and hidden courtyards of his own stomach. But she had never before seen him so alive, so connected to the world around him as when he was back in the mundane sphere again. It was a perplexing contradiction.

Jiana rummaged through the dresser until she found the sliver of soap. She poured some water into the basin and wetted her head. As she lathered, she watched Toldo.

His head tipped slowly forward, excruciatingly slowly. He opened his eyes half way and focused on her.

Jiana scraped the razor across her scalp; the bristles were just long enough that they cut easily, not so long that they pulled.

"How do you sleep?" asked Toldo.

Jiana froze in mid-stroke for an instant; then she continued.

"Like the dead."

He watched her through eyelids still at half-mast.

"No more frightening dreams?"

She waited an equivalent moment before her own reply. Recent conversations had sounded like two mountain-climbers shouting across a valley.

"No more dreams."

She moved the razor in long, purposeful strokes. It soothed her, both the noise and the feeling of coming clean.

"Graveslipper can be deadly, Jiana."

Jiana's eyes widened momentarily, then she regained control. Toldo had seen; she was certain.

"I was not aware you knew I was using it. Don't worry. I monitor the dosage very carefully."

"I am sure you do. But there is a purpose to dream-sleep; you cannot stopper your stomach forever. Soon or late, it will burst forth, and, ah, *demand to be heard*, as it were."

"Toldo, I first beheld that dream when I turned thirty-two. Something will happen, happen thrice, before I turn thirty-three. Toldo, how long has it been since that first dream?"

"I don't know. What's today?"

"I was in the Market. A man asked the date. Before I could stop my ears, that damned fishmongner blurted it out."

Toldo watched her longer than usual.

"Well? What's the date?"

"In five days I'll be thirty-three."

She finished shaving in silence. She washed the remaining soap off of her head, and toweled off. She had paid for a mirror, and she was glad now. She took it into the light, and in the burnished surface she saw that her Warrior's Strip was as long and silky as it was back in Bay Bay, before this adventure began, a thousand thousand turns ago.

"Has it been so long?" asked the priest, "but it could not have been! You said you journeyed with the caravan for . . . what, four moons?"

"Four and a half. Then a half-moon on the raft *before*, two weeks after, and a moon and a half here in Hak'sha. The only gap was the time spent 'over the Edge,' as Radience calls it."

Toldo looked dubious. "Ah, I know we've been a bit out of touch since we landed, but can we have spent *five moons* in the Summerland? Would we not have noticed how out of synch we were with . . . well, with the seasons, for example?"

"Seasons? In Door? There's hot and hotter on alternating days. Have you asked anyone the date?"

He started to answer, then closed his mouth.

"Me neither, rotund one. Maybe we already knew the answer, and didn't want to hear."

A sudden flaw in her image, an imperfection, caught Jiana's attention. She looked closely into the metal, turning it left and right to catch the waning, afternoon light.

Right at the front of her hair, along the left side of the strip, was a clear though narrow streak of grey. Incredulous, she reached up and fingered it, separating it from the rest of the hair.

Nameless Serpentine . . . I'm only thirty-two! Or thirty-three. Snakeshit, what will it look like in ten turns, or fifteen?

One by one, Jiana separated the strands of grey and yanked them out of her head. Upset, she threw them out the window. She turned back; Toldo was watching her curiously.

"Uh, got something sticky in my hair," she explained, feeling her face flush.

"Jiana, the dream is urgent, or you would not have it night after night for nearly a turn. It will come out. It *will* out."

Jiana turned back to the mirror and searched for any more traitorous strands of grey; liars and dissemblers that falsely claimed she was an old woman when she was only thirty-two. *Thirty-three.*

"Then it will have to come out while my lids are wide open, for I'll not stop taking the Graveslipper."

Jiana inhaled deeply from the *huk* pipe and passed it to Radience.

—*thousand thousand horses hooves spruckling gingurgently 'gainst the sandy.* . . .

At once she is weeping, sad, both Jiana and Jianabelana. She cried for what was lost, found, leaving, taking, trickling. Radience this time, but Jiana in another time.

Old holds young; old endures, young impures. Sadness a mournpipe on a ruined castle wall. Grief a lake with a single, black treefinger pointing up at the loss. The madweed helped.

Jiana holds her but from behind, holds the girl's mouth over the chamberpot as she vomits a million years of compromise onto the floor. Bile burns her throat, stomach rejects all the little losses and ladle-leavings that add up to one gruff grief. Jiana understands. Filled her own share of chamberpots.

She. Was. Radience, Jiana. She was both. She held the apprentice's trembling body—not mother, just friend.

Radience held the stone straight out from her stomach, elbow locked. Jiana watched. At the slightest drop, the field captain said "pick it up, apprentice," punctuated with a rap on the girl's head.

Radience held it in her right hand, her strong hand. It was a tiny thing, a stone that weighed less than a teacup filled. It was a mountain, crushing her down like the grief, but a physical one she could fight. She ignored it and visioned an orange; her thoughts wandered as they had not for weeks.

The warrior is not her sword. The warrior is not her armor. The warrior is not her outfit, her unit. She is not her feet, her heart, her stomach. She hovers not overhead, does not buoy you up. RAP!

The warrior is the deepest part, nothing more than iron. Pick it up, apprentice, pick it up! RAP!

The warrior is the slayer? Radience thought.

"The warrior is not slayer, though sometimes she slays."

The warrior is the defender?

"The warrior is not defender, though often she defends."

Help me, I don't know where the warrior is! RAP!

"Then you have found the warrior after all, for the warrior is No Where. The queen does the finding; the warrior *carries on* until the queen wins. The queen endures; the warrior carries on."

The rock sank a notch and the image of the orange wavered.

"Pick it up, apprentice. Pick it up."

The warrior raised the rock, and Radience opened her eyes, quiet and aching. Jiana had turned into a huge, round orange. Radience laughed, and the image dissolved.

Jiana threaded her way through the tapestry of Hawkers and betrayers in the Hak'sha Market, fingering a cloth, staring at a silver breastplate, entranced. She sought something; she sought someone.

He was there, somewhere in the market. He was there, lost in Hak'sha. He was alive, shadowed in Door, in the middle kingdom, mid from the ocean, mid from the mountains, mid from the sewer-river Jambajala, giver of life, mid from tangled jungle to the south.

The market was a disappointment, after the stories she had heard. Jewels? Gold? Books by the thousands? Nothing but the maze of Bay Bay blown to ten times size, with all exotica removed! One hour in the Hak'sha Market and she'd seen everything. Everything except . . .

The sky darkened and the colors dimmed. She was glad for the greys, for she did not have to name them anymore. The winds picked up, and the merchants packed their smells and sweets away. Closing up, she heard trunks filling and booth-covers closing.

She shivered in the breeze, wrapped her cloak more tightly about her. It was dusty, grey with dust. Her lips were dry; she tasted the salt-sand, kicked up by the night breeze.

One lonely man stood at his booth still. Grief filled his eyes, too, and she felt at kindred touch between them.

"What are you selling?" she asked in Tooltak.

"A rug. It's a most wondrous, fine rug." But his voice was flat as the Five Sands.

"It is a wondrous rug," Jiana admitted. The texture was rough, but patterned; all of the pieces interlaced and connected, a bug inside a fish inside a bird. Even in the waning light, the rich greys blended into feelings and friends long gone.

At the center was a radiant woman, lines coming from her head. Her outstretched hands held night on the left and the sun on the right. Another figure depicted a terrible demon frightening a crowd of sinners, all save one man whose back was turned. He gazed upon a tree, serene and untouched. Its roots tangled both his own feet and that of the central figure.

"I have no spot for this rug."

The man nodded; his rug was unsold at the end of a busy day.

Jiana moved on, looking back once at the man who had woven such a rug. His loom sat ready, loaded with threads for the light of tomorrow.

She zagged her way through a score of boarded-up stalls, hearing the echos from within as families ate dinner in their tiny shops, which had now become even tinier homes. Quiet lights hung from some of the crossbeams, but in the chill no one came outside to share the night with Jiana. Far away, she smelled jasmine.

Her footsteps crunched on the gravel. The merchants

laid it generations ago to cut down on the sand clouds, but it was a lonely, hollow sound.

I'm just carrying on, she thought. *There is no queen within me. Just a warrior. What can I teach her? Only the queen can free the slave.*

Jiana shook her head, disagreeing with herself.

"That's a melancholy, a frivolity. I have my queen; she's just asleep."

"You have me," said the Jianabel voice in her ear.

"You are my sister, but I'm still missing parts of myself."

The sun set. Blood filled the western sky. The Great Moon stood directly overhead, obscured by clouds, and the Less Moon peeked over the horizon.

Jiana stepped around a big stall, stones laid upon stones, perhaps a jewelry mart. A figure loomed out of the dusk, and she froze, heart pounding.

They stared at each other, spirits in shadow; neither could see. Then he reached forth a hesitant hand, and whispered, "Jiana?"

The clouds parted, and the Great Moon burned the ground, illuminating the man in a flash of yellow.

It was Lord Dilai, her old lover. He covered his mouth in shock and shame. He wore the green sash of a Market hawker.

4

Jiana and Dilai walked slowly, untouching. The deserted market grounds were less oppressively hot at night. Jiana smelled jasmine again, but the smell of Dilai was stronger and overpowered the sweetness.

He reached out and touched her hand. He did not hold it; it was enough to touch it once. Jiana shivered at the touch, and her heart jumped. She pulled her hand away.

I am not in love with Dilai. He's a friendly face, he's a loved one. I don't love him.

From a boarded stall, a voice behind her ears: *make a deal—make a deal—make a deal.*

"Late shopping?" she asked, pretending she had not

seen the sash. He paused a long time before answering,
finally opting for truth.

"Things haven't gone well."

"It's been but a few moons."

"It's been a turn since I sold you to the Caliph; it hasn't
gone well. I've . . ."

He was about to tell her something dreadful; she heard
it in his voice, in the strain behind his words.

"Jiana, it's all gone."

"All gone?"

"Everything. Everything I have. Everything I had."

She stopped and stared at Lord Dilai.

"Oh gods. Shit. How could you lose—? It's *all* gone?"

Dilai turned away and put his hands over his face in
shame.

"A ship. A damned ship, a storm. Tear my tongue out,
and I won't tell you."

She reached out, but stopped just short of his neck; she
hesitated a moment, and then pulled her hand back again.

"How did it happen?"

"I know why they sent me out here now. Why they
were so eager to accept my application for the foreign
service. Alanai, that barbaric usurper, that lumbering savage! He could not *wait* for me to leave the country to
confiscate my estates! Nationalized. Took it in God's name,
for the Eagle and for the *people*." He spat the word.

Dilai began to sob. This time, Jiana did not hesitate; she
wrapped her arms around him and held him from behind.

"When I found out I—I went mad, I suppose; it's the
only explanation. I had some funds still, those which I
brought with me. Desperate, I invested all in a spice ship
sailing back up towards the Water Kingdom. Damned
captain. Who could expect a freak hurricane, this early in
the season?"

"A spice ship? Everything? Why the slithering hell did
you do that?"

"I . . . thought I had an inside track. A special edge."

A thought leapt to Jiana's lips. "Sorcery?"

Dilai nodded, eyes squeezed shut. "A powerful magus

promised me—well, indicated it was a propitious time to take a white flier."

"Who?" she asked, already suspecting the answer.

"Maug, he called himself; Potentate of Athnoor Door. He said."

"Pale-skinned, with black hair, blood-red gash of a mouth, features of a spoiled child? A dwarf?"

"He wasn't a dwarf, but he did rather resemble a child. What difference does it make? I'm ruined."

"Toq," she declared, swallowing a mouthful of anger. "Dilai, I'm sorry. I don't know what to say. You got caught in crossfire between me and a sneaking, weasely little godlet. Are you—don't take this the wrong way—are you *working* here in the market?"

Dilai nodded, listless and distracted.

Jiana pressed her face against the back of his neck and looked into the blackness. For as long as she had known him, Dilai was rich. He was not a fop, not a profligate; but he was generous to his friends. He was sometimes generous to total strangers, though never foolishly so.

There was no justice in such a sudden and final catastrophe in Lord Dilai's finances.

"Dilai, I can only promise you a warm bed and food, but you've already taken care of that. I have nothing else, except . . ."

Dilai said nothing, but Jiana heard the question in his silence.

"No, don't even ask. You must find your own light, your own reasons why."

"Jiana, light is what I need, more now than I ever have."

"It's dangerous. It's a shortcut, when what you need is long reflection. Damn it, it's a cheat."

And you are all against cheats, aren't you, dearest? Care to pick up a white-hot coal now?

No, please, don't let him! Don't do it, sister—remember our pact, our truce!

Dilai turned and grabbed her, his face twisted and ugly. "Jiana, do not deny me! WHAT DO YOU HAVE?"

Sleepy voices hollered protests from inside the stalls; a dog barked, and a window opened.

"I won't deny you anything that is mine, Dilai. Take it. Take me—right here and now, if you want. Only *do not ask someone else to free you.*"

"Jiana, I beg of you! Freedom is what I seek, but I don't know where to find it! Free me from this misery, this absurd despair. It was only money, in my stomach I know that. But in my heart, I lost *everything.* In my heart, I lost my soul! If you have something that will teach me, open me up to the rest of the world, to all that lies outside this mortal prison, then for the Eagle's sake, for pity's sake give it to me! Please!"

"Who told you to demand this of me? Are you still seeing that maggot, Toq? Or Maug, whatever he calls himself?"

Dilai's skin was sallow; even in the lantern light, Jiana saw his paleness. He had been quite tanned in Bay Bay. As she watched dumbfounded, he lowered himself to his knees and held his hands out to her, as if she were his leige-lord.

"I beg of you . . . I have nowhere else to turn!"

She recoiled from the debasement, stunned that the mere loss of a fortune would so tear a man to pieces. *Snakes and dog piss, I've won and lost more than I can count! Dilai, what have you done to yourself?*

"Please," he begged again. He laid his face into the gravel, hands at her feet. He trembled.

Jiana stared, her mouth open. She felt a hole open in her stomach. *This THING at my feet—how can I possibly still love it? I'm as sick as Dilai! Have I so little dignity left?*

"Deel, get up. You don't know what you ask."

"Help me."

"Free yourself."

"Help me."

"Help *yourself!*" she screamed, backing away; he was a stranger in the lamplight mist that blew between them.

Are you not choosing for him even now, sister mine? Why do you not offer him that which he demands?

Betrayer! You know the danger as well as I. You were there when I stole Toldo back from the friggits!

I remember also that he found what he sought. Maybe Dilai will do so, too.

Traitor!

Eater of souls!

A force pressed against her stomach, and she swelled like a balloon—not in the corporality of her body, but in her straining, thinning spirit. It was Jatjaka, throwing himself against the walls of his prison. Thin ice, he pushed, he beat! Once, she remembered, once she was skating, she fell through a hole . . . *grey light above, the cold, tearing through her skin like razors under the flesh. Fingers scraping rough ice from deep deep below begging for a hold, lungs straining bursting the air explodes out of them, and in rushes the molten water. All is black. All is warm. But who is this one?*

Jiana wrapped her arms tightly around her, pushing back the vision. Dilai stared up at her, his eyes two brittles of blue ice, his frozen, black hair flurrying like smokelines in the breeze.

Resistance was too hard. A doom hung over her head, a ghost lurked in her stomach. *What will be, will be.*

"Come with me." She turned and led a path back to the inn, her mouth too dry to spit.

She did not look back even once; his need would draw him. She did not look ahead; the future was a glacier, crushing all the paths of might-have-been under the inexorable weight of forward motion.

The streets were filled with beggars. They grew silent at the sight of her and drew back into the shadows. No warrior today. Today, Jiana was puffed full of the breath of the serpent. Today she was priestess . . . gave absolution to the fallen lord.

She reached the inn, stretched forth her hand. The latch worked itself before she could touch it. The hardwood door shied from her hand to swing wide.

Jiana crossed the threshold as the moons turned red. Holiness dripped hot ash from the sky. Rats scurried from her path, disappearing into the walls in terror.

She closed her eyes, but the Power had risen within her, and she saw all, and more than she should have. Too many dead. A thousand turns dead. No one in the hall, for they were all buried before their children's children's children were born; the dead lay silent, cold winding sheets their only caresses.

Hands held apart, nearly a prayer, touched the walls on either side. She crossed the room, scattered cold sanctity with booted feet. Up crystalline stairs. One step follows another. Looping cobwebs formed a circular tunnel through which she passed.

Low chanting, a long, drawn-apart note. It was the first sound of life she had heard. It was life at the end, an old man at the end, memories of an old man looking back to the beginning and wishing himself into a new babe's first piercing yowl.

Came to her own room at last. Blackness out the windows, furniture looms like solid shadows: a dresser, two chairs. Pegs on the wall for clothes and weapons. A wash basin, a chamberpot.

A bed. All furnishings furnished by Harouk Nadore, Esq., keeper of the Dangling Jamal. Dark, ancient furniture that was cold to the touch.

Jiana lit a lantern, burning her fingers when the tinder caught. She heard music through the window, the end of a refrain. The last notes, war-pipes across a battle field too far to hear, borne on warrior-winds. The charge, break, collapse of the center.

The horse is missing. They push through, scatter the enemy, but at last they are gone, and even the groans and death-cries of the wounded fade, and then there is no more alone time to sit on the back of a horse and look at a valley. Then, only then, do you hear the pipes. You shudder, you look back over your left shoulder, you look for the moons, but they are gone—what, did they flee, too? —and you know that the pipes you hear are the hiss of the Slithering One, the Nameless Serpentine, Death the Final Bit, come to git.

She heard *those* pipes in her room.

He was gone; Toldo was gone, but he left Dilai's awakening upon the dresser. *So simple; a handful of paste, roll it in a slice of brown bread, fall out of the Dreaming.*

Fall awake.

Without a word, she scooped the paste out of the mortar with her knife. She turned and held it out to Lord Dilai.

He looked frightened, but he knew he could lose nothing more than he had already squandered. He scraped it off onto his own knife.

"Wrap it. It's vile."

He looked around helplessly; she walked into the pantry, took down some bread and cut a slice. She handed it to him, and he was grateful.

Dilai spread the paste upon the bread; he rolled the slice into a bread-ball. He kept licking his lips, and rubbing the side of his hand against them, too dry, too wet. He closed his eyes and ate the ball, all in one bite.

"Now come to me," Jiana demanded. She pulled her tunic off over her head.

"How long until . . . ?"

"Fuck off. *Attend to me.* You'll slide soon enough, Serpent knows." She rubbed her fingers gently across her brown nipples, and sat down. She removed her boots, first the left then the right.

Dilai watched her like a frightened schoolboy. He touched his penis, just barely; at least it was responding appropriately, even if he was not.

Jiana pulled her pantaloons off and stood nude before him.

"Strip," she suggested, gestured impatiently. His hands shook. She helped him unbutton his blouse.

Jiana pulled his luxurious, black wig from his head, used his unholy-expensive silken shirt to wipe the powder from his face and neck, crushed-berry eyepaint from lids and lashes.

She kissed him, biting his lips and tasting blood and cherries. She grabbed the back of his close-cropped hair, his own hair, with a savage grip of longing. She pressed her tongue far back in his mouth.

Dilai distractedly ran his fingers up her legs, starting at the knees and ending between her thighs. A lustless, desultory caress; rote exercise.

Jiana's atavism flowed into Dilai's ascetisicm and the balance they struck was an equitable dance. Jiana forgot what could be and focused on what she had. She had Dilai, and this time that was enough.

She reached around and bit his neck, not quite hard enough to break the skin. She ran her tongue lightly across the fold of flesh stretched tight by her teeth.

Dilai took hold of her buttocks, sinking his fingers inside, touching the tiny, black hairs. Almost despite his intention, he grew excited and rubbed himself against her thigh. She spat out face powder and kissed him again. He responded, and their tongues entwined.

At the edges of her hearing the pipes still blew, still faint but louder. Closer—the Slitherer coiled back, scales rumbling the ground beneath their feet.

Jiana had swallowed a balloon, and now it expanded within her. It contained many rooms: a room for Jianabel, and a room for Jatjaka, a room for her mother, a room for Dida, and a very large room for Dilai. The last was empty, for the Lord had left home and a stranger warmed her bed.

Another room there was, locked with an iron bolt, sealed with five great runes, buried beneath a mud mountain, and sunk beneath an ocean of *aparts* and *detaches*. There was a window in the room, hole in the bars, gap through the runes, tunnel in the mountain. An underwater cave rose through the ocean. Down this hole, she dimly saw a dark, hairy-knuckled hand reach out, loving.

Jiana turned her head, averted her eyes.

Dilai gasped and arched his back. Jiana pushed him back, back across the room and onto the soft bed, covered in warm fur blankets. Two lovers sank like children in the tall wheat of White Plains.

Jiana kissed his bare chest, tugging hairs with her teeth. She ran her tongue down Dilai's belly, and unbuttoned his thrice-woven trousers.

Sedge sedge, he thought, and Jiana jumped when she heard it. *He is a glass, I see through him to the roundy world beyond.*

Sounds: the roarwhoosi of the feckle wind, blowing acrues the battleplains, accepting the suckrifaces, the thousand whiting dead, breach their bowns in the umercibake son.

Sounds: the roar of the fickle wind, blowing across the battleplains. *Drones, chanters, mockers*, she thought. *I hear them, angels of angles bend and pluck us from the ground, woven of bodies and parts, remains of The Crew What Never Sleeps, the soldiers of Didńa'win!*

They blew their pipes, rode ever closer. No trick of the wood, trick of the night; they blew *above* Reality Prime, in the Oversphere that swam into her ken, now and again.

Dilai fell into the play even as he fell out of the dream. Again he spasmed, again the little death fired his inner landscape into Jiana's receptive stomach.

The plains opened before him, spread wide, a bowl to an ant at the center. The vision spun, mountains reeled; he sees the mountains, he does not see them, he sees.

Glass arching overhead, the bottle (the sky). The goose strains; goose is trapped. What is inside *and* outside *when there is* only *one* side?

Jiana has his cock in her hand, squeezes it hard, hard enough. She is all. She is all for him. For her, his thoughts reach out and pull her into the nightmare with him: *Sedge, take me back, smoke calls me out, reaches for me* (hand— whose hand?—she sees it still, *must* look. It belongs to—no, it is no one's now!).

Jiana felt a trickle run down her thigh; she needed him then, and she did not care where the rest of him was. She straddled Dilai and pushed him deep inside. For a moment she stayed perfectly still, felt him so large, swollen. One clear voice spoke: not Jianabel, not Toldo, no part of her stomach but herself. Her thoughts.

Jiana, you cannot *turn away. For a thousand years you have denied the final vision of this dead part of your life. Sister, you must look. You must learn the truth about me, about you.*

No! she cried, *leave me ignorant, you bitch! I'm afraid. How can I be a master when I'm filled with such fear?*

Dilai gripped her savagely and breathed rapidly as the Waking began. At last, the young lord had broken through the mountains of hallucination and found the abyss they hid. Toldo's potion exploded in Dilai's stomach. The voice would not be stilled.

Poor, little hero, it is because of your fear that you can be a master! To feel it burn every tiniest atomie, every germ of your flesh, and still stamp a foot and say No! This is what makes the sky blue.

But what am I, what am I? I see everyone but me—Toldo with his mushroom, Radience with her freedom. Where is my liberation?

You helped them to what they have. You have it too. The fear of death is the beginning of slavery—the death of fear is the beginning of slavemongery. To go warriorwards—what a campaign!—is to touch the fear, but let it not touch you.

Jiana rolled with Dilai. She knew him, but he was a stranger. The Waking poured through his body, turned him from her.

This is whoring! she accused. *I don't know him.*

This is worship, responded the voice. *Your touch is shaking him awake. Whose hand did you see? Whose dark hand has reached out to you for more turns than you've reached for Wave?*

Liar! Deicide!

You know; you have always known. You know you did not kill your father!

Jiana pushed her hands under Dilai's thighs and pulled him deeper inside. He was warm and solid. He pushed her spirit up, pushed everything aside to make room. Jiana rocked back and forth with rhythm.

You lie. He died. I saw him die!

But you did not kill him.

He died on my knife! He killed the little girl, Daddy with his hands, roving hands, hands so touchy—

Daddy is here with you.

Daddy raped me!

Yes.

I killed him!

No. You know *who killed your father.*

I killed him, damn you! I killed, killed, I kill them all! I killed a thousand in Deh Bid, burned them, killed Rethe my friend Rethe killed Dida killed Toldo killed—I don't want to hear!

You know. Who killed your father?

I did!

Who killed him?

Jiana sobbed, sorrows of woman of worlds of spheres of turtles of fishes of trees and rocks, of Totality burst forth from Jiana's stomach in one convulsive sob. "Daddysnakes fighter biter suicider *you didn't need to fucking* end it *like that!*"

Dilai came. Jiana felt powerful thrusts, and a great laceration split her belly from crotch to sternum. A savage *Ahhhh!* burst forth, a swollen troll gobbles one heart too many and explodes into a dense fog of trollops!

Warpipes raged *inside* Jiana's room. Coming, coming for Dilai!

Jiana was inside him. Even as he was inside her. She looked *out* through Dilai's eyes, heard with his ears the pipes that called him up, out. *The Waking calls . . . him out . . . Toldo's apothic . . . burns, pulls. . . .*

He rises. Rises up out of his body. Rises up, the himness of it, looks down—*Jiana my love, farewell—my time—learned what it is to have, learned what it is to lose.*

Rise above her and what was once mine. Rise, cross the room, stretch out their hands to me. Pipes, I hear you! I hear them!

The end. Last days. In the truth. rise, I walk across the room, drift in the smoke, drop in the ocean. She is behind me; Dilai my body once me too is behind me.

Door opens, I pass through. Stairs—brush fingers along the wall I glide, look through the doors on either side, thousands and millions of doors. Closed, but I know I could open them. Don't want a door. Down the stairs, pipes drone to wake the dead, shake the living.

Great hall, they're all there. Slave girl at the fire, no a warrior now nearly. Priest in the big chair—he sees me. How can he? He watches—

—as I go by, eyes follow me. Secret smile signs to me that he knows, rather. Smile back, happy. Wealth is what was, richness what is. Lift a hand. Going home. Going Dilaiwards at last!

Pipes and horns, shells and huzzahs, ribbons and bunting, lanterns, fireflicks! Surround me, crowds on the wide smooth road. Stamp of thousands of millions of feet. Dancers at the door in red robes and jeweled slippers, welcome me with outstretched hands, I TAKE—

Last door—

—only door I want—

—only door I open. It's over. . . .

Jiana held him close. Dilai stiffened, relaxed a long, slow outbreath. Pipes died slowly as the windbag emptied.

They tripped gaily, gaily down the stairs. She heard them in the great hall, heard them outside her window. Heard them over the desert, the battlefield, fading like wind through hollow reeds. She held him close in the dark, on the bed, inside her. No inbreath.

Jiana gritted her teeth, rocking his limp body back and forth and back, holding him up, her Krakshi, her rag doll. No bloodbeat. No inbreath.

Tears . . . she touched her cheek, astonished. *What's this? What is this? What was he to me, what more than the others? What more than Dida, than Tawn, than that bitch in Two Rivers who threw herself on my fucking sword?*

Damn you, Wave! Damn damn you, Radience and Cascade and Toldo and all the everyone on this fucking bloody sphere!

I hate you all for loving me. Hate you for tearing the heart from a dying bear and leaving nothing but a hole. Oh god-Tooqa worldserpent I hate You too for not being here to help me! I killed them all myself no help from any of you, man, girl, or god!

She kissed what once was Dilai, once a lord, once her

love. The lips were cold, though he died but an instant before. Pipes were silent. Dilai was dead.

But a laugh began. Slow at first, a mere chuckle; it grew and rolled, now from here, now there. She knew that laugh.

It became a howl of hilarity, a madness of mirth, a rage of rowdy knee-slappery. *Who but one?* she thought, dead as Dilai in her stomach.

She turned her head. The light in the room faded, leaving only a dull, blue glare coming from the lantern. All the colors paled in the blue, as if the Less Moon had fallen into the room and snuffed out its enemy, the lantern sunfire light.

Out of the blue folded the pasty, white boy-god, Toq.

Jiana watched him; she still held Dilai's body to her breast; she made no move to slide him out of her. "Twice," said the god, admiring his fingernails; he tore them from his fingers, one by one, as they talked.

"You did nothing to hurt him," countered Jiana emotionlessly. "I was with him, within him as he died. He died knowing himself. I killed him without your useless help."

"*His* life was not what I promised to blot."

"His own choice. Dilai knew the risk. I saw the desperation in his face, the only choice he could make!"

"He's gone, thing. You will never, ever, ever see him again. And there is worse—much worse!"

She watched him silently. Then she pressed Dilai's icy cheek to her own and closed her eyes. "There is worse," continued Toq, cheerfully. "You already realize how much worse, deep within you . . . say, a bit deeper than you have that Jatjaka chap captive. You know as well as I what is *really* behind your pious feelings of sorrow.

"Can you idenetify that feeling? Do you know that emotion? It's your very favorite, Jianabelana!"

Still, she said nothing. But her stomach flexed tightly for an instant. She knew. Toq continued joyfully. "It's Envy, creature! You *envy* the poor, dead Dilai. You know why?"

A horrid voice suddenly whispered in Jiana's ear. It was Dilai's voice, but flat, devoid of life. His lips moved mechanically, like the card-reading, instrument-playing automatons of Doctor Crugitti, he who once passed through White Falls when Jiana was eight turns old.

"I-know-something-you-don't-know," croaked the voice of her dead lover, "but-you-will-learn-as-I-learned. Exactly-as-I-learned." Then it grinned, its lips curling back as if they had been flayed away.

Jiana dropped the body, staring in horror. It reached a cold, dead hand up and took hold of her breast.

She yanked her chest away from the hand as Dilai's corpse began to laugh like a broken water clock, chiming the hour endlessly, "hu-hu-hu-hu-hu . . !"

Then even the blue light faded to black. The lantern sack turned to ash, the corpse died again. Toq was gone, and poor Jiana was left alone. She knelt on the bed and wept, wished she, too, could die that moment. Wished she could hear her own warpipes. Wished someone, *anyone*, would hold out a hand so Jiana could follow the thousands she had sent along the smooth, wide road in red robes and jeweled sandals.

Wished that she *knew*.

"Goodbye, Dilai," she said at last, her voice breaking, "alright, damnit. I lu-love you. More than the others. Safe passage." She reached out in the dark and closed his eyes.

Chapter X

The inexorable weight of forward motion

1

Radience watched from the doorway, silent as a tomb. She had watched for a long time, swallowing her heart down her throat again and again.

She watched Jiana strip, every inch as thrilling as the girl had visioned. She watched her take *that man* inside her, every inch as repulsive as Radience had imagined. The girl nearly cried out then, but clamped hands over her mouth instead.

She watched Dilai die, watched him reanimate; Radience felt ice between her thighs. She watched the show, silent as a grave, until a cry was ripped from her when Toq's evil animus passed directly through her. She recognized him, the Teenja-Overman *daeva*.

The field captain looked back at her. Jiana's eyes caught the lantern light and shone like a cat's. The warrior watched Radience like a predatory animal, but the girl met the gaze without flinching.

Radience trembled all over, but she did not know whether it was out of fear or anger. *Betrayal! doesn't she* know *what she means to me?*

Radience stepped into the room from the doorway. She hungered to be where the dead man was, with Jiana's naked, sex-drenched body straddling her. Radience desperately wanted to feel Jiana's hands touching her the way the dead man felt them, wanted it so much her gut ached. Tears leaked down her cheeks, and she pressed her lips together to stop the shaking.

"All this time . . ." she said at last, her voice unable to produce more than hoarse whisper, "all this time, damn you, you *knew!* You must have known!"

Jiana dropped her eyes, glowering, not responding.

Finally, Radience found the volume she needed.

"THEN HOW COULD YOU FUH-FUH-FUCKING LET ME GO ON HOPING, YOU BITCH!" The last word rose into a shriek; the tears flowed freely down her face.

Jiana did not respond, but she closed her eyes and turned her head aside.

"I loved you! I *needed* you!"

Radience turned and stumbled blindly, blinking the salty drops out of her eyes, feeling for the wall. She pounded upon it, again and again, beating out her hurt, her anger, her frustration. Soon her right hand was numb and bleeding. One of her knuckles was broken and swollen.

Jiana spoke, not as the field captain, not as the warrior; she spoke as one woman to another woman.

"Radience . . . I'm sorry. I'm not—that way."

The girl laughed, without mirth.

"Ever try it?"

"Yes. More than once. I like—I can only do this with a man. I'm sorry. Really." She did not sound sorry.

"Stuff it."

Radience rested her head against the cool wood. Her hand began to throb. She kneaded it with the small hand; it felt raw and swollen.

"He's dead, you know," Radience said.

"I know."

"How did he die?"

"At peace," said Jiana.

Radience wiped her wet cheeks on the rough, wooden panels. She could not stop grinning at the perfection of the humiliation. *She prefers men. She prefers* dead men *to me!*

She reached across with her left hand and drew out her knife. She breathed deeply, calming herself, slowing her heart as the field captain had taught her.

Slowly, she brought the tip of the blade up until it just touched her chest, directly underneath her sternum, pointing slightly upward.

A tiny thrust; a spasm. . . .

"If you're going to do it, apprentice, then *do it*," said Jiana angrily. "Don't stand there like a virgin with her first mouthful of cock."

The girl's mouth fell open in astonishment; she visioned what Jiaña had just said and closed her mouth abruptly.

She let her arm drop and the knife dangle, though she did not let go completely. The lantern was immensely bright, all of a sudden. *What a stupid, what an incredibly stupid way to die!*

"Am I that transparent?" she asked.

Radience laughed, a real laugh. She could no longer take herself or the situation seriously. There sat the field captain, naked as a mid-day lie, mounting a corpse—while her crippled apprentice watched breathlessly, one hand up her shirt, the other clutching a suicide knife!

Radience fell to her knees, giggling hysterically. The more she laughed, the lighter she felt, until she was certain she would float up and out the window, never to be seen again. *In a fairy song, that's exactly what would happen*, she thought.

She rolled around, planting her back against the wall.

"Damn the Seer's eyes," she swore, "but you are beautiful!"

Jiana stood, allowing the dead man's penis to slide out. She stepped off the bed, facing Radience. The warrior stood unashamed of her nakedness, even after what Radience had revealed.

"Someday," Jiana said, "the sun will turn black, and the earth will shake. The heavens will split, and the Nameless

Serpentine will slither forth to make his nest among the ants that crawl upon the surface of this sphere.

"Someday, the oceans will boil, and the whirlwind will level all the mountains. We will stand upon the great plain of Agtor, you and I, watching the kneeling ones, the cowering ones, the crawling ones, as the Great World-Serpent swallows them up like mice and lizards.

"On that day, I shall look Tooqa the World Serpent in his ice-grey left eye, and you'll look him in his fire-red right eye, and we will defy that huge, bloody, worm and tell him to go crawl back into that egg whence he came, that egg we call the Less Moon.

"On that day, we shall be equals.

"But until that day . . . GET YOUR FUCKING ASS UP AND AT ATTENTION WHEN I TALK TO YOU, APPRENTICE!"

Radience staggered to her feet, caught rubber-legged by the raw violence of her outburst.

"Start packing your shit, apprentice. We're bugging out of here tomorrow morning at sunrise."

Radience snapped to attention and saluted.

"Aye, ma'am!" she said with an unwarrior-like grin, and quick-marched back to her own room. She bounced on her toes, feeling a great energy surge through her. The terrible weight of the future had fallen off back in the field captain's room, and Radience willingly left it there.

2

"So what do I do with you now, my love?"

Dilai did not answer, though the echo of his horrid, mechanical laughter rattled around Jiana's stomach.

She could not call the *hostelator;* he would have them all thrown out in an instant, and they needed the night. In any case, she wanted to burn Dilai's body, as befitted a Lord of Bay Bay, but the Doorian Guard would take the remains as evidence and try to convict the three of them of murder. He was too young to die without a mark upon him.

She would have to walk the corpse down the stairs herself, pretending he was merely drunk, and take it to an Eagle temple. Toldo could help, both with his size and his connections . . . if he would ever return.

I ain't going to do that in the nighttime, she decided. Not that she was afraid, she hastened to assure herself; but there was too much danger of tripping and falling down the stairs, or being stopped by the Guard.

This left the uncomfortable necessity of sleeping alone with Dilai all night, but Toldo might soon return, and he slept next door. And Radience was a shout away—in case Jiana needed to move Dilai, of course.

Twice, she thought; *twice the son of a bitch has blotted my life, like slapping me across the face with a leather strap.* She was filled with a cold anger at Toq, the nasty, little boy-god; Toq, of the raging temper and sick humors.

Feeling weak and a bit nauseous, Jiana stepped up to the bed, grabbed Dilai around his middle, and hauled him off and onto the floor. She dragged him across the room, straining every muscle in her arms, belly, and back. Thin as Lord Dilai was, he was a very tall man, and he nearly weighed more than she could carry.

She dragged him into the far corner and sat him down as gently as she could. His head fell forward, followed by the rest of his body. By propping up his knees, Jiana manipulated him into a position which was stable.

Like a leather strap across the face . . . like a mailed fist . . . hu-hu-hu-hu-hu. . . .

"No!" she said, and all at once she understood, "not a leather strap, a gauntlet!"

Jiana stood slowly, massaging her naked shoulder. "Damn it, was I *blind?*" So obvious, now that she thought of it; the universal challenge of the *code duello:* three slaps across the face.

So the fucker wants to fight. Still wants revenge for a quest four turns ancient. She laughed, dry as Radience in her mirth. A challenge!

But what were the rules, where was the field? Jiana

stretched forward and turned out the lantern, plunging the room into blackness.

The moons played hide-me-find-me behind a cloud; she could not even see her own hands, so dark it was.

And in the corner, surely now staring at me with those dead, blue eyes popped open again, sits my once-a-time lover.

So when does the third boot drop?

Three times, Toq had said; three times before she turned thirty-three.

She sat cross-legged on the bed and visioned herself young again, as she was when she quested for the World's Dream. Then, she was a young woman, fighting and training far across the sea, in the Flower Empire.

Soon she was back, but before she had left. Bay Bay again, for the first time; first days in the harness, strutting and proud—*soldier-girl! Hah, step back, jump back you fags and fuckers, and keep your shit-soaked hands off my body you still want 'em stuck to your wrists want to live forever still be able to smack yer snakes*—But the confidence waned (not yet grown), the harness grew big (for she had not yet grown into it).

Other birthdays she had had: other parties, raising a glass, running a gauntlet, and then she was seventeen seasons old at an orgy with five guys, two girls, and ten pots of strongtea.

Then the light blew out, days grew short and overcast, irongrey clouds and clods unrivaling the sin, twice the brackness of the Waifwolf Whore. When Jianabelanabel luved.

How many turns in the wolfish desert, dating from the time Daddy—*no! turn away, stay back! danger lurks!*—from the time Daddy got his hands in one too many snakeholes, yeah that's the story now—*dragged himself unwilly unnilly up the altar steps, dragging two, too-long snakearms a dozen and more dozens of feet behind like horrid anchor ropes pulling him back back back away from the sacrifice, laying down on the altar with the*

*lifeprick above in the paws of She What Done It All and
cables of lifeline straining to pull him back. . . .*

But no—

It didn't—it wasn't—

DANGER! BEWARE! *STOP THE THOUGHTS NOW!*
*(yes I know I killed a thousand innocents yes kill me for
it nail me upside-down by my feet that's the real crime
that's. . . .)*

Too late. The warning fell unheeded. Jiana broke a
twenty turn pact with the Less Moon, Mother Memory.
Jiana remembered.

She remembered nights of terror, dreading a moment
she knew would come. Dreaming a footstep on the stair, a
drunken stumble against the bannister. Crying a silent
prayer that tonight, just this *one* night he would pass on
by. The step mounts the stairs. Deep voice slurring curses
at officers, paymasters, stockade guards.

Pause. Floorboards creak. Start to recede, pause and
turn back.

Hand on the doorlatch.

She hated the feel of him, hated the smell of him. Afraid
to tell, just *our little secret,* Mom never understand afraid
to tell anyway just making it all up sick little girl oh my
God *what have you done to your teeth?!*

No, not that; she remembered all that long ago. Never
truly forgot, just buried.

No. Deeper. *(No deeper!)*

I sacrificed him. I led him, lured him up to the attic—

*No, dearest. It's time. Time to remember what really
happened.*

Suddenly she was She again. She as a lonely, frightened
little girl, seven turns, two seasons perhaps.

She was she. Sobbing on the bed in an inn in Hak'sha in
clothing many times too big holding a sword far too heavy
(always too big, always too heavy). *How am I here? What
is this? Dilai is still dead but I am young enough to be his
daughter . . . Tooqa, Nameless Serpentine please I do not
want to remember this!*

Her mother was sick. She lay in bed, unable to move.

Daddy crippled, left arm severed many moons past.
Useless.

They pensioned him out; spit and a biscuit, not enough
for half a turn, after half a life in the service.

So what to do? Rent piling up. Housing not free, not
even in White Falls, New River Area.

Still on the rolls, though. Still on the rolls until the Wolf
Run, still half a moon away. Muster them out on the third
day of the Run, give them their spurs and a hearty slap on
the back. *Good luck, don't trip over the spittoon.*

Still on the rolls of the Citizen's Protection Committee
Militia, and if one were to *die* in service. . . .

But it has to be clean; no sudden thrust from a sword,
no falling off the cliff at the falls. None of them are stupid,
not about such scams.

Has to be clean.

So cold . . . so cold . . .

Tiny Jiana crouches at the window. She stares out into
the white, stares into the wolf weather, slush-snow alter-
nates with freezing rain.

Stares at her father. Watches him stand in the river.

Stand still as a statue, as if he were frozen himself.

(Do you think they can tell?)

Hour after hour he stands, knowing what will finally
catch him. *(Do you think they can guess?)*

Momma doesn't know. Lays in the bed, doesn't recognize Jiana, doesn't look for Neis in the water.

*Daddy lays in the bed now. Coughing, wheezing. No
breath. Can't breathe.*

*He slips. Further. Breath a gurgle, blowing bubbles in
the bathwater. Pneumonia, influenza, who knows? Heal-
er's on the other side of his circuit.*

*Do you think? They'll figure it out? Do you think they
can tell?*

Will I ever tell?

*I hate him. I hate him for touching me hurting me,
loving me hurting me. I hate him for dying for me!*

I killed him; yes, that's easier.

I did him. Up in the attic. No, no I'm not Jiana, really

*I'm not; silly, you know me . . . you know Jianabel! Today
I'm alive, today I'm the Wolfish Queen, and afterall Daddy,
your fingers were just into everything, you know!*

*Who is that man that stands outside my window on cold
nights, stands in the icy river watching with hungry eyes?*

Sleep falls like a curtain; a lonely, guilty little girl weeps.

3

Awakened by a kiss. . . .

Jiana dreams, dreams she is awake, awakes to find she
dreams. Is she awake or asleep, dreamer or dream? Is a
mountain?

Awakened by a kiss. . . .

She opens her eyes. Dilai kisses her a third time.

For a moment, Jiana froze. Then she rolled out of bed
on the opposite side, grabbing for Wave. She held the
sword in front of her, but the tip wavered and shimmied
like moonlight on the ocean.

Dilai, clothed only in his wig and powder, stood across
the bed from her. He grinned, and one of his teeth fell
from his rotting jaw. His tongue was black and swollen.

"Honey-I'm-home," he intoned mechanically.

Jiana curled her lip.

"Schoolboy pranks now, Toq? What's next? Going to dip
my hair in an inkpot?"

"Do-you-know-what-tomorrow-is." It was a moment before she realized it was a question, flat as the voice was.

"Sunny. It's always sunny here. Ghosts vanish into va-
por in the sunlight. It must be almost dawn; hadn't you
better get dissolving?"

"Tomorrow-you-turn-thirty-three."

"Snakeshit!"

"Tomorrow-you-turn-thirty-three."

"It has *not* been a turn. It has *NOT* been a turn!"

Dilai continued to grin, but his head rolled sideways,
the neck fractured.

"I-made-you-a-promise-do-you-remember."

It was Dilai. It was not Dilai, it was the nasty, little

boy-god, Toq. But it was Dilai, and she could not close him out, not completely.

"Three times," she answered in spite of her resolve.

"Three-times-would-I-blot-your-life."

"I count only twice: the fire worms and your own death. Dilai's death. I know what you do, and the challenge is accepted."

"I have not finished."

"You have only one night. Nothing else you can do will hurt as much. Want to kill Radience? Toldo? Makes no difference; both have already found a piece of themselves, due to me. Damn you, I accomplished something, even if they both die tonight!"

One eye stared at Jiana; the other rolled slowly in his head, as if detached from its muscles and nerves.

"Well, what then?" Jiana took a powerful, warrior's posture, ready to attack or defend as necessary.

"You already know. And you have already died one of your deaths."

"One of?"

"You are destined to die many times, Jiana."

Toq-Dilai lurched his hand up and extended it to her. His fist was closed, holding something. It could only be one thing.

"What is in your hand?" she asked, turning her face slightly.

Toq-Dilai did not speak; he did not move his hand.

As if compelled, Jiana reached her own left hand out and held it beneath his. He opened his fingers. A roll of Toldo's magical paste fell into Jiana's palm. The paste was shaped like a snake.

So it's come to this, eh? No one to stay awake for; no one to die for. My choice, at the last.

Don't do it, sister! Remember what he said—on the day you taste this false answer, you shall follow Dilai down the Jambajala!

Her palm glowed with a malignant, blue light; the power

So? What's the point?

of the Waking, had all by itself shifted her consciousness into the magical sphere.

It's just another pasture to graze, explained another, unbidden voice in her stomach. Concentrating, Jiana could almost hear the horsey-snort, the shuffle of hooves.

Don't listen to him! We're fine as we are, Jiana!

"I'm *not* fine. But I am a 'we,' a plural. Snakeshit. That's my problem."

His mission completed successfully, Dilai's body became at once nothing more than a dead body. It collapsed into a tangle of limbs next to the bed. Jiana's hand began to tremble beneath the weight of the Waking.

Like a battlefield where a thousand armies meet, the voices all converged upon Jiana. She did not know where Toldo was, but his thoughts invaded her digestion now. Radience was asleep across the hall, but her noisy spirit filled Jiana's ears.

Don't run, don't become another. I need you as you are!

I have seen so much, such an explosion of comprehension. And all because of a tiny, misshapen fungus.

Don't be silly, we have so much to stay alive for!

"Stop . . ."

Yes, you take, you try! Try and die, free me from this prison of betrayal, yes yes!

So much I never knew, so much I can never put into words. . . .

Jiana? Help me . . . help me find my way back, I your first love. . . .

—*merging into a closed consciousness of Unity*—

—*follow you, no matter what*—

—*roundable spherism of thinkism*—

—*blood of the Earth*—

—*free! Be free, shall I be free when you*—

—*uniting with Universal stomachspirit*—

—*always loved you, ever since you drew me from Outside, from another, from far*—

—*Coward. Human*—

—*find me . . . fix me . . . fuck me*—

"*SHUT UP!*" she screamed; "all of you! Jiana—*must*—be—*first!*"

She clapped her hands over her ears, and the abrupt silence tore her, thunder shattered her ears and rendered her deaf and mute.

So it's down to this. Down to me. Down to this.

She unclenched her fist; the snake shape was obliterated into four fissures left by her fingers.

"I have decided," she whispered, as if afraid of who might overhear. "I know now; I see what must be. I *must* taste totality—at least once. At most once."

Jiana's breath came ragged and fast. Her heart beat like a rabbit's. She raised the Waking to her lips.

There she froze. Her heart raced so fast that she felt faint. She could not catch her breath. Her hand dropped.

She tried again, pulling the magical paste up to her mouth, but again, the terror seized her, and she dropped her hand and fell heavily on her side.

"Damn it, I *will* do it!"

She opened her mouth, wide as a snake swallowing a toad. She focused her gaze upon her hand and brought it excruciatingly close to her tongue. But the shaking in her hand grew more and more violent, and she whimpered involuntarily.

"*Why can't I do this?*" she cried.

She tried; again her will failed.

Too quickly to lose her nerve, she brought her hand up and shoved the wad in her mouth. She swallowed without chewing.

At once, the long-suppressed Toq-dream erupted in her stomach. The Waking stirred and came to life; it twitched and squirmed in her throat and crawled madly about her stomach like a maddened living thing, a cockroach.

Her stomach heaved, rejecting the Waking. She doubled over and vomited the paste upon the bed. She continued to heave, again and again, as the last drop of sputum was forced up her burning throat and onto the bed where Dilai died.

She lay on her belly, sick and dizzy, refusing to whimper or cower. Her face rested in a pool of sour, sticky fluids.

Jiana opened her eyes; the acid from her stomach stung them, and she was glad for the pain and the shock of the smell. She saw the paste-wad, the Waking. It laid on the bed, glistening with last night's supper, both undigested.

The meat she had eaten crawled slowly across the bed— living roaches without legs. Jiana was paralyzed, even when one of the cursed hunks of living flesh humped across the quilt and began to crawl up her face.

I failed. I feared. I'm the real slave, not her.

She was not ready to Wake; she still needed dreamsleep, like everybody else.

God, Tooqa, doesn't this ride ever *quit?*

Tears of frustration and fright streamed down her face. Her skin felt unclean where the piece of steak crawled. She was again a girl of fifteen, of ten, of five. A child, a lonely, frightened, indecisive, undergrown child. She was Jiana, not Jianabel. She had never been Jianabel—that was another. Toldo was right, Toldo was wrong.

Where's your warrior-spirit now, butcher? You stink of mud and blood and the soul of a beast.

Turns. A lifetime. Battles great, battles small, an ocean of blood and hundreds of innocents sacrificed to my lust to know. Yet after all—after all of it—to fear such a tiny thing as dying!

Jiana blinked, and the night vanished. She lay curled in the bed, pieces of sleep gluing her eyelids together. She no longer wept, but ancient tears still drowned her thoughts.

The red light of day shone through the shuttered window, casting long streaks of fire across the floor, the blood of the Earth.

Dilai's body did not lie beside her bed. He was still in the corner where she left him.

There was no wad of paste and no vomit on the bed, but no Jiana, either. Her soul had drifted away during the night, leaving only an empty suit of armor with pale skin and raven-black hair. The third boot had dropped; Toq was vindicated.

"So I *am* a coward after all," she said. No emotion colored her words. She examined critically, no sense of talking about *herself*. "I wondered. Now I know. Of all the things to fear . . . dying!

"The fear of death is the beginning of slavery," she quoted. "Welcome to the leash, Jiana Analena."

She watched the door. The bare room was bleak in the morning light. Soon *they* would come, those who *did it* to her: Toldo, Radience, all of them.

Jiana stood, donned the mask, played her part. Reflexively, she reached to touch her throat, surprised when she felt no collar.

So what happens next? Toldo will drift away, sell enlightenment at ten claws a throw. Dilai will be wrapped in a winding sheet and thrown into the River of Life. Or burned. Or buried for maggots.

Radience will go with me, I'll go with Radience. Together we'll go like flame and fuel. Head where, head who knows, head Warriorwards. Will she guess? Depends on how bright she is.

But we four will not—will not come—not come, ever again.

The sun rose. Jiana turned thirty-three. She greeted the dawn with Rethe's obscene gesture.

4

Radience crept silently with utmost awareness, as she had been taught, into the room, the quarters of her field captain; she held the weighty trunk of clothes and weapons close to her left side, so her good arm would be able to help, too.

The trunk was wooden, bound with iron; it was ugly and heavy. No slave could carry it, even with two good arms. It was her freedom trunk.

Pressed against her side as it was, the trunk also offered excellent cover against a long dagger, sharp as a needle, unexpected as the blessings of the Seer.

I'll never be a slave again. Never!

She silently pushed through the wooden door; weeks of training to live up to the field captain allowed her to pass through with not a scrape, not a single, wooden creak.

Jiana was asleep, laid upon her bedclothes, curled like a babe in the womb, fingers just touching the hilt of her weird, snake-like sword, Wave (it was inscribed with words from the Flower Empire which some said were the trapped souls of those Jiana killed).

The warrior girl stepped closer, a strange, unfamiliar serenity soothing her; she rolled her weight from back foot to front foot, for she *had* been taught. Holding her breath to not flutter Jiana's eyelids, she leaned over and studied the face of the woman for whom she would kill.

Jiana's eyes were wide open.

Before Radience could react, the air cracked and lightning flashed, and the field captain caught her by the throat and half drew deadly Wave.

"You're getting good, apprentice."

Radience said nothing; all she could have managed was a hoarse squawk, with the deathgrip Jiana held. The field captain released her.

"Toldo up yet?"

Radience coughed, and massaged her neck.

"Not back yet."

"Where did he go?"

The girl shrugged. The priest was gone when she got back to her room, after leaving Jiana and the dead man. She hoped to talk to Toldo, ask him to explain. But she discovered she did not need him; everything was all right.

For the first time in her life, Radience accepted tragedy and *moved on.*

Piss on the Seer, she thought. *It's not that big a crime. I won't die from it. Damn it, she has no taste . . . but I can surely live with* that!

"Should we wait for him, ma'am?"

"Of course. He's a brother. Check on Cascade, I'll get us some food and find a box for . . ." she looked back at the body of her friend, Dilai.

"What are we going to do with him?"

The field captain shook her head, still upset.

"I've decided we'll go north. North of Bay Bay, by ship this time. I'll lay him to rest in the ocean. I don't want any of those bastards to ever know whether he's alive or dead. Don't want them to have the satisfaction."

"Um, field captain?"

"Speak."

Radience hesitated. She had been about to ask "am I a warrior yet," but something stopped her. She had never been tested; not really, not in the world.

Over the Edge doesn't count, she thought.

"How many days out will we bury him?" she asked instead.

Jiana thought for a moment, looking at Dilai. Radience could tell it was more than a friendship; at one time, he must have meant as much to her as she did to Radience.

"We'll wrap him in five layers of oil-soaked cloth, set him alight at sea."

"Cloth—oil—box—horse. Got it." They exited the room, and Jiana closed and locked the door behind them. They descended the stairs into the common room. Toldo was not there.

"What if he doesn't show?"

"He's a brother," said the field captain, patiently.

Radience asked the tea-master about boxes, and he directed her to a sundries store, across the street. Jiana gave her a silver Achram, which Radience held tightly in her hand as she pushed through the crowds, ignoring the blind, the crippled, and the maimed that threw themselves at her feet, begging for somebody else to free them.

She found no box; but a tightly-fitted barrel looked big enough. She filled it with the cloth and three bottles of oil, and still got a few grains of change from the Achram. She started rolling the barrel back along the street.

A carriage rounded a corner bore down upon her. Radience saw the danger and rolled nimbly with the impact. She was only slightly bruised; the barrel was untouched. The carriage door was adorned by a goblin-grinning boy-god, inlaid in gold. The face looked familiar, but Radience shrugged off the memory as the coach sped into

the morning sun, its passenger cackling like a madman
under the full moon.

She heard a footstep behind her. A man was following
her—little more than a boy, actually.

She looked back at him, and caught him staring at her
crippled arm, which she used to guide the barrel while
her right hand rolled it.

He curled his lip, and took an instant stance that Radience
recognized all too well: he was about to utter something
terribly witty.

"So," he sneered, "need a helping *hand* with that?
Think you can *handle* it all by yourself, missy?"

"I'm sorry?" she asked, as if she had not understood the
reference.

"I *said*, if you'd clean out your ears, is that barrel going
to come in *handy?*"

He was dressed as some sort of a soldier; a group of
similarly-dressed young men behind him laughed very
loud (and very forced) at the boy's humor. They sounded
like braying donkeys.

"Hey, hey, she better not let it roll over her," interjected
another donkey, in a whining, nasal voice. "She don't want
to come to no *'arm!*" They brayed again, and Radience
could almost see them kicking back their hind legs and
wiggling their ears.

For an instant, Radience wondered whether she should
draw her knife and make them pay for their cruel remarks.
But she was one, and they were six; she had a knife, and
they had swords. They were armored. And more important, why should she allow such children to set the agenda
for Apprentice Radience?

Smiling, she turned away to complete her task. The
field captain was standing in the doorway, but she was not
looking at Radience. Jiana stared over the girl's head, at
the soldier-boys. Her mouth was pressed in a tight line of
anger, then it relaxed into the dangerous warrior's calm.

By His beard, does she know *these clowns?* the girl
wondered. She looked back.

The first boy, the one that started the incident, noticed Jiana; he gasped, and took a step backward, startled.

Reacting quickly, Radience rolled the barrel to the tearoom door, moving it and herself out of the line of fire . . . just in case.

She watched the unfolding street-theater intently, feeling some concern. *Should I move around behind him? Should I draw my knife?* One thing Radience did *not* want to do was to escalate an exchange of words into a bloodletting, but neither did she intend to allow Jiana to face six thugs alone.

Jiana strode calmly towards the boy. He did not flee, did not realize his peril.

Or maybe he does, Radience thought; just before Jiana reached him, he turned away from the field captain and approached Radience instead.

"So," he said, curling his lip in a self-conscious, practiced sneer.

"So?"

"So!"

"This conversation is getting quite dreary," said Radience. "Can't you say anything other than so?"

"So, now I see where you get all that arrogance! You must be Jiana's new slave."

Anger flashed through Radience, but it was followed by a powerful inner voice: *Anger dulls the sword and hobbles the feet . . . Don't give the fool that power!*

"I am her apprentice. Who," she asked, "are *you?*"

"Slave! You're her new slave, like she tried to do to me!" He spoke to Radience, but he was actually turned towards Jiana, who watched him impassively.

"How do you come to know the field captain?"

"Field captain?" The boy turned back to Radience. For a moment, he was just a young boy; an edge of innocence flickered in his face, quickly extinguished by hot army air. "So! Now she calls herself a field captain, hunh? Funny, she used to be a full-blown *hero* back when I—when I let her sleep with me a couple of times."

Again, Radience stiffened, clenching her fists in a spasm

of fury. *Hah!* crowed the voice, *this boy sure knows how
to blow dust up your robes! Remember the* jamal, *sticking
its nose under the tent—how hard it is to get the beast out
once it's gotten as far as the hump? Anger is that* jamal!

Radience let the anger drain. "She is a warrior, I'm her
apprentice. She taught me. She obviously never taught
you . . . I'm sure she tried, though."

Now it was the boy's turn to rage. His face turned red as
if she had slapped it, and he drew his sword. It was a
soldier's hacking tool; Radience realized uneasily that he
might decapitate her before Jiana could even react.

"My honor demands satisfaction!" cried the boy, jug-
gling his sword from one hand to the other. "Draw your
sword, you little pile of horsedung!" He bared his teeth
like a nasty, predatory monkey, and struck his "superior"
posture again; he thought of a "good one."

"I'm the offended party so I choose weapons," he continued. "I choose swords. But tell you what—I'll let *you*
choose which hand you want to use! Haw!"

Radience, alarmed, glanced over at Jiana. The field
captain looked at her for a moment, then incredibly, she
turned her back upon the girl and her predicament.

Radience understood: this was her own fight, and no
one else, not even the field captain, was going to fight her
fights for her. *It's me*, Radience thought. *It always comes
down to me*.

Preternatural peace descended upon her spirit. Her
ears grew until she could hear her own heart, hear the
faint buzzing of a wasp in the eaves of the inn, hear the
sweat dripping down the boy's back.

"I have no sword," she said, utterly calm.

"So? That's your fault! You said you were a warrior—
choose which hand, cripple!"

Her eyes widened until she could see his chest rise and
fall with each ragged breath, see in the same instant every
expression of each of his friends and what each intended to
do in the next hour or the next moon.

Her stomach expanded, and a single word, an unimportant bit of data rose to her lips, the name under which this creature masqueraded.

"Which hand would you *like* me to use . . . Dida?"

Dida paled when she spoke his name. His eyes widened; he knew the moment she spoke that she had not learned the name from Jiana, just as Radience knew that Dida was not the name he currently used.

Fear raised Dida's arm; fear flowed into fury, and he charged, aiming a vicious cut at her head. Fear demanded a silence, where once there was a word.

The world slowed. Radience had time, time enough to hear, to see, to sense the word. Dida, not a boy, not a man with a sword: he was a line of energy, a *wave*. Radience was another wave.

As waves they were shaped, moulded, and projected. The lattice of crystal spheres (of which Jiana often spoke) was another wave, a more complicated wave, with many swirls and eddies, cascading over rocks and winding around trees.

A wave could either fight the current to move in a straight line, or it could flow with the tide of the spheres, dissipating none of its precious energy in bootless lunges and splashes.

The sword descended, slow and stately as a cresting breaker. Radience stepped into the flow of the sphere, and bent gracefully *around* the sword blow. It whistled harmlessly through the space where once she stood.

The current of the spheres was full of eddies. Radience chose the one that intersected with Dida's diaphragm. Serene, she drove her fist forward up to the wrist. She neither noticed nor cared that he wore an armored breastplate.

A monstrous thunderclap shook the ground and rattled her teeth. Dida's breastplate cracked in two beneath her blow; his face turned red as the sands of Deh Bid.

Dida staggered backward, his sword falling to the street with a thud when he could no longer grip his hand. He looked up at Radience with a shock of recognition, and collapsed to his knees.

He tried to breathe, and realized for the first time that he could not. Radience, still caught in the web of serenity, turned and walked back to her barrel without a backward glance. She honestly did not care in that moment whether he lived, or died of suffocation. She was not about to apologize.

She maneuvered the barrel through the door and began walking it up the stairs.

5

Jiana watched Radience depart. She smiled; another turn, and now she was thirty-three, the age of Oninan Toiduko when he left the world of men and women to walk alone through the Jagged Chasm.

She approached Dida, her hands thrust deep into the pockets of her pantaloons. She spared a glance for his "friends"; they watched him writhe on the ground for a few moments, then they turned away in disgust and continued down the street. Dida's career in the army, whosever army it was, was ended.

She stood over him, one big, rawhide boot on either side of his face. He was frantically trying to inhale.

He saw her boots; he looked up and saw her pantaloons, her banded-leather tasset, studded gambeson, unbuttoned to the waist, vambrace on her right forearm, wire-wrapped shoulder pad, white throat, pale face, and ink-black warrior's crest. He saw her face, impassive, granite.

Help me, his face pleaded. *Save me.*

Jiana spoke quietly, but she spoke through the oversphere, speaking directly into Dida's stomach.

Only Dida can save Dida. A slave is a man waiting for somebody else to free him.

I'm going to die!

"Convictions make convicts," says the Tunk Maklypse. Breathe like a sleeper, find the rhythm.

I can't breathe! She murdered me!

All things are true in some sense, false in some sense, and meaningless in some sense. Breathe like the ocean waves; find the pattern.

Dida's lips turned a ghostly blue, as if he had eaten too many plurberries. His eyes were as wide as a snake's mouth, tiny tongue-dots of pupils.

I can't. Breathe. God help me . . .

. . . as wide as his heart had once been.

God is crazy. Her name is Jiana. Feel the womanblood pulse within you; feel the pattern; feel the rhythm. We all ebb. We all rise. The world contracts to a point, She blinks Her eye, then She opens wide, and we expand into a new world again.

This is Her womb. You feel the contractions, She's birthing a new Dida. When you are born again, all the old, rotten Dida will be ripped from you like the uterine sack, the waters, and the afterbirth. Find the flow. Breathe like the heartbeat of the world.

Dida took a breath. It was feeble, a mere mouthful; but he realized he was not, finally, going to die today. His face lost the hopeless terror. As he breathed again, and again, it twisted instead in the Underdwell of self-loathing.

At last, Dida was able to rise to his knees. He fumbled at the buckles of his broken breastplate, nerveless fingers unable to work the mechanism. Jiana reached down and unstrapped him.

He stood unsteadily, wrapping both arms around his mid-section. His face was still white, but he breathed. Again.

Dida hung his head, unable to meet Jiana's eyes.

"You've grown," she said.

"No, I haven't," he whispered.

She put her hand on the small of his back and pushed him toward the inn. He walked slowly, looking neither left nor right.

"I want you to meet someone; you have a lot to learn from her, and she has one or two things to learn from you."

They mounted the stairs slowly, pausing often for Dida to regain his breath. Jiana pushed open the door; Radience was pushing the lid of the barrel down on its gruesome contents.

"Talk to him," Jiana said. "Use your talent. He needs you more than he needs me."

At first Dida said nothing to Radience; he was frightened and embarrassed at what he said in the street, while the madness of manhood still gripped him. Jiana smelled the burn of magic.

Radience reached out her left hand and touched Dida on his forehead, and he began to talk. Jiana listened for a moment, then she began to feel uncomfortable, like a burgler beneath a bed, accidentally overhearing sweetdrips between a woman and her husband.

She turned away to her kit, and rummaged inside; she found a leather case and drew it out.

Radience paid attention only to Dida; she did not see Jiana gently lay the razor on top of the girl's pack. *She'll see it when she's alone*, Jiana thought; *that's how it should be.*

The elder warrior withdrew silently with utmost satisfaction, for she, too, had been taught. Jiana ghosted down the stairs, visioning Radience and Dida and Toldo and Cascade and . . .

Toldo stood at the bottom of the staircase, waiting patiently for Jiana.

. . . and Jianabel, who was not *simply a cold, sharp part of her own stomach. The fat, old bastard was wrong, for once!*

"We have a ship," he said.

She raised her brows into two black question marks.

"It's headed north, past Bay Bay. Way north."

Jiana nodded. "Good. I have a present to return, as soon as we're to sea."

"Ah. And unless I've fouled the calendar along the way . . . merry birthday. Thirty-two?"

Slowly, she held up three fingers, then she pressed on by the great buffalo of a man. He did not see her bend all but the middle finger down.

To hell with Jianabel. To hell with the girl. To hell with Dida and Dilai and Toldo and that horse and Tool and Door and water and air and blood and piss. Snakeshit, but no one *should be expected to evolve on her thirty-third birthday! Give me a glass.*

For all this warrior crap, still a Briar inside. Give me a martyr, a cause to lose! Snakepiss, just give me a glass.

Jiana strode into the common room and demanded breakfast, in a quiet voice that made the whole place jump.

Feel the pattern; feel the tides. She blinks her eyes, and we are birthed anew.

> *I'll be seven years a-ringin' the bell,*
> *But the Lady above may save my soul*
> *From portin' in hell*
> *At the well below the valley-o!*

After the Ending . . .

In the stables attached to the Dangling Jamal, Cascade rocked from his left to his right legs in satisfaction, anticipating the ocean voyage, the touch of his mother, Magadauthan Full-of-Oceans. Perhaps he would finally discover why he had been summoned to the side of the master human.

Content, he leaned down and ate the stomach out of the stables-slave who had annoyed him with a rope's end.

The End

Jiana will return in *Jiana the Dead* . . .